THE ORDEALS OF ELLY ROBIN

VOLUME ONE OF
"The Ordeals of Elly Robin" Series

THE ORDEALS OF ELLY ROBIN

by P.D. Quaver
with illustrations by the author

BOOKS BY P.D. QUAVER

Unplugged

"The Ordeals of Elly Robin" Series:

Visit P.D. Quaver at pdquaver.com

In memory of my mother

Contents

LIST OF ILLUSTRATIONS

\

Author's Note

Anyone reading source material from the earliest decades of twentieth-century America will find the ethnic and racial slurs we now so abhor being tossed around with breathtaking casualness. So the occasional inclusion of these repellent words in the dialogue of my characters stems not from any wish to offend, but a simple desire to recreate the authentic speech of the period—that sense, the holy grail of the historical novelist, of having gone "back in time."

For the same reason—and despite the act of writing dialect having recently become a minefield of potential offense—I have done my best to accurately render the colorful speech patterns of a diverse, polyglot and often poorly educated populace. Because giving voice to people different from oneself is surely at the heart of the novelist's craft. And I believe anyone reading these passages with an open mind will realize my attempts at Appalachian twang, pidgin-English, Yiddish-inflected speech and Afro-English patois are intended not to mock or belittle, but to *celebrate* this rich diversity.

—P.D. Quaver

CHAPTER ONE

EAVESDROPPING

The whole problem, Elly would later decide, arose from her confusion about what it meant to murder someone.

"Oh, didn't I just murder em tonight!" her friend Esta would often say, prancing off stage after her final curtain call. So Elly had deduced that murdering was something one did to an audience, and (judging by their rapturous applause) something they very much enjoyed having done to them.

But the Colonel and Mr. Burns had talked about a *girl* being murdered, which left Elly perplexed. Of course, she could have *asked* them what they meant. But Elly disliked speaking; if forced to communicate, she preferred to nod or shake her head. And asking them was also a problem because they'd had no idea she was even listening.

Her mother had told Elly (told her in fact many times) that eavesdropping was "not a polite thing to do." But Elly found it a hard habit to break, because adults talk differently when they don't know a child is listening, and one can learn so many interesting things! She had learned, for instance, that John Humphrey Davies, the troupe's tragedian, made six times as much money as Elly and her parents, gave himself airs, and was (in her mother's words) "an odious man" (a phrase Elly had rolled around on her tongue in private with great relish). And she was certain that only by eavesdropping would she ever learn how a man could possess a bosom—a concept that continued to elude her.

She'd learned about the odiousness of Davies by pretending to be asleep in their hotel room while her parents were getting ready for bed, *pretending to be asleep* being a very important weapon in the arsenal of the eavesdropper. But there were others as well, and this was another reason Elly found it so hard to break the habit: she was so very good at it. She was small and quiet and had a knack for making herself unobtrusive. And she was alert for eavesdropping opportunities. Which is why she had overheard the conversation between the Colonel and Mr. Burns, because the very best place in the world for eavesdropping is a train.

Elly had spent her entire life traveling around on trains. Being entirely comfortable with them, she also enjoyed traveling around within the trains themselves, moving around from car to car in search of interesting and exciting things. She had successfully trained her parents to let her do this on her own ("Cooped up for so many hours, she needs her freedom," her mother had reasoned. "Another way of saying we can't stop her anyway," her father's tart reply). And all you have to do, to eavesdrop on a train, is find a pair of empty seats behind two people who are talking, press your face into the narrow crack between them, and you can hear *everything*!

So this was how she had overheard the Colonel and Mr. Burns talking about murder. And if she'd only known what the word really meant, she'd have realized this was quite the most interesting and exciting thing that had happened to her all day! But the journey from Omaha to Denver had yielded so many other marvels that, if there had been a contest inside her murder-ignorant self, one of them would surely have won instead.

There was, for instance, the astonishing fact she had learned that morning regarding sausages.

Bright sunlight had melted all the ice on the windows of their car, and Elly had been lying on her back with her head in her mother's lap and her legs across her father's knees, watching the telegraph wires go *zoop zoop zoop*, rising and falling in hypnotic procession like a rhythmically writhing snake. Each sinuous repetition was about three times slower than the *click-clack* of the train tracks (but not exactly), and every twenty-seventh *zoop* coincided with a *clack*—

Which gave Elly a thrill.

Zoop one thousand two hundred seventy-six, *zoop* one thousand two hundred seventy-seven—

"Whatcha reading, Jane?"

Elly's mother must have just pulled a book from her valise. Elly was still counting and tried not to listen to them.

"*The Jungle*," continued her father in his teasing voice. "Sounds so fierce. I'd no idea you had a hankering for the primitive."

(*Zoop* one thousand two hundred ninety-four...)

"Jack, you're a goose," replied her mother mildly.

"What—what'd I say?"

Elly could picture her father's face, the funny way he would be making his eyes bulge and the tips of his mustache twitch. But she kept her eyes resolutely fixed on the window. *Zoop...Zoop...*

"If you read anything besides the sporting pages, you'd know *The Jungle* is about the meat packing industry."

"What, hyena meat? Filet of snake?"

"Stuff!" cried her mother, acting impatient (but amused in spite of herself, Elly could tell). "It takes place in Chicago, and the writer, this Upton Sinclair, is comparing the city to a jungle."

"There *were* a lot of apish-looking characters in the audience last week."

"Jack, you *are* a goose!" Her mother playfully slapped her father's shoulder, jostling Elly and almost making her lose count. "Everyone's talking about it, how it shows all the awful things they're putting into our sausages these days. Even the president's up-in-arms."

"Teddy's always up in arms about something. What things?"

"Well, I've not read much yet. Terrible talk of sawdust, even rats—"

"Rats! In the sausages?"

This was such astounding news that Elly couldn't help but look up at them.

"Oh Jack, now you've done it," said her mother, stroking Elly's cheek. "Elly, don't listen to us."

"Elly listens to everything," said her father, grinning down at her. "Don't you?"

Elly nodded glumly, wishing for once it weren't true. Sighing, she looked out the window and began again. *Zoop* one (rats in the sausages), *zoop* two (rats in the sausages)…

Her parents were still talking. The sky was the same blue as her mother's eyes. Elly had her mother's pretty features and flawless ivory complexion—everyone said so. But Elly's eyes were like her father's, dark as coffee beans. And instead of her mother's golden locks, Elly had her father's black hair as well. Worse, it was wild and snarly (her father's was the same before he oiled it), and hurt when her mother brushed it.

The telegraph poles were flashing by more slowly. The distant shriek of the train whistle. She sat up and looked out the window. Ramshackle houses, weedy backyards littered with trash, patches of gray snow in the shadows. A livery stable from which an old sway-backed horse stood gazing at the train—

They were coming to a town.

She scrambled down from her bed of knees, endured being bundled into a coat, cap and mittens, and skipped down the aisle. The "drummers"—traveling salesmen with sample cases full of eggbeaters and corsets, garters and gadgets—sprawled with their derbies pushed back, reading newspapers and smoking cigars. She raced past them toward the rear of the car, threw herself against the legs of a gangling young man sitting in the last seat, and stared up at his startled face.

"Elly! You are quite the little firecracker," exclaimed the young man, whose name was Albert Jenning. Albert had a funny way of talking because he was from England. He had a funny face, too—long, like a horse's, with sad eyes that somehow made him even funnier. Which was good, because Albert was a comic, the funniest one Elly could remember.

"So, is it time to look again?" asked Albert.

Elly nodded eagerly. The whistle shrieked again and the train came to a juddering halt. Albert donned a pair of earmuffs and a scarf, replaced his derby, unfolded his long, stork-like legs, and shakily stood. Elly snatched his hand, pulled him toward the rear door of the car, and they stepped onto the crowded platform. It was as fine a day as one could hope for on the high plains in February, and the sun had already melted most of yesterday's snow. But the wind was still icy, and a line of people stood in the lee of the station house, sheltering themselves from it. Elly led them through a gaggle of ladies carrying carpet bags and clapping enormous hats to their heads against the wind, past a colored porter pushing a handcart piled with baggage, a man in patched clothes selling roasted peanuts.

"Ah, Nebraska," Albert rhapsodized, "the very name stirs the blood. Desperados, buckskin buckaroos, Comanches, Kiowas, Apaches—they're here, I tell you! I can almost smell them."

He pushed his derby back, scratched at his hair, which stuck up like the weeds sprouting from the dirty snow, and peered around uncertainly. Elly looked with him. They were searching for Red Indians. Albert had never seen any, because there were no Red Indians in England. They had been searching ever since Des Moines. In Omaha they had found one leather-skinned old Indian wearing dusty blue jeans and a Union cap begging on the streets, but Albert had pronounced him a "sorry specimen."

"I shall not rest until I have seen war bonnets and loincloths," he had told the Colonel. The Colonel replied that Albert had better prepare himself for eternal insomnia.

"Or go buy a ticket to Buffalo Bill's show," suggested Mr. Burns. "See enough half-naked savages to last you a lifetime."

Now Elly was urgently tugging on Albert's hand.

"What, Elly?" murmured Albert, striding in the direction indicated. "Is it—well, by Jove!"

An Indian family was huddled against the wall of the station, silently watching the bustle all around them. The woman was young, with a broad, impassive face, and wrapped in a colorful blanket. A baby with a face like a dried apple and a mop of shiny black hair peered from a shawl slung from her shoulder. A young man wearing buckskin leggings along with a beaded vest and headband completed the trio.

The black eyes of mother, father, and child widened in alarm at the gangling figure advancing on them.

"Well!" cried Albert. "How most entirely delighted I am to have found you all!"

The young man scowled and moved closer to his wife.

"Might I ask—that is, if it's not unduly presumptuous on such short acquaintance—with which tribe are you affiliated?" continued Albert, peering at them hopefully.

The baby screwed up its face and began to silently weep. The man herded his wife and child away, looking back fearfully over his shoulder. Albert looked down at Elly with a long face, like he was about to cry himself, which gave Elly a fit of the giggles—then something caught her eye that drove all thoughts of Red Indians out of her head.

Across the platform, half-hidden by the station building, was a locomotive. She ran toward it, then stopped abruptly in wonder. Bits of the huge engine were strewn about the platform.

It was a fantastic stroke of luck.

Elly was fascinated by machines. She had been told that locomotives were powered by steam, and had seen for herself they needed vast amounts of water, and coal to make the water boil. But that something as insubstantial as the friendly puffs of white vapor from a tea kettle could make a big heavy train move seemed absurd. She had worked out that the long rods connected to the wheels were pushing them and making them turn in circles. But what was pushing the rods? There was some secret, some magic she had yet to understand. And now, it seemed, was her chance—

"Elly!"

Albert had caught up with her just as she was reaching out her hand to a long, greasy metal cylinder lying on the platform half-disassembled.

"There you are! Best not touch that, you know. Your mother would box my ears if I let you get oil on your mittens—"

The train whistle blew a long shriek, and the engine made chuffing noises. Elly jumped up, grabbed Albert by the hand, and the two of them raced around the station house and across the platform. Groups of people waving or idly watching impeded their progress. They snaked their way through the throng and reached the train just before the caboose flew by. Elly leaped aboard, skirts flying, followed by Albert, clutching his derby to his head.

"Shaved it rather close there, we did," he muttered, mopping his face with a handkerchief.

Elly hardly noticed, already absorbed in planning her next adventure. In just one morning she had discovered the truth about sausages, come upon three genuine red Indians, and explored a dismantled engine. How many more interesting and exciting things could one day possibly yield?

She decided it was time to pay a visit to Smiley Hobson.

Smiley Hobson was the best dancer Elly had ever seen (and she had seen a lot of them). Since Smiley was a colored man, he got to ride in the Colored Car. And since the Colored Car was at the very front of the train, Elly got to run its entire length to get there. She liked to do this as quickly as possible, so she skipped ahead of Albert, opening all the heavy doors herself by hanging on their handles, raced through first class, slowed down briefly for the dining car (having once upset an entire dinner tray, an experience she had no desire to repeat), rushed through second class (pausing to toss her coat, hat, and mittens on her mother's lap), sprinted through third class (artfully dodging several other stray urchins), on through the Menagerie (pausing again to bark a brief greeting to Binky), and arrived, panting at the Colored Car.

Since it was at the very front of the train, the engine was thrillingly loud; in warm weather hot cinders sometimes flew into the open windows, which make it even better. She looked around for Smiley, and found him sitting in the midst of an animated little group.

"Elly!" he exclaimed, displaying the mouth full of gleaming white teeth that gave him his name (they looked even whiter when he put on his black-face make-up, which always struck Elly as silly because his face was already so dark). Smiley was a featured artist and always dressed like a sharp. He wore a shiny green suit with a yellow vest, spats and four-in-hand, matching yellow derby, and was (as usual) the center of a circle of admirers, including a pretty young woman who was glued up against his side. She had on a tight velvet dress the color of strawberries and a hat with big white feathers. She smiled at Elly and Elly quickly looked away.

"This here is Elly Robin," said Smiley, setting Elly on his knee. The two gentlemen across from him were Mr. Pitts, who had a gold tooth that Elly concentrated on when he looked at her, and a man named Saint Louie, who was fat, wore a plaid suit, and was smoking a long cigar. The woman was Miss Olive.

"Pleased to meet you, Elly," said Miss Olive in a soft voice that Elly liked. "Don't she talk?" she asked Smiley.

"Well now, Miss Elly can talk when she's of a mind to," said Smiley, directing his famous smile at Elly. "Can't she?"

Elly nodded, avoiding his eye.

"Only thing," added Smiley, "she ain't of a mind to all that often."

Saint Louie pulled the cigar from his lips. "Not a bad trait in a woman."

They all laughed.

"Thing is," continued Smiley, "Miss Elly here, she don't *need* to talk. Cause she can say everything she needs to say with ten little fingers and eighty-eight keys." He picked up Elly's hand and squeezed it.

"Whatchoo on about?" said Mr. Pitts. He pulled a silver flask from his pocket and drank from it.

"What—you mean this little slip of a girl here can play the piano?" said Miss Olive. "How old are you, Elly?"

Elly would generally respond to factual questions. "Six," she replied.

"Six!" exclaimed Miss Olive. "And already you're learnin the piano!"

"Folks, you are entirely non-assimilatin what I am tryin to impart to you here," said Smiley Hobson grandly. "This 'slip of a girl,' as you put it, is a *prodigy*—a child genius!"

"Sakes!" cried Miss Olive.

"So," Saint Louie waved his cigar at Elly, "you sayin she's in the show?"

"In the show?! Why she's a feature. Brings down the house every night."

Miss Olive exclaimed again, and reached over to pet Elly.

Mr. Pitts took another pull from his flask and wiped his mouth. "So what she doin up here with us folk?"

"Why," Miss Olive stroked Elly's dark, crinkly hair, "she tryin to *pass!*"

This started the four of them laughing so hard that Mr. Hobson's knee jiggled and Elly almost fell off.

"Don't,"—Miss Olive tried to catch her breath—"don't pay us any mind, Elly. So what's it like, up there playin on that great big stage for all them folks?"

But talk of being a piano prodigy bored Elly, and she slid from Smiley Hobson's knee and skipped away. She had never understood what was so wonderful about doing something she found so simple. And in this same car there was a girl her own age who could do much more wonderful things than play the piano!

Lying on a mat on the floor at the very front of the car was a tiny Chinese girl in faded red pajamas named Ah Lin. Her father, Ah Wing, was kneeling over his daughter and twisting her legs into all kinds of impossible positions that Elly was certain must be very painful. But Ah Lin and her five older brothers went through this every day, and she lay there with an impassive face.

Ah Wing and his family were the Seven Wonders of Shanghai, and their acrobatic feats opened the show. During their routine, tiny Ah Lin got to fly around the stage in shiny yellow silk pajamas with sleeves that billowed out like the wings of a butterfly. At the act's conclusion, Ah Wing supported all five of his sons, and Ah Lin was tossed from one son to another until she stood on the youngest son's shoulders, high above the stage. Watching from the wings each night, Elly knew true jealousy.

At the sight of Elly, Ah Lin's impassive face broke into a broad smile.

Her father looked up. His head was bald except for a long braid tied with a ribbon. Elly had often wondered if it actually grew out of his head, or was just stuck on somehow. She had a strong desire to pull it and find out, but had never dared.

"Ah, Missy Elly," said Ah Wing, nodding. "Missy Lin, she velly busy now." He pushed his daughter's feet behind her head and locked them in place. "Velly velly busy."

Elly reached into the large pocket especially sewn in her pinafore where Mr. Hoppy lived. Mr. Hoppy was a stuffed frog. She pulled his long green legs up until they framed his face, just like Ah Lin's. Ah Lin began to giggle.

"Wha?" said Ah Wing. He looked up at the twisted frog.

"Mr. Hoppy," said Elly.

Ah Wing turned the name over in his mind. "He Mistah Hoppy," he finally concluded, "cause he velly hoppy."

Elly was delighted that Mr. Hoppy had finally acquired a first name, and marched off singing, "Mr. Velly Hoppy, Mr. Velly Hoppy" (to a tune of her own devising), back through the Colored Car and into the Menagerie.

The Colonel had dubbed it "the Menagerie" because the animals and the musicians rode in it together, the Colonel claiming he "failed to see the distinction." The animals were stacked in their cages at one end of the car, along with the troupe's props and backdrops. The musicians lounged around on old ripped seats in shirtsleeves and suspenders with their collars off.

"Heya Elly!" said Shorty. Shorty played trombone. He was drinking from a flask and squatting in the corner near the stove with Smitho and Jingles, who played saxophone and drums, and throwing dice against the wall. He held his flask out to Elly. "How bout a nip?"

Smitho punched him in the shoulder. "She's just a kid, ya dope!"

"Ow!" said Shorty, rubbing his shoulder. "Just a joke."

"Hey Crawley," Jingles called to a group nearby playing cards, "Crawley, you gotta meet Elly."

A pale young man with a high forehead and dark, curly hair glanced up from his cards.

"Elly, this here's Mr. Crawley," said Jingles. "New cornet player."

Elly regarded Mr. Crawley as a whole, avoiding his eyes. "Mr. Schwartz," she murmured to no one in particular.

"Ya, um, well, seems Mr. Schwartz got the old razoo in Omaha," said Jingles.

Elly was spurred by this dire news into loquaciousness. "Why?"

Shorty began to explain (with help from Jingles and Smitho) that Schwartz had gotten the old razoo "because Mr. Burns caught him sneaking a girl up to his hotel room and called her a floozie—"

"Which she was."

"Full-fledged."

"—and Mr. Schwartz being at the time somewhat spifflicated—"

"Positively stinko."

"Girl too."

"—so Mr. Schwartz decided he was John L. Sullivan and took a swing at Mr. Burns—"

"Too bad he didn't connect."

"Musta gone over his head."

"—and that's why the Colonel gave Mr. Schwartz the ol razoo," concluded Shorty, "and Mr. Crawley here's takin his place."

You didn't have to eavesdrop on musicians to learn interesting things.

"You'll like him," said Jingles hopefully. "Got a nice, sweet sound."

But Elly had quite liked how Mr. Schwartz played "Jeannie with the Light Brown Hair," and was dismayed that he'd gotten the old razoo. She regarded Crawley anew with cool eyes.

Mr. Crawley smiled back uncertainly.

"Blow her a note, Crawley," suggested Smitho.

"Yeah," said Shorty, grinning. "Pick a note. Any note."

Crawley stared at them in confusion. Realizing they were serious, he pulled a paper bag from beneath his seat, and extracted a battered-looking cornet. He blew through it tonelessly, fluttering the valves with his fingers, then played a long, shimmering note.

All the men looked at Elly expectantly.

"Sharp," she said.

"Um, no," said Crawley, looking embarrassed. "Actually it's a concert C *natural*—"

"It's a C natural, and it's sharp."

The car exploded with laughter. Crawley went pink, and flashed a twisted smile at Elly.

She continued to gaze at him with cool, unfocused eyes. "Play 'Jeannie,'" she said.

Crawley looked around uncertainly.

"G'wan, you heard the lady," said Shorty. He took a pull from his flask. "'Jeannie with the Light Brown Hair'—ya know it, don't ya?"

Crawley nodded. He put the cornet to his lips—then, thinking twice, pulled the tuning slide out a bit (to another round of laughter). He blew a few notes, adjusting it and glancing at Elly until she nodded her satisfaction. Finally he closed his eyes, and began to play...

His sound was different from Mr. Schwartz's bright, silvery peal, the notes warmer, more rounded. They floated over the train's *clack-clack* like a balloon wafting over a rocky field. When he reached the high note in the last phrase, he held it in a way that made the dogs in their cages whine, and gave Elly that tingly feeling.

The last note died away. Everyone looked at Elly. Mr. Crawley took the horn from his lips and stared at her with all the rest.

She looked directly into his eyes for the first time, flashed him something close to a smile, and skipped away.

"Haw!" said Shorty. "Kid—you're in!"

In fact, Elly had found the young man's playing magical enough to add to the day's growing catalogue of interesting and exciting things.

Her decision to pay a visit to Esta Sangley would add yet another.

Like John Humphrey Davies, Esta was a headliner, and the two of them had adjoining apartments in a private Pullman car. Esta lived with her maid, Molly, and sometimes Elly slept with Molly when Elly's parents (for some reason she had never figured out) wanted to sleep alone. But this was fine with Elly, because Molly was pretty and funny and acted like a child herself sometimes, even though she was sixteen and all grown up.

The Pullman car was the very last one before the caboose, so Elly got to run all the way through the train again. This time she didn't have to pause to remove her coat (though her mother gave her a look when Elly flashed by), and she was near to setting what was surely a new record when she was brought up short by the tall, imposing figure of John Humphrey Davies.

He was sauntering with studied nonchalance from the dining car back to his apartment, so Elly was forced to fall in step behind him. A pretty young woman in first class glanced up at Davies demurely, fluttered her eyelashes, and said something. He stopped so abruptly that Elly almost bumped into him.

They called Davies "The Great Profile," and Elly's mother had explained what it meant. As he leaned over to sign his autograph, she was able to study this alleged attribute at short distance. His nose was indeed prominent, graceful, majestic: a proud beak. But his eyes were dark and piercing, the young woman twittered nervously under their scrutiny, and Elly had the uncanny impression of a great bird of prey poised to devour a defenseless rodent.

Suddenly his head swiveled and his gaze fell on Elly herself.

She gave a little squeak, rushed around him, and arrived at Esta's door, breathless. She knocked loud enough to be heard over the noise of the train. The door opened and Molly's freckled face appeared. She raised an eyebrow.

"Tis the dwarf," she called over her shoulder.

"Ha!" Esta's resonant voice.

Elly rushed past Molly and threw herself on top of Esta, who was reclining on a velvet divan in a green silk wrapper and purple harem pants.

"Oof!" said Esta. "Hiya Elly-Belly. How's tricks?"

Elly made a comfortable perch out of Esta's soft stomach and kicked her legs.

"Here, have some of these." Esta handed Elly a bowl of grapes and Elly proceeded to eat them, collecting the seeds in one hand. Molly sat in the corner and resumed sewing sequins onto one of Esta's costumes. Since so many were lost in each performance, it was a task she never seemed to finish.

"Elly," said Esta in a conspiratorial voice, "wanna see somethin prime?"

Elly nodded eagerly.

Esta thrust out her hand. An ornate gold ring glittered on her middle finger. Set in the center was a bright green stone nearly as big as one of the grapes.

"Ain't it just the snappiest thing ya ever seen?"

Elly gazed at it with wide eyes.

"Sure, showin off your ill-gotten gains," said Molly, who talked funny because she was Irish.

"Hmph," retorted Esta. "It's an emerald!" she confided to Elly in a stage whisper. "Gent who give it to me owned the biggest meat-packing plant in Omaha."

"Broke the gentleman's heart, she did," said Molly.

"Well, he wanted me to marry him," said Esta.

Elly's eyes widened even further.

"Old as Methuselah, he was," sniffed Molly.

"True, he weren't no pup," admitted Esta. "But dignified."

"Sure, there's nothing so dignified as a well-dressed corpse."

"But hey, I thought about it."

Molly made a face.

"Yeah, I know," said Esta. "But you're still a young chick. I've been at this game for more'n twenty years, since I was just your age. Think I'm gonna totter around the stage singin 'I Don't Care' when I'm a toothless old hag? I'm already losing my looks." She plucked a hand-mirror from the side table and examined herself doubtfully.

Elly was stricken. A sentence formed in her mind. She turned it over and over like she always did before speaking unprompted.

"You're beautiful," she finally said.

"Ooh, Elly-Belly!" cried Esta, tossing the mirror aside and hugging Elly. Molly looked up quickly and smiled.

"She don't talk much," gushed Esta, stroking Elly's hair, "but when she does, she makes it count!"

"Sure, she'll make for a politician someday," said Molly, resuming her sewing—then tossing it impatiently aside to answer another knock on the door.

"Hello Molly," Elly heard her mother's voice, "I'm sorry to bother you—"

"She's in here, Jane," yelled Esta.

"Oh Elly," said her mother, "I've been looking all over—what sort of deviltry have you been up to?" she asked mildly.

Elly tried to assume an innocent expression.

"I suppose I'll never know," said her mother, regarding Elly indulgently. "I'm afraid I've long given up trying to put a rope on her."

"Twould needs be a long rope," observed Molly.

"Esta, would this be a good time—?"

"Sure, hey, bang away all you want," said Esta, waving toward the spinet piano bolted to the floor in the corner on which Elly was often allowed to practice. "I gotta go change anyways. Ain't we about there?"

"Soon, I should think," said Elly's mother.

"Denver," mused Esta. She lifted Elly off her perch and languidly stretched. "Easy house. Laugh at anything, if you get em on your side. But heaven help you if them cowboys turn against you," she added as she padded toward the bedroom. Molly sighed, laid down her sewing, and followed. She caught Jane Robin's eye and pointed to the wall behind the piano—the wall shared by John Humphrey Davies.

"Play *loud*," she said.

~

After her practice session (during which Elly indeed tried her best to penetrate the adjoining apartment with her exertions), she suffered herself to be led by the hand back to her seat. But Esta's emerald made Elly only more on fire to see what else might be discovered on this red-letter day. So no sooner had her mother laid down her book and closed her eyes than she slipped from her seat and set off in search of eavesdropping opportunities.

And that was when she spotted the Colonel, sitting in front of two empty seats, and conversing with what appeared to be yet another empty seat. But a wisp of cigar smoke hovered over it, and Elly knew it must be Mr. Burns.

Stealthily she crept behind them and pressed her face between the seats to listen. Except that with the Colonel and Mr. Burns this wasn't even necessary, because the Colonel's voice was so nasal it sounded like he was speaking through a kazoo, and Mr. Burns had the loudest voice of anyone Elly had ever met. He was also the shortest man she knew, resembling a boy who'd tried to disguise himself as a man by donning a derby and pasting on a fake mustache. It added to the startling effect when his foghorn of a voice suddenly boomed forth. At the sound of it, small children had been known to weep; when he bawled out hotel clerks for overcharging the troupe, they generally went pale and adjusted the bill without a fight just to shut him up.

Elly had been hoping to hear more about the Colonel giving Mr. Schwartz the old razoo, but was just as delighted to find them discussing John Humphrey Davies:

"…but what I wanna know," brayed Burns, "is what the devil all those rubes out there"—he waved a stubby arm at the flat, featureless landscape—"what the devil do they see in him? I mean that act of his, it's pure claptrap!"

"My dear fellow," buzzed the Colonel, "you must never forget that, although Davies's name has penetrated even these yokelish hinterlands, a selection of Shakespearean soliloquies—his true métier—would sail right over their hickish heads. No, it's claptrap your yokel craves, and the chance to view the celebrated profile. Bilge water, as it were—but served in a champagne glass."

Elly was making a mental note to find out what "bilge water" was, when Mr. Burns, affecting to drop his voice (but still loud enough to turn heads), suddenly said:

"Say, I forgot to mention: when I went around to the theater this morning to supervise the loading, there was a commotion up the street. Crowd a people, buncha policemen. Walked over to investigate, turned out they found a girl, murdered."

More heads turned.

"Murdered, you say?" said the Colonel.

"Got it straight from one a the cops. Found her in the alley, in a trashcan. Like garbage."

The Colonel shook his head. "And Omaha seemed such a peaceful, wholesome sort of burg. A paragon of sober, yawn-inducing virtue."

"Just goes to show," brayed Burns.

"It does," buzzed the Colonel. "It just goes to show."

Just goes to show what? wondered Elly. The conversation had been disturbing yet nonsensical. Why on earth would a girl decide to hide inside a trashcan, and why was everybody so worked up about it? Without the true definition of murder (which she quickly added, along with bosoms and bilge water, to her list of things to be thoroughly investigated), she had no idea this was by far the most interesting and exciting thing that had happened all day.

Especially considering the way things turned out.

CHAPTER TWO

HANDMAIDENS TO
THE WUNDERKIND

Elly stood in front of the food stand as the vendor handed over a long, greasy sausage wrapped in waxed paper to one of the drummers on the train. She watched breathlessly as he raised his meal of mustard-slathered rats to his mouth—only to freeze at the sight of the little girl gazing fixedly at him with wide-eyed glee.

"What's up, kiddo—ya hungry?"

"Don't pay her no mind," said the vendor. "Been standin there twenty minutes, rubber-neckin all my customers. Touched, I reckon."

"Elly!"

Elly looked up to find Molly staring down at her with flashing eyes. Bright red curls escaped from the confines of her hat. She grabbed Elly's hand.

"By all the saints," she muttered, pulling Elly roughly through the crowded station, "sure you may be a prodigy, but you are a prodigious botheration to boot."

They passed by the stagehands unloading trunks and rolled-up backdrops and crates full of props. Through the din Elly heard excited yelps and monkeyish chatter and caught a glimpse of Mr. Barnhold directing the unloading of his animals. The animals were all her friends, and she tried to stop. Molly made an exasperated sound and gave her arm another yank.

The musicians were standing around a pile of instrument cases. Shorty poked Mr. Crawley, the new cornetist, in the ribs and pointed with his chin in their direction. Molly brushed at her loose curls with her free hand and took no notice of them. But it seemed to Elly they were walking slower.

Up ahead she saw her parents and the Colonel talking with a man in a fedora holding a notepad.

"Elly!" cried her mother. "You're an imp. Where on earth was she?"

"Sure, she was watching a man eat a sausage," said Molly, "like it were a command performance and she the queen."

Elly saw her parents exchange a glance. Her father started a laugh, which turned into a cough. Molly rushed off to join Esta.

"So," said the newspaper man, turning in their direction, "is this the kid?"

He stared down at Elly like a cat at a mouse. She turned to avoid his eye. Esta, followed by a porter wheeling her enormous trunks, was slicing through the sea of people like the prow of a ship, Molly trailing in their wake.

The Colonel cleared his throat importantly. "This, sir, is Baby Elly Robin, the *Wunderkind*. That's German for Wonder—"

"Wonderchild, right, I got all that. And she, what, studied with Paderooski?"

The Colonel looked slightly pained. "Not only did she study with him, but Miss Robin is the one-and-only true protégé of the great Ignatz Paderewski."

"Uh-huh," said the newspaper man, writing and stifling a yawn.

Mr. Paderewski was a pianist. Her parents had taken Elly to Carnegie Hall to hear him play, and she had instantly decided that someday she too would play beautiful songs all alone on a stage in a beautiful theatre for people dressed in furs and diamonds. After the concert her father had somehow gotten them into Mr. Paderewski's hotel room (though it had seemed to Elly that he didn't want them there) and made her play for him. She had played the minuet that Mr. Paderewski himself had written, playing the treble part while her mother played the bass. When they started, Mr. Paderewski had looked bored. But when they finished, he had laughed and picked her up and called her *"ein echt Wunderkind."*

Which meant that she was a *real* wonderchild. But Elly had never quite figured out why she was also Mr. Paderewski's one-and-only true protégé. Or even what a protégé was.

The newspaper man was talking to John Humphrey Davies now (or really, just listening to him). Davies wore a sealskin coat trimmed with white fur. He stood with his chin tilted up and one foot thrust forward, and his deep voice echoed through the station. An excited crowd, most of them female, had gathered around him.

"Let's skidoo before he does his whole act," whispered her father.

~

Most of the troupe was assembled in the omnibus Mr. Burns had hired to take them to the hotel. (Elly knew that John Humphrey Davies and Esta would both take cabs, and Davies would stay in a suite on the top floor; Esta, being a headliner, could have done the same. But she preferred being on the same floor as the rest of the troupe because it was "more sociable.") Smiley Hobson and Ah Lin and her family always stayed in a special hotel for the colored people, just like they rode in the colored car.

Behind the omnibus was a dray loaded with all the crates and trunks, including the animals in their cages. Elly slipped from her mother's hand and ran to see Binky. Binky was a wire-haired terrier and the star of "Barnhold's Animals." At the sight of Elly he jumped up with his paws on the side of his cage, yipping excitedly. Mr. Hoppy came out of his pocket and began yipping back at him. They had just gotten a nice conversation going when someone grabbed Elly by the waist, hoisted her into the omnibus, and set her between her mother and Albert Jenning. Albert tipped his derby to her. She held up Mr. Hoppy, and Albert tipped his hat to him as well. Elly giggled and kicked her legs.

"...and vat I gonna do, I just dunno," said a mournful voice behind her. She twisted in her seat and found Mr. Barnhold sitting between Mabel and Millie, the Twin Sisters (who were neither twins nor sisters).

Snuggled against Mr. Barnhold's broad chest was a hairy form Elly recognized as Miss Koko.

"Can't ya give her castor oil or sumpin?" said Mabel.

"Yeah, some kinda monkey medicine," said Millie.

"I dunno, I just dunno," said Mr. Barnhold again, shaking his head. He had a round, fat face the color of raw beef, eyes so large and protruding they looked to Elly like eggs poking out of his skin, and he never smiled. Which Elly thought strange, since he taught his animals to do so many funny things.

He saw Elly looking at him.

"Elly, Elly, vat I gonna do? Miss Koko, she done got sick."

Miss Koko lifted her head from his chest and directed a bleak expression at Elly.

"She don't look so hot," agreed Mabel.

"Maybe she's just lonely," suggested Millie. "You know, needs summa dat jungle lovin'," she added, quoting from their act.

"Capital idea!" said Albert, turning around to join the conversation. "Acquire a chimp Lothario for Miss Koko."

"I tink," said Mr. Barnhold, ignoring them, "I tink she got da vorms."

"Forms?" said Albert.

The driver jerked his reins, and the omnibus jerked into rumbling, creaking motion, cutting their conversation short.

Elly had seen Denver before but had been so young she didn't remember it. The late afternoon sun made the dust rising from the streets sparkle. Between the buildings she caught glimpses of pale lavender mountains in the distance. The streets were full of people enjoying the sun's last rays on this unseasonably warm day, an interesting mix of women wearing stylish hats or old-fashioned bonnets and men wearing derbies, cloth caps, or Stetsons. She saw a Chinese man, his wife following several paces behind him, and a dog jiggling on the back of another dog, which drew a laugh from the men in the orchestra sitting behind her.

They turned a corner onto a main thoroughfare and found an entire herd of cattle being driven toward them by men on horseback.

"Oh, by Jove," cried Albert Jenning happily, "it's the genuine article all right!"

The driver of the omnibus made a disgusted sound and reined in his team to wait for the herd to pass.

A roaring, sputtering noise came from the other direction. Elly turned and saw a shiny green motorcar, driven by a young man in a stylish checked cap and goggles, motoring straight for the herd. She watched its approach with great interest, for motorcars fascinated her almost as much as trains. Once she had seen someone point to a very small motorcar and say it was powered by "seven horses." She had tried to imagine seven tiny horses hidden somewhere inside. But, like locomotives powered by steam, the concept seemed nonsensical, and again she knew there had to be some magic involved.

The men from the orchestra began whooping and yelling things at the young man.

"Hey, get a load of Casper!"

"Ride em, pardner!"

"Five bucks on the cows!"

The motorcar was now motionless amidst a sea of cows. The cattle made strangled noises and rolled their eyes as they flowed around the smoking, sputtering vehicle. The young driver stood up, looking as fearful as the animals swarming around him. The cowboys were yelling and whistling above the noise of the machine and herd, trying to control the panicked beasts.

"Get a horse!" yelled Shorty.

"Horse, hell—get a *cow*!"

There was a terrific BANG as one of the cattle careened against the stalled vehicle. The driver flipped backward with his feet in the air and disappeared behind the seat.

The men from the orchestra cheered.

"Goodness gracious," said Elly's mother mildly.

"There's a moral there somewhere," remarked her father. "But I don't know what it is."

·   ·   ·

"Elly," said her father, setting her on his lap as he sat by the window of their hotel room and her mother unpacked their trunk, "look at those mountains over there."

Elly looked at the mountains, silhouetted by the setting sun.

"All right, now look at that streetcar—can you see it?"

Elly located the streetcar and nodded.

"OK," said her father, running his fingers through his hair. "So now—look at me."

Elly raised her eyes to her father's face, focusing on his sleek black mustache.

"No, that's not what I mean—"

"Jack," said her mother. She had stopped unpacking and stood watching them.

"Elly," said her father in a tight voice, "what I mean is, I want you to look me in the eye."

"Jack, we have had this conversation."

Elly sat rigidly, staring at the wallpaper, her face hot.

"All I'm saying," said her father, his voice rising, "is when someone from the newspapers asks her a question, the least she could do is look him in the—"

"Jack," cried her mother, in as forceful a tone as she ever used, "Jack, I *will not have it!*"

Elly took out Mr. Hoppy so he could look at the wallpaper too. It was covered with a pattern of hearts and diamonds. They began to count the hearts, starting at the far corner. A little tune played in her head to go with the counting: One (Mr. Velly Hoppy la la la). Two (Mr. Velly Hoppy la la la). Three…

"And now look at her…" was the last thing she heard her mother say before their voices faded away. Instead, she remembered a conversation she had once heard when she was pretending to sleep.

"…and she never talks."

"Jack, of course she talks."

"You know very well what I mean. Other children her age are full of questions nineteen to the dozen."

"She is not like other children."

"Jane, you have said a mouthful."

"Oh Jack, I know she can be somewhat…trying."

"Trying! If only she were just trying! But what she seems to me at times is…*unnatural.*"

"Jack! You must never say, nor even think such a thing! Your own flesh and blood—"

"Look look, I know, I'm sorry. It's just…"

There was a long silence.

"What I know," said her mother at last, "is that Elly's gifts, and the ways she is not like other children, are so connected they cannot be separated. And I love her dearly, just the way she is."

.   .   .

Three hundred sixty-seven (Mr. Velly Hungry, la la la)…

Elly realized it was her mother's lap she was sitting on now, her mother gently rocking her. For some time now the word "hungry" had been popping into her song.

"Elly, sweetheart," said her mother in a soft, patient voice, "are you hungry?"

Elly decided she was, and nodded.

As they started for the dining room the door to the Colonel's room suddenly opened, and the Colonel and John Humphrey Davies emerged. Both were dressed to the nines. Davies, with his dark good looks, might have been an advertisement for elegant evening wear, while the Colonel, with his paunch, bald pate and luxuriant mustache, resembled an aging walrus in a dinner jacket.

"Ah Jack, Jane: an opportune moment to invite you both to my quarters later for a discreet celebration, ritually marked by the decanting of some vintage bubbly, of a certain nascent event, which unfolded some three score years ago."

Elly enjoyed the Colonel's mellifluous speech, even when it didn't seem to be about anything. Her father looked equally mystified. Davies lounged against the door jamb, smoking a cigarette.

"Your sixtieth birthday," her mother smiled.

The Colonel bowed. "Shall we say, tennish? Meanwhile, Davies and I are off to dine at some establishment said to be, *hrm*, a cut above—"

"A cut above the sordid fare one is normally reduced to in these barbaric outposts," drawled Davies.

"You mean," said Elly's father, "like the stuff we're about to eat."

"Quite," replied Davies with a smirk. He crushed out his cigarette on the door jamb, pulled a gold flask from the pocket of his dinner jacket, unscrewed the cap with long, perfectly manicured fingers, and took a drink.

Another door down the hall opened and Albert Jenning started toward them. Davies and the Colonel had their backs to him and the thick carpet muffled his footsteps.

"…and if you should run into Esta and Albert," the Colonel was saying, "I should like them to attend as well—"

"What—that vulgar clown?" said Davies.

Albert was only a few feet away, and stopped dead. Something in her parents' faces made the Colonel look around.

"Everything about the man's so-called act," continued Davies, savoring his own words, oblivious, "is an affront, a perversion of my noble calling—"

"Albert!" cried the Colonel much too heartily, "I'm having a bit of a celebration this evening, and I should like to invite you—"

"Oh," Albert doffed his derby and put a hand over his heart, "but I would never *presume* to share the same room—nay, even breathe the same air!—as our *great tragedian!*"

He minced the phrase, salaamed Davies in a fawningly obsequi-ous manner, smiled at Elly and her parents, donned his derby again, and strode off with a long-legged, flat-footed gait—a pantomime of clownish-ness that made Elly giggle, but nobody else seemed to find funny.

Davies waved his flask at Albert's departing figure, sneered "I rest my case," and drank.

"The old bird's seventy if a day," said Elly's father, "but I'll still drink his champagne."

"I tell you, Jack," her mother's mild voice had an edge to it, "after that little exhibition I myself can hardly bear to be in the same room with that man."

That odious *man*, Elly felt like adding, certain now she knew exactly what the word meant.

"I suspect Davies may have been a little the worse for drink," replied her father. "And you know this thing between him and Albert has been coming on for some time." They stepped out of the elevator and crossed the lobby. "Look, just stay long enough to have one glass and toast the man who is, after all, our boss. Then you can slip away."

Her mother sighed, and nodded reluctantly.

As soon as they entered the dining room, they saw the Twin Sisters sitting at a table toward the back with Sadie Jacobs.

"Oh Lord," said her father under his breath, "pretend you don't see."

"Oh Jack," said her mother, "I know Sadie does go on. But the poor dear means well. Besides, it's too late anyway."

Sadie had already spotted them, and was waving toward the empty seats at their table.

"Well," her father fixed his face into the semblance of a smile, "at least we won't have to think of things to talk about."

Sadie Jacobs was a very fat woman with large, expressive eyes and two chins. Usually they were both wobbling, because she always seemed to be either talking or eating or both at the same time. In her act she put on different hats and bonnets and talked like she was all different people and sang in a loud, sobbing voice while waving her arms around. On the train she usually sat alone because she dribbled into the next seat so there wasn't room for anyone else. But there was room for Elly, and sometimes Sadie would snag her as she rushed by and make her sit beside her. She smelled like flowers sweating and hugged Elly too hard and called her funny names like *Bubbeleh* and of course she talked and talked. But some of her stories were interesting (Elly knew many of them by heart), and she always shared the gumdrops that she kept in her purse.

"Get the cutlets," said Sadie through a mouthful of cutlet. "How's the *Wunderkind* today?" She smiled at Elly.

"Oh," said her father, "the *Wunderkind* thrives—"

"She was running up and down the train all day, up, down, up, down—*oy*, enough to make you dizzy! If she's not careful she'll get so pepped up she'll have a fit like my aunt Miriam, she had fits, she once had a fit while she was taking a chicken out of the oven—"

"Elly's just full of natural high spirits," Millie suggested.

And she threw the chicken into my nephew Marty's crib, Elly finished in her head.

"She's a pistol," agreed Mabel.

"Well if she's a pistol," said Sadie, "she's an awfully *quiet* pistol! I mean," she turned her soulful eyes on Elly, "I worry about the child sometimes."

Elly felt her mother stiffen.

"I once knew a boy," said Sadie, sawing at her food, "who was using a knife to eat beets from a can and got beaned on the head by a baseball and cut off his own tongue so surgically perfect, the doctor said he couldn't have made a better job of it—"

A waiter with a stained cloth draped over his arm had arrived to take their order: veal cutlets for her parents; hamburger steak and mashed potatoes for Elly. She listened anxiously until her mother said the words, "Well-done, and no gravy please."

"—but even that boy made noises," continued Sadie as though the interruption had never occurred. "I mean it wasn't like talking"—she imitated his weird grunts and groans, the part Elly liked best—"but at least it was *something*—"

"So Sadie,"—Millie managed to cut in—"what's Denver like?" Elly's mother looked at her gratefully, even though Elly had gathered (from eavesdropping) that her mother didn't like the Twin Sisters because they were "too fast." They did dance awfully fast, but Elly somehow guessed that wasn't what her mother meant.

"Oh, you gals will go down a treat," said Sadie, chewing away, "once those cowboys get a gander at your garters. But me and my act—*oy vey*, not a prayer! Ever since Chicago, I've been *dying* up there."

There was a collective rolling of eyes. Elly quietly pulled Mr. Hoppy from his special pocket and began playing with him under the table. They all knew the speech by heart. How Sadie's song "Come Backa, Antonio!" had slayed them in Newark ("of course New Jersey's got more wops than Rome") but the same thing in Des Moines "you could have taken that audience out and buried them." How "Yiddisha Mama," Sadie's showpiece, had them bawling in Buffalo "but in Cedar Rapids they actually *laughed* at me…"

Everything she said was true—it was why Sadie was at the bottom of the bill. But it was always the same, and Elly was only half listening (though she marveled how the big woman could talk without stopping *and* eat a whole plate of food).

Their own food came. Elly frowned at her plate: her hamburger steak was on the wrong side, and someone had put a leaf on top of her mashed potatoes. Her mother rotated her plate and removed the offending sprig of parsley. So Elly was finally able to begin the important job of using her spoon to shape her mashed potatoes into the perfect circle they needed to be in before they could be eaten.

"She sure do like them hamburger steaks," observed Mabel, interrupting Sadie's flow of words.

"And mash patatahs," put in Millie. "I ain't never seen her eat nothin else."

"And you never will," said Elly's father, laughing. "If it's not on the menu, Elly would sooner starve. And those potatoes had better be in a perfect circle…"

His voice trailed off. Elly glanced up and saw her mother looking at him in a funny way.

"Well, when *I* was a little girl," Sadie pointed her fork at Elly, "all six of us had to eat whatever was put before us—and mighty thankful we were to get it! Did I ever tell you about the time…"

·   ·   ·

The week's run would start with tomorrow's matinee, which meant tonight was free. So Elly knew it was a night for practice.

Elly couldn't remember a time she couldn't play the piano. Her parents told people of how she sang along with her father's violin playing when she was just a baby and could pick out melodies on the piano before she was two. And as soon as she knew the names of the notes, they found she could name any note—even a fistful of random notes—without looking.

Except for this, she never spoke. Until the day (she'd heard the story so many times) her mother was brushing Elly's snarled hair more impatiently than usual, and Elly had stated matter-of-factly: "I don't like my hair."

This was when she was three, before one of her first appearances on stage.

Her father was "Jack Robin and his Golden Violin." Elly loved listening to him play the violin more than anything in the world, because the sound of it made that same world dissolve into shimmering colors—not just gold, but red, blue, green—all the colors of the rainbow. When the music stopped, she always had to look around to remember where she was.

Her mother played the piano with her father, and sang as well. Her voice was high and sweetly pure, and could decorate a melody with glittering ornaments like a lady putting on her diamonds. They had taught Elly to play a simple accompaniment to one of her father's solos, bringing her on at the end of the act. The audiences would chuckle indulgently when Elly, in a short dress and bonnet, was carried by her father onstage and placed on the piano bench, and she had to kneel to reach the keys. But they made a different kind of noise when she began to play.

It took Elly some time to work out that the strange noises coming from the theatre were gasps of amazement.

Her mother started teaching her in earnest then, snatching hours on backstage pianos, pianos in hotel ballrooms, churches—whatever they could find. To Elly it was child's play. She only had to hear a melody, and she could see all the notes playing in her mind; all she had to do was push them down. Yet soon she was not only onstage during the entire act: it seemed she had become the star.

"Nobody comes to hear us anymore, Jane," her father had teased. "We've become nothing but handmaidens to the *Wunderkind*!"

The hotel had an upright piano in a corner of an empty ballroom. Her mother had checked it already and found it was in decent tune, because Elly had been known to burst into tears at the sound of a badly out-of-tune instrument. That afternoon in Esta's Pullman car, they'd done nothing but scales, which her mother insisted Elly play every day to strengthen her fingers. Elly thought playing scales was like running as fast as you can and not going anywhere, like Alice and the Red Queen. To make them more interesting, she'd begun playing them in time to the rhythm of the train, thirty-two notes to every click-clack of the track.

"I hear what you're doing," her mother had said, raising an eyebrow.

Elly had gotten a sly look.

But tonight they would play through her new showpiece. It was called the "Fantasy-Impromptu" and was by Chopin, which was pronounced "Show-PAN."

"Like the North Pole in here," said her father, shivering in the dark, cavernous ballroom. Elly's mother made her play through the piece slowly to get her fingers warmed up while her father put rosin on his bow and tuned up his instrument. She sat on her special cushion on her side of the piano bench, dividing the notes of the melody between two hands as her mother played the left hand part and worked the pedal.

Elly's lips were set in an angry pout. On the second page her mother stopped abruptly.

"You don't like playing it so slowly, do you?"

Elly shook her head.

"You're ready to play it fast, aren't you?"

Elly nodded and kicked her legs.

Her mother glanced up at her father. He shrugged, her mother played the two booming bass notes again—and they were off.

There was nothing Elly liked better than playing fast, and she threw herself into the music. The notes rippled and cascaded down the keyboard as she passed the melody from one busy little hand to the other, and her mind filled with flashing colors as the beautiful chords her mother rang out melted into one another. After a really exciting passage (in which Elly got to tear down the keyboard like a roller coaster), they arrived at the slow part. Her father played the melody, Elly played a harmony with him (exactly like they had practiced), and the chords were the same lovely green as Esta's emerald ring...

A repeat of the opening led to a new section where Elly's part jumped all over the place (which was fun!). Finally her father played the slow melody again, the merest echo of it, like a field of grass disappearing in the rain...

A small crowd of people at the door of the ballroom burst into applause.

Her father had his hand over his face, laughing. "I'd...I'd say we ate her dust," he managed to sputter.

"My Lord, Jack," said her mother, hugging Elly, who sat red-faced and panting, kicking her legs, "d'you know she never fingers it the same way twice?"

Her father called her a "damn monkey," which made her mother frown but Elly thought quite funny. The people who had been clapping had crossed the dimly-lit ballroom and stood in a little group, staring at Elly with expressions of incredulity.

"I say," said her father, "I say tomorrow we give er a whirl."

.   .   .

Normally Molly would have stayed with Elly while her parents attended the Colonel's birthday celebration. But her mother intended to stay such a short time, it wasn't considered necessary. Elly changed into her night-gown, her mother tucked her into the cot in the corner of their hotel room, kissed her, whispered for her to go to sleep, turned out the light, and left, locking the door behind her. But tearing through the "Fantasy-Impromptu" at top speed had gotten Elly all pepped up, and she wasn't a bit sleepy. Besides, she was almost never alone in their hotel room. It was too good an opportunity to pass up, and a mischievous plan formed in her head.

Elly knew her parents were somehow responsible for her own existence. But neither of them ever talked about the time before her miraculous arrival on the scene. Until now, this had scarcely bothered Elly; she had always been with them, so it felt as if her parents must have always been with her. But hearing Esta talk about her marriage proposal reminded Elly that her father must once have proposed to her mother. And that (hard as it was to imagine) her parents had once been born themselves, grown up with parents of their own, lived lives apart from each other.

Of course, she might have just asked them about these prior lives. But she sensed there was a reason for their reticence. Besides, Elly much preferred discovering things by eavesdropping or snooping. And she knew just the place to begin her search.

She climbed out of bed, switched on the light, and opened her mother's trunk.

On top was a large removable pasteboard tray containing Elly's own things. Everything was carefully arranged—her shoes, picture books, hair ribbons in a pretty heart-shaped box—and fit together in a jigsaw-puzzle sort of way she found deeply reassuring.

With great care, she lifted out the tray and set it on the floor.

Beneath it were her mother's things. Many of them were already hanging up or put away in the hotel bureau, including her traveling frocks and gown for performing, neatly rolled stockings, and fascinating lacy underthings. But there were still boxes containing shoes, clothespins, an electric hot-plate, tortoise-shell combs, and the heavy iron her father said would "be the death of some poor porter." And, in the very bottom of the trunk, one final box Elly had never looked inside, a box that had once contained candy. But her mother had stopped Elly from opening it, saying that it now held "personal things."

Knowing she was stepping beyond the pale, she pulled it from the trunk and lifted the lid.

On top was a pretty satin bow the same blue as her mother's eyes, and beneath that a small stack of letters. But the cursive writing that covered them Elly was unable to decipher. There were also two postcards, one of a gleaming white city labeled "Columbia Exposition, Chicago Illinois," the other of a long pier with the title "Lakeside, Ohio's Summer Playground." Neither had anything written on the other side.

There were a few more odd mementoes—a card with a menu printed in gold letters, featuring *Roast Prime Rib of Beef* and *Peaches ala Melba*; a bronze medal with a man's head and the legend "Theodore Pressler Music Award"; another ribbon, this one red with "Ohio Wesleyan" printed in black lettering. But what riveted Elly's attention were the two photographs at the bottom of the box.

One was of a pretty, pale-haired little girl not much older than Elly. She was dressed in a tight, embroidered bodice and full skirt with an apron, and demurely posed before a painted backdrop of an Alpine lake. Her hair was coiled into braids, and she wore a queer starched cap. But her dimpled smile had a mild, unflappable quality that made Elly gasp aloud:

Her mother.

The other photograph showed a well-dressed, middle-aged couple. They stood on the sidewalk of what looked like the main street of a small town. In the background were signs: HECKMAN DRY GOODS, BLUMENTHAL CAFÉ AND BAKERY, WERTZ SAVINGS AND LOAN. The woman was handsome rather than pretty, with a hardness to the set of her jaw. But the man's blond hair, round face, and bland, pleasant smile left Elly in no doubt about who they were.

She stared at them for a long time, then put everything carefully away.

CHAPTER THREE

DISGRACE AND TRIUMPH

The following evening's performance would stand out in Elly's memory from all the hundreds of others in her short life as one of her greatest triumphs. But it did not start that way at all. In fact, it started rather badly.

Elly wasn't in the matinee show, because the manager of the house slipped the word to the Colonel there was a Gerry in the audience. The Gerries were members of the Gerry Society, also known as the Society for the Prevention of Cruelty to Children. The way Elly understood it, the Gerries thought it was a bad thing for a child her age to be on a stage, and—if they caught her—would do something terrible to her.

But the Gerries usually came just for the Monday matinee, which meant the rest of the week she was safe. Her parents did their act without her, and Ah Lin and her family spent the afternoon practicing their routines in a corner backstage, even though it was unclear (Elly once heard someone say) whether the Gerries really cared about a "bunch of chink kids." Elly spent much of the matinee peering from behind the curtain trying to spot the Gerry, whom she imagined to be a bestial, hairy man with the eyes and appetite of an alligator, waiting to snatch and devour any child whose misfortune it was to wander onstage.

Vaguely disappointed when no monster materialized, she set off in search of Mr. Barnhold.

"Barnhold's Animals" was the last act of the show, because after the last headliner (which was Esta), people started to leave; since it was a noisy time, an animal act was good. After the animals left the stage it was time for the "chasers." These were flickering images projected on a white curtain by a kinetoscope—fascinating moving pictures of ships being launched, men boxing, marching soldiers. When they finished, the show started all over again. So you could say that it never really stopped.

She found Mr. Barnhold in a remote area backstage, surrounded by his animals in their cages. The animals watched him silently, making no noise while the other acts were onstage; they were professionals. But since their cages often needed to be cleaned, they were usually banished to a place far from the stage and close to the stage door. This made it easy for Mr. Barnhold to take them outside in the mornings for exercise and training. This process fascinated Elly; she had watched Mr. Barnhold coax Binky into standing on his hind legs while pretending to conduct an orchestra, and Miss Koko into daintily drinking from a teacup with her pinky in the air and smacking her lips.

But today Mr. Barnhold sat on an overturned bucket, wearing his blue uniform pants with the gold stripes and a dirty undershirt, cradling Miss Koko in his beefy arms. Elly crouched beside him and stroked Miss Koko's glossy fur, which was hot and damp.

"Ja, it's da vorms, da vorms for sure," he murmured sadly. "I give her da medicine, but it gonna take time. I can get by widout her most of da act—but what I gonna do bout da paddy wagon, eh? Oh, dat paddy wagon, she's da sticker, all right."

The paddy wagon, a miniature replica of the real thing, was pulled onstage by a team of dogs and driven by Miss Koko, dressed as a policeman, to arrest the inebriated Binky. It was the end of the act, a real showstopper, and always got a big hand.

The sound of footsteps. The erect figure of John Humphrey Davies, scrubbed of make-up and wearing his fur-trimmed coat, walked past them and opened the stage door. A cluster of young women squealed at the sight of the famous matinee idol, waved programs to be autographed, and quickly engulfed him before the door closed again.

Mr. Barnhold frowned and shook his head, then turned his attention back to his ailing simian prima donna.

"Miss Koko," he crooned, "can you do dis ting, dis one little ting, for Papa?"

Miss Koko opened a bleary eye and stared up at him mutely. Mr. Barnhold stroked the monkey's face and kissed her tenderly on the forehead.

But Elly never got to see if Miss Koko rose to the occasion, because after her parents finished their act (to rather mild applause, she couldn't help but notice), they all went to a café across from the theatre for some dinner. Coming back, she spotted Smiley Hobson on the sidewalk ahead of them. He wore his sharp green suit, yellow derby perched at a rakish angle, and swung a gold-tipped cane as he strode along. Elly raced ahead of her parents to catch up with him.

She was almost there, eagerly anticipating his smiling surprise, when one of a trio of men in blue jeans leaning against a building stuck his leg out and sent Mr. Hobson sprawling on the sidewalk. He landed gracefully like the dancer he was, even as his cane flew through the air and his derby went rolling away on its brim. The men all laughed, Mr. Hobson picked himself up and smiled at them like it was all a fine joke, the derby rolled into the street—

And Elly ran after it.

There was a confusion of loud noises—hooves on cobblestones, the squeal of brakes on steel wheel rims, people screaming—but she ignored them all and doggedly pursued the spinning hat until it finally lay motionless. She was just reaching for it when it was flattened by a horse's hoof. She let out a squeak of dismay—then found herself being grabbed roughly by the waist by someone who turned out to be Smiley Hobson, except he wasn't smiling at all. And then her mother and father rushed up, she was in her mother's arms, and everyone was yelling.

"Oh Lord, sweet Lord, oh sweet Jesus." Mr. Hobson mopped his face with a yellow handkerchief. Elly twisted in her mother's arms, saw the derby still lying in the street, flattened and forlorn, and burst into tears.

"Oh Elly, Elly," said her mother, rocking her.

"Mr. Hobson," she heard her father say, "I would like to thank you for saving my daughter's life."

"Oh Mr. Robin, Mizz Robin, don't you know it's all cause of me that—"

"Nonsense, Mr. Hobson," said Elly's mother.

"Please, Mr. Hobson," said her father.

"He's shakin hands with the nigger," said a disgusted voice.

The men leaning against the wall were watching them with stony faces.

"Don't pay them any mind," said Smiley. He picked up his cane and pulled at his shirt cuffs. "So, what do you folks say we make a bee-line for that theater over yonder? Cause I do believe we got a show to do."

And he flashed his famous smile at Elly.

.   .   .

The strains of a Chinese march drifted from the open stage door; the second show had already begun. They met Mr. Burns rushing out of the theatre.

"Ha—Jack!" he boomed, buttonholing her father and pulling his cigar from his mouth. "Jack, you shoulda seen it! Barnhold's damn monkey—scuse my French, Jane—damn monkey fell off the paddy wagon before it could even arrest the dog. Looked like it was the *ape* was drunk. Funniest thing I ever seen!"

"Oh, poor Miss Koko," murmured Elly's mother.

"Audience howled. Barnhold's all tore up about it though. Told him he should keep it in the act. He about bit my head off. Funny bird."

"I believe the monkey is ill," said Elly's father.

"Huh," said Mr. Burns, jamming his cigar back into his mouth and rushing away. "Shaping up to be a rough crowd," he called over his shoulder.

Elly dashed ahead of her parents, in a fever to see Miss Koko. Often at the end of a performance there were children gathered around the animals, and Mr. Barnhold would let them pet his four-legged stars. But today she found him alone with his charges, bent over Miss Koko's pros-trate form. He lifted the monkey's head and tried to make her swallow a spoonful of caramel-colored liquid, then turned his huge protruding eyes toward Elly. They glistened in the dim backstage light and seemed to stare right through her.

The sight was so horrible she ran away.

The "Seven Wonders of Shanghai" were just finishing their act, and she stood in the wings to watch. Ah Wing stood centerstage, shirtless in yellow silk pantaloons, his compact, muscular body trembling from the effort of supporting his entire family on his shoulders. Little Ah Lin was being tossed from brother to brother, pajama sleeves aflutter, looking more like a butterfly than ever. Elly pulled out Mr. Hoppy so he could watch as the tiny girl made her way to the top of the human pyramid. In the orchestra pit, Jingles played a continuous snare roll, punctuating each swoop of her little body with a rimshot. Finally she reached the youngest brother. Crescendo of snare as she carefully balanced on his shoulders, extended her arms to the rafters (crash of cymbal, applause), suddenly caught sight of a stuffed frog waving to her from the wings, giggled—

And fell.

Pandemonium as her brothers reached out to catch her—and the entire human edifice collapsed in a disorderly mass. People screamed, bodies thumped on the hard stage. At the last second Ah Wing caught his daughter in his arms. The orchestra struck up the Chinese march at a furious tempo and the curtain came thundering down. Ah Wing herded his dazed and limping sons offstage, carrying Ah Lin, who appeared con-fused but unhurt.

Elly was watching all these developments with interest when a pair of hands suddenly grabbed her shoulders and spun her around.

"Elly!"

Sadie Jacobs stared down at her in full stage make-up, face bright pink, eyes rimmed in black, a fairy tale witch.

"Oh, you *meshugana* little girl, don't you know you could have *killed* someone with a stunt like that!" Her words rained like blows, she shook Elly to punctuate them. "What on earth is wrong with you—"

"Sadie, please!"

Elly felt someone pulling her from Sadie's grip.

"But did you see—"

"I saw," said her mother tersely as she lifted Elly into her arms. "I'll talk to her."

Elly pushed her face into her mother's shoulder and sobbed. The orchestra struck up Sadie's theme song. She heard people talking, her father's voice ("What the devil's got into her today?") as she was carried past them. The jumble of voices and music faded away until it was just her and her mother, and her mother was rocking her, rocking her, and only her mother's voice was left, whispering in her ear.

"Elly, Elly, sweeter than jelly," she crooned, "ate a piece of cake and it went to her belly," over and over. As Elly listened her breathing slowed. Finally she lifted her face and watched her mother's pretty mouth as she softly sang. In the distance the orchestra was playing "Under the Bamboo Tree."

"Elly, do you want to go watch Mabel and Millie?"

They found her father watching the Twin Sisters from the wings. By now they had shed their long dresses and frilly parasols and were down to green skirts that ended above their knees, showing most of their pretty legs in green tights, and were capering around the stage singing "Where did Robinson Crusoe Go with Friday on Saturday Night?" in their not so pretty (but spectacularly loud and piercing) voices.

"They sound like two polecats in heat," Elly had once overheard her father tell the Colonel.

"Yes, well, the, *hrm,* vocal gymnastics of the Twin Sisters," the Colonel had replied, "are not the, *hrm,* focus of their thespian endeavors."

The audience was cheering with gusto, whooping whenever the sisters twirled so that their skirts flew up, and when they sang the line "where there are wild men, there must be wild women" (while bumping their bustles together in rhythm), the yelling threatened to drown out the orchestra.

"Really, very tastefully done," said Albert, sidling up to Elly's parents as the sisters finally came high-stepping offstage. "The magical fairy dust of art."

"Oh stuff!" said Elly's mother, smiling at him. Albert's checked suit so tightly encased his skinny limbs he resembled a cross between man and praying mantis; an absurdly tall derby completed the comic effect. As the orchestra segued into his silly signature tune, he flashed a grin at them all—then tumbled onstage to the usual laughter.

A large crowd, including the Twin Sisters, still gasping and panting, had gathered in the wings to watch. Because (unlike all the other comics Elly had seen, who were always the same) you never knew what Albert Jenning might do.

Inspired by the riotous reception received by the sisters and their gyrations, Albert began dancing to his theme song, shimmying his hips in a ludicrous imitation of them. The audience whooped. When the orchestra stopped at the usual place, Albert put on a long face, peered down into the orchestra pit, and suddenly began conducting in an exaggerated fashion. The orchestra gamely struck up the tune again—Elly could almost hear them laughing through their instruments. Once again Albert began happily shimmying to the music, became so engrossed he forgot to conduct, and again the music ground to a halt. By now the audience was convulsed with laughter. Albert looked around, bewildered, put his hand on his hip, then began conducting again at a comically frantic pace...

"Criminy," sputtered Mabel between fits of laughter, "where does he come up with this stuff?"

"He's sumpin, all right," said Millie.

Elly wanted to stay and watch, but knew it was time to change into her outfit.

The tiny dressing room stank of grease paint and sweat and was festooned with the hastily-shed street clothes of the Twin Sisters, whose untidiness exasperated Elly's mother. Sadie Jacobs was at the mirror taking off her make-up. Normally she would have been complaining a blue streak about her act's poor reception. But tonight the big woman was silent, and stared at them in the mirror with big, sorrowful eyes. Elly avoided their gaze, and stoically submitted to being changed into her stage frock and having her face made up; it was a part of life. Her mother changed into her own costume, all the time listening with one ear to Albert's act as it progressed through its various musical interludes. She pinned a huge bow to Elly's hair, retouched her own make-up with practiced efficiency, effected the temporary surrender of Mr. Hoppy (a painful separation to which, after three years, Elly was still not inured), and the two of them were just stepping out of the dressing room when they heard a sob behind them.

Fat tears were dribbling down Sadie's cheeks.

"Oh Elly," she blubbered, "I…I didn't mean to scare you!"

Elly's mother hurried back to her, pulling Elly by the hand, and Elly was forced to endure a smothering hug and a wet kiss that smeared her make-up before the sound of Albert's theme song sent them rushing out the door again.

They found her father already by the piano, tuning his violin. There was just time for him to grin at Elly (and remind her that the new piece was replacing the "March of the Tin Soldiers") and her mother to seat herself at the piano and hand Elly her lollipop. The orchestra segued from Albert's music into Fritz Kreisler's "Liebesleid," which was their own theme song. The curtain separating them from the audience began to rise, flooding the stage with light. The orchestra stopped after the first phrase, and her parents picked it up.

Elly stood between them dutifully licking her lollipop. This wasn't much fun, because it was made of brightly-painted wood (they'd tried real ones, but they always seemed to end up stuck to Elly's frock). Her father, tall and handsome in his swallow-tail coat, played the lilting melody with his usual expressive grace. But Elly could feel the audience growing restless, and they finished the piece to middling applause.

This was the cue for Elly to tug at her mother's skirt and say "I wanna play *too!*" as loud as she could. It had taken tedious and tearful hours of coaching before she could be induced to speak in anything but her usual soft monotone, and was the part of the act she most dreaded. But she delivered her line successfully (eliciting the line, "No dear, you're still too young" from her mother). Her father smiled condescendingly, then plunged into the terrific descending chromatic passage that begins "The Flight of the Bumblebee," and her mother joined in, playing the staccato accompanying chords with military precision.

Now Elly was supposed to tug at her mother's skirt with growing impatience and (Elly knew the exact moment) push her off the bench. She had no problem at all with this part of the act and performed her role with gleeful gusto. Her mother tumbled off the bench with a shriek, the audience laughed, and Elly leapt up to take her place. Since her cushion was not yet in place, she had to kneel. Without missing a beat, she attacked the same chords with furious intensity. Her father fiddled on, seemingly oblivious…

Enthusiastic applause.

Now it was her mother's turn to lift Elly from the bench and take her place—then for Elly to push her mother off the bench again. Laughter and applause greeted each upset. Then came the big moment. Her father turned around, pretended astonishment at finding his daughter at the piano, then played the seven *pizzicato* notes that marked the middle of the piece. Elly echoed him, the orchestra took up the chordal accompaniment—

And she began to play the wickedly fast melody herself.

This usually drew furious applause, and tonight was no exception. Elly was now in her element, dividing the continuous chromatic passage between both hands. On the last ascending run (suggestive of a bee disappearing into the distance), her father joined her, whipping his bow triumphantly into the air after the last note to a thunderous ovation. Elly stood on the bench and performed her curtsey (another part of the act that had taken more practice than the piece itself) as her parents held their arms out to her and her father shouted over the applause, "LADIES AND GENTLEMEN: BABY ELLY ROBIN, THE *WUNDERKIND!*"

They had them now.

Her father gave the speech about how she was "the one-and-only true protégé," etc., etc., and they did Paderewski's minuet. Elly sat on her special cushion now, and her mother played the bass and worked the pedal. Then it was time for her mother to sing the "Doll's Song" from *The Tales of Hoffman*. To imitate a clockwork doll, she wore a giant key

strapped to her back and moved in jerky motions while Elly and her father accompanied her. Each time her mother ran down (which she did in an eerily mechanical way that Elly loved), Elly leapt from the piano bench and helped her father wind her back up, while Jingles in the orchestra turned a mechanical ratchet that made a wonderful winding noise.

Finally the showstopper, which tonight would be, for the first time, the "Fantasy-Impromptu." Fearlessly Elly plunged into her part, even faster (in her excitement) than they had practiced it. The audience was with her—she could feel that special kind of silence—and when she and her father played the lovely, deep-green melody together, she felt the world disappearing in the way that she loved…

Suddenly it was over. Her parents lifted her together and held her up to the crowd as the orchestra played "Liebesleid" once again, and Elly blinked in the blinding spotlight and tried (with no more success than usual) to smile as the curtain came down.

"Elly," said her father, tears in his eyes.

"Oh, Elly," said her mother, hugging and kissing her on the cheek (and smearing Elly's make-up yet again).

All around them stagehands were moving the grand piano and hauling papier-mâché statues and artificial shrubbery on stage for John Humphrey Davies's soliloquy. Elly paid no attention to her parents' caresses or to the commotion around them, focusing instead on "Jeannie with the Light Brown Hair," which was floating over all the noise.

Molly was peering through the curtain at the orchestra pit, a rapt expression on her pretty freckled face.

"Sure, twas sweeter than previous," she murmured to no one in particular.

"It's that new boy on cornet," said Elly's father.

The curtain rose to reveal Davies leaning against a plaster column, his noble profile displayed to advantage. The rest of the cast had long tired of his monologue—something about a "fallen woman"—and few people in the wings paid him any attention. But Elly was still trying to puzzle out exactly where and how the woman had fallen (as well as a tantalizing reference to the male bosom), and only gradually became aware of another person standing beside her, equally absorbed in Davies's act:

Albert Jenning.

After the scene she had witnessed the previous evening, it made no sense. She scanned his face for evidence of bitterness or loathing. But his gaze was curiously blank and unwavering, like someone trying to understand the workings of some complex piece of machinery.

Her mother led her back to the dressing room to change out of her frock. As the last of her make-up was being wiped off she heard the orchestra playing off Davies. She grabbed Mr. Hoppy and rushed back to the wings just in time to watch Smiley Hobson, resplendent in top hat and tails, go prancing on stage.

Elly tried never to miss Smiley's act. The music, with its bouncing rhythms, did something to her insides. And she was determined to learn how he did those things with his feet, so every night she stood in the wings trying to match his steps. But so far the secret had eluded her.

Yet tonight something was different, and she knew at once it was the new cornet player. All day she'd been listening to him. But he must have been unsure of himself, still learning his part. Because now she could feel him cutting loose, punching out the melody of the "Ragtime Dance" in a way that made her feet move of their own accord, as if bewitched. Smiley's smile stretched so wide it seemed in danger of swallowing his face, and he danced as Elly had never seen him dance. And when the band played the "stop-time"—staccato bursts of melody that Smiley echoed with his feet—it was like he and the cornet player were having their own private conversation.

"Ain't the band just crackerjack tonight, huh Elly-Belly?"

It was Esta in all her finery, an awe-inspiring confection of sequins, tassels, and frills, all contriving somehow to highlight and adorn Esta's equally awe-inspiring bosoms (Elly did know what the word meant). Elly's eyes flashed a smile, and she flung herself against Esta's skirts. Sequins went spinning off in all directions.

"Saints preserve us from the affections of the dwarf," muttered Molly, bending to retrieve them.

Smiley cakewalked off stage to wild applause, smiling at Elly as he passed by, and the band segued into "I Don't Care." At the first three notes of the melody, the crowd began to roar.

"Well, here goes nuttin," said Esta, and then she bounded on stage, prancing back and forth to her theme song. Surprise and delight flashed across her expressive face, and she began blowing kisses to the audience. And the audience (like every audience Elly had ever seen) redoubled its efforts to show Esta just how much they loved her.

Esta was the "I Don't Care Girl." Everyone knew her song—a huge seller in both sheet music and the cylinder Esta had recorded—and audiences loved to sing along with it. Just as they were doing now:

"They say I'm crazy, got no sense—" sang Esta, cupping a hand to her ear.

"BUT I DON'T CARE!" sang the audience as one.

Esta paused, smirking, hand on hip. The orchestra paused with her.

"I may or may not give offense—"

"BUT I DON'T CARE!" roared the audience.

"Jack, I just cannot fathom it," Elly's mother had once remarked (unaware that Elly was only feigning sleep). "Esta can't really sing, she cannot dance (though Lord knows the poor dear does try), her jokes weren't funny a hundred years ago when they were new—just where does her appeal lie?"

"All true, Jane, all true," her father had answered, laughter in his voice. "But you know, I can't even think of Esta without smiling—and maybe that's her secret: you've just *got* to like her!"

But Elly liked Esta's jokes, because she could mostly understand them. Like the one she was telling now:

"Ya know, a gent stopped me by the stage door just now and said 'Hiya cutie. How's about a bite tonight after the show?' I told him I was busy tonight, but I ain't doin nothin now. He said fine. So I bit him."

The audience laughed and clapped, delighted, and Elly giggled with them.

And then she remembered Miss Koko.

~

Mr. Barnhold's animals were all dressed in their wonderful costumes. There were dogs in bonnets or top hats, dogs in skirts or trousers, everything ingeniously secured with bits of elastic. The animals sat patiently, only the swishing of tails betraying their impatience to be on stage.

Mr. Barnhold, his braided uniform coat as tight on his lumpy body as a sausage casing, stood over the only member of his troupe not in costume. She lay with her mouth open and eyes closed, a sheen of sweat on her glossy fur.

Barnhold shifted his mournful gaze to Elly and sighed.

Elly saw Miss Koko's little uniform coat, police cap, and rubber nightstick lying neglected in a corner—and in a flash she had the solution. She grabbed the cap, fastened it under her chin, and stood in front of Mr. Barnhold.

Mr. Barnhold's huge, protruding eyes popped out even further.

· · ·

Binky was a consummate drunk. In his battered derby and seedy coat, he lurched around the stage on his hind feet, tottering, his every lurch underlined by a lick from Shorty's slide trombone. Respectable dog couples in top hats and parasols strolled past him on two legs, snouts in the air. When at last Binky reached the lamppost downstage he fell heavily against it. The audience tittered, and he regarded them with a bleary eye.

The orchestra launched into a brisk "Stout-hearted Men," and a miniature paddy wagon entered from stage right pulled by a team of matched Schnauzers. A little girl in a police coat and cap held the reins. The Schnauzers hit their marks, and the little girl jumped down and belabored poor Binky with her rubber nightstick. Binky collapsed, the girl dragged him to the paddy wagon, and (with some effort) hoisted him inside. Then she climbed back up and, as the curtain fell, drove the paddy wagon offstage to laughter and applause.

It was Elly's greatest triumph.

· · ·

On the following day Miss Koko made a miraculous recovery, and the rest of the week's run was uneventful. That is, until the final matinee, when fate (as if to make up for the tragic curtailing of Elly's fledgling acting career) dropped the eavesdropping opportunity of a lifetime in her lap.

Again it was the Colonel and Mr. Burns she overheard. But this time even Elly's mother couldn't have blamed her, because it was *they* who came to *her*, as if eager to share their conversation. And the eavesdropping gods even insured they were unaware of her presence.

It was early in the show, and Elly was playing in a room full of old props and costumes she had discovered. Listening with one ear for Albert's theme music (the cue for her to put on her outfit), she was crouching behind a pile of dusty furniture, trying on a selection of papier-mâché crowns and helmets and wishing she had a mirror, when she heard the door suddenly open.

"What the hell ya drag me in here for?" brayed Mr. Burns.

"Funny the light's on," murmured the Colonel. The door shut. Elly held her breath. "My dear fellow, your stentorian manner of speaking is singularly unsuited for matters requiring the utmost discretion."

"Yeah yeah, I know I talk loud—so what's the big secret?"

The Colonel heaved a heavy sigh. "I have just this morning received a stack of newspapers from the head office. Reviews of the show from various cities. Here's one from last week, in Omaha."

Rustling of newspaper, a minute of silence, then Burns began to read aloud in a sarcastic voice:

"'…but a dramatic recitation by the well-known thespian John Humphrey Davies gave an uplifting note to the evening, and exposed our fair city to the high culture of which, judging by the audience's vociferous response to the lewd gyrations of two half-dressed young women, it is sorely in need.' Lotta tripe."

"Yes, and about the best publicity we could have received."

"Ha! Hadn't thought of it that way."

"But that's not what I wanted you to see. Look here, on the next page."

"'Girl Found Murdered,'" read Burns. "But—why, it must be that one I…only sixteen years old…huh, went to our show with some friends, then got separated…never made it home…doesn't say if she was interfered with."

"For that you need the *Police Gazette*," said the Colonel dryly.

Elly listened intently, trying to make sense of it all.

"Hanging's too good for the son-of-a-bitch," Burns was saying.

"I believe the British used to, *hrm,* disembowel people alive, then draw and quarter them."

"That's the ticket! So, it musta been somebody in our audience, huh?"

"So one would assume," said the Colonel. "Now look at this."

More rustling of newspapers.

"*Pittsburgh Courier,*" murmured Burns.

"Skip the review—read this."

"The devil—another murdered girl?!"

"Who was also at our show. Also found a block from the theater—"

"—and also just a kid—Christ, fifteen it says here—"

"—and also strangled. Just like the one in Omaha."

The men went silent. Elly felt sick. *Strangled.* She was pretty sure what the word meant. And wished she wasn't.

"Good holy Christ," muttered Burns, more softly than Elly had ever heard him speak. "So you're thinkin…?"

"What other conclusion is there? Both murders committed on our last night, just before we left town—the coincidence is too much."

"Christ," said Burns again. "So…who do you figure?"

"I haven't the slightest idea."

"The police—"

"My dear fellow, the police are the last thing we need."

"Yeah, what was I thinkin. Keep it under our hats, like."

"And keep our eyes peeled."

"Nothin else we can do."

"I'm afraid not… Well, I just felt you should know."

"Sure, sure. Except I kinda wish I didn't."

Elly felt exactly the same way.

CHAPTER FOUR

AN INTERESTING VISIT

And hast thou slain the Jabberwock?
Come to my arms, my beamish boy!
Oh frabjous day! Callooh! Callay!—

"**H**e *chortled in his joy,*" finished Elly's father. "I think I got the whole thing memorized." He dropped the sporting pages to grin at Elly as he sprawled on the bed in pajamas and dressing gown. "Musta heard it about a thousand times by now."

"Then soon it shall be a thousand and one," murmured Elly's mother. Elly sat on her lap in a chair in the corner in her flannel nightgown for her nightly story time. She had not cared for *Alice's Adventures in Wonderland*, finding the constant shrinking and expanding both disturbing and tiresome. But when her mother finished reading *Through the Looking Glass*, Elly had decided it was everything a book should be and immediately turned back to the first page, looking up at her mother expectantly.

This was before she was talking. After her famous first words, her mother began pointing at words in the book, trying to get Elly to say them, but she stubbornly refused. Nevertheless, having noticed how fixedly her daughter watched her finger when it followed beneath the text, she continued to read to her that way. Until the day, when Elly was four, she had picked up the book and, in her curiously toneless voice, began to read it perfectly, just to show that she could. What she had never revealed, though, was that now she did indeed have the entire book memorized—afraid that if her mother knew, she might stop reading it aloud to her.

They finished another chapter. Her father had thrown his paper aside and was jiggling his foot.

"Elly, sweetheart," said her mother, "do you want to go visiting until Molly comes?"

On the last evening of a week-long run, it was the custom to leave one's door open as an invitation to socialize. Elly nodded eagerly, slid from her perch, snatched Mr. Hoppy, and was out the door before her mother could change her mind. The Colonel's door was cracked open and she could hear his voice. But it reminded her of the disturbing conversation she'd overheard that afternoon, and she quickly fled down the hall. Then she spotted another door ajar—the door to a room whose occupants were almost never at home at this time of the evening. She stood and listened a moment, but heard only the rustling of bedclothes and squeak of mattress springs. Abruptly Mabel appeared in the doorway, dressed in a peach-colored silk nightgown.

"Elly! Come on in, I was just about to close the door but you can watch."

Millie was sitting up in bed in a satin robe, drinking something with a lovely purple color from a flask-shaped bottle and smoking a cigarette.

"Hey ya Elly, have a seat." She patted the bed.

Elly kicked off her slippers and launched herself across the bed.

Mabel had closed the door. She laid a towel on the bed, lay down on the other side of Elly, hoisted up her nightgown, and stretched her bare legs out on the towel.

Elly stared, transfixed. She had never seen a grown woman's bare legs before—not even her mother's. The closest she had gotten was when they went to Ocean City during their summers off and her mother wore bloomers that, when wet, showed their lovely, rounded shape. So she was doubly lucky to have found the Twin Sisters not just at home—a rare event—but Mabel's bare legs in the bargain.

Mabel rubbed some lotion into her skin, then began scraping her leg with long languid strokes of a safety razor, checking for errant stubble with her other hand and wriggling her toes. Elly decided it was the perfect opportunity to pursue the subject that the search of her mother's trunk had only made more tantalizing. Still staring at Mabel's legs, she murmured, in her flat little voice: "How did my parents meet?"

"Wow!" Mabel's razor stopped mid-stroke. "Spooks me when she talks—I just about cut myself."

"She don't even know?" asked Millie.

"It's weird how secretive Jack and Jane are about it all. Jeez," Mabel resumed shaving, "six years old, isn't that right? She should know by now. I mean what's to hide? Such a romantic story," Mabel sighed. "Like Romeo and Juliet. Feel," she commanded Elly.

Elly stroked Mabel's leg, thrilled.

"If I didn't do this, I'd look like a wooly mammoth."

"Them tights is thin," agreed Millie.

"Them tights is *tight*!"

Millie laughed and took another drink.

"So Elly," said Mabel, "the way your parents met—"

"Maybe we shouldn't," said Millie. She held out her bottle to Mabel.

Mabel took a swig and passed it back. "Who's she gonna tell?"

"Ha!" said Millie, coughing cigarette smoke.

"So," continued Mabel, "so, your papa's on the road in Ohio—"

"I heard it was Pennsylvania."

"No, it was Ohio, some little burg. And his piano player gets sick, see. So they looks around in this little burg for someone to fill in—"

"And it was your momma!" said Millie, squeezing Elly's leg for emphasis.

"*I'm* telling it! Right, it was your momma. Except she wasn't your momma yet."

Millie snorted.

"And it was love at first sight," continued Mabel. "Except your momma's family, they were the rich folks in this little burg, her father owned some big business—"

"Big fish in a small pond," sniffed Millie. "Germans, I heard."

"That's it, rich Germans. And they didn't hold with their daughter marryin a—"

"A musician," said Millie quickly, giving Mabel a look.

"Yeah, that too—what, you think she don't even know what she is?"

"Besides," said Millie, "I don't even think she really is, anyway. I mean, not if her momma ain't."

"Yeah yeah, has to be on the mother's side, our rabbi used to go on about it." Mabel snatched Millie's cigarette and used it to light her own. She took a long drag on it while considering Elly, then let the smoke out slowly through her nose. "Still say she's one of us. Got her father's hair." She grinned and playfully stroked Elly's head.

Clues all over the place, thought Elly.

"Whatever," said Millie. "So anyways, your folks got married—"

"Eloped."

"Right, so they eloped. And ain't neither one of their families ever forgiven em."

"We don't know that for sure," said Mabel. She took another long drag on her cigarette and studied Elly again. "Elly, did ya ever meet any of your parents' folks?"

"You know," added Millie, "grandparents and such?"

Elly shook her head.

"See!" said Millie.

There was a knock on the door. Millie jumped up to open it and revealed Molly.

"Ah, the dwarf in hiding," cried Molly with her usual exasperation.

"Hiya Molly," said Millie. "Come on in and have a nip." She held up the bottle.

"Sure, you know I'm only sixteen," said Molly, coming in anyway and shutting the door. She squinted at the bottle. "What is it?"

"Plum brandy," said Mabel.

"Gwan, try it," said Millie.

"Yeah, come on in and get comfy," said Mabel, patting the bed.

Molly joined them, sitting on the edge of the bed. She wore a quilted robe, and her long red hair was twisted into a braid.

"Just a sip," she said, accepting the bottle.

"So Elly sleeps with you tonight, huh?" said Mabel.

"She does," said Molly. She took a drink and made a face. "Plums, you say?"

"Better take another sip," said Millie. "Like, to make sure."

Molly shrugged and drank some more.

"So I guess her folks wanna be alone sometimes," suggested Mabel.

"Ha!" said Molly. "Sure the door was closed when I got there. 'She's out visitin, Molly,' Jane calls out to me."

"What—they never even opened the door?"

"So romantic," sighed Millie.

Clues thick on the ground, thought Elly. Emboldened by the success of her detective work, she took a deep breath, and asked the question she'd been brooding about all week—even as she had a terrible suspicion she already knew the answer.

"What's murder?"

Molly spewed plum brandy all over her robe.

"She's a regular motor-mouth tonight," marveled Mabel.

"Why you wantin to know about stuff like that, Elly?" asked Millie. "Stuff that's not very nice?"

"Maybe she wants to kill somebody," suggested Molly.

And just like that, Elly's worst fears were confirmed.

~

On the way to Molly's room a door opened, and Brett Crawley emerged in his shirtsleeves carrying the paper bag Elly knew housed his cornet. At the sight of Molly he stopped short and his high forehead went bright pink.

Molly stopped as well, and the hand holding Elly's squeezed her tighter. "Um," Molly pulled her robe together with her free hand, "sure you're Mr. Crawley, the new trumpet player?"

"Cornet," said Crawley, pulling the bell of his instrument out of his paper bag. "Everyone calls me Brett."

"Ah," said Molly.

Brett Crawley stared at her for a long moment. "So, what's your name?" he finally blurted.

"Oh!" Molly put her hand to her face (which was as pink as his) and shook her head. "Doyle. Molly Doyle."

"I'm pleased to meet you, Molly Doyle."

"And likewise, Brett Crawley. Sure I am pleased to meet you."

"It sounds like you're from Ireland."

"It's discernin you are, Brett Crawley."

Crawley went pale now. "Hey, um, I didn't mean..." he sputtered.

Molly squeezed Elly's hand so hard it hurt. "You play pretty."

"Gee, you think so?" said Crawley, letting out his breath and smiling. "Sometimes I get nervous as the dickens."

"Uncommon pretty."

There was a long moment of silence. Molly brushed at a loose strand of hair.

"Hey," said Crawley, seeming to notice Elly for the first time, "ain't she a little wonder though!"

"Sure, there's no wonder to it," said Molly, her green eyes flashing. "She's but a dwarf."

"Ha! That so?" said Crawley, grinning. There was a wide-eyed openness to his face that Elly decided she liked. She was a bad judge of age but guessed he was younger than the other men in the orchestra.

"Yes, well, I must be off," said Molly.

"Oh yeah, right," said Crawley.

She turned to leave.

"Hey," said Crawley suddenly, "I'm goin down to blow some tunes with the guys"—he held up his paper bag again—"if you wanted to come listen…"

"So late?"

"Um, yeah, down in the ballroom. You wanna come?"

Molly lifted Elly's hand ruefully. "Sure, I cannot."

"Oh yeah, sure, I forgot," said Crawley. "Sorry."

They turned to go again and got halfway down the hall.

"Hey!" said Brett Crawley. He was still standing in the same spot. "Maybe some other time?"

Molly squeezed Elly's hand. "Perhaps," she called back. "Yes, perhaps some other time," she repeated, almost to herself, with a funny and (Elly thought) very interesting smile.

•   •   •

Over the next few weeks, through the runs in Salt Lake City, Boise, and Seattle, Elly furtively watched the members of her troupe, searching for the murderer in their midst. She assumed such a being must be clearly malevolent, a drooling beast of a man (Burns and the Colonel seemed certain it was a man) just itching to get his hands around your neck. But everyone appeared the same as always, it seemed more and more preposterous that one of them might be strangling young girls in his spare time and stuffing them in trashcans, and her quest gradually lost its urgency.

Developments on the romantic front were decidedly more satisfactory. Molly spent much of her time backstage peering through the curtain at Brett Crawley in the orchestra pit, and Elly had spotted them walking together through the streets of Boise. Then, one memorable evening when she was again sleeping with Molly, she awakened to find Molly facing away from her, a pair of masculine hands roving over the back of her shirtwaist. For some time Elly watched, spellbound, as Crawley's fingers bunched up the material, then smoothed it out again. Until Molly suddenly looked over her shoulder, and announced in a disgusted voice: "The dwarf awakes."

Whereupon (despite Elly's intense disappointment and Crawley's plaintive cry "Who's she gonna tell?") Molly made him leave.

      •   •   •

In Portland, Albert received a telegram with an offer to join Karno's comedy troupe for an appearance at the London Palladium (which, it was explained to Elly, was like "The Palace of England"). It was a big step up, and, everyone but the Colonel agreed, worth breaking your contract for. So Albert was leaving tomorrow, and tonight would be his last show.

He asked Elly if she could ever forgive him for "leaving her in the lurch" (she decided she could) and promised that someday they would meet again. "And Mr. Hoppy too," he added, which made her happy. And that afternoon they went on their last expedition together.

They no longer looked for Red Indians (they'd seen so many in Colorado, Utah, and Idaho that Albert had pronounced himself "quite surfeited—though I do still long for a loincloth"). So they wandered the Portland waterfront, looking for nothing in particular. The sky was overcast and the balmy April air rich with the smells of tar, fish, pine needles. Husky men unloaded barges full of barrels onto waiting drays.

The seedy waterfront streets were lined with pawn shops, Chinese laundries, and rough-looking saloons. A man suddenly stumbled out of one of them as though the building had spit him out. He was big-bellied and stocky, dressed in filthy canvas pants and knee boots with flapping soles, with a beard so thick his eyes resembled an animal peering out of a bush. Taking no notice of them, he began walking in the most extraordinary manner, swinging his legs from the hip with a corkscrew motion while lurching now one direction, now another, like a ship tacking against the wind.

Albert began following the man, mimicking his gait. Elly fell in behind Albert, doing her best to ape both. The three of them formed a sort of drunken parade, and people on the street were laughing and pointing. Startled by this attention, the man looked over his shoulder. Albert assumed an innocent pose. The man blinked at him, then staggered on. Again they began dogging his footsteps. Albert's imitation was so

wonderfully perfect that Elly began to giggle. Suddenly the man whirled on Albert, knocked him down with a powerful blow to the chest, and staggered away, mumbling to himself.

She rushed to Albert's side. He looked up at her, dazed but happy.

"Oh Elly, such a lovely walk he had. And now," he exulted, "now I've *got* it!"

She retrieved his derby and perched it on his head. Shakily he stood up and dusted himself off. "About time we started back," he said, looking around. "This looks like the fastest way…"

They started down a narrow street toward the avenue where the theater was. At the next corner a group of young sharps were leaning against the side of a building. One of them nodded in Elly and Albert's direction and the rest turned hard faces toward them.

Albert squeezed Elly's hand and they walked faster. Picking their way past piles of horse droppings, they passed a pool hall and a barrel house. From its open door came raucous laughter and the sweetish reek of alcohol.

"This is beginning to look like not such a bright idea," murmured Albert.

A woman stood in the doorway of a dilapidated hotel. She wore a wine-colored silk dress and was garishly made-up. She eyed Albert in a funny way, as if they shared some delicious secret—then caught sight of Elly.

"If you ever wanna try one a bit older, dearie, look me up."

She was still cackling as Albert hurried away, tugging on Elly, almost colliding with a very tall man stepping out of a saloon with a very short woman hanging on his arm.

It was John Humphrey Davies.

At the sight of them Davies froze. The young woman stumbled and looked up at him, frowning. For a moment Davies's oily insouciance deserted him and he seemed genuinely at a loss. But an instant later the actor in him was back at the helm, and he appeared his usual smirking, preening self.

"So I hear tomorrow you shall be relieving us of your presence?"

Since their falling out, Albert had begun referring to Davies as "the Great Tragedian"—lately shortened to "the G. T."—and he continued to watch Davies's act with the same bemused attention. But they had never spoken a word.

"Yes, I'm off to join an entire troupe of vulgar clowns," Albert simpered.

Davies forced a laugh, and the young woman scowled. Elly couldn't stop looking at her. She had a small, pinched face and her cheeks were heavily rouged. She was dressed in a pink satin gown with many bows, a large bustle, and a mud-stained hem, and her hat was covered in artificial roses. But it was too big for her face, and her gown hung loosely on her small, bony frame, like a little girl playing dress-up.

"Yes, well be careful with those pratfalls," Davies was saying, "or someday you're liable to break your neck."

The girl yawned hugely and tugged on his sleeve.

Till now, Albert hadn't really noticed her. His eyes widened, and his habitually mild expression fled. He looked hard at Davies.

"I know clowns whose boots you are not fit to lick."

A kind of madness blazed up in Davies's eyes, he moved as if to strike Albert—but the girl tugged on his sleeve again and said, "Come on!" in a whiney little voice. Davies's expression softened into a sneer. He spat, turned on his heel without a word, and led the girl down the street and into the hotel they'd just passed.

All the way back to the theater, Albert never said a word.

·   ·   ·

Albert Jenning's final performance with the troupe was a memorable one.

He had finished his act and changed into his street clothes. Elly and her parents had just come offstage, and were standing in the wings with the Colonel and the Twin Sisters. Albert joined them just as the curtain rose on John Humphrey Davies in his usual pensive pose. In a resonant bass, Davies began to intone: "Full many a stoic eye and aspect stern, Mask hearts whose grief hath little left to learn…"

As usual, no one paid the slightest attention to him.

"How shall I describe her?" cried Davies with rhetorical fervor.

Albert stepped away from the group and struck Davies's exact pose, ludicrously exaggerated.

Millie tittered.

"How picture to the mind that gentle-eyed, confiding creature that stood before me," continued Davies.

Albert was now mouthing Davies's every word, exactly synchronized.

"—her ruby lips, her rosy cheeks, her graceful and elastic step—"

Still mouthing the words, Albert pursed his lips, pinched his cheeks, and took a mincing step while wriggling his hips. Elly's mother had gone bright pink. Mabel and Millie were both gasping, and the Colonel was making curious snuffling sounds.

"And yet," continued the oblivious Davies, "that form, once so full of grace and beauty"—Albert delineated a curvaceous shape in the air while lewdly winking—"now stiffened and cold, and those once so bright and laughing eyes now glazed and fixed in death—"

Albert went slowly cross-eyed. Mabel emitted a stifled shriek.

Davies paused. A pained expression flitted across his brow. Taking a deep breath, he plunged on...

And so did Albert. Mabel and Millie clutched each other and did a sort of spastic dance. Elly's mother had her hands over her face and was taking deep breaths. Smiley Hobson had joined them in his costume and black-face make-up; in the gloom his smile seemed to float in space like the Cheshire cat's.

It was now so noisy backstage that Davies began to fluff his lines. The audience had grown restless, and when Davies cried out, "Oh, that I might die as well and join her—" someone yelled out, "Go ahead!"

"I believe he may already be deceased," murmured the Colonel.

Finally Davies delivered the lines referring to his own bosom (the concept that continued to elude Elly), and flung himself against the gravestone of his beloved.

Albert flung himself against a folding chair, which collapsed with a bang.

The curtain fell. Davies leapt up and stormed offstage, pausing to glare at them all, his eye lingering on Albert.

"The head office shall hear about this," he hissed to the Colonel.

The Colonel seemed unperturbed. In fact it looked to Elly like, beneath his mustache, he was actually grinning.

.   .   .

But Davies's anger had the opposite effect on Elly, because it reminded her again of the scene she had witnessed that afternoon.

She could not stop brooding about it. In an instant, Albert's insult had transformed Davies from matinee idol to madman; to imagine him actually throttling Albert was the shortest of leaps. But what to do about her awful revelation? It was hard enough for her to talk about anything, and this would stretch her powers to the limit. Worse, the only people she could tell were the Colonel and Mr. Burns. And this would mean revealing the truth about her shameful eavesdropping…

The rest of the troupe, including her parents, were taking Albert out for a farewell party, and Molly was supposed to escort Elly back to their hotel. But Elly's dilemma had put her in a funk. In the final show that evening she shouted out her line ("I wanna play *too!*") with a vehemence that startled her parents, and suffered the removal of her outfit and make-up with more than her usual bad grace. And when her mother ran off to fetch Molly, Elly snatched up Mr. Hoppy and (knowing full well how naughty she was being) left the dressing room.

She had a vague notion of catching John Humphrey Davies in the act of strangling one of the young girls who always hovered outside the stage door after his performance, and set off in that direction. The stage door in this theater was even farther away from the stage than usual. She threaded her way past rows of thick curtains and backdrops hanging to the floor, took a turn, and found herself in a large, dimly lit space. Gathering her courage (for to leave the theater alone was truly stepping "beyond the pale"), she pushed open the heavy door. But the alley behind the theater was empty, and she realized she was too late.

She realized as well what a silly idea it had been.

As she stepped back inside she heard little yips of excitement coming from around a corner, and knew Mr. Barnhold must be feeding his animals.

Just as the human members of their troupe usually headed out for a bite to eat after the show, Mr. Barnhold always fed his animals after their final appearance. As they ate he would stroke and pet them, praising their performances. Elly loved to watch this frisky exhibition of tail-wagging divas, and was just turning the corner, when she heard Mr. Barnhold's voice:

"Dey know ven I am feeding dem de show is over, and dey can cut loose."

He chuckled—a sound Elly had never heard before—and somebody laughed. She peered around the corner. A single lightbulb cast a dim light over Barnhold and his charges. A young girl stood next to him. She wore a sailor blouse, and was at an age Elly found interesting, with the face of a girl and the body of a woman. Neither she nor Barnhold had yet noticed her. On a whim she stayed in the shadows and listened to them.

"And vich one is your favorite?"

"Him," the girl said at once.

"Ah, dat is Binky. You may pet him if you like."

Eagerly the girl knelt down to stroke Binky's wiry coat.

"He's very handsome," she pronounced.

"Oh ja. But don't say it too loud, it vill go to his head."

The girl laughed. Mr. Barnhold guided her hand gently up and down Binky's back.

"And so, do you haff a name?"

The girl giggled and nodded. "Gertrude Wade."

"Gertrude, is it? Den it is Gertie I vill call you."

"That's what my father calls me." Mr. Barnhold made her hand stroke Binky's muscular flank. The dog writhed in ecstasy.

"So Gertie, your mudder, she is waiting for you out front?"

She shook her head. "I came with my friend. But she went off with a boy." She wrinkled her nose in disgust.

"Ja, dose boys, you got to look out for dem—"

"Excuse me, Mr. Barnhold?"

Her mother's voice.

"You haven't seen Elly, have you?"

"No, I haff not seen her—"

Guiltily Elly emerged from the shadows.

"Elly!" Her mother made an exasperated face. "Why did you go running off like that? You know Molly's waiting for you." She took Elly's hand, paying no attention to the other girl.

Mr. Barnhold was staring at Elly with his bulging eyes.

Her mother pulled her by the hand and led her away.

CHAPTER FIVE

AN EARTHSHAKING EXPERIENCE

"Just what was it Sadie was yelling after the lights went out?" asked Elly's mother.

"Ha!" said her father. "Stuff that would offend your delicate sensibilities. It's a great language for those kinda words."

"It did sound rather as though the Yiddisha Mama had turned into a Yiddisha fishwife," mused her mother mildly.

Her father laughed again. Elly sat on his lap, holding the reins and proudly driving the buggy. The rhythmic motions of the horse's dappled rump were punctuated by lazy flicks of its tail.

They were on a holiday because the lights in the theater had gone out at the beginning of the Saturday matinee, right in the middle of Sadie's act. In the sudden darkness the band had fallen apart. Above the audience's restless murmuring, Sadie could be heard yelling in that funny language she often spoke—a language Elly now realized her father could understand.

There had been a lot of fuss. She heard Mr. Burns braying backstage that the theater's brand-new electrical lighting system "wasn't worth a bucket of warm spit," and the Colonel declared that gaslight suddenly possessed a "more than nostalgic appeal." To calm the restless audience Brett Crawley struck up "The Man on the Flying Trapeze," and the rest of the band joined in, improvising in the dark. Finally the house manager carried a portable, battery-powered light on stage and announced the matinee was canceled, tickets would be refunded or exchanged for a later performance at the door, and if everyone would please remain seated, the ushers would be by to escort them out of the theater.

Groans from the audience. The manager stalked offstage, scowling. His light flashed on Elly and her parents. She looked up at her father's face. He grinned down at her.

"What say we skidoo," he suggested. "Before he changes his mind."

.   .   .

A free afternoon without having to journey to the next city was a rare luxury and put the troupe in a holiday mood. Elly watched Brett and Molly stroll off into downtown Sacramento, arm-in-arm. Esta, the Twin Sisters, and the rest of the band opted for an excursion boat on the river. Elly wanted to go along; she found steamboats as fascinating as steam locomotives and could easily have spent the entire afternoon watching the paddle wheel go around. But her father wanted to rent a buggy from a livery stable and take them for a ride. And with the promise that Elly could drive, all thoughts of steamboats were driven from her head.

They had left downtown behind. Crowds of Saturday strollers were promenading along the tree-lined riverbank. Sailboats dotted the river's bright surface. An excursion boat was paddling upstream. From across the water came the faint sounds of a band playing a waltz.

A muscular man riding an old-fashioned penny-farthing bicycle drew abreast of them. He looked down his nose at them from his lordly perch above the machine's enormous front wheel, then flew past, leaving a cloud of dust in his wake.

"What say we pick up the pace?" suggested her father.

"Careful, Jack," said her mother, smiling. "You know she's a demon for speed."

But Elly was already gleefully shaking the reins. The horse abruptly shifted its gait to a brisk trot. They overtook the cyclist and left him in their own cloud of dust. Her father laughed and squeezed Elly's waist.

~

They parked the buggy near the river and ate a picnic lunch beneath a grove of shade trees. Her mother had bought sliced ham for Elly; it was one of the few non-hamburger steak foods she would eat—and then only after aligning the slices perfectly with her bread. But she would not touch the deviled eggs or potato salad, and her father teased her by eating an entire can of sardines, dangling each oily fish by its tail and lowering it into his mouth like a sword swallower, to Elly's fascinated disgust.

"Jack, you are a goose," said her mother. She lay on her side with her head propped on her hand, smiling at them both. Her hair had come undone and cascaded in golden ringlets around her pink, shining face; Elly couldn't remember her looking any lovelier.

Her father grinned, washed down the sardines with a swig of beer, and offered the bottle to her mother. She accepted it (something Elly had never seen her do) and took a ladylike sip. She passed the bottle back to her father and brushed at a blonde ringlet. A look passed between them.

"Hey Elly—how's about you run off and explore for a while?" asked her father.

Elly nodded eagerly. Her mother helped her take off her boots and stockings and told her she needn't worry about getting her old traveling pinafore dirty.

"Don't go far," her mother called after her.

She ran to the river and began splashing through the reeds growing along the bank. Mud squished deliciously between her toes. Something sailed through the air and plopped into the water in front of her. A long-legged shadow glided beneath the water back to the shore, and a pair of yellow eyes emerged from the water's surface and blinked at her. She made an excited lunge, but the creature leapt from her grasp, plopped into the water, and again kicked its way to shore.

She splashed after it…

~

Her mother lay on the grass on her back. Her father lay almost on top of her, as though they had been wrestling and he was the winner. They were kissing.

Normally Elly would have stood still to savor this exciting event, but she was too excited herself. She approached and stood over them, proudly dangling the wriggling creature by one webbed foot. Her father's head moved to one side and revealed her mother's face. Her eyes were closed, her cheeks were pinker than ever, and her lips were parted. A drop of muddy water splashed on her cheek, and her eyes fluttered open.

She screamed.

Her father's whole body jerked and knocked against Elly. She fell on her bottom, the frog leapt from her hand, and she burst into tears—even as her parents were helpless with laughter. Her mother took her on her lap and hugged her, exclaiming over how wet and muddy she was. A moment later her father put the squirming little creature back in her hands.

"See Elly? I've caught him for you again," he said, stroking her head. She cradled the little frog, felt his heart flutter, and was happy again. She pulled Mr. Hoppy from the pocket of her muddy pinafore, and introduced him. Her father declared the other frog must be Mrs. Hoppy, and her mother laughed.

"Oh, but poor Mr. Hoppy," she exclaimed, examining the doll. "So wet and muddy—and look! His seams are coming apart. I'll have to sew him back up."

"Just how old is that old thing, anyway?" asked her father.

"Old thing!" chided her mother. "You'll hurt poor Mr. Hoppy's feelings. My mother sewed him for me," she said in a different voice. "When I was a little girl. Just about Elly's age."

Elly was amazed to learn that Mr. Hoppy'd had a prior life—nor had she ever heard her mother talk about her own mother. She began to listen carefully.

"I'll never forget," said her father, laughing. "When I watched you unpack that first time, and you pulled out that doll! That's when I knew I was really robbing the cradle."

"Jack, you're a goose," said her mother, slapping him playfully on the shoulder.

"Was that when you eloped?" said Elly.

Her parents froze.

"Elly," said her mother at last, "Elly, how on earth—"

"Someone's been talking to her."

"Oh, I wish people would mind their own…" Her mother's voice trailed off. She looked off into the distance and brushed at her hair distractedly.

"Jane, perhaps it's time—"

"Yes yes, Jack, I know, only…" Her mother took a deep breath. "Yes, Elly. That was when your father and I got married—that's a much nicer way of saying it."

"She had the right word." Her father opened another bottle of beer and drank from it.

"Oh, Jack." Her mother settled Elly on her lap and stroked her hair. "So, Elly… what else would you like to know?"

Elly thought. "Do you have a mother and father?"

Her mother sighed. "Yes, sweetheart. I do."

"Are they German?"

"Someone's really been at her."

"Yes— No— Their parents all came from Germany. So they are German-American, I suppose."

"Are they my grandparents?"

"Never heard her talk this much in my life," said her father.

"Yes, sweetheart. They are your grandparents."

Mrs. Hoppy squirmed in Elly's hands. "Can I meet them?"

She felt her mother stiffen. She stopped stroking Elly's hair and put her lips to her ear. "Someday," she whispered. "Maybe someday…"

"Elly," said her father in a brisk voice, "how'd you like to play with my watch?"

Elly's eyes opened wide. She put Mrs. Hoppy down as her father pulled out his pocket watch and handed it to her. With practiced motions she released the catch that opened the glass case, then pushed another small lever. The numbered face flipped open, exposing all the marvelous inner workings. There were shiny brass gears and springs and a piece that jiggled back and forth, making one of the gears move in tiny increments, a ticking sound accompanying each rhythmic motion. That gear connected to all the other gears (Elly had deduced), and they were all turning as well, she had decided—but much more slowly... Tick...tick...tick...tick... She stared and stared, fascinated, hypnotized. And never noticed when Mrs. Hoppy finally hopped away, or the protective way her father was hugging her mother—

Or the tears on her mother's face.

.   .   .

"Hey, how's about what happened with the animal act tonight!"

"Sure, tis my fate never to see Barnhold's beasts tread the boards," replied Molly, "as I am always then engaged in removing her majesty's gown."

"Hey, that's right, I forgot they go on right after Esta's act. Did you see, Elly?"

Elly nodded. She liked that Brett Crawley talked to her like she was all grown up, and decided she would someday have a sweetheart just like him. Her fantasy was sometimes brought wonderfully to life, because he and Molly had relaxed their scruples about being observed by Elly, and she had been allowed to watch them kissing on a number of occasions. And tonight Brett had talked Molly into going to a party that a girl Shorty knew had heard about, which he said was sure to have dancing.

"But the dwarf," Molly had sighed. "Sure I cannot just leave her. Such mischief and mayhem she is capable of; twould be my job."

"Hey, but what if we just brought her along? After all—"

"—who's she gonna tell?" finished Molly, laughing. And, to Elly's delight, she had given in.

So here she was, sailing through the streets of San Francisco in the middle of the night, carried in Brett's arms like a princess in her litter. The night was wonderfully mild and smelled of the sea. She wore her flannel nightgown and slippers and held Mr. Hoppy (newly washed and seams doubly reinforced). Molly tripped along beside them carrying Brett's cornet in its paper bag.

"And so what wonders did Barnhold's beasts perform, then?" she asked.

"Well, that's just it. They didn't perform *any* wonders. I mean, they didn't perform period, did they, Elly? Barnhold about had a conniption trying to get them to walk on their hind legs and do all the usual stunts, but those dogs just weren't having any. Running all over the place, nervous as cats—Ha! Monkey jumped off the paddy wagon and started in beating on Barnhold with the rubber nightstick—I tell you, me and the boys were laughing so hard we could hardly play!"

Molly mused on this information. "Sure, what would make them all forget all their lines like that, in a manner a speakin?"

"Can't imagine. Took sick, maybe?"

A thought occurred to Elly.

"Vorms," she said.

"Huh?" said Crawley.

"Sure, she does speak on occasion," said Molly. "but it's not always worth the waitin."

"Ha! But then again"—Crawley's voice turned serious—"nobody was on the ball tonight. Not after that man Weaver and all his talk. Imagine, Esta forgetting the words to her own song!"

"Sure, it's so horrible, it put her majesty in a state."

"I swear, me and the boys were all looking sideways at each other all the time we were playing, trying to figure out which one of us was Jack the Ripper."

"Christ Jesus, those poor girls..."

Elly twisted in Brett's arms, electrified by Molly's words.

"Hey remember," Brett jiggled Elly, "we got a little pitcher here—"

"—with very big ears," finished Molly. She tweaked one of Elly's ears playfully.

Elly was sure they were talking about a strange man she had seen wandering around backstage that afternoon, talking to people. He wore a fedora and carried a notepad, so at first she'd dismissed him as a reporter. But whatever he was saying made people look shocked and shake their heads, and the photographs he was passing around made them do the same thing. For once Elly's eavesdropping skills had failed her, and every time she'd gotten close enough to listen she'd been chased away.

Molly still couldn't stop talking about it, and Elly listened carefully.

"But do you really think—God in heaven, could it really be one of us?"

"How else can you figure it? All four of em went to our show, and all of em were found close to the theater. And all of em came to the show on the last night of our run, so we were gone before they were ever found. Just seems like too much coincidence."

Four of them now, thought Elly.

"But, I mean—how on earth did he ever suspect?"

"It was parents of the one in Omaha, hired him when the police came up empty. And still for the longest time he didn't have a clue. Kind of a last resort—a shot in the dark—he finally wired some other cities where we had played to see if there were any unsolved crimes during the time we were there. And he learned about the ones in Pittsburgh, Springfield, and Portland. But still the police wouldn't act—called it 'far-fetched'—so he came out here on his own."

"Oh, it's just too much to take in, that there could be such evil in the world. But we'd better stop our gabbin or the dwarf shall be havin nightmares."

She reached up and patted Elly's cheek. Elly frowned, and fretted over whether to tell them about John Humphrey Davies. But despite her best efforts, over the last two weeks she'd still never caught him actually doing anything. She watched him carefully when the man showed him the photographs, and there seemed to be a gleam in Davies's eye. Yet he'd appeared completely relaxed…

They'd begun climbing a hill so steep that Brett was puffing when they reached the top. The city twinkled beneath them like a mirror of star-strewn sky. Looking back over Brett's shoulder, she saw a flash of light over the distant horizon that made no sense to her. She was still puzzling over it when they came to a clapboard house alive with the sounds of voices and laughter and piano music. Shadows danced across the curtains, and shadowy figures lounged on the front steps.

"Abandon hope all ye who etcetera, etcetera," said one of them, holding up a glass.

Inside the front door, three girls with drinks in their hands were shrieking with laughter at a man dancing in a feather boa with a woman's hat on his head. The air was hot and thick with smoke. Brett Crawley set Elly down and helped Molly off with her coat.

"In there," said one of the girls, pointing to a door slightly ajar.

Inside a dark room was a bed piled with coats. In one corner two people were entwined in an easy chair. Molly spread her coat on the far side of the bed and laid Elly down on top of it. She leaned over and hissed, "Sleep!" Then she kissed Elly on the forehead and left, shutting the door behind her.

Elly suspected the two people in the chair were kissing. She sat up to try and watch them, but it was too dark to see anything, and with all the noise outside she couldn't hear them either. What she could hear was a piano playing and someone singing "The Sidewalks of New York" (a song she knew) in a very loud but very lovely voice, and laughter, and pounding feet…

Before she knew it she was up and out the door, following the music. It led her into a smoky room packed with people. Through the legs of the people in front of her, she could make out other people dancing in the middle of the room. She squeezed through the crowd to where a beefy, red-faced man with a drink in one hand was leaning against a player piano and singing (in what was truly the loudest voice Elly had ever heard) a different song now:

> *Come away with me, Lucille,*
> *In my merry Oldsmobile.*
> *Down the road of life we'll fly,*
> *Automo-bubbling, you and I…*

The keys of the player piano were going down as though played by some invisible spectre. A group of people, most of them women, were standing around the singer, listening. One of the women nudged another and pointed at Elly, just as someone picked her up from behind and turned her around.

"Elly!" said Shorty. "How the deuce—"

The music ended and everyone clapped. The dancers stood in place, waiting for more—all but one red-haired girl who was striding toward Elly with an expression between a scowl and a laugh.

"Sure, I should have known it was hopeless."

"Hey," said Brett, grinning behind her, "you can't keep ol Elly away from the music!"

Elly was still sitting in Shorty's arms, and watched with interest as a short, thick young woman with black ringlets and a powdered face streaked with perspiration began licking his ear.

"Didn't realize Oscar was coming," said Brett.

Elly followed his eyes and saw Mr. Barnhold sitting on the floor in the corner. His thin hair was pasted to his skull and his beefy face redder than ever. He was drinking from a bottle, looking at nobody, and seemed terribly out of place.

"Yeah, havin his animals all go bananas musta put him in a state, he was lookin so down-at-the-mouth I dragged him along."

"He ain't looking too frisky," agreed Brett.

"Needs to join in the dancin. You know, get him up on his hind legs, like his dogs."

"Ha!"

"Twas uncommon loud," said Molly. "The singin."

"Well, I guess it oughta be," said Shorty. "Fella here is only a singer with the Metropolitan Opera! Here, lemme introduce ya…"

Elly had heard a lot of talk about this Metropolitan Opera, which had opened the same night as their troupe and had a man named Caruso singing with it. She wondered if he might be that same "Robinson Caruso" the Twin Sisters sang about.

"Riley—hey Riley, these folks here are with the vaudeville down at the Orpheum."

Riley turned a red, round, friendly-looking face toward them.

"Oh yeah? Pleased to meet you all."

"Brett Crawley here, he plays the sweetest cornet you ever heard. And this little lady"—Shorty jiggled Elly—"kid you not, she's one of the headliners! Plays pianah."

"You don't say!" said Riley, miming astonishment.

"Sure, I'm nobody in particular," muttered Molly.

"Oh hey, and this here is Miss Doyle, she's Esta Sangley's, ah, understudy."

"Esta Sangley! She here?"

"Probably at Delmonico's with your pal Caruso eating oysters," said Molly, eyes flashing.

"Hey, Caruso's no friend of mine, I'm just a lowly spear carrier. Except tonight I was a *picador*. Still a kind of spear carrier, I guess," mused Riley, laughing and taking a drink.

Two women had been rummaging through a cabinet full of piano rolls, and brought some over for Riley's inspection.

"How about 'In the Good Old Summertime'?" one of them suggested.

"Sure sure, we could do that one, though April's jumpin the gun a bit. So, this little girl here can really play the piano?"

"Surest thing you know. Here, Elly,"—Shorty sat her on the piano bench—"go ahead, show em your stuff!"

Elly had spent her entire life playing for thousands of people and wasn't at all shy. The song about the "merry Oldsmobile," was still going through her head, and on a whim she began to play it. From behind her came the usual gasps and cries of, "Get a load of this!" But she paid no attention, focused on playing the song just the way she had heard it.

The people around her applauded wildly. Riley gaped at her.

"How the devil can she know that tune? It's almost brand new!"

Shorty laughed. The woman leaning on him smiled at Elly vaguely. "I bet she never heard it before—did ya, Elly?"

She shook her head and kicked her legs.

"No, I don't believe it," said a woman in the crowd surrounding her (all of whose eyes she was avoiding).

"Folks, you are looking at Baby Elly Robin, the *Wunderkind*," said Shorty grandly. "Watch this." He untangled himself from the black-haired woman and sifted through a pile of sheet music atop the piano. "Here, Elly—play this."

The song was called "On the Banks of the Wabash." Molly had found a cushion for her to sit on, and she played as many of the notes as her small hands could manage (though without her mother there to push the pedal down the music sounded terribly choppy to her ears). On the second verse Mr. Riley joined in, and it was much better.

There was a big crowd of people around her now. Someone gave her a bottle of Coca-Cola (which her mother didn't allow her to drink because it got her "too pepped up"), and Brett took out his cornet and they played "The Ragtime Dance." People danced and the floor sounded like a big drum. Between songs everyone clapped, and she drank her Coca-Cola. When she finished it, someone gave her another…

They played a lot more songs, then took a break and put more piano rolls on. Everybody was drinking and loud and laughing. Shorty picked her up and danced with her, whirling her around the room, and Brett was dancing with Molly. Her freckled face was bright pink and her long red hair had come undone; she looked happier than Elly had ever seen her.

Shorty put Elly down so he could dance with the black-haired young woman, whose name was Rose. The room was still spinning around, making Elly dizzy. When it finally settled down she suddenly caught sight of Mr. Barnhold, still sitting in the corner with his bottle. He turned his head and stared at her without seeing, like a blind man. The sight chilled her, and she ran away.

She began wandering from room to room, trolling for interesting conversations. A man in a cloth cap said the working man's time had come and he knew Jack London personally and the people around him seemed very impressed. But Elly wasn't, so she went into another room where the door was closed and it was dark. Two people were on top of a bed, and a man's voice said, "Hey, can't ya see we're busy in here!" and a woman's voice giggled.

In another room two women were dancing in what looked like bed sheets, dancing in a fluttery way that didn't go with the piano music in the distance. A lot of people (mostly men) were standing around watching them. One of the women exclaimed how heavenly it was to dance with one's corset off, and a man said, "Hell, go ahead and take the sheet off too!" and the other woman laughed so hard she slipped and fell. Her bed sheet flew up, revealing she had no stockings on at all—the second time in a month Elly had seen a woman's bare legs. The men helped her up and gave her something to drink, and everyone just seemed to be having so much fun.

Sometime later she went looking for her friends, and found them on the front porch. After the heat and the smoke of the house the balmy night air was refreshing. Rose, Shorty's girlfriend, was sitting on the floor leaning against the house. She smiled at Elly and beckoned her over and she lay down with her head on Rose's soft, roomy lap.

Elly's body was tired, but her brain was still pepped up. The condition was perfect for eavesdropping, since everyone thought she was asleep. But the conversations around her were hard to follow because everyone was talking funny and laughing too much, and she guessed they were all pixilated.

Shorty was teasing Molly about being Irish.

"…and this whole country's awash now in paddies. Everywhere you look, another spud-eater."

"Sure, there's hordes of us," crowed Molly. "No more spud-eaters if you please— We're full up!"

"And send some of the surplus back while you're at it."

"But not me," said Molly, "because you see I've already turned AMERICAN! Why, not one month off the boat and I was feelin American enough to massacre a whole Indian tribe!"

A whoop, then the sound of a bottle breaking on the lawn. Laughter, followed by a lull in the conversation.

"Talk about killing people"—Brett's voice—"makes me…Lord, I just can't get those poor girls outa my mind."

"Christ," said Shorty, "why'd ya have ta…all night I been tryin to forget about em."

"Forget about em?!" exclaimed Molly, indignant. "Bejesus, someone needst *mourn* the poor things."

"What in the world are you folks on about?" said Rose, yawning, and making Elly's head go up and down.

"Gosh, the photograph of that one in Portland," said Brett. "Only fourteen, Weaver said—"

"Looked even younger," said Shorty. "If I ever find the son-of-a-bitch—"

"*What* son-of-a-bitch?" said Rose, exasperated.

"Some private dick came round today. Showed us photographs of four girls who got murdered—"

"Murdered!"

"—in cities that we played in. And all of em had been to our show. Found their bodies just a block or two from the theaters."

Elly's heart beat fast. Involuntarily her body twitched. Rose stroked her head absently.

"So how bout you, Oscar," said Shorty, "Weaver show you those photos?"

There was a pause, then someone murmured "Ja." Elly realized Mr. Barnhold must have joined them.

"You recognize any of em? You're right back there by the stage door, maybe they—"

"No, I did not recognize dem—why, are you accusing me?"

He had raised his voice. There was a short silence.

"No one's accusing you, Oscar," said Brett.

"I figure it was Sadie," said Shorty. "Talked em to death."

"If you can't be serious," said Molly, disgusted.

"Whoever did it," said Brett, "I'm guessing he hid the body back-stage, then came back to get it when everybody—"

"Sure, we're all a pack of ghouls," said Molly. "To talk about the poor things this way."

"*Ach,* so beautiful dey all was!" blurted Mr. Barnhold. "Sweet liddle angels." He sounded near tears.

"It's that one in Portland I can't shake," said Brett. "Gretta—wasn't that her name?"

"Gertrude," said Shorty.

Gertrude, is it? Den it is Gertie I vill call you…

Instantly Elly realized that all her assumptions about murderers were wrong. As if the terrible revelation were helium, she found her head rising from Rose's lap and turning in the direction of Mr. Barnhold's voice. A lone streetlight illuminated his beefy, flushed face.

He was staring straight at her. Remembered Elly had been there. Saw she'd recognized the girl's name.

"The dwarf!" exclaimed Molly. "What the devil time is it?"

"Must be after four," said Shorty.

"Saints preserve us"—Molly got unsteadily to her feet—"we must needs get her back to the hotel before she turns into a pumpkin, or my job is forfeit!"

Mr. Barnhold's bulging, unblinking eyes were still locked on Elly. For a long, terrible moment she stared back at him, then buried her face again in Rose's lap. An instant later Brett picked her up. She clutched at him and peered over his shoulder. Mr. Barnhold had gotten to his feet as well. He was still staring at her.

Molly gave Elly Brett's cornet in its paper bag for her to carry, and the five of them set off for their hotel. Rose staggered along next to Shorty, for she had decided to come along. In fact, everyone was having trouble walking, and twice Molly had to go in the bushes to be sick. There was a lot of talk about how they were going to sneak Rose into their hotel (with increasingly nutty ideas—"disguised as a buffalo"—which provoked a lot of laughter), and Elly sensed they were all trying to forget their previous conversation. Mr. Barnhold walked behind them, never speaking, hardly stumbling at all.

Whenever Elly dared to look at him, his eyes burned into hers.

"By all the saints," said Molly, catching sight of Elly's wide eyes, "why is the child still awake? Twill be my hide!"

By the time they got to the street with their hotel, the sky was going green at the edges, and the crescent moon was fading. A herd of cattle appeared at the end of the street, being driven toward them.

"Huh," said Brett. "Guess they're probably being led to market."

"Sure that's why they call it Market Street, ya ninny," said Molly.

"Say, where was that other herd of cows we saw," said Shorty. "Ones that crashed into that automobile?"

Everyone laughed at the memory. Elly risked lifting her head from Brett's shoulder.

Mr. Barnhold was still staring at her.

All at once they heard an awful sound, a deep roar coming from everywhere and nowhere, and the ground beneath their feet began to move.

"Holy Christ!" cried Brett.

He stumbled—Elly felt herself almost dropped—then managed to steady himself. But the world refused to steady itself as well. Over Brett's shoulder she saw Shorty and Rose fall to the ground. The surface of the street was rippling, and Mr. Barnhold seemed to be dancing on its undulating surface. Molly screamed "Sufferin Jesus!" as she and Brett staggered along together. Elly dropped Brett's cornet, but her squeal of dismay was lost in the clatter of falling stone and shriek of twisting metal. Dust choked the street as though a giant were shaking out a gigantic carpet. Through the thick gloom Elly glimpsed people pouring out of doorways and cattle running down the street.

"Mother of God!" screamed Molly—and disappeared in a shower of bricks.

Elly was thrown to the ground. She scrambled around on her knees and found Mr. Hoppy. Where Molly had been was a pile of rubble with feet sticking out. Brett was bent over, his face contorted, frantically pulling away bricks.

The sound all around them was like the roaring of ten thousand lions. Shorty and Rose were gone. In the choking dust she could make out Mr. Barnhold on his knees. He tried to stand up but was knocked down by a man racing by in his pajamas. He staggered to his feet again, shaking his head—and spotted Elly. They stared at each other for what seemed an eternity, even as the world reeled drunkenly around them.

Then he started toward her.

She shrieked and ran into the street.

The surface was like an ocean mid-storm. A black snake spitting blue sparks writhed toward her. She scrambled to get away from it. Maddened cattle emerged from clouds of dust, their terrified bawling barely audible over the tumult, and she darted between them. The ground rose up; it was like running on the back of a surfacing whale. Suddenly the earth in front of her split open. A team of terrified horses dragging an empty wagon came charging toward it and were swallowed up. She teetered on the edge of the abyss, and a hand clamped around her arm.

She turned. Mr. Barnhold's bulging eyes glared down at her with a pure madness—then his hand was abruptly wrenched away, throwing Elly to the ground. She looked up. A monstrous bull had impaled Mr. Barnhold on its horns. She watched, stupefied, as the massive animal pawed the earth, shaking him like a ragdoll. Then it bore his bloody body off like a grisly trophy and disappeared in a cloud of dust.

For an instant she sat, dazed, then the roar started up again and the ground began to shake. She grabbed her doll and scrambled to her feet. Bricks were jumping out of the street like popcorn. Through the dust she could dimly make out her hotel. She was running toward it when a pair of trolley tracks rose up in front of her and began waving around like insect feelers. She screamed and ran around them. Water was pouring into the street from a hole in the ground, and she sloshed through it. The hotel was just across the street, she started toward it—

An awful, cracking, exploding sound. The bottom of the hotel suddenly jerked like a rug had been pulled from underneath it, and the ground floor folded under like a house of cards collapsing. Mixed in with the roaring and booming, she could faintly make out the screams of people being crushed. Above the rising cloud of dust she watched the top of the hotel jerk down again like a man dropping to his knees. Another wave of screaming like a distant roar of surf. And still the ground trembled, the hotel fell yet a third time, disappeared in a great cloud of yellow dust…

And, as she watched the building that contained her mother and father collapse, something inside Elly's mind collapsed as well.

CHAPTER SIX

HOT POTATO

Joining the militia was the most exciting thing that had ever happened to Zeke.

He and Dewey had headed downtown because their neighborhood got off light, and they wanted to see some real destruction. They saw plenty, all right, and dead people too. The clouds were tinged a lurid red, ash was falling from the sky, and people were saying the whole city might go up. The air was like a dragon's breath, with a faint odor of roasting meat. Dewey declared it was people they smelled, nodding wisely like he knew about such things. Zeke argued how could he be so sure if he weren't no cannibal?

They were dynamiting buildings to stop the fire from spreading, though it seemed like a lost cause to Zeke. They stood and watched some men carry a barrel of powder into one building.

"Silly buggers doing it all wrong," said a stocky, bearded fellow standing next to them. He had a red cross pinned to his sleeve. "You got to put the charge next to the walls, not in the center of the building."

Sure enough, when they set it off, the walls were still standing, and they only succeeded in starting yet another fire that began devouring the building from the inside.

The stocky fellow spat, then turned to Dewey and asked if he wanted to join the militia.

"Hell yes!" exclaimed Dewey. He pointed to Zeke and said, "What about him?"

The man looked at Zeke and hesitated. Zeke felt himself blush; though as old as Dewey, he was scrawny and still looked like a kid. But the man finally nodded. A few minutes later they were lined up with a bunch of others, sworn in, told they were now members of the "Golden Gate Vigilante Committee," given guns, ammunition and armbands with red crosses on them, told to "help keep good order, shoot any looters"—and turned loose.

They took off on their own. The gun was heavy and had a bayonet fixed to the end. Zeke had never shot one and had to get Dewey to load it. They fired a few bullets into the air, whooping.

The streets were thronged with people dragging their belongings. It was like a mad circus; you never knew what you'd see around the next corner. They passed a man standing on a wrecked wagon preaching the end of the world, and he had a few takers. They saw a small girl trying to drag a heavy trunk out of a building. When Dewey asked her why didn't she get her folks to help, she said they were both dead and just kept on trying to drag that trunk with a stony face. Zeke wanted to help her, but Dewey pointed across the street to where some other militia men had broken into a liquor store. They ran over to join in the fun, but the place was already cleaned out. One fellow had a whole case of whiskey on his shoulder, and they begged a bottle off him.

They had a few pulls from it, then continued on. They ran into a fireman standing with just a dribble of water coming from his hose. He nodded down the street, and they saw where the hose had burst. A man had led his horse up to drink from the spillage.

"Hey, you can't do that," Dewey told him, "that there's guv'mint water."

"Go to blazes," said the man. Dewey lifted his rifle and shot the man's horse dead. They walked away, the man and the fireman staring after them, speechless.

"Why'd ya do that?" asked Zeke.

"Felt like it," said Dewey.

They drank some more whiskey. There were lots of looters around, but they all had red crosses on their arms and carried rifles. They came upon a barefoot woman carrying a half-dead baby with what looked like two broken legs, trying to beg some milk off a dairy wagon. The driver refused, so Dewey shot his horse too. The dairyman took off after him. Zeke jumped into the wagon and passed some milk to the woman. She said thank you with her eyes and scurried away.

He caught up with Dewey around the St. Francis Hotel, which was still standing. A man with one of the powder crews told them they were going to dynamite the buildings nearby to try to save the hotel, and enlisted Zeke and Dewey to help clear them all of people.

"How long we got?" asked Dewey.

The man pulled out his watch. "Another half hour," he said.

They took off at a run for one of the buildings, but there were already militia men coming out with armloads of stuff, and they heard it was about picked clean. They went on to another whose ground floor had been a furniture store. Most of the stuff was too heavy to carry, but Dewey got a big clock for a mantelpiece and Zeke found a brass lamp shaped like a naked woman. It was big and heavy, a real find. Dewey wanted to trade him for it, but Zeke said in a pig's eye.

They could hear the approaching fire roaring like a freight train and feel its heat. Every now and then a dynamite blast came from somewhere. There was so much smoke in the air it was getting hard to breathe. Dewey said he figured the time was about up and started back, but Zeke decided to poke his head inside another building. It was already half-fallen down, the inside dark and full of fallen debris. He yelled, "Everybody out!" in a voice that cracked and turned to leave—then spotted a tiny figure squatting amongst the fallen beams.

"Out! Time to go! Vamoose!" he yelled, but the child remained motionless. It was a girl, he could discern now, a little nigger girl just sitting there in the gloom. Zeke realized the only way she was going to move was if someone carried her out. But there was no way could he carry both her and the lamp.

He had about decided to just leave her and hope the powder men saw her when they laid the charge (though it was doubtful; he was surprised he'd spotted her himself), when a huge explosion came from somewhere nearby. The building shook, some bricks clattered down around the child—

Still she didn't move.

Cursing, Zeke threw down his lamp and started picking his way through the rubble.

.   .   .

Lucy Fisher thought of her as the "Wonder Baby."

"We pulled away a bunch of broken beams an' stuff," said the man who brought her in, "and there she was lyin in her crib just suckin on her bottle and starin up at us, content as you please."

Though charmed by the tale, Lucy pointed out that—there being nothing wrong with the baby—she hardly belonged here. But the man was already walking away.

"Well," said Elspeth, running her hand through her hair distractedly and pushing her nurse's cap even further askew, "put her with that other girl, I guess—the one with the feet."

"I'll do it," said Lucy, trying to discreetly point out to Elspeth that she was giving orders again—then chastising herself. Really, this was no time for such petty thoughts.

The "girl with the feet" had been found in one of the buildings being dynamited to stop the fire (was it her imagination, or were those ominous thunderings—so like the sounds of distant battle—getting louder?). A scrawny youth with a gun that looked too big for him (one of those riff-raff they were calling a "militia") had found her sitting barefoot in the rubble. She was wearing a filthy nightgown and clutching a shapeless, soot-blackened doll. Her hair was singed, her face so dark that Lucy had taken her at first for a pickaninny—and her feet were cut to ribbons.

She had stared vacantly into space as Lucy picked glass and rubble from her feet—but screamed piteously when Lucy tried to take her doll away prior to removing her nightgown. So she let her hold the pitiful object while she cut away the filthy garment. Surprisingly, the child turned out to be white. Lucy had washed her, treated her cuts and bruises, and bandaged her feet. Then, using stuff they'd commandeered from nearby clothing stores, she'd dressed the child in a clean gown. But in the crush of new cases she hadn't given the girl another thought.

The baby slept peacefully in her arms as she scanned the huge pavilion, trying to remember where they'd put the girl. An improvised hospital of more than a thousand beds, thrown together in a couple of hours in a building that covered an entire city block—Lucy was still astounded. She saw the girl at last and was starting toward her, when an older nurse accosted her. Leaning in close, the nurse said in a low voice:

"Pass the word—very quietly you understand. The roof of the pavilion is on fire, and we shall have to evacuate. They've brought a crew to help"—she nodded in the direction of a group of men already beginning to empty the beds nearest the exit. "There's transport being arranged to the ferry. We're decamping to Oakland General."

She rushed away without another word.

Lucy continued on (pausing to pass the word to another nurse) and found the girl clutching her doll and staring at the ceiling. She picked her up with her free arm and carried both children toward the exit. On the way, she passed two men carrying an old woman whose feet were in even worse condition, surely burned beyond saving. She beamed beatifically up at Lucy.

The wonders of morphine, thought Lucy distractedly.

Outside, she had only a moment to register the awful sky and motley assortment of carriages, ambulances, and automobiles parked in a long line, before a harried man with an abrupt manner steered her toward a green automobile with shiny trim, pushed her into the back, slammed the door—and off they drove.

She found herself crushed up against a man with what looked to be two broken arms. His face was pale and rigid, his eyes tightly shut. The old woman sitting on the other side of him appeared to be in a bad way. In the driver's seat was a very young man in a cap and goggles whose face was alight with, Lucy thought, an unseemly excitement. The man sitting next to him wore a bloody gown, and when he turned around she recognized him as one of the surgeons.

"Helluva thing," he said. He looked both exhausted and unnaturally alert.

"Gosh, yes," said the young man, even as he sped up and overtook a carriage full of patients on stretchers. "Biggest thing to ever hit the U.S. of A.!"

They were slaloming around dead animals and debris, Lucy could have reached out and touched the things that were whooshing by—then, to her alarm, they sped up even faster. Really, was she going to survive an earthquake and a fire, only to be killed in an automobile wreck?

To distract herself, she told the story of the "Wonder Baby." To her horror, the boy turned around to look at the baby, narrowly missing several pedestrians. The entire city seemed to be on the move. Baby carriages and child's wagons were piled high with household goods. Children carried puppies, women lugged sewing machines, men pushed trunks directly over the pavement like so many Sisyphuses. A vast cloud of smoke glowing red at the base hovered over the already surreal scene like some monstrous living thing.

They turned down a side street—only to meet the fire head-on—then reversed to try another. The boy drove with a fixed, manic grin, swerving to avoid twisted wires, fallen bricks, wrecked carriages. Over and over Lucy was thrown against the man with the broken arms; he grimaced but said nothing.

At last they rounded a corner, and found the mob scene Lucy had feared. Thousands of people and their belongings were converging on two ferry boats. Other automobiles had already arrived, and men carrying stretchers were trying to fight their way through the crowd to the nearest boat. They parked as close as they could. The man with broken arms was still able to walk, while the old woman leaned against the surgeon. Lucy staggered along behind them with the two children. The people around them were haphazardly dressed; she saw a man in a dinner jacket and pajama bottoms, a woman in a bathrobe and a feather boa. At the edge of the crowd a group of people stood around a wagon loaded with casks, carousing. The women wore satin dresses that Lucy guessed had never seen the light of day, for the waterfront was notorious. They sang along to someone playing the fiddle.

"Like Nero," she murmured to herself.

The surgeon laughed over his shoulder.

"If you want I can carry her," said the young driver, coming up behind her and pointing to the girl with bandaged feet. Gratefully Lucy handed her over, for the ferry was still far away, and the "Wonder Baby" was really a very fat, healthy—and heavy—baby.

"You're a little wonder, you know that?" she said, stroking its face.

She never thought of the girl with bandaged feet again.

~

Jack Pedersen had just reached the end of a long line of patients waiting to board the ferry when he suddenly spotted his friend Henry, driver of one of the other motorcars—a Cadillac, and a dandy. He fought his way through the crowd.

"Henry!" he yelled.

"Jacko!" Henry's face lit up. "Isn't it just the corkingest thing!"

"Surest thing you know!" said Jack. The girl's trailing gown hid her bloody, bandaged feet, and he set her on the ground so he could shake his friend's hand. "I'm afraid the city's for it though…"

They talked for a long time, excitedly relating their separate tales.

When Jack looked for the girl again, she was gone.

~

Ginny Pleasance suggested the fellow with the fiddle play "A Hot Time in the Old Town Tonight," which got a laugh. Gamely he struck up the tune. Or something like it; by this point Ginny was too drunk to tell.

Scates had liberated another bottle of champagne and was pouring it around. As she lifted her glass, she spotted a pathetic little waif standing nearby. She wore a shapeless gown, and clutched something that looked like a burnt chicken with its legs hanging down. But what caught Ginny's eye—gave her the willies, really—was the way the kid was staring at the fiddle player. Staring at him with big tears running down her cheeks, like the sound of a fiddle was just the saddest thing in the whole world…

Ginny shivered and drank her champagne.

When she dared to look again, the child was gone.

.   .   .

"All the way from Italy. Then working like a dog for three years to bring you and the children over. Then work like a dog again for five years, and this"—he waved his hand at the tent over their heads—"this is what I got to show for it."

Isabella Frigo let her husband rant on without interrupting. She knew him. Knew he was a good man, just letting off steam, exhausted from dragging that heavy trunk through the streets. And she knew as well that they would survive this. Perhaps open another vegetable stand in some other city. She left off piling clothes into a pallet for the children to sleep on, and furtively caressed the shape of the money bag pinned beneath her skirts.

Yes, they would survive.

"The tent is already dry again," said her husband, pressing his hand to the canvas. "I should—"

"I'll do it," she said. As long as the wind was blowing sparks in their direction, the tent had to be regularly dampened to keep it from catching fire. She laid her two youngest, both exhausted and already asleep, on the pallet and dragged the precious tub of water the soldiers had given them outside again. All around them were thousands of other tents, thousands of families in the same desperate circumstances. Next to them was a couple, very young, from Germany, she thought. The wife had been sobbing ever since they arrived; she was at it again now. Last night, in another nearby tent, a Chinese woman had given birth.

Sighing, she lifted the dipper to douse the tent—then stopped at the sight of a little girl squatting nearby and watching her with a fixed expression. She wore a filthy frock and clutched something black and repulsive-looking. Then Isabella realized the girl was staring not at her, but at the dipper in her hand.

"You wanna?" she said, holding up the dipper. "You wanna some water?"

The child made no move to approach, so Isabella brought the dipper over and held it to her lips. Her hair was a singed, tangled mess, and she drank with an urgency that shocked Isabella. Where were her people? Why weren't they looking after her?

That's when she noticed the girl's feet.

~

"Bella, what the hell are you doing? You think we've got food to spare?"

"There's a child outside," said Isabella, refusing to meet her husband's eye and leaving the tent with a piece of cheese they had scavenged from a store.

The girl was still squatting in the same place, cradling the thing Isabella had decided must have been a doll. Isabella held out the piece of cheese. The child stared at it for a long moment, then took it and held it up to her doll as if for inspection. Finally she began to eat. Never once did she look Isabella in the eye.

Her husband had emerged from the tent, and stood frowning at the scene. "*Madre mia*," he muttered, "Who the hell is she?"

"I don't know. I just found her sitting here."

"Well, where are her people? Why aren't they taking care of her?"

"How should I know?" said Isabella impatiently. "All I know is, they aren't."

The child had finished the cheese. Isabella offered her another dipper of water, and she drank it greedily.

"Perhaps she's Italian," mused her husband.

"Could be. The hair."

"Hey? Are you Italian?"

No response.

"Where you-a from?" he asked, switching to English.

The child held it up to her doll, as if for inspection.

The child gave no sign she even knew they were there.

"I think there's something wrong with her."

"Look at her feet," said Isabella.

"What? What about her feet?"

Isabella showed him.

~

The girl was like a feral animal, and it took a long time for Isabella to coax her inside the tent. She unwrapped the bloody rags from the child's feet, made clean bandages from an old pillowcase, and found an old frock of Sonia's that fit her. Finally, when the child lay comatose in the corner from what was clearly utter exhaustion, Isabella slipped the doll from her fingers. Using some of their precious water, she discovered, beneath the soot and grime, a frog with a red vest and button eyes.

All the time she felt her husband watching her.

"Bella, we gotta get rid of her," he said softly.

She ignored him. He tried again, talked of all the mouths they had to feed. But she refused to meet his eye. As she hung the doll up to dry, he finally sighed and gave up.

In the morning when she awoke, she looked for the doll and discovered it was gone—and so was the girl.

Now it was her husband who would not meet her eye.

.   .   .

Sergeant Lucas Hudson knew he should have taken the girl straight to the Missing Persons Bureau.

She had been handed to him by an exhausted-looking private. "Some dago foisted her on me," he said, disgusted. "As if I ain't got enough to do already, what with babysittin a whole city full of tents."

Hudson had accepted the girl and promised to deal with her. He looked at his watch; it was almost eight, and he was due to get off the night shift. It would take a long time to take the girl to the authorities, wasn't on his way home at all, probably a lot of papers to fill out. Wouldn't hurt to take the girl home with him, just for today. His wife wouldn't mind.

Yes, he was quite sure she wouldn't mind.

.   .   .

Melinda Hudson was sallow, overweight, already graying at thirty-nine—and childless.

When her husband brought the little girl home, he carefully explained the circumstances, emphasizing how important it was that the authorities pursue every avenue to find the child's family.

"Yes of course, yes," said Melinda, even as she took the little girl tenderly in her trembling arms. "But…but surely we should keep her for a little while. At least," she added anxiously, "until she's feeling better?"

"Yes, of course," mumbled Lucas. "Probably a good idea."

But a look passed between them that sent Melinda Hudson's heart soaring.

The next day, Lucas didn't comment on the pretty frock the child was now wearing. (Where had Melinda bought it, with the city in such a state? Or had she, perhaps, always had it?) Nor, in the weeks that followed, did he say anything about the other frocks, hair ribbons, and expensive dolls that began to accumulate. Not to mention, when the child's feet had finally healed, her collection of pretty new boots. But even befrocked, be-ribboned, and expensively shod, Maude (as Melinda had begun calling the child) seemed little more than a full-sized doll herself. She spent her days rocking and staring into space and refused to even look at them. As for all her costly toys, Melinda might have saved their money, for the stuffed frog she had come with was her fixed and unchanging plaything, and she would only eat something—really, the child was intolerably picky—after showing it to her idiotic doll.

As for Melinda, the failure of the child to acknowledge her—even look her in the eye!—had turned her beautiful dream of motherhood into a bitter mockery. And bitterest of all was the one time she finally seemed to get the child's attention.

Her maternal fantasy had always included the singing of lullabies to her little girl. Settling Maudie on her lap, she began to croon "All the Pretty

Little Horses" as best she could. True, she was no singer (she couldn't really hear what her problem was, but people had hinted as much). But for the child to screw up her face in such a horrible way and burst into tears…

Perhaps it was this that had decided things. For the day came when Lucas, with tears in his eyes, told his wife they must face facts: the child was an imbecile. And Melinda had retired to her room, sobbing, as Lucas led little Maudie away.

But she hadn't really tried to stop him.

·   ·   ·

It was beyond believing, thought Georgina Snelling crossly. Her work finally complete—and then this child dumped in her lap.

Weeks she had spent placing all the children orphaned by the earthquake. Some had merely become separated from their families in all the tumult, and by combing through missing person reports, she had been able to effect tearful reunions; these were her greatest triumphs. For those truly orphaned, the older children were often able to tell about other relatives, and even the babies usually came with addresses pinned to their clothing. Often it had taken a lot of detective work, weeks of telegrams and typewritten letters to far-flung provinces, but she had usually been able to find relatives willing to take the children in. As for the rest, she had—sometimes with great difficulty—finally managed to place them all in the state's overcrowded orphanages.

And now this girl!

She'd no idea where the girl was found, never even got a straight answer as to why it had taken so long for her to come to light. Given the delay (and the child's costly outfit), Georgina half suspected that her family had used the earthquake as a pretext to rid themselves of the girl, for the child was clearly a mental defective.

Sighing, she searched her files again, and despaired. All the orphanages were full to bursting, she couldn't imagine them taking even one more. And then there was the child's imbecility, hardly an inducement. Finally (with great reluctance), she turned to an institution calling itself the "Marysville Benevolent Christian Asylum for Unfortunate Girls."

On the face of it, the place sounded ideal. Church sponsored, quite small, fewer than a hundred and fifty mentally deficient girls, housed in a stately old home outside the city. And yet Georgina had never before considered it, for all the state inspections had shown it to be clearly substandard; indeed it had been repeatedly threatened with having its license revoked. She scanned the report, shaking her head—really, the place must be quite abysmal. Though there was something about a new doctor they had just hired, young and trained in Europe, versed in all the latest techniques.

And besides, thought Georgina, casting her eye once more on the little girl rocking in the corner and staring into space, it really didn't much matter one way or the other.

She began to type the letter.

CHAPTER SEVEN

THE TROLL FINDS A FRIEND

Hello my honey, hello my baby,
Hello my ragtime gal!
Send me a kiss by wire,
Baby, my heart's on fire...

Mr. Hoppy delivered the song in his ringing baritone, twisting the fabric of his froggy face into droll expressions. The band played an instrumental chorus, and—to Elly's delight—her talented doll began to prance across the stage on the tips of his toes. The footlights added a sunny glow to his green corduroy skin. At the edge of the stage he executed a smart pirouette, came prancing back, spread his arms and opened his mouth to sing the second verse—then collapsed in a heap.

She shook him and squeezed him, even though she knew it was useless.

Oh look, Miss Bland, Maudie's shaking her doll!
Don't like him cause he's lost all her marbles.
Oh Gladys, you're not making any sense. Besides, I'm sure she
    must love him dearly—don't you agree, Miss Bland?
Well, um, yes... I should rather think...

Owe-ee freh.
Oh Drooly, you're so right! He is her only friend...

Elly kept her gaze resolutely fixed on Mr. Hoppy, and tried to ignore the voices. But it was impossible to ignore the fact that Mr. Hoppy was again nothing but a doll lying motionless in her lap. And that the brilliance of his colors came not from footlights, but a buttery oblong of sunlight cast by a window.

He was changing himself back into a doll more and more now. It was irksome, because all Elly wanted to do was watch him sing and dance and tell his stories. He was so good at it! He could play the violin as beautifully as her father, and read to Elly in her mother's soft voice. Sometimes his long frog fingers would fly over the keyboard (he knew every song Elly had ever played) conjuring up lovely colors. And just yesterday he had performed Albert Jenning's entire act. In her mind Elly had laughed and laughed.

But where were they all? Where were her mother and father, Albert, Molly, Esta? Why didn't they come and rescue her from this terrible place? She searched Mr. Hoppy's froggy face for an answer. But he only stared back at her with button eyes. And she again found herself alone in this strange place where nothing made any sense.

It was rather like a school, Elly supposed (though she had never actually been to school), because there were two old ladies who seemed rather like teachers, and she had to wear a uniform—a coarse, scratchy woolen frock and scuffed boots that didn't fit. But it was all girls, and all of them were scary in one way or another. Some couldn't talk and only moaned. Some couldn't walk and had to be pushed around in chairs with wheels. And she sometimes wondered if perhaps she really *had* turned into a different girl named Maude. And traveled, like Alice, through the looking glass, to some different, nonsensical world.

The thought made her hug Mr. Hoppy even tighter, because he was the only one who knew she was still herself.

The voices had stopped talking about her. The old woman seemed to have left. And since the young woman with the snuffling voice wasn't around, things should have returned to their usual state of chaos. But the late afternoon sun had made the room a stifling box, and all the girls were probably as sweaty and listless as Elly herself.

Two girls who sounded like one girl sitting in two places (so that Elly had decided they must be twins) were reciting long numbers in a secretive fashion. Another girl who always moaned the same thing (it hurts, oh it hurts!). And beside Elly the moist lump of a girl whose fat hands Elly had learned to dread.

All these girls she had never properly seen. Because it was dangerous to look at anyone, unspeakably dangerous to look them in the eye—and, of course, *unthinkable* to ever speak.

These facts were so obvious she didn't think to question their logic.

So she tried to keep her eyes resolutely fixed on her doll. But her blinkered condition meant she experienced this new world as if she were sitting in the audience of a play, blindfolded. Yet it was still a fascinating and complete world in its own way, with the most marvelous and life-like sound effects, and a cast of characters whose names, over time, she began to learn.

But at first she only identified them by their attributes.

There were, for instance, the three girls she liked to sit beside. One said obscure or silly things in a countrified voice; another spewed barely intelligible words after what sounded like enormous effort. But the third girl especially interested Elly, because even though she talked faster than anyone Elly had ever met, the things she said sounded almost normal. The other day she had even read aloud to the other two.

But today it was clearly too hot to read.

She heard the horse and buggy, which left every afternoon around the same time, returning. Someone led them to the stable; she could tell when the door closed, muffling the sound of the horse's hoofs.

Suddenly a commotion. A girl moaning. Two pairs of boots running around. A chorus of gleeful shrieks. The girl who talked in a foreign language said something in her incomprehensible tongue—then suddenly fell silent.

Screams.

Oh Drooly, did you see? She ate it!
Gah!
An it was still a-wrigglin.

.   .   .

The sun was gone.

Shline up! The young woman who had a funny snuffling way of talking and liked to beat them.

A mad scuffle as the girls rose in a disorderly mass and spilled out into the hallway. Elly tore her eyes from Mr. Hoppy and followed behind one of the wheelchairs. She was fascinated by the turning wheels (as she was by any machinery), and it gave her something to watch when she had to walk somewhere.

They collected outside the dining hall.

THE SNUFFLER: Two by two! Two by two! *(The girl next to Elly keeps poking her in the ribs.)*
THE SILLY GIRL WHO ECHOES THINGS: Two by two! Two by—
(A loud shriek—the Snuffler must have boxed her ears.)

The doors were finally thrown open. An assault on Elly's nose. All discipline fled as the girls stampeded inside. Elly found a seat, then realized with dismay the fat lump of a girl was sitting beside her. Quickly Elly grabbed her bread, and managed to gobble two of her prunes before a fat hand grabbed the rest, along with the meat from her plate. But it was all right, because the meat was so fatty that even by Mr. Hoppy's newly-relaxed standards it was inedible.

A sudden hush: the old lady with the grandmotherly voice must have come in. Elly stood with the rest of the girls, knowing (from bitter experience) that if she didn't, she'd be hoisted to her feet by the Snuffler and get her ears boxed.

The old woman read a passage from the Bible in her melodious contralto, and finally murmured "Amen." Sounds of girls attacking their food with slobbering gusto. Elly showed the piece of bread to Mr. Hoppy in her lap. He told her it was all right—but not the loathsome stuff that looked like butter but wasn't. She held the bread under the table and furtively scraped it off with her spoon, but managed only a few bites of the leathery black stuff before the girl next to her snatched it away.

She took a sip of rust-flavored water from her metal cup to wash down the bread. Normally she would now have gone back into her dream. But with Mr. Hoppy mute, there was nothing to do but stare down at him and listen to the things around her. A man hurling pots and yelling in some incomprehensible tongue—a Chinaman perhaps. The sounds now loud, now soft, suggesting a door opening and closing.

It hurts! Oh it hurts so bad!
Oh, it shlurts, it shlurts!

The girl carried off by the Snuffler. From the hallway a single muffled shriek, as if someone had stepped on a cat's tail.

The girl next to Elly seized on this distraction to snatch her spoon.

The old woman (or women—somehow Elly sensed the other one was there as well) left the room. The girls shuffled out, were herded back down the hall, stood in long lines for the toilets. Finally Elly pulled off her frock and crawled into bed, hugging Mr. Hoppy and waiting for dreams. Because no matter how bad they might be, they couldn't be any worse than life itself.

·   ·   ·

With nothing else to fill her time, Elly began to gather clues from the conversations swirling around her, and work out the intricacies of this cock-eyed community. As if it were a machine, she analyzed its parts and put names to its various cogs and gears.

The two women who presided over their meals and church services were Miss Bland and Miss Pitts. Both were old. But they could not have been more different.

Miss Bland was an insubstantial wraith of a woman who drifted in and out of their lives. She seemed to have been tasked with organizing games and pastimes for the girls. But her attempts to explain whatever crack-brained diversion she had come up with were so dithering and obscure, it was quickly clear she was spectacularly unfit for organizing anything—least of all a mob of unruly and half-witted girls.

The fact that she was "not quite all there" gave Miss Bland an un-flappability that was, under the circumstances, something of an asset. Though the way the girls ran roughshod over the poor old woman made Elly inclined to feel sorry for her. Only last week she had been trying to recite "The Owl and the Pussycat" in her low, fluting voice (and mixing up all the stanzas) when she suddenly gasped. An instant later, a wooden block rolled onto the floor by Elly's knee; she guessed Miss Bland had been beaned. A moment later the old lady got creakily to her feet and tottered off, mumbling to herself.

Miss Pitts was another kettle of fish entirely.

She clucked at them in a grandmotherly way, as if she were a loving old hen and they her poor wayward chicks. Yet when she walked among them, addressing them by name, questioning or gently correcting them, the girls seemed to shrink from her. And Elly began to suspect the crooning concern was only a mask concealing the *real* Miss Pitts.

But whoever the real Miss Pitts was, she was clearly running the show.

She addressed the young woman who snuffled and beat them as "Frieda" or "Miss Klee." She seemed a sort of lieutenant to Miss Pitts's general, tasked with enforcing discipline. Her relish for the job had caused the girls to nickname her "The Bruiser." It seemed an excellent name, and Elly adopted it in her mind.

MISS PITTS: Dear Hattie, and how are you today?
(The girls all go quiet, animals in the presence of a dangerous predator.)
FAST-TALKING GIRL: *(in a bright, brittle voice)* Oh I'm
    quite well, thank you, Miss Pitts—just ever so well!

MISS PITTS: Well I'm just so glad! No desire to throw one of
  your beastly fits today?
HATTIE: Oh no no no no—no fits, Miss Pitts!
THE BRUISER: Sheesh a poet and don't know it!
MISS PITTS: So very indulgent, those fits of yours. If you
  would just learn to exercise more self-control—
(Commotion. Moaning. Something banging against the wall.)
MISS PITTS: Frieda!
(A flurry of movement. A girl sobbing. Her voice fading away.
The room seems to collectively shudder.)

There were other people working there as well. whose names Elly
began to learn. The girls called the impatient Chinaman in the kitchen
"the Chink," and his equally short-tempered wife they dubbed "Mrs.
Chink"—but never to their faces. Elly wasn't surprised by this; her mother
had made a pained face whenever anyone used that word to describe the
Chinese acrobats in their troupe. So she listened carefully, and — after
overhearing Miss Bland once flutingly refer to "Mr. and Mrs. Wong" —
resolved to henceforth call them that in her mind.

Mrs. Wong washed clothes during the day and slept outside their
bedroom at night. If anyone made so much noise they woke her, she
would come storming in and smack them with a wooden paddle. The
room where they slept had a ceiling of pressed tin, the staircases had ornate wooden banisters, and Elly had the impression the building must
once have been a very large and grand house. But much of the woodwork
had been painted over, linoleum had been laid over the fine oak floor-
ing, and bars on the windows had converted the old home into a sort of
prison. While shuffling through the hallways, they passed locked doors
leading to remote, mysterious areas. And Elly guessed the two old ladies
must live somewhere in the building.

Sometimes, as they stood waiting outside the dining hall, a door
would open at the end of the hallway. And Elly fancied she could make
out, beneath their own hubbub, the sounds of distant shrieking.

Besides Mr. Wong there were two other men working there.

One was a colored man named Henry. He spoke so seldom that for a long time he was only a glimpse of dark skin in Elly's peripheral vision. Until one day:

MISS PITTS: Henry, the door to the pantry is sticking.
HENRY: Yes'm. I get on it.
MISS PITTS: Then you may hitch up the buggy.
HENRY: Yes'm.

So Elly now knew it was Miss Pitts who drove off every afternoon, and returned two hours later. And that Henry was the one who brought the buggy in and out of the stable, and did odd jobs around the building.

The third man who worked there was Dr. Phelps.

He sounded young—perhaps as young as Elly's father. They encountered him but seldom, usually bustling down the hallways. Staring at the floor, Elly would see the edge of a billowing white smock flying by, cuffs of tweed trousers, large feet loudly clomping. A curious gait, as if he were battling a headwind.

Once a week he came to see them in the dayroom. With Miss Pitts and the Bruiser for a retinue, these occasions had the flavor of state visits. At these times Dr. Phelps examined such girls deemed worthy of his notice. Elly had an impression of magnified eyes behind thick spectacles.

The girls shrank from his attentions even more than those of Miss Pitts. But it soon became apparent that only certain girls attracted the doctor's interest. The others might as well have been invisible, and Elly was determined to remain in this second group. So when Phelps approached her one afternoon, she stared steadfastly at Mr. Hoppy and pretended not to notice him.

DR. PHELPS: And this one, Miss Pitts? No change?
MISS PITTS: *(sighing)* I'm afraid not, Doctor. In her own
    world, poor lamb. Perhaps—perhaps a treatment might be
    in order?

DR. PHELPS: I'm reluctant to try it on a child so young. The
   technique is still in its infancy, so much we do not yet
   understand...

Miss Pitts fluttered around Phelps in such a grotesquely girlish manner that Elly was forced to revise her theory, and decided the doctor was
actually the mainspring driving the entire operation. Especially when, at
the visit's conclusion, one of the girls was helplessly borne away by the
Bruiser.

.   .   .

Every day Elly sat near Hattie, the fast-talking girl, and her friends Gladys
and Drooly, just for the pleasure of overhearing their conversations. She
was now aware that Hattie wore something on her head, but had not quite
figured out what it was. Gladys sometimes said very strange things, and
seemed always to be twitching, but Elly had decided she actually had most
of her brains. Drooly sat slumped in a wheelchair, and at first Elly was
inclined to discount her almost unintelligible utterances. But she soon
realized that the enormous effort Drooly expended to speak—the words
wrenched from the center of her being and heaved into the air like heavy
weights—meant each word had been chosen for maximum impact, and
Elly learned to pay close attention to them. Though she still had to rely on
Hattie's translations most of the time.

   The girls often speculated about Elly as if she weren't right there listening. In fact, that was often precisely what they speculated about.

HATTIE: But she's not like the Troll, Gladys. She understands
   us, I'm just sure of it. Don't you, Maudie?
*(The Troll was what they called the enormous lump of a girl
sprawled on the other side of Elly, the one who stole her food.)*
GLADYS: *(twitching)* Troll don't understand diddly.
HATTIE: *(impatient)* But Gladys, that's exactly what I'm
   saying—
DROOLY: What-chess.

HATTIE: Yes Drooly, it's true—the Troll watches everything. *(addresses the Troll)* Isn't that right? Nothing escapes those beady little eyes.

(The Troll is silent.)

DROOLY: Lie a dock.

HATTIE: *(clapping her hands)* Oh yes! She's quite like a dog, isn't she? Perhaps a big friendly Saint Bernard—

GLADYS: Big friendly hippo.

(Laughter. Elly feels a spray of something on her cheek.)

HATTIE: Oh Drooly, you splattered! But really, *(movement; Hattie probably wiping Drooly's face)* I wonder if there's anything at all going on inside the Troll's head? I mean she doesn't do anything. Just sits there like a rug. Or an ottoman.

GLADYS: Moves quick enough when there's food.

(Elly was in fact amazed by the Troll's ability to snatch food, while—presumably—monitoring the eyes of Miss Pitts and the Bruiser; that she never got caught suggested a kind of intelligence.)

HATTIE: *(speaking again of Elly)* But this one here, why I'm just convinced she understands every word we say. She only refuses to let on. Isn't that right, Maudie?

But Elly remained mute on the subject.

·   ·   ·

Time passed in increments fixed by the unchanging routines of Elly's strange new world. Every morning the awful awakening in frigid half-light. Mrs. Wong yelling, "Chop-chop! Chop-chop!" Long shivering lines for the toilets. A savage hair-brushing by one of the older girls.

Those that were able were supposed to make their own beds. One day Elly decided to undertake this task herself, and found a pale satisfaction in making sure her blankets were absolutely square and wrinkle free.

But the process took her so very long, she was at the tail end of the line when they were finally herded to breakfast. This consisted of a bowl of lumpy oatmeal with a dab of congealed molasses, another noxious concoction that Mr. Hoppy had unaccountably decided she could eat. But she managed only a few spoonfuls before the Troll gobbled the rest.

She soon discovered it had been a big mistake to start making her bed.

Despite the bleakness of their environment, the building was kept scrupulously clean. In fact, Miss Pitts had a mania for cleanliness; their weekly baths were harsh and thorough, and every morning any girls deemed able were put to work cleaning. So one morning after breakfast, instead of being allowed to sit by herself trying to coax Mr. Hoppy out of his lethargy, Elly found herself transformed into a drudge.

At first she was put with the gang that scrubbed floors and toilets. But she was so slow and painstaking at anything she did that the Irish maid who oversaw them boxed her ears for dawdling. And soon she was switched to the crew that hauled buckets of horrible, stinking diapers from the wing where the babies were kept.

This area, an awful bedlam of squalling infants in iron cribs, was a revelation to Elly, as was the dark room off the side of the kitchen where Mrs. Wong presided over steaming cauldrons of laundry like some oriental witch. Mr. Wong Elly would glimpse from the corner of her eye, chopping things and muttering to himself, and she tried to hurry past before he spotted her—just as she tried to hurry past the babies, for she had the distinct impression that all of them were malformed in some way. She couldn't help but wonder what further horrors the building might hold.

A different Irish maid was in charge of the babies. She was quite young, and looked as slack-jawed and simple-minded as some of the girls. Because the bucket was too heavy for Elly to carry by herself, she was paired with Gladys. But Elly refused to look anywhere but at her feet, Gladys twitched, and the bucket's loathsome contents often slopped on the floor. Whenever this happened the maid gave them a tongue-lashing, swatted their behinds, and made them mop it up.

So the inedible mid-day meal came as a relief.

Then the long afternoon, when they were abandoned to the day-room as though they were so many broken and useless objects, like the toys and torn, coverless books littering the floor.

Many of these, Elly learned from Hattie and her friends, had been destroyed by a girl named Rena.

> HATTIE: Have you ever really looked at her face? It's like someone split it down the middle and glued it back together and made a bad job of it—no wonder she's so crack-brained!
>
> *(Drooly sputters with laughter.)*
>
> GLADYS: She gots a chest on er.
>
> *(More laughter)*
>
> HATTIE: *(mopping Drooly)* Well, she *is* the oldest one here. Still, why must she be such a bully! We got so close that time to finishing *The Wonderful Wizard of Oz*—then to tear out the last chapter!
>
> GLADYS: *(wistfully)* I liked that dog.

.   .   .

One day Elly decided to sit next to the twins, whose bizarre obsession with numbers fascinated her. Their gnomic exchanges followed a fixed pattern:

> FIRST TWIN: *(slowly, savoring the words)* Three thousand one hundred sixty-one.
>
> *(A long pause)*
>
> SECOND TWIN: *(with appreciation)* Mmm!
>
> *(Another long pause)*
>
> SECOND TWIN: *(slowly, savoring the words)* Eight thousand one hundred sixty-one.
>
> *(Long pause)*
>
> FIRST TWIN: *Mmm!*

As Elly was fascinated by the twins, so Hattie seemed to have become fascinated by Elly herself, and had taken over the job of brushing Elly's tangled mass of hair every morning. It was still a painful ordeal, for Hattie brushed hair in the same frenzied, jerky way she did everything. But there was something affectionate in the way she fitfully caressed Elly as she worked, an echo of her own mother's attentions. And, since Hattie was still convinced Elly could understand her, she often chattered as she worked.

> HATTIE: *(fingering one of Elly's chicken bone arms)* How skinny you are, Maudie! But of course, we're all skinny, aren't we? I can't imagine why they don't feed us more. But then you're lucky to be alive at all, you know.
> *(Elly somehow betrays her curiosity.)*
> HATTIE: But don't you remember? It was when you first got here, and you tried to take your doll into the dining hall! Well of course Miss Pitts wouldn't have it, and took your doll away as a corrective. But since it seems you must always show your food to your doll before you eat anything—quite silly of you, you know, *(shakes hairbrush in Elly's face)* but I suppose you just can't help yourself… Anyway, you stopped eating at all, and got so weak you just lay in bed all day. And, well, everybody knew you were going to die.
> *(Elly vaguely remembers lying in bed, the world becoming very dark, terrible dreams of wandering lost and alone through a shattered, burning world.)*
> HATTIE: But then Miss Bland brought your doll back to you. And you ate again—we all brought you food—and when you became strong enough to walk to the dining hall, Miss Bland insisted you be allowed to bring your doll with you. Can you imagine? Miss Bland standing up to Miss Pitts!
> *(Elly tries to imagine it, and cannot.)*

HATTIE: So really, *(gives Elly's unruly locks a final yank)* you
    owe your life to Miss Bland.

This bit of news electrified Elly, for it gave her a glimpse of a period
of her life she could scarcely recall. She had no memory at all of her arrival
here. She could remember performing with her vaudeville troupe in San
Francisco. But that had been April, and now it was September. It meant
she was now seven, for her birthday had been in May. She had misplaced
several months of her life as casually as one might lose a handkerchief.

It was also a fascinating new view of Miss Bland, who had always
seemed as impotent as a cloud. So when the doddering old lady favored
them with another visit that very afternoon (only to prove as easily ma-
nipulated as ever), Elly was inclined to be indulgent with her.

It was Hattie herself—bright, articulate Hattie—who most delighted
in derailing whatever crack-brained plans Miss Bland had made to entertain them.

HATTIE: What's that, Miss Bland—a puzzle? Oh but it looks
    so easy, and besides, it's sure to be missing pieces… Why
    don't you tell us about your pioneer days instead?
MISS BLAND: *(dithering)* What's that? Pioneer days? Do you
    really want to hear?
HATTIE: Oh yes, please!
DROOLY: Yeh!
(Gladys twitches.)
MISS BLAND: *(sounding rather pleased)* Well! My mother
    came here in a covered wagon—part of a "wagon train,"
    they called them—in 1842.
HATTIE: To Marysville, Miss Bland?
MISS BLAND: Yes, all the way from Saint Louis to
    Marysville.
DROOLY: *(with much effort)* Etch.
HATTIE: Drooly wants to know her age.

MISS BLAND: *(confused)* Her age? Well let's see, my mother was sixty-five when she passed away—

GLADYS: When she come here.

MISS BLAND: *(brightly)* Oh yes! She was only eighteen, and I was born on the way here. Can you imagine!

(Elly struggles to imagine Miss Bland being born in a covered wagon, and fails. One of the shufflers trips and falls against Miss Bland's chair with a shriek.)

MISS BLAND: *(jarred into speech)* Donner Pass. That's where we came through those mountains. *(She waves an arm vaguely.)* Of course, it wasn't called that yet. It was two years before that awful… *(Miss Bland's voice trails away. She hugs herself.)*

HATTIE: *(scenting conversational prey)* That awful *what*, Miss Bland?

MISS BLAND: *(still hugging herself)* Well, two years later there was another wagon train, led by a man named Donner. But they started too late, and got caught in a blizzard before they could make it over the pass. So they had to spend the entire winter in the mountains.

(A long pause. Miss Bland does not seem inclined to continue.)

HATTIE: *(taking up the slack)* Oh, but doesn't it sound like fun? All cozy in your wagon, waiting for the snow to melt.

GLADYS: Snowball fights.

HATTIE: Yes! And they could…they could make hot mulled cider! *(Hattie gesticulates in her jerky way.)* That is, if they had any apples.

MISS BLAND: *(dreamily)* But they hadn't any, you know. That was what was so awful.

HATTIE: *(tactfully)* Oh, I see. How awful for them.

DROOLY: No…foo.

MISS BLAND: *(for once understanding her)* Yes, they had no food at all.

> HATTIE: *(amazed)* But…but how did they live? What did they eat?
>
> MISS BLAND: *(mildly)* Well, one another. Yes, they ate one another.
>
> HATTIE: Goodness gracious!
>
> DROOLY: Gah!
>
> GLADYS: *(snickering)* Did they et all the dogs 'n cats?
>
> MISS BLAND: Oh, they did! They ate all the cats as well—oh, those poor little kitties! *(She noisily blows her nose and picks up her sad puzzle.)* Perhaps…perhaps some other time.
>
> *(She totters away.)*

When the shock wore off, a lively discussion ensued, with the girls concluding they might ease their constant hunger pangs by devouring the Troll. They tried to decide how best to cook her, Hattie plumping for slow roasting.

The Troll was silent as ever.

A commotion, girls all running toward the window. Unable to contain her curiosity, Elly joined them and peered through the bars.

Frieda Klee and Dr. Phelps were bundling a girl out of a curious closed carriage, something like a milk wagon. She was strapped into a heavy canvas coat with no sleeves. They could hear her screams even before Miss Pitts unlocked the door and helped wrestle the writhing, kicking girl inside.

"DAMNED!" the girl cried in a ravaged voice. "I'm DAMNED for all EE-TER-NI-TEEE!"

The girls rushed across the room and spilled out the door to the hallway to watch the drama unfold. The Bruiser gripped the girl, who continued to rave about her damnation. Dr. Phelps opened a black bag, pulled out a long syringe, and advanced on the girl.

"Here shcomes shlucifer," snuffled the Bruiser. "Shcomin to *git* ya!"

"*AAARGH!*" shrieked the girl. "LOOO-CIFER!" Her eyes rolled wildly. The Bruiser gripped her while Miss Pitts unstrapped the canvas coat and pulled out an arm. She held it as Dr. Phelps plunged the long needle into it. The Bruiser cackled, and Phelps flashed her a reproving look. Finally they frog-marched the distraught girl down the hall.

For several days after, when they stood in line waiting for their meals, they could sometimes hear her agonized cries—"DAMNED! DAMNED for all EE-TER-NI-TEE!"—echoing from what sounded like a thousand miles away.

Then they came less and less often, and disappeared altogether.

.   .   .

HATTIE: *(reading from a book)* "Alice thought she had never seen such a curious croquet-ground in her life. It was all ridges and furrows; the croquet balls were live hedgehogs, and the mallets live flamingoes—"
THE GIRL WHO ECHOES THINGS: Flamingoes! Flamingoes!
(Drooly rolls her eyes.)

Since watching the new girl arrive, Elly had begun to furtively peer around, looking at all the things she had only listened to. She found Hattie, Drooly, and Gladys to be all rather repulsive. Poor Drooly's body was all twisted, not to mention the affliction that had inspired her loathsome nickname. But her eyes were quite nice, and Elly learned to focus on them. Hattie wore an ugly leather helmet, and her face was so thin she seemed all eyes and teeth. While dumpy little Gladys was constantly twitching, grimacing, or scratching herself.

Across the room, sitting facing them with her breasts pressed up against the back of a broken chair, was a girl Elly identified (from Hattie's description of her crooked face and jealous references to her large bosoms) as the odious Rena Jacobs. Dancing around her was the girl who echoed whatever she heard, a skinny redhead hopping from foot to foot; Hattie had told Elly her name was Bertie McPhee, devoted acolyte of Rena.

Elly was still afraid to look directly at the Troll.

HATTIE: "…and the soldiers had to double themselves up and stand on their heads and feet, to make the arches."

BERTIE: Arches! Make the arches!

TWO IDENTICAL VOICES: *(in chorus)* Shut up! Shut up!

(They are indeed twins, with round faces and stick limbs.)

GLADYS: *(pulling a finger from her nose and inspecting it)* What's arches?

HATTIE: Oh, you know, those hoop thingies you hit the croquet balls through. *(She frantically sketches an arch in the air with her free hand.)*

GLADYS: What's croquet balls?

THE GIRL WHO ALWAYS COMPLAINS: It hurts! Oh, it hurts just so bad!

(The girl who constantly wails this refrain has mousy brown hair that covers her eyes.)

HATTIE: *(sighing)* "The chief difficulty Alice found at first was in managing her flamingo"—a *flamingo*, Drooly! They're playing croquet with flamingoes as mallets! Oh isn't it just the queerest, funniest thing?

(Drooly twitches agreement.)

Hattie continued reading, striding around the room and gesticulating wildly with her free arm as she described the absurdities of trying to hit a reluctant hedgehog with a twisting flamingo. Drooly shut her eyes as though trying to see it all in her mind.

Elly, too, was listening. She had never liked the first Alice book, but—just like Drooly—she relished anything that took her out of this place. Yet the constant interruptions were most irritating, while Hattie had a habit of losing her place, and was apt to repeat entire pages. Besides, Rena Jacobs was now grinning at them in a crack-brained way. How long before she grabbed Hattie's book, ripped out the pages, and spoiled their fun?

HATTIE: "The hedgehog was engaged in a fight with another
    hedgehog—"
BERTIE: Hedgehog! Hedgehog!
HATTIE: "—which seemed to Alice an excellent
    opportunity—"
*(A flurry of movement as Rena leaps from her chair—knocking
it over—snatches Mr. Hoppy, and bears him triumphantly
away. Like a shot, Elly is up and after her. The room erupts in
shrieks and moans. Rena throws the doll across the room, and
soon poor Mr. Hoppy is being gleefully tossed from person to
person as Elly frantically chases after him.)*
BERTIE: *(catching Mr. Hoppy and dancing around on her toes)*
    Off with his head! Off with his head!
*(She flings him back to Rena. Who turns to Elly and, grinning
dementedly, grabs Mr. Hoppy's head as though preparing to
twist it off)—*

Only to be knocked off her feet.

The Troll! The Troll, who never did anything but sit and lurk, had
crawled toward Rena, grabbed her legs, and pulled her down. Mr. Hoppy
went skidding across the floor. Elly ran and clutched the poor traumatized
frog to her chest.

The Troll grinned at her.

She was a huge, moon-faced girl, with cascades of greasy black hair
and dark, beady little eyes pressed deep into her face like raisins in a bun.

Their eyes met.

For several long, thrilling seconds, Elly did not look away.

Rena scrambled to her feet. She glared down at the Troll, and made
as if to wallop her. But the Troll stared back at her, and the malignant grin
on her moon face promised more of the same if Rena dared to lay a hand
on her.

Rena backed away.

.   .   .

Nobody ever wanted to sit next to the Troll in the dining hall. But that evening at dinner, Elly deliberately chose the seat next to her. And, before the Troll could snatch her bread, she picked it up and laid it on the Troll's plate.

The Troll stared at the bread. Tears pooled in her beady little eyes, and her fat lip trembled.

She had made her very first friend.

CHAPTER EIGHT

A FIT AND A FITTING

Every Sunday those girls deemed capable of sitting for an hour without disgracing themselves were herded into the chapel. This was a small, rather dismal room full of folding chairs and not much else, other than the lectern where Miss Pitts read Bible passages and improving sermons in a mellifluous voice of which she seemed rather vain. The Bruiser stood at the back, ready to whisk away any girl who lost control of herself, while Miss Bland sat to the other side of Miss Pitts, looking lost.

Since Elly had begun peeking at them, she knew the Bruiser was a powerfully built young woman with blond braids. She wore a brown and white striped uniform with brass buttons, an apron, and a small white cap, and her broad face reflected the unseemly glee with which she discharged her disciplinary duties.

Miss Pitts was stout and solidly built, with a sweet smile that failed to reach a pair of shrewd eyes. Eyes which always seemed to be assessing them, as though they were all defective merchandise offered at a bargain price. Miss Bland, on the other hand, was a tall stick of a woman, often as not haphazardly groomed, her hair in disarray, her sweater inside-out.

At the conclusion, Miss Pitts closed her Bible, the girls all stood, and she coaxed them into joining her as she warbled "Onward Christian Soldiers" in a wobbly contralto. Because even the most dim-witted of the girls knew this signified the service's end, they would lustily bray (at whatever pitch came out of their mouths) any words that popped into their heads; the resulting cacophony so ravaged Elly's musical soul she would often find herself paralyzed with horror. So she was still sitting in the back of the room one Sunday as the rest of the girls filed out, and she overheard the two old ladies talking.

> MISS BLAND: *(in a querulous voice)* Oh Beulah, such a dismal, *dismal* sound! If only… Couldn't we ask the deacons this year…?
>
> MISS PITTS: Hazel, dear Hazel, I'm so sorry. But I've gone over the budget and once again, we've no money to spare. Especially *(she chortles)* for anything so frivolous as a pump organ.
>
> MISS BLAND: *(with more emotion than Elly has ever heard from her)* Oh, but how could one call such a thing frivolous! To bring a bit of music into their dreary lives!

But the question was rhetorical, for Miss Pitts had already collected her Bible and sailed out of the room.

·   ·   ·

One day Miss Pitts led a new girl into the dayroom.

> MISS PITTS: *(trilling gaily)* Girls, I'd like you all to say hello to Brenda. Brenda darling, go on and get acquainted—they won't bite!
> *(Elly knows this to be not strictly true.)*
> *(Miss Pitts exits.)*

With Miss Pitts gone, Elly dared to look up. She saw a look pass between Hattie and Drooly, and turned her attention to the new girl. She was quite pretty, with a sweet but rather vacant smile that marked her as a shuffler. Indeed, she had already drifted toward one of the walls, hugging herself and rocking in place, looking at no one at all. It came as a complete shock when Elly suddenly recognized her as the girl who had arrived several weeks earlier, her face twisted in terror, shrieking of Lucifer and being "damned for all eternity."

Hattie sighed, picked up her coverless book, and flipped through it with jerky motions. "So, Drooly, where were we?"

Elly saw Drooly roll her eyes and shared her despair: Had Hattie forgotten that today they were finally to begin the second Alice book—were they doomed to hear about that awful croquet game yet again?

"Oh Drooly, *now* I remember!" cried Hattie, clutching at her helmet as though to jog her brains. "How silly of me—today we start the new book, yes we do, the new new NEW book, cock-a-doodle-DOO book…"

She prattled on while feverishly flipping through the pages. The twins yelled at her in unison to "Shut up!" and the girl who talked in a foreign language began an animated dialogue with herself.

"Here it is, here it is, here it IS!" Hattie triumphantly displayed the titled page to Drooly and Gladys. "*Through the Looking Glass—and What Alice Found There.*"

"Found there! What Alice found there!" piped Bertie, who had kicked off her boots and was dancing around in her stocking feet.

"Found her pitcher," suggested Gladys. "Pitcher of her face."

Elly had decided that, even though Gladys had most of her brains, they were rather haphazardly assembled.

"'One thing was certain,'" began Hattie, "'that the *white* kitten had had nothing to do with it—it was the black kitten's fault entirely…'"

Gladys began dreamily picking her nose. Drooly closed her eyes and looked like she was becoming lost in the story. Elly was flooded with warm memories of sitting on her mother's lap and listening to her read the very same story—so many times that Elly had it memorized. Since Mr. Hoppy was sitting in her own lap, she began moving her lips with the words, as if reading the story to him:

> "Here are the Red King and the Red Queen," Alice said in a whisper for fear of frightening them. "And there are the White King and the White Queen—"

Suddenly she realized Hattie had stopped reading, and was staring at her open book with her mouth agape. Gladys had pulled her finger from her nose and Drooly had twisted in her chair—and both of them were staring at Elly. And it dawned on her that she must have spoken aloud.

"Oh Drooly," whispered Hattie, "she got every word right. It's just not possible…"

She dropped to her knees in front of Elly. Elly stared intently at her doll, her face burning.

"Oh dear little Maudie"—Hattie stroked Elly's face—"here we were thinking you couldn't even speak! Oh Drooly," she cried over her shoulder, "what if she's got the whole book by heart? Do you, Maudie? Here, let's test you…"

She flipped frantically through the book and began to read at random.

> By this time it was getting light. "The crow must have flown away, I think," said Alice. "I'm so glad it's gone. I thought it was the night coming on…"

She stopped and waited breathlessly. Elly tried to resist. But the next words of the story were like a pressure building inside her brain. In a soft but audible voice, she continued "reading" to Mr. Hoppy:

> "I wish I could manage to be glad," the Queen said—

"Oh Drooly, I was RIGHT!" Hattie jumped up and thrust the book at her friend, jabbing at the passage Elly had just recited. "She's got ALL of the ENTIRE BOOK by HEART! Oh isn't it just the queerest, most wonderful thing?"

"Kweeah," sputtered Drooly. Even as she looked at Hattie with, it seemed to Elly, a resigned sadness.

"Oh, shan't we have such FUN now with MAUDIE to play with?" cried Hattie all in a rush. "Surely she's the SMARTEST one here, don't you think?! I mean I couldn't learn an ENTIRE book by HEART, could you? No no NO NEVER in a THOUSAND years, never in a MILLION BILLION years—"

"Billion years! Billion years!" echoed Bertie.

"SHUT UP!" cried the twins.

"—and I'm sure Maudie is just a WHIZ at reading, don't you think? Oh she MUST be to have an ENTIRE BOOK by HEART! I must write my parents and tell them to send MORE books, yes EVER SO MANY books…"

Like a wind-up toy suddenly let loose, Hattie's torrent of speech was accompanied by frenzied gesticulating. Then abruptly her face became stricken, even as the spate of words rushed on:

"Oh but Drooly WHY don't they ever VISIT me anymore, they did once no twice no THREE TIMES they visited me, oh I'm SURE they did, you remember, why did they ever PUT ME in this HORRIBLE PLACE oh they've FORGOTTEN all ABOUT me, I'm just SURE they have—"

With a convulsive jerk of her arm she hurled her book across the room. The other girls were becoming more and more agitated, shrieking, crying, laughing, moaning—a mad chorus to Hattie's mad aria.

"—and even though they still send nice things to me they NEVER answer my letters and Mother NEVER even BOTHERS to SIGN HER NAME to ANY of the cards, she makes SOMEONE ELSE do it—"

Her words now came so fast they were almost impossible to understand and seemed to be approaching some sort of climax:

"—they've forgotten about me FORGOTTEN FORGOTTEN and every day I'm FORGETTING FORGETTING more and more I'm like Alice I've gone THROUGH THE LOOKING GLASS and I'm NEVER COMING BACK no NEVER NEVER NEVER—"

It was now that Elly finally learned the purpose of Hattie's helmet as, still gibbering, she began to hurl herself headfirst against the wall. Energetically, with full force, as if longing to break her neck. Over and over and over…

The Bruiser rushed into the room, closely followed by Miss Pitts. Elly watched with horror as, under Miss Pitts's direction, the big muscular woman wrestled Hattie into one of the armless canvas jackets, then carried her, still writhing and shrieking, out of the room.

The sounds of her screams echoed down the hallway, then finally faded. Perhaps twenty minutes later there was another kind of sound, and Elly was at the window in time to watch Dr. Phelps drive up in his motorcar.

She had heard it many times before, and already deduced that Phelps must not live in the building, but somewhere nearby. He usually parked it in the stable, and she had never before seen it. But this time he drove it up to the front door, leapt out, and rushed inside the building. And Elly had time to savor the vehicle's gleaming brass work and elegant lines before Henry ambled over and pushed it into the stable.

·   ·   ·

A few days later Hattie suddenly reappeared—or a girl with the same leather helmet and greasy auburn hair as Hattie. But this girl was even skinnier and had none of Hattie's nervous animation. Instead she spent long hours staring dreamily into space, and for a few days Gladys had to poke her in the ribs when it was time to go eat.

Gradually Hattie came out of her trance and began to converse again with her friends. But there was a new gracefulness to her movements that was altogether startling, and the frantic spate of words when she talked or read aloud had been replaced by a decorously calm and pleasant voice; if it weren't for that same irritating tendency to read the same page twice, she might have been a different person.

"You...diff–reh," Drooly sputtered. And managed to ask what Dr. Phelps had done to her.

Hattie had wiped her friend's face, smiled sweetly, and agreed that yes, she did feel different.

"But I swear, I can't remember anything at all about what happened to me."

Hattie returned to reading aloud. This time Elly was careful to keep her mouth shut, and it soon became clear that Hattie had even forgotten the event that had indirectly ignited her own fit. So when Gladys pointed at Elly and suggested that Hattie "make *her* tell the story," she had only laughed, thinking it a joke.

Then one day, just as Hattie was opening the book and preparing to read, she mentioned to Drooly she'd had the strangest dream about "Maudie reading the book aloud." At once Drooly began sputtering it had been no dream. Hattie was amazed. But when Gladys cryptically assured her that Maudie "got the book in her head," she was finally convinced. She was trying to get Elly to repeat her performance (and Elly stubbornly resisting) when Dr. Phelps arrived for his weekly visit.

As always when Phelps and Miss Pitts were around, Elly was careful not to look up from her doll. So she again experienced the visit as though listening to a play, blindfolded (with occasional moments when she dared to peek):

HATTIE: *(rushing up to Phelps)* Oh Dr. Phelps! Dr. Phelps, you won't believe it, but little Maudie can actually speak! Not only that, she knows the entire second Alice book—the one about going through the looking-glass—by heart!

PHELPS: *Mmm,* does she now?

(Dr. Phelps has thinning brown hair, a weak chin that makes his nose seem even more pointed, and green eyes disturbingly magnified by thick spectacles.)

HATTIE: Oh, but it's bothersome. She just refuses to speak at all today. But she did it before, I remember now!

PHELPS: *(gazing at Hattie as if his spectacles were a microscope and she a specimen on a glass slide)* So your memory's coming back, is it?

HATTIE: *(smiling)* Oh yes, I remember it quite clearly. But isn't that wonderful? To know an entire book by heart!

PHELPS: Wonderful!

MISS PITTS: *(sidling up to Phelps and laying a hand on his shoulder)* Oh Doctor, it's not just wonderful—it's *miraculous*, nothing short of!

(Neither of them is paying the slightest attention to Elly; it's clearly Hattie herself at whom they are marveling.)

HATTIE: *(pointing at Elly)* Perhaps…perhaps if *you* were to ask her?

PHELPS: *(ignoring her)* So, Hattie, how do you feel?

HATTIE: Oh Dr. Phelps, I feel just *oodles* better! Do you think—do you think soon I might be able to take off this beastly helmet?

MISS PITTS: Doesn't fidget at all. Talks at a normal rate—

PHELPS: Yes yes… Changing the wave form and duration of the pulse…my God, perhaps the breakthrough I've been… But this bizarre delusion…

(He finally deigns to gesture toward Elly. Elly quickly drops her eyes to her lap.)

HATTIE: But it's not a delusion! I remember perfectly clearly. *(She drops to her knees in front of Elly, opens her book, and reads aloud a random passage.)*

(Elly stares stonily at her doll.)

HATTIE: Oh Maudie, please *please* show Dr. Phelps I'm not having a delusion! Don't you see, *(close to tears)* if you show them how smart you are, they might let you out of this place! Isn't that right, Miss Pitts?

MISS PITTS: *(clears throat)* Well, surely, um…I mean if it should actually prove to be *true*…

Perhaps it was Miss Pitts's doubt that piqued Elly. Or maybe it was the tears of frustration glistening in Hattie's eyes. Still staring at Mr. Hoppy, she recited the rest of the passage in her flat little voice.

Hattie leapt to her feet and triumphantly held her book up to Dr. Phelps.

"My stars," he murmured. He took the book, knelt in front of Elly, and tested her again. His magnified eyes terrified her. But the wild hope had been kindled inside Elly that this might actually get her out of this place, and she dutifully completed the paragraph.

> PHELPS: *(standing up)* Utterly remarkable.
>
> MISS PITTS: But…but it hardly seems *credible*—
>
> PHELPS: Not at all. Hattie, I do owe you an apology. But no, Beulah. Remarkable—but *not* incredible. A young savant. They're often capable of quite astounding mental feats. What did you say the girl's name was?
>
> MISS PITTS: Maude…Smith. Yes, that's it.
>
> PHELPS: And her background?
>
> MISS PITTS: I'm afraid she came to us with very little documentation. But I understand they found her in San Francisco.
>
> HATTIE: *(crowing)* So you see how smart she is! I mean surely she doesn't belong here!
>
> PHELPS: I'm afraid, Hattie, it's unwise to confuse such mental feats with true intelligence. Indeed, such cases are often referred to as "*idiot*" savants" for that very reason. So, even though she responded to the stimulus of hearing the book she has memorized in an automatic way, I doubt she even hears us. *(Again he kneels in front of Elly. Tries to get her to speak to him. Waves a hand in front of her eyes. Incensed at being referred to as an idiot, Elly keeps her eyes fixed on Mr. Hoppy and stubbornly ignores him.)*
>
> PHELPS: *(sighs and stands)* Yes, it's as I said. A classic state of catatonia, her ability to perceive outside stimuli inhibited. The result of hysteria, perhaps brought on by some sort of trauma… San Francisco, did you say, Beulah?
>
> MISS PITTS: Precisely, Doctor.
>
> *(Elly struggles to make sense of this cryptic exchange.)*

PHELPS: *(suddenly expansive)* Whereas you, my dear Hattie, if your wonderful improvement proves permanent—that is, if there's no relapse—I see no reason why you might not soon be returned to the bosom of your family!

HATTIE: My family? But didn't you know? My family doesn't give a FIG about me. They haven't visited me in TWO YEARS, not once in TWO WHOLE YEARS! And all of the nice books Mother sends me have cards written by her secretary, she doesn't even bother to SIGN HER NAME—"

(She throws her book on the floor and bursts into tears.)

MISS PITTS: Dr. Phelps, I should have warned you: The subject of her family is Hattie's great bugaboo; I'm afraid the child uses it as an excuse to lose control of herself.

PHELPS: Yes yes, I see. Well, what about this, Hattie: if there's no relapse in the next month, I'll write your parents personally and tell them what wonderful progress you've made.

(Hattie takes her hands from her face and stares at him.)

PHELPS: And *(reaches out and fingers her ugly headgear)* and we'll take off this "beastly helmet" as well, hmm? What do you say to that?

(Hattie smiles through her tears. Dr. Phelps and Miss Pitts exit.)

MISS PITTS: *(twisting around as they leave to hiss into Hattie's ear)* Remember: *no more fits!*

.   .   .

At the rear of the building was a large area where, on nice days, they were allowed outside to exercise. The ground was barren but for a few scraggly trees, trampled into hard dirt by girls' boots. A tall iron fence topped with sharp spikes surrounded the space and added to its grimness.

On the other side of the bars the horizon was crowned by an undulating range of mountains like the frozen waves of a lavender sea. In the clear autumn air, they looked close enough to touch. It gave an illusion of freedom so delicious that Elly longed to run around without having to worry about dropping Mr. Hoppy.

She went in search of the Troll.

The two of them had an understanding. They sat beside one another in the dining hall, and the Troll didn't steal Elly's food (though Elly was always careful to give a portion of it to her anyway). When they sat together in the dayroom, the Troll protected Mr. Hoppy from his enemies. It was a job she took very seriously, her beady little eyes constantly darting around at everyone in the room. As a reward for this diligence, Elly sometimes let her play with her precious doll.

She found the Troll sitting in a heap. The Troll grinned savagely and clutched Mr. Hoppy to her chest.

Satisfied, Elly ran off to explore.

She squatted in the dirt beside a new girl who was examining something in the palm of her hand with an expression of rapture.

"Look!" she said, holding out her hand. Cupped inside her palm was a pair of moth's wings etched with delicate brown and gold filigree. They reminded Elly of one of Esta Sangley's silk wrappers. She nodded her appreciation, and the girl flashed her a smile of uncommon sweetness. She was as short as Elly. But something about her squat, thick body made Elly suspect she was older, and her broad face and slanted eyes reminded Elly of Mrs. Wong. She was so stupid she was unable to make her bed, and ate so slowly that her food was mostly stolen before she could get it in her mouth; soon she would be as skinny as the rest of them. But she seemed to have an ability to find beauty in the most obscure corners of their sordid existence.

Elly was still savoring the perfection of the lovely wings when her glance fell on something crawling laboriously across the dirt at her feet:

A crippled insect searching for its lost wings.

She stood up and wandered over to where Hattie and Drooly and Gladys were gathered around Brenda.

Brenda had emerged from her trance as obsessed with Lucifer as ever. But she no longer raved about him, instead offering her shocking bulletins from the netherworld in urgent and secretive whispers delivered in a lilting Irish brogue.

"He kissed me last night," she once revealed. "Lucifer."

"Gah!" was Drooly's response.

"What was it like?" asked Hattie politely.

"Tasted of licorice," whispered Brenda.

She talked not just of Lucifer, but also of ghouls, leprechauns, faerie folk, and beasties, all of which the world appeared to be teeming with.

"Sure, tis only the chosen can see em," she remarked somewhat smugly.

Elly found them gathered beneath one of the scraggly trees, sorting fallen leaves into pretty piles according to color, and speculating on the ghosts known to infest the building. From outside one could see how very large it was, and all the turrets and gables and ornamented recesses were surely enticing to ghosts. Hattie said you could sometimes hear them playing ghostly music, but Elly had yet to experience this.

According to lore passed down among the girls over the years, the ghosts belonged to the girls who had died here. There was a stretch of earth along the back of the iron fence where they were said to be buried, and none of the girls would play there; if one of the stupider ones wandered in that direction, the others would shriek an alarm, like a herd of elephants trumpeting danger, until she wandered back.

The mysterious screams and moans faintly echoing through the building's hallways were said to emanate from the place to which girls were whisked away by Miss Pitts and the Bruiser to be murdered (the same place, they thrillingly theorized, from which Hattie and Brenda had somehow managed to return). But whereas Hattie had no memory of the experience, Brenda claimed to remember everything. Elly found her in the process of relating the lurid details to her skeptical yet enthralled listeners.

"Stripped me stark naked, they did. A pack of devils. Poked and prodded me with their forks until I screamed and bled. Sure, twas right there—"

She pointed to a turret on one end of the building sprouting wires like hairs from a mole. The wires drooped to a pole standing beside the building, then connected to a series of poles receding rhythmically into the distance.

"—and the wires, sure that's how the devils send their messages to Lucifer."

Elly found the explanation both silly and thrillingly plausible.

"Does he write back?" enquired Gladys.

Drooly rolled her eyes; it was something she did very expressively.

"Listen!" cried Hattie suddenly. "There it is!"

They listened intently for a minute.

"I hear it too!" said Brenda.

Elly heard nothing. Then suddenly the hairs on her arms prickled as, faintly audible beneath the shouts and shrieks of the other girls, she detected the sound of someone playing a piano.

"Lucifer," Brenda nodded knowingly. "He's a-playin his devil's music to set the faerie folk a-dancin."

Again they went quiet, listening. The sounds were so faint they were scarcely there at all, like music in a dream. But Elly heard enough to come to a surprising conclusion:

The Devil was a shockingly inept musician.

·   ·   ·

Ever since Dr. Phelps—by whatever mysterious method—had cured Hattie of her fits, he had become her hero. And she was counting the days until he would write her parents and remove her hateful helmet.

"He's not been here very long, you know, Maudie—less than a year. He must be quite wealthy, don't you think? To drive his own motorcar. And he's ever so smart—he studied in Europe and speaks German. Miss Pitts says we're ever so lucky to have him."

Such nuggets of information Hattie dispensed as she brushed Elly's hair every morning. Because no matter what the "ever so smart" Dr. Phelps had said, Hattie was certain Elly understood her perfectly well.

"But one can't help but wonder about some of the other girls who've gone away. I mean it's clear he must do something to them. Because when they come back—well, if they're no longer as wild as they were, it's only because they're no longer much of anything at all."

It was true, Elly reflected. At least half of the girls were incapable of speech, and seemed quite lost.

"And then there are the ones who don't come back. Like that poor girl yesterday—she'll *never* be back, I promise you."

Elly shuddered at the memory. One of the shufflers had dirtied her drawers. The expression on Miss Pitts's face when she entered the room and encountered the stench! For a long moment she had stood frozen in a pantomime of utter horror—then rushed about like a maddened bloodhound, sniffing out the offender and yanking up her frock.

"You *filthy-dirty* girl!" Miss Pitts had shrieked. "FILTHY-DIRTY!"

The poor girl had let out a dismal howl as the Bruiser carried her away.

"No," repeated Hattie grimly, "we'll never see *her* again. And as to what happens to the ones who don't return, well I really don't believe Miss Pitts *murders* them"—Hattie laughed nervously—"but some of them do die, you know. One of these nights, I'll show you."

      ·   ·   ·

Meg, the Irish maid who looked after the babies, had banished Gladys for twitchy ineptitude, and Elly was now teamed with Brenda. Meg herself was only sixteen, and the two Irish girls got along well. Though Meg was quick to take offense when Brenda referred to the pathetic and misshapen waifs under her care as "Satan's spawn."

"For shame, Brenda Moran. Sure they're as much God's children as you or I. The pore little mites, I'd coddle every last one of em all day long, had I only the time."

Now that Meg was saying things (other than Irish curses), Elly soon realized it was not stupidity, but sheer exhaustion, which made her so slack-jawed and glassy-eyed.

"She makes me do the work of three," she said of Miss Pitts. "All five of us curse the day we came to this place." She was referring to the other maids, all of whom had come over together from County Cork. "Five years we signed on for, to pay back our passage. Had I known what was in store, I'd have prayed the ship would sink."

She crossed herself at this blasphemy and rushed back to her squalling charges.

Brenda didn't twitch. But she was much taller than Elly, and this lopsidedness still made them occasionally stumble. And one day they had the terrible misfortune to drop the bucket of dirty diapers right in front of the kitchen's open doorway.

Mr. Wong had been chopping something with a cleaver. He turned around and glared at them. Brenda rushed away to fetch the mop. Elly began stuffing diapers back into the bucket, her face burning.

Mr. Wong turned back to his work, chopping furiously. His skinny body jerked, and his long queue swung like a pendulum. Brenda returned and began mopping. Suddenly Mr. Wong whirled around.

"You!"

They both froze.

"You no likee my food?" His sweaty face was twisted into a frown, and he swung his cleaver menacingly.

Brenda was saucer-eyed, no doubt certain that Lucifer himself was preparing to chop them into mincemeat.

Mr. Wong's face suddenly relaxed and he smiled grimly. "Sure, you no likee. Nobody likee my food. But what I can do? Miss Pitt, she gimmee not nuff money. You savvy? She makee me buying bad food"—he bent and seized a sad-looking cabbage from a basket on the floor—"you lookee—bad food! Not nuff food! Makee you all too much skinny! But what I can do?"

He hurled the cabbage back into the basket, turned his back on them, and started chopping more ferociously than ever. Brenda seized the opportunity to scurry away with the mop.

Suddenly Mr. Wong threw down his cleaver, reached up to a shelf, and pulled something from a jar. He turned around and held out his hand to Elly.

In his sweaty palm lay two peppermint sticks.

"You takee!"

He glared at her until she took them.

"You eat!"

She dared to lick one of them.

He nodded, satisfied, and returned to his chopping.

When she offered the other stick to Brenda she was aghast.

"Sure, it's full of devil's pizen!" she gasped.

So Elly ate it herself.

·   ·   ·

Saturday was bath day, a dreaded ordeal in which the girls were made to strip, then stand in a long line waiting to be doused with cold water and washed by Mrs. Wong with all the gentleness of a hog being scrubbed for market.

But today something was different. The weather had turned wintery, they shivered as they waited in line, and the water was sure to be icy. But even that couldn't explain the volume of the shrieks echoing from the bathroom.

A pungent reek filled the air as Elly drew closer, and she hesitated at the threshold.

"Chop-chop!" barked Mrs. Wong, grabbing Elly and pulling her into the bathroom. "Close eyes!"

She dunked Elly's head in a vat of kerosene.

A moment later Elly was standing with a group of naked screaming girls, screaming as lustily as the rest. Her head felt like it was on fire, so when the icy water was finally poured over them, it came as a relief. Then instead of itchy and threadbare frocks, they were handed pretty new uniforms, along with thick, new stockings. Eagerly Elly put them on, relishing the warmth and the feeling of the soft material against her skin. And her scalp was no longer crawling with the itchy bugs that had plagued them all for several weeks.

Perhaps—she dared to hope—perhaps things were getting better!

She was soon disabused of any such notion by Hattie.

"It's only for the inspection I'm afraid, Maudie," she sighed as she combed the snarls from Elly's damp hair. "Every year some men come to look at us to see if...well, if everything's hunky-dory in this place, I suppose."

It was only recently Elly had discovered what exactly "this place" was. A new girl named Tussie had just arrived. She had lank, mouse-colored hair, thick glasses, and the protruding teeth of a large rodent. But she seemed to have some of her wits, and Elly had overheard Hattie telling her things.

She learned that Hattie and Drooly were both twelve, Gladys was nine, and Brenda was eleven. Drooly had been here the longest of the four, arriving five years ago. But the Troll was already here when she came and seemed such a permanent fixture that nobody speculated on her age, or had any idea of her real name.

And that's when Elly learned that she was in the Marysville Benevolent Christian Asylum for Unfortunate Girls, named for the nearby city of Marysville.

GLADYS: *(between grimaces)* It's a hunnert miles away.

HATTIE: Oh Gladys it isn't any such thing, it's only a few miles—

GLADYS: *(scratching obstinately)* Hunnert miles. Hunnert miles, very least.

HATTIE: Oh now, Gladys, how could that be, when Miss Pitts drives into town most every day to market, and back again—

GLADYS: Makes two hunnert.

TUSSIE: *(echoing Elly's own thoughts)* What's a 'sylum?

GLADYS: Booby hatch.

HATTIE: Oh Gladys, that's such a hateful word! Tussie, you
    mustn't listen to her—

GLADYS: You's a booby, I's a booby. We's all boobies.

Yes, that conversation had certainly been food for thought.

"That's why," Hattie continued explaining about the inspection,
"they've gone to all the trouble of painting the building."

For the previous two weeks the girls had watched a gang of Chinamen in ragged, paint-stained tunics swarming over the building on
rickety ladders and scaffolds, like pirates in the rigging of a Chinese junk.

"So the inspection is nothing but a sham," concluded Hattie. "Because after it's done, Miss Pitts will pack away all these pretty frocks for
another year. But at least"—Hattie sighed philosophically and brushed
the last snarl from Elly's hair—"at least we'll get one good meal out of it."

        •   •   •

Hattie's cynicism was softened by a most surprising development. For
that very afternoon, she and Elly were plucked from the dayroom by
the Bruiser, and—with a gentleness unprecedented in the girls' experience—escorted through one of the doors that was always kept locked into
a sort of parlor. There they found Miss Pitts, Miss Bland, and Dr. Phelps
all waiting, along with a hard-faced woman they had never seen before.

Elly's eyes were immediately drawn to a stack of expensive-looking
party frocks arrayed on the sofa, before she remembered to stare at her
doll. Breathlessly she followed the ensuing conversation:

MISS PITTS: Well! You girls are indeed fortunate—

PHELPS: Hattie, what would you say if we were to remove
    your ugly helmet a week ahead of schedule? I mean, it's

hardly the sort of thing one wears to a dinner party, eh Beulah?

MISS PITTS: *(laughing merrily)* Indeed not, Doctor!

HATTIE: *(in disbelief)* A...a dinner party?

Phelps explained there was to be a private dinner after the inspection. And that he'd like Hattie to demonstrate her remarkable recovery to the two deacons and the state examiner—and thus the efficacy of Phelps's revolutionary new treatment—by eating and socializing with them.

PHELPS: While Maude here shall provide a sort of...*diversion*, I suppose one would call it, by demonstrating her remarkable memory. That is, if you think she can be coaxed into it?

HATTIE: *(beside herself)* Oh, I'm sure she can!

PHELPS: *(clapping his hands)* Splendid, splendid! Well then, I'll leave you ladies to it. *(He exits.)*

(Hattie begins tearing at the straps of her helmet. Miss Pitts clucks and nods at the Bruiser—who quickly undoes them—then clucks again at the sorry state of Hattie's hair, clumped around her head like a second greasy helmet.)

MISS PITTS: Frieda, if you would be so good as to take Hattie and give her hair a thorough washing. Mrs. Faircroft, what do you have that might fit this one here?

Mrs. Faircroft was now revealed to be a seamstress, and Elly spent a giddy hour being fitted with a frock of apricot-colored satin with puffed sleeves and lace trim. While Mrs. Faircroft sewed the hems, Miss Bland went to work arranging Elly's hair. She smelt of sweat, talcum powder, lavender, and onions, and the way her fingers flitted about Elly's head felt like a mouse had got loose in her hair. But the results, when Miss Bland held up a mirror, were very pretty.

Hattie returned, arrayed in a similar confection of green silk. When her long auburn locks had been brushed, prettily arranged, and adorned with a bow to match her frock, the resulting transformation, from ugly duckling to fairy princess, astonished them all.

The finery of both girls was carefully removed and set aside for to-morrow. As Frieda began to lead them away, Miss Pitts grasped Hattie's arm and hissed in her ear:

"Do not disgrace us!"

CHAPTER NINE

A SOCIAL OCCASION

On the day of the inspection, Hattie's prediction of "at least one good meal" was supported by the savory aromas wafting through the building's hallways. It put the girls into a fever of anticipation, and Drooly quite earned her nickname. But their excitement was tempered by the fierce attentions of the Bruiser, who stood guard all afternoon, lest the girls pull the ribbons from each other's hair, tear off their nice new uniforms, or otherwise disgrace themselves before the arrival of the inspectors.

At last a rather old-fashioned and grand looking carriage drove up. A short time later, Miss Pitts swept into the dayroom with Dr. Phelps and three strange men in her wake, Miss Bland trailing behind like an after-thought. Elly sat pretending to stare at her doll, and peered stealthily at them. The two old ladies wore gowns she had never seen before—Miss Pitts's of burgundy silk, and Miss Bland's of black velvet with a sadly drooping bodice. Phelps had exchanged his tweeds for an elegant black suit and scarlet waistcoat, which failed to disguise his gangly figure.

At once he strode toward Hattie.

"And this, gentlemen, is Hattie Limburg—the girl I've been telling you about."

He proceeded to introduce Deacons Radcliffe and Diddy, and Mr. Fisk, the state examiner. The three men murmured greetings, even as they inspected Hattie in a way Elly thought rather rude, as if she were a horse they were thinking of buying.

Hattie preened and tried a curtsey. Neither she nor Elly were yet dressed in their party frocks; they would change while the other girls were at dinner. But Miss Bland had redone their hair, and without her helmet, Hattie's narrow face had gone from starved-looking to greyhound-sleek. In addition, she had regained much of her former animation—but without the nervous fidgetiness—and her radiant smile seemed to charm the men.

"Why, she seems perfectly normal!" exclaimed Deacon Radcliffe, a very fat man with a florid complexion and a large nose ornamented by a spider's webbing of fine purple veins. "And once, you say, she suffered from fits?"

"A kind of mania," said Phelps. "Periodic convulsions, quite severe—"

"But I remember the girl," said Mr. Fisk. He had thinning blonde hair atop a perfectly oval face, with features so blandly simple they might have been sketched in by a child. "She had a fit while I was last here. In fact, I seem to recall you had her wearing some sort of headgear—"

"For three years I had to wear the most *beastly* leather helmet!" wailed Hattie, making a comic face.

"So you saw the poor child before we began her treatments," said Miss Pitts. "Whirling like a dervish, talking nineteen to the dozen, throwing her head against the wall—"

"I once saw a dervish," mused Deacon Diddy, an ancient-looking man with a bald dome fringed with limp white hair and a long drooping mustache. "Calcutta, I believe it was. Some filthy *souk*… Or was it Cairo?"

"Were there pyramids?" asked Miss Bland shrewdly, sidling up to him. Her cheeks and withered lips had been rouged, to ghastly effect.

Diddy beamed fatuously. "You know, I believe there were!"

Mr. Fisk had broken away from them, and seemed intent on justifying the title of State Examiner by examining everything in the room. Elly watched him take in the coverless volumes in the bookcase and the sad miscellany of broken objects in the toy chest, before turning his attention to the broken girls themselves. Most of them had been watching the visitors warily, and shrank from his bland blue-eyed gaze or giggled nervously. But many were oblivious, hugging themselves and rocking or shuffling in place. Fisk peered at them all before rejoining the group.

"You know," he offered, in a voice as colorless as the rest of him, "I keep imagining I smell mothballs."

Dr. Phelps shot a quick glance at Miss Pitts, who laughed nervously.

"I must say, Doctor," continued Fisk in the same bland voice, "I'm surprised at how very many of the girls seem…well, to use layman's terms, 'not quite all there.'"

"Girls who were once wild banshees," retorted Miss Pitts, "have become, thanks to our treatment, docile and manageable—"

"*Our* treatment, Miss Pitts?" Phelps voice was quietly acid.

"And surely modest, quiet deportment," continued Miss Pitts, ignoring him, "can only be considered a step toward salvation for the poor creatures."

"Hear hear," rumbled Deacon Radcliffe.

"And cleanliness," remarked Deacon Diddy. "Next to Godliness, don't you know."

Phelps suggested they pay a visit to the part of the building where he gave his treatments. "You'll have seen nothing like it, I assure you," he added, ushering them out.

Not long after this, all the girls but Elly and Hattie trooped off to the dining hall while Patty, the Irish maid who helped Mr. Wong in the kitchen and served the old ladies their tea at dinner, led the two of them off to be changed. She was a thin, nervous girl with a pinched face and wore an elaborate starched uniform Elly had never seen before. She dressed them, then left them alone in the same parlor as yesterday. Faintly the sounds of the other girls eating in the dining hall could be heard. Patty bustled in and out with a tray of empty glasses and decanters full of wine. Finally she brought in a large tray laden with small pieces of fresh-baked bread topped with fragrant slices of ham and cheese.

"Don't ya dare to touch em," she snapped. "She'd have me head."

She bustled away again.

Mr. Hoppy had already given Elly permission to gobble up the entire tray, and the admonition was almost more than the starving girls could bear. They tried to distract themselves by marveling at the rich oriental carpet, plush velvet upholstery, fresh flowers in delicately cut glass vases, and other splendors so foreign to their own tawdry domicile. Hattie held in her lap the book with which Elly's fabulous memory was to be displayed, and was nervously chattering that passing through the locked door into this wing of the building was "just like going through the looking glass," when the thunder of fifty pairs of girl's boots heralded the conclusion of their dinner. A few minutes later, they heard approaching voices and stood as the adults entered the room.

"Well now"—Deacon Radcliffe filled the doorway and beamed at them—"aren't these two a pretty sight!"

He crossed the room and reached for the tray. Elly watched balefully as two of the delectable morsels disappeared between his thick, sensual lips.

Miss Bland entered the room tottering coquettishly on the arm of Deacon Diddy. Dr. Phelps and Mr. Fisk were in the midst of a spirited conversation. Elly stared at the floor.

PHELPS: …then after Vienna, I continued my studies in
    Geneva. Worked with a man named Battelli. Continuing
    the work begun by Duchenne, the great French
    neurologist—
FISK: Duchenne… Didn't he take those photographs, men
    being made to grimace?
PHELPS: Precisely! But we took it so much further!
    Fantastic experiments, extending the frontiers of scientific
    knowledge—
FISK: *(mildly)* Experimenting on human beings?"
PHELPS: Well, er, actually, no, it was…dogs. Dogs we were
    working with…
*(The girls are allowed to sit down again. Elly stares at the food
on the tray. Miss Bland sits on the end of the sofa next to Elly.
Deacon Diddy takes the easy chair beside her.)*

DEACON DIDDY: Now don't those look tasty! *(Elly watches his palsied hand reach for a slice of the bread.)* Perhaps the girls would care for some?

(Elly gobbles up four slices before the wonderful flavor even registers on her senses.)

DEACON DIDDY: Good heavens!

(The entire room has gone silent.)

DEACON RADCLIFFE: *(finally finding his voice)* Do you not feed them enough? I mean, I couldn't help but note, during the dinner we just observed, the rather…*unseemly* voracity with which the girls devoured their roast beef.

MISS PITTS: *(sorrowfully)* Ah, Deacon Radcliffe, if you only realized the difficulties involved in civilizing the behavior of these poor creatures whom God, in his mysterious wisdom, has denied the full flowering of humanity.

DEACON RADCLIFFE: *(gravely)* Yes, of course.

DEACON DIDDY: Perhaps give them knives. With which to cut their meat.

MISS PITTS: *(nonplussed)* Knives?

FISK: Speaking of poor creatures, isn't it true, Doctor, that you have been lavishing all your time and expense on certain girls. At the *expense*, as it were, of the many desperate cases in the west wing—

PHELPS: *(with bravado)* Yes, I freely admit it. Why should I waste my time on incurables? When there are others—formerly considered equally hopeless—who are now, thanks to a scientific breakthrough, eminently treatable! *(Elly senses Hattie preening beside her, and guesses Phelps is smiling at her.)* A breakthrough that, I venture to add, is about to put this institution on the map.

DEACON RADCLIFFE: Hear hear.

DEACON DIDDY: *(befuddled)* But surely you are already marked on *some* maps?

FISK: *(with quiet doggedness)* But your quite appalling death rate—how do you explain it?
PHELPS: *(in a tight voice)* As I mentioned before, there was an outbreak of typhus.
FISK: And yet there has been no such epidemic in any of the neighboring communities.
MISS PITTS: *(brightly)* Doctor, perhaps it's time for that little diversion we've arranged?
(Miss Bland has been furtively feeding Elly slices of bread, and she is caught with a mouth full of food. She tries to choke it down.)
PHELPS: …a sad case, they found her in San Francisco, don't you know—
DEACON RADCLIFFE: Indeed!
PHELPS: —after the event. And the trauma rendered her catatonic.
DEACON DIDDY: *(wisely)* She does look a bit feline.
PHELPS: *(coughs)* No, what I mean is…

Dr. Phelps concluded his explanation of Elly's condition—and her extraordinary talent—then asked Hattie to open the book at random and read a passage. Elly balked at having to perform like some trained parrot. But the thought that she might be denied the wonderful meal, whose aroma had already penetrated the room, trumped her distaste, and she dutifully mumbled the rest of the sentence.

Gasps of amazement.

Soon everyone was passing around the book for a turn. All the time she avoided their astonished eyes by staring at her doll.

Deacon Diddy was the last one to read to her. After she completed the paragraph he had started, there was a long silence.

DEACON DIDDY: *(bemused)* Is it a trick?
FISK: Astonishing. And you say she is otherwise mute?

PHELPS: What's more, she is utterly unaware of anything we
say. A purely automatic response…

PATTY: *(in a quavery voice)* Beggin yer pardon—dinner is
served.

Elly risked peering around. She saw Dr. Phelps rise and gallantly
offer Hattie his arm. Miss Pitts, Deacon Radcliffe, and Mr. Fisk followed,
then Miss Bland leaning on Deacon Diddy (or was it the other way
around?) and holding Elly's hand.

Miss Pitts had been whispering something in Deacon Radcliffe's ear,
and now circled back to walk beside Deacon Diddy.

"I'd forgotten to mention," she said in a low voice, "please don't ask
Hattie about her family. It's the one subject that might…well, she finds it
difficult to talk about."

"Her family," Deacon Diddy nodded sagely. "Yes, of course."

The fine china, crystal, and silver cutlery adorning the dining room
table's snowy surface glistened in the flickering light of a silver candelabra
and cheerful fire. Hattie was seated between the two deacons (the better,
Elly guessed, for her to charm them). Miss Bland sat on the other side
of Deacon Diddy, and Miss Pitts to the other side of Deacon Radcliffe.
Elly was not expected to charm anyone and had been negligently stuck
between Dr. Phelps and Mr. Fisk. She and Hattie faced each other across
the table.

Patty went around filling wine glasses (grape juice for the girls), and
there was a general murmur of appreciation for the elegant setting. Miss
Bland and Deacon Diddy had fallen into a lively discussion, but in all the
hubbub, Elly couldn't quite catch the subject. Some sort of salads were
served. But the only edible element, according to Mr. Hoppy, was walnuts,
so she began to pick them out with her fingers.

FISK: Does she always do this? Show her food to her doll?

MISS PITTS: *(sighing)* Yes, I'm afraid so. Such a repulsive
object! We tried to break her of the silly habit—

HATTIE: *(conversationally)* But then she began to starve to
death, so Miss Bland gave her doll back to her.
(Miss Bland bleats a laugh.)
PHELPS: And quite right, under the circumstances. Had I
but known about it—
DEACON DIDDY: *(tapping his wineglass with his spoon)* Yes,
er, excuse me everyone, but I have a little announcement:
Dear Hazel—Miss Bland—has just been telling me how
very keen you are to acquire a pump organ for your
services. An excellent idea, if I may say so, Miss Pitts.
*(Elly peers at Miss Pitts. She has a wide-eyed look, and jerks a
nod.)*
DEACON DIDDY: Well! It so happens I know of a church
in Fresno that has just purchased a pipe organ. And they
have an old pump organ I'm sure they'd part with for a
very nominal sum!
*(Miss Bland simpers her thanks, and Deacon Diddy pats her
hand. Miss Pitts twists her mouth into a ghastly smile.)*

Elly had never played an organ. But she knew they had keyboards,
and her heart did a little dance.

The salads were removed and plates with thick slices of roast beef,
mashed potatoes, and green beans were placed before them. Elly would
have scraped the green beans onto the tablecloth if she'd dared. But the
rest of the meal was close enough to her ideal that Mr. Hoppy had only to
give the plate a perfunctory glance before she set about the inviolable (and
keenly pleasurable) ritual of sculpting her mashed potatoes into a perfect
circle. There was a desperate moment when Mr. Fisk tried to spoon gravy
onto her plate—but she pushed the spoon aside in the nick of time. In the
single-mindedness of her attention, she failed to notice that the gravy had
been diverted onto the tablecloth.

FISK: *(laughing uneasily)* Well, she seems to have definite
preferences.

PHELPS: Fascinating. Like the doll, some sort of obsessive ritual…

Elly's anticipation of the crowning moment when she would begin to devour her beef was at its apex. But it proved impossible to cut with a spoon (the implement she had always used on her hamburger steaks), and she suffered having it cut into small pieces by Mr. Fisk.

Finally that first heavenly bite!

Her attention was now so utterly focused that for some time the conversations swirling around her hardly penetrated her consciousness. She was vaguely aware of Hattie, charming the deacons with bright chatter, and Dr. Phelps and Mr. Fisk volleying words over her own head as though she were a tennis net. But not until she had eaten the final carefully-synchronized bites of roast beef and mashed potato did she really begin to listen to the two men.

They were speaking in low tones, so as not to be overheard by the others, and—from the sound of their tight voices—engaged in some sort of argument.

FISK: …appallingly understaffed. Along with a truly extraordinary number of girls in the west wing in a vegetative state, most of them malnourished—emaciated, even. In addition, I observed scars on some of their wrists, hidden by the long sleeves of what I suspect are not their regular uniforms, which suggests that—

PHELPS: You forget I have been here less than a year—

FISK: Those poor girls are still your responsibility.

PHELPS: *(makes an exasperated sound)* My dear man, let me be honest with you. I am a scientist. And I came to this institution expressly that I might continue my work, this monumentally important work—

FISK: I see.

PHELPS: No, you do *not* see. I have no time to play nursemaid to incurable imbeciles. Not when I am deeply involved in working out the optimum combination of a multiplicity of factors. I've had to constantly adjust waveforms and voltages, the lengths of each session, time between sessions, placement of the anode and diode. So many variables—

FISK: *(blandly)* So I imagine there have been quite a few failures.

PHELPS: With science, nothing that adds to our understanding can be termed a failure. And so concentrated have I been on my research that it is only recently I became aware of the many shortcomings of this institution—

FISK: Oh now surely Dr. Phelps, you protest too much. In fact, I would guess you deliberately sought out a place with lax standards. A place willing to turn a blind eye to things many would call unethical. Because I submit you have been engaged in nothing less than subjecting hapless girls to the same experiments for which you once employed dogs—

PHELPS: My dear Mr. Fisk, *(Phelps leans so close Elly can smell his beefy breath, see his magnified eyes in her mind)* they are no longer experiments. I am on the verge—scratch that, I have *arrived*—at a breakthrough so revolutionary it is sure to galvanize the scientific world, and save the souls of thousands of people like this young girl here. And you would quibble over a few…

(Phelps waves a dismissive hand, sits back, and drains his wine glass. Elly peers at Hattie. She is animatedly acting something out for the two deacons. They listen raptly. Fisk nods, as if conceding a point.)

MISS PITTS: *(brightly)* Whatever have you two been talking about so intently?

FISK: Oh, um, I was just asking the doctor about his European travels.

DEACON RADCLIFFE: You were in Vienna for a time, were you not? Put any stock in the crack-brained theories of this Dr. Frood?

(A silence. Then Phelps bursts out laughing.)

DEACON DIDDY: Did you, per chance, ever make it to Bayreuth?

PHELPS: Ha! Sir, I am the most *devoted* Wagnerite! It's a sort of religion—or perhaps a disease. Made the pilgrimage every year. Heard Nikisch conduct *Parsifal* the last season I was there—

DEACON RADCLIFFE: But isn't that the most ungodly endless one of all?

PHELPS: Six hours, during which almost nothing happens. But the music—sublime!

MISS PITTS: *(gushing)* I saw Sarah Bernhardt play Joan of Arc in Paris. The very definition of sublime!

PHELPS: *(offhandedly)* Speak French do you, Beulah?

MISS PITTS: Well…not really. But it was hardly necessary. The expression on Miss Bernhardt's face as they burned her at the stake! A combination of agony and ecstasy…

(Elly risks a glance at Miss Pitts, who has screwed her face into an alarming expression, as if at the same instant she had both won a prize and been bitten by a dog.)

DEACON DIDDY: Oh, Bravo! Hattie here has also been entertaining us, acting out all the roles from *Alice in Wonderland*. (His fatuous smile flickers, and he turns to Hattie with a quizzical expression.) Wasn't there something I was supposed to ask you about? But I can't seem to recall…

DEACON RADCLIFFE: *(patting his formidable belly)* A truly memorable repast.

MISS PITTS: So kind of you. I have taken pains to wean our cook from a dismaying preference for decadent oriental spices. But I must agree that Mr. Wong has surpassed himself this evening.

DEACON RADCLIFFE: Indeed he has. But now, if you don't mind, *(dabbing his lips with a napkin)* we've had a very long day. Perhaps it's time we started back—

PHELPS: I could give you a ride in my motorcar.

DEACON RADCLIFFE: Oh, I'm afraid Deacon Diddy and I are fuddy-duddies and really prefer that charming old carriage we rode out in—

MISS BLAND: *(obscurely)* A moonlit drive.

MISS PITTS: I'll have Henry prepare it immediately. But while you are waiting, you simply *must* have a slice of my pecan pie! I gave Mr. Wong my mother's own recipe.

DEACON RADCLIFFE: *(quickly)* Oh well, if you insist…

Miss Pitts ordered up both carriage and pie, and Elly soon found a slice sitting before her. She felt full to bursting, but couldn't resist hazarding a tiny bite. And quickly decided she had to find room for it.

But for murmurs of appreciation and the sounds of forks on plates, the room had fallen silent. Suddenly Deacon Diddy exclaimed aloud:

"*I* know—I was supposed to enquire concerning your parents!"

"My parents," said Hattie in a flat voice.

Elly looked up from her pie.

"Yes, I mean"—Deacon Diddy floundered—"are they well?"

Hattie laid her fork on her plate. "Oh, quite well!" she chirped.

"Would anyone care for some brandy?" said Miss Pitts in a rather loud voice.

"Well, I'm so glad!" Deacon Diddy smiled, nodding. "So they visit you quite often?"

Elly felt like she was teetering with Hattie over the edge of an abyss.

"Often?" Hattie turned her head toward Miss Pitts. "Would you say they visit me often, Miss Pitts?"

Miss Pitts wiped her lips with her napkin. "Not so very," she said quietly. "I really think a bit of brandy might go down a treat—"

"I'd not be averse," said Deacon Radcliffe, looking uneasily at Hattie.

"Actually"—Hattie turned glittering eyes on Deacon Diddy—"they *never* visit. Not once in two years."

"Have...haven't they?" Diddy looked terribly confused.

Hattie jerked her head back and forth as though trying to work out a kink in her neck. "But they've sent me ever so many nice books and games and pretty things—"

"Oh indeed, they have!" agreed Miss Pitts quickly. "Very nice things!"

Phelps was watching Hattie closely. Miss Bland had become suddenly alert, like an animal that vaguely senses danger.

Hattie had frozen in place, her smile a grimace; if you struck her, thought Elly, she might have shattered.

"Well!" Miss Pitts clapped her hands. "I just heard Henry calling, the carriage must be ready—"

"But...but wasn't there to be some brandy?" asked Deacon Radcliffe with a frown.

"*I* didn't hear anything," said Deacon Diddy in a querulous tone. "And I've not finished my pie!"

But Miss Pitts was already standing. "Come now, no dilly-dallying, gentlemen! Your carriage awaits!" She flashed Phelps a desperate look.

"Yes yes," agreed Phelps, jumping to his feet, "we must seize the hour..."

Together they herded the three bemused men out of the room. Miss Bland tottered out on Deacon Diddy's arm. Fisk glanced once over his shoulder with an unreadable expression before the door closed behind them.

Except for Patty clearing the table, Elly and Hattie were alone. Hattie was still staring into space with the same icy smile. But her eyes blazed, and Elly guessed that the litany of her parents' transgressions—the unanswered letters, the cards signed by her mother's secretary—was circling endlessly through her mind, like a dog chasing its own tail. She was a ticking clock, a bomb about to explode...

She began to bang her head violently on the table.

Patty screamed and dropped a full tray of dishes onto the floor. A minute later Phelps came rushing back through the doorway, followed by Mr. Wong. A terrible interval during which the two men—joined by Miss Pitts and the Bruiser wearing only a nightgown—struggled to control the violently convulsing girl. She was still wriggling like a snake, blood streaming down her forehead, when Phelps and the Bruiser finally carried her away.

Miss Pitts stared after them for a moment, poured herself some brandy, then sat down heavily across from Elly. Patty cleaned up the mess from the floor then scurried away.

Phelps reappeared, poured himself his own snifter full of brandy, and collapsed into a chair.

For a long minute they sat without speaking. Despite the horrors she had just witnessed, Elly's half-eaten pie was calling to her, and she returned to taking tiny bites and letting each one slowly dissolve in her mouth.

MISS PITTS: *(sighing heavily)* Well, that was a narrow squeak.

PHELPS: *Mm.*

MISS PITTS: And it seems, Doctor, your treatment is not quite so effective as you'd thought.

PHELPS: So it's *my* treatment now, eh Beulah? And on the contrary—this only proves how very close I am to success. For she was able to fight off her fit for several minutes.

(A pause)

MISS PITTS: *(perhaps noticing Elly for the first time)* Why is this child still here?

PHELPS: Oh for God's sake, let her finish her pie. She can't hear a word we're saying anyway. Which is just as well, because believe me, I've got a few words for you.

(Elly keeps her eyes on her plate, resolved to listen carefully.)

MISS PITTS: I can't imagine what you—

PHELPS: Oh please shut up. I have never been so mortified! First being forced to spout all those lies about the imbeciles in the west wing—then having to sit through that dinner, trying my damnedest to distract three men from the sight of fifty girls devouring their food like ravening wolves! Oh, you may have pulled the wool over the deacons' eyes with all your flim-flam about "poor creatures denied the full flowering of humanity," *(Phelps recites the words in a mincing sing-song)* but that Mr. Fisk wasn't so easily taken in. Oh no, he saw exactly which way the wind blows!

MISS PITTS: *(coolly sipping her brandy)* And what way, pray tell, would that be?

PHELPS: I'm only talking about systematic starvation, criminal negligence—oh what a fool I've been, not to bring you to heel before this! And what a fool *you* are—

MISS PITTS: *(in a melodramatic voice) All I ask is to be left alone to do my work.* Did you not get your wish, Edgar?

(A pause)

PHELPS: *(reluctantly)* Yes, I must say—

MISS PITTS: Have I ever been anything but supportive? Even assisted you in undertakings others might perhaps have termed…distasteful?

PHELPS: *(exasperated)* Yes, I have to admit—

MISS PITTS: And have you forgotten it is my skill in running a tight ship that pays for you to sport around in a fine motorcar?

PHELPS: Yes yes, and I'm grateful for…for everything. But my God, Beulah! We are on the verge of attracting a fantastic amount of attention to this institution. I guarantee you people will soon be flocking here to receive my treatments! And some will surely be of a class that expects their daughters to be well clothed and fed—and what's more, willing to pay for it. So it's beyond foolish, it is in fact sheer idiocy, to be so penurious, so niggardly about doling out the most basic comforts—

MISS PITTS: *(in her Sunday sermon voice)* And what about *spiritual* comforts, Edgar? Do you not think those are also impor—

PHELPS: *(laughing raucously)* Such humbuggery! And all this talk about "a tight ship"—do you think I don't know exactly what's going on here? Would you care to let me examine your books?

(A pause)

MISS PITTS: Just what are you insinuating? The deacons were perfectly satisfied—

PHELPS: Bah! Prize ninnies, the pair of them! No no, it's time for this sham of a place to make some changes, big changes in the way—

MISS PITTS: Sham of a place! Oh Edgar, to bite the very hand that has fed you all these years.

(Elly is still trying to work out what books Miss Pitts is so reluctant for Dr. Phelps to examine, when the conversation takes another turn.)

PHELPS: And speaking of shams, what in God's name am I supposed to tell that poor girl about her parents? I mean it's terribly ironic, wouldn't you say, that it was an *actual* outbreak of typhus that killed them both, as opposed to the sham epidemic you forced me to invent—

MISS PITTS: It was only the same understanding we always had with dear old Dr. Smythe—

PHELPS: Ha! And how much did you have to pay that senile old codger for his bogus diagnoses?

MISS PITTS: I seem to recall a couple of death certificates you yourself wouldn't care to have too closely examined.

(A pause, during which Elly eats the last bite of her pie.)

PHELPS: *(clearing his throat)* And why you never bothered to inform me that Hattie's parents died *two years ago*, until after I'd already promised the poor girl I'd write to them—

MISS PITTS: It had never been necessary for you to know—

PHELPS: More to the point, why didn't you tell her in the first place? She has to face the truth sometime! How much more terrible to face it now, when she's so full of hope—

MISS PITTS: At the time, it seemed less cruel—

PHELPS: *(in a strangled voice)* Cruel! You truly are the limit. Having yourself appointed the child's guardian has given you access to her family's fortune, and thus every reason to retain her here indefinitely. And you dare to talk of cruelty?

MISS PITTS: *(coolly)* Yes, and what about you, Edgar? Wouldn't you prefer she stay here, as an example of your wonderful treatment?

The final bite of Elly's pie turned to bile in her mouth.

CHAPTER TEN

A COZY RELATIONSHIP

Hazel Bland gazed into her mirror and applied a spot of rouge to each cheek. Then dabbed on a bit more, for it was a very special day! As she worked the color into her withered skin, she began humming "How Great Thou Art," her favorite hymn. And the one that would open the very first service she would play on her new pump organ!

Really, after so many years of asking, she could hardly believe it had finally arrived. And against Beulah's opposition, oh yes, Hazel had seen right through her claim there were "not enough funds." But still, it had taken real courage for Hazel to petition Deacon Diddy directly. The look on Beulah's face!

Hazel's excitement was not untinged with a certain apprehension, for she knew she was not the musician she had once been. She remembered the time she had played "Marching through Georgia" for the assembled guests in their home when she was only fourteen. On a rosewood Nuns Clarke piano from Cincinnati, which her mother had carried all the way to California in their covered wagon—the same lovely instrument that had pride of place in Hazel's parlor. Such a success she'd had! She kept the piano religiously oiled and tuned, and tried—oh, she tried!—to keep her skills up. But of late her fingers seemed disinclined to obey her, and were apt to go wandering off on their own errant adventures.

"How great thou art, how GREAT...THOU...ART!" warbled Hazel. She pinned up a few more stray gray hairs and reflected that, really, it was all Beulah's fault. For Hazel had only to play a single note, and Beulah would begin pounding on their adjoining wall. So Hazel had been reduced to playing when Beulah took her daily buggy ride.

Perhaps what her fingers needed was a fortifying dose?

She reached for the bottle, which she always kept close at hand, and carefully doled out a spoonful of the ruby red liquid. And, as the wonderful warmth and peace spread through her body, Hazel once again thanked the good Lord for Dr. Pinkham's Celebrated Elixir: the medicine that was keeping her alive.

This fact had been driven home to Hazel the time Mr. Schmidt, the druggist, had been late getting his shipment in. Just two days deprived of her elixir, and she found herself beset by palpitations and waking nightmares. Frantically she made Henry drive her to every druggist in the city (and discovered, to her surprise, many other people in the same desperate straits). But it was two more days—terrible days in which the imminent breakdown the elixir had clearly been keeping at bay stood nakedly revealed—before it finally arrived.

Ever since then, she had been careful to keep a large supply on hand.

Now in a wonderfully cozy frame of mind, she finally headed out the door—only to return a moment later to pick up the music that, in her excitement, she had left atop the piano. On her way out again, she stopped on a whim, plucked a sprig of lilac from a vase, and pinned it to her hair.

For this was a special day—a *very* special day!

She found Beulah standing at the lectern and putting place marks in her books. Beulah glanced up, took in the flower in Hazel's hair, smirked, then returned to her task without a word of greeting.

Fine, thought Hazel—two can play at this game.

She settled herself on the organ bench, placed her music on the rack, began pumping the bellows with her feet, and hazarded a few wheezing chords.

The expression on Beulah's face was priceless.

The tramp of ill-fitting boots heralded the arrival of their congregation. Like a defeated army they shuffled in, some pushing others in wheelchairs. But their usual disorganized boisterousness was subdued by Frieda's hulking presence—and by the novelty of the sounds issuing from the huge thing Hazel was energetically flailing away on. In the hope of a majestic sort of sound, she had pulled out all the stops. Well, it *was* loud at least, thought Hazel, in that tiny part of her mind not desperately trying to command her really quite impertinent fingers. But surely enough of the notes were correct for the melody to come through…

Elly could dimly make out that Miss Bland was trying to play "How Great Thou Art." But she recognized it the way one might recognize a person maimed by some terrible accident. The other girls must have felt something similar, because two of them burst into tears.

Miss Bland ceased torturing the instrument, and directed a vague smile over her shoulder at them, as though hoping for applause. Bertie McPhee began laughing hysterically. The Bruiser pounced and pulled her out into the hallway by her ear.

Miss Pitts stood waiting for the noise coming through the door to die down. Miss Bland stood up from the bench, looking rather crestfallen, and began thumbing through a stack of music atop the instrument.

The happy thought suddenly occurred to Elly that, if only they were to hear her play, they would surely know she didn't belong in this place. And now that the bench was empty…

Frieda Klee re-entered the room. Her cheeks were red, her eyes merry. Beulah nodded to her, glanced down at her text, took a breath—

From the back of the room a tiny figure streaked toward the organ, leapt upon the bench, and—flinging her doll down beside her—began furiously working the keys with her small hands. But her feet couldn't reach the pedals to pump the organ's bellows, and the instrument yielded only a mechanical clicking noise.

The sound was quickly drowned out by a chorus of shrieks, moans, and laughter. Frieda was already striding through the unruly throng like some female Moses parting the Red Sea. She plucked the tiny malefactor from the bench and headed out the door with her. Beulah directed a steely

gaze at the girls until the room quieted. The shrieks coming through the door would have wrung Hazel's heart, if she hadn't been in such utter shock.

She went through the rest of the service in a sort of trance. She scarcely heard a word Beulah said, hardly noticed the discordant sounds issuing from beneath her fingers. Instead, her mind returned again and again to what she had just witnessed. Because even though Hazel's days of musical glory were far behind her, she still retained a basic knowledge of the keyboard. Enough, at least, to realize one thing for certain:

What she had just seen was impossible.

.   .   .

"Miss Klee," intoned Hattie in a low, fruity voice, "this child is one of the assets of this institution. Only a *smidgen* of chastisement was called for—not wanton brutality."

It was a ripe imitation of Miss Pitts. Elly felt the mattress shake as Brenda and Gladys tried to stifle their laughter.

All three girls were squeezed together in Elly's bed. Every night, when Mrs. Wong began to snore, girls would stealthily leave their beds to visit one another. Rena slept in the bed beside Elly; almost every night Bertie climbed in with her and they would keep Elly awake with their giggling and noises. But all of them were careful not to make so much noise they woke Mrs. Wong—and thus provoke an encounter with her wooden paddle.

Elly never had to worry, because nobody had ever come to visit her. Until tonight.

They had raced back after dinner to check on her. She felt them gazing at her, heard Gladys pronounce that she was "right beat up." When Hattie asked Elly if she could hear them, she'd managed to crack an eye open.

"See!" crowed Hattie. "Maudie knows what I'm saying! But oh, Maudie, what on earth got into you? Why, it looked like—"

The rather unnerving arrival of The Troll silenced them all. She produced a greasy slice of bread and dangled it over Elly's face. Elly reached for it, showed it to Mr. Hoppy, and began to quietly chew it.

The Troll seemed to smile (it was hard to tell) and lumbered off.

"We'll come back and visit you tonight, Maudie," suggested Hattie. "If you'd like us to."

Elly cracked an eye open again. It was close enough to an assent that Hattie smiled broadly.

"Chop-chop!" yelled Mrs. Wong, clapping her hands. "Chop-chop!"

The girls all scampered away to get ready for bed.

There followed a long interval as Mrs. Wong went through her evening ritual.

Mrs. Wong was short and squat, and her fat cheeks squeezed her narrow eyes so deeply into her face that Elly wondered how she could see. But now her eyes were closed as she lay back with her feet propped up, sipping from a bottle of what was said to be plum brandy, while a pair of specially selected girls massaged her tired feet. Occasionally she would emit a deep growl of pleasure. Sometimes the girls would tickle her, and she would laugh—a low gurgling chortle—and slap at them playfully. But finally she dismissed them and doused the lights.

A short time later she began to snore.

So now they all lay together beneath one of the thick new blankets they had been given, wearing warm flannel nightgowns (another recent improvement in their lives), and Elly decided it was wonderfully cozy to be cuddled up with one's friends. Even though Gladys's elbow sent shooting pains through Elly's bruised body whenever she twitched, and Hattie's helmet kept bumping against her head.

All of them were still atwitter about the events of that morning.

"But you know, Maudie," said Hattie, "even though everyone was laughing at you... well, I had the queerest feeling that if only your feet had been able to reach the pedals, we would have heard real music!"

"She was wallopin it," agreed Gladys.

"'Twas Lucifer got into her," was Brenda's predictable response.

"Oh fiddle-faddle," said Hattie.

"Sure, tis him, and his evil minions—"

"If you are going to say such things," Hattie interrupted primly, "you really must say them softer!"

Brenda may have been mad, but she was no fool. She dropped her voice to a breathless, urgent whisper:

"Last night Satan came into my bed, pushed up my nightgown, and kissed my breasts!"

Hattie had to muffle her scandalized shrieks in the blanket. Gladys snickered and prodded Elly with her knee. While Elly was confused. For she knew breasts to be the same as bosoms, and Brenda hadn't any.

In the bed next to them, Rena and Bertie snorted and giggled.

"Oh Brenda," gasped Hattie, "sometimes you're— Ooh, is that a light?"

She pulled herself up to peer out the window. "Oh, it is! Oh Maudie, you must see this—"

The four of them crawled toward the front of the bed, knelt beneath the blankets, and looked out the window. Wisps of cloud above the distant snow-covered mountains had been transformed by a full moon into cottony haloes, and its soft light illuminated the exercise yard. Three figures were walking in a ghostly procession toward the back of the iron fence. One carried a lantern, another a large box and a shovel.

"Oh, isn't it just the spookiest, scariest thing!" said Hattie in a thrilled whisper.

The figures had stopped. The one carrying the box put it down and began to dig. By the lantern's light, Elly could make out that it was Henry. Miss Bland was holding the lantern. Miss Pitts carried what looked like a large book.

"Dead booby," said Gladys. She extracted a finger from her nose and examined it in the moonlight.

"Gladys, I do so wish you wouldn't use that word," scolded Hattie. "It's a very small coffin—one of the babies, I'm sure."

"Baby boobie," amended Gladys.

Elly couldn't help but think of Meg's "pore little mites."

All around them, girls were kneeling on their beds to watch. Rena and Bertie emerged from beneath the blankets with their nightgowns all askew.

Henry finished digging and laid the box inside the hole. Miss Pitts began to read from her book. A cloud passed in front of the moon, obscuring the scene.

"Sure, Satan's a-comin now, a-ridin up from purgatory on his black steed—"

"Oh Brenda, do be quiet—"

"It HURTS! Oh it HURTS SO BAD!" cried an anguished voice.

Instantly Hattie, Gladys, and Brenda scurried off. Everywhere girls were racing for their own beds like cockroaches scattering in the light. The door to the hallway burst open, silhouetting the squat form of Mrs. Wong.

Holding her paddle.

·　　　·　　　·

Two days later the unsightly greenish-purple bruise on one side of Elly's face had faded enough for her to join the other girls in the dayroom.

It had been a month since the inspection, and the weather had turned bitter. The girls had all been allowed to keep their nice new uniforms, and given warm leggings as well. But the radiators were off (they were only on, Elly had noticed, on the days Dr. Phelps was there), and it was almost cold enough to see your breath. She found her friends all huddled together for warmth. She squeezed in between Brenda and the Troll, whose big pillowy body radiated heat like a roasted marshmallow.

Hattie had been reading from a book Elly hadn't seen before.

"Oh Maudie, it's so nice to have you back—you look ever so much better!"

"Cept for that shiner," said Gladys.

"And look," gushed Hattie, "I just got this pretty new book. It's called *Little Lord Fauntleroy*, and it's all about a boy named Cedric, whose father is the son of an English lord—"

"Only he's not a boy at all," confided Brenda, wide-eyed. "But a little faerie lass in boy's clothes!"

"Oh Brenda, that's so much drivel!"

But Elly had to agree that the boy on the book's cover looked remarkably girlish. She turned to the frontispiece, and came upon an inscription, written in a florid hand with many flourishes:

To Hattie, from Mother
With Boundless Love

Hattie snatched the book away and flipped nervously through the pages, looking flustered. She cleared her throat, and began to read…

But Elly wasn't listening. Instead she brooded on the terrible knowledge that the inscription was a counterfeit. And not because (as Hattie still believed) her mother had made some secretary write it for her.

The things Elly had overheard that night still confused and tormented her. Where did they come from, all the nice things Hattie was sent? And how could they keep lying to her this way, Miss Pitts and Dr. Phelps?

Hattie had been in tears when she was again made to wear the dreaded helmet.

"But…but can't you give me another treatment right away, Dr. Phelps?" she had pleaded. "I'm just sure it would make me stop having fits—"

"Hattie, Hattie," Phelps gazed at her through his thick spectacles and patted her arm, "I completely empathize with you. But you are my prize exhibit, and I'm afraid to go any faster. It might jeopardize all the wonderful progress you've already made."

"But I don't want to be an *exhibit*," Hattie said, pouting. "I want you to write to my parents, like you promised—"

"Yes yes, and that I shall certainly do," answered Phelps smoothly. "And the best way is for us to proceed carefully."

"Like"—Hattie braved a smile—"like the tortoise and the hare?"

"Precisely! Slow and steady, wins the race!"

"And then, you'll—"

"And then," said Miss Pitts, who had been hovering over them, "I'm sure your parents will be eager to come visit you."

It had made Elly almost angry enough to speak! But how could you tell someone their parents were dead? She could hardly imagine such an awful thing. At least she knew her own parents were still out there somewhere, searching for her.

Hattie's reading was interrupted by the arrival of Dr. Phelps in his motorcar. (Had Miss Pitts actually bought it for him? The things Elly had overheard were so confusing.) They ran to the window and watched as a new girl was bundled out of the back by Phelps and a man wearing a white jacket. She was strapped into a canvas coat and would have run if they hadn't held her. The Bruiser joined them, and together she and Phelps dragged her into the building.

The girls ran to the hallway. Miss Pitts was helping to hold the girl, and they got a close look at her. She was at least Hattie's age, with curly brown hair and a snub nose, and would have been very pretty if her face hadn't been distorted by terror and rage.

"Oh Lord, oh get me OUT of here!" she shrieked. "Let me GO—Ah'm not CRAZY, Ah don't BELONG HERE—"

"She don't shbelong here!" cried the Bruiser in a mocking voice. "Sheesh too fine a SHLADY!" She plucked at the expensive-looking material of the girl's frock where it emerged from beneath the ugly coat.

Miss Pitts pursed her lips. Phelps was searching through his medical bag. Miss Pitts said something to him and shook her head, and a moment later the Bruiser dragged the girl down the hall.

"Beulah"—Phelps closed his medical bag, stood up, and ran a hand through his hair distractedly—"must we have this conversation again? If you continue to keep the building at an arctic temperature, we really *shall* have an epidemic. Only this time it will be pneumonia!"

From far down the hallway they could hear the girl's screams, accompanied by the sounds of splashing water—water Elly knew to be ice cold.

Dr. Phelps strode angrily off and drove away. A moment later they heard Henry leading Miss Pitts's horse and buggy from the stable.

The girl's screams had died away. The Bruiser pulled her out of the bathroom and back down the hall. She was dressed in one of their frocks and trudged along, sobbing quietly but offering no resistance. Her curly hair was plastered to her head in dark ringlets, and there was a bruise on her temple.

Miss Pitts stood near the door. She was dressed in a heavy coat of navy blue and black leather gloves. A jaunty feathered hat was tied under her chin with a black scarf.

"Dear Amelia," she said in a kindly voice, stroking the girl's face, "are you going to give us any more trouble?"

The girl clutched herself, shivering. Slowly she shook her head.

"Sheesh losht all her shpunk!" cackled the Bruiser.

The girl collapsed in a corner with her head on her knees. Hattie knelt beside her and said something in a soothing voice. The girl jerked her head up and recoiled at the sight of Hattie's ugly helmet.

"Ugh! Get AWAY from me!" she cried. "All of you, don't even TALK to me, Ah don't want to KNOW you. Ah don't want to BE here, Ah don't even BELONG here—"

She laid her head on her knees again and sobbed.

Outside, Miss Pitts cracked her whip, and they heard her drive off. As if on cue, Miss Bland came drifting through the door. With all these exits and entrances, thought Elly, the dayroom was beginning to feel like the stage set of a rather hectic play.

"Miss Bland!" Hattie rushed up to the old woman. "Miss Bland, look! We've a new girl, her name is Amelia. But she's in a terrible state because the Brui—I mean, Miss Klee, had to discipline her."

Miss Bland cast an uneasy glance at the girl sobbing in the corner.

"Yes, um, well," she murmured.

She looked away, then cast her eyes around the room until they fastened on Elly.

Quickly Elly looked down at her doll.

"Yes, and Maudie's back!" chirped Hattie. "None of us can fathom why she should have misbehaved like that, I'm sure she'll not—"

She broke off. In fact the entire room had gone quiet. From the corner of her eye, Elly saw the old woman's boots had stopped in front of her. An inch of sad gray slip poked from beneath the hem of her skirt.

Miss Bland took her gently by the hand and led her from the room.

~

Miss Bland's atrocious organ playing had rather turned Elly against her. But she remembered the old lady had once saved her life, and allowed herself to be led down the hallway.

They came to the door that, the girls had surmised, must lead to where the two old ladies lived. Miss Bland unlocked it, led Elly inside, then locked it again. They climbed a narrow staircase to another long hallway. It was deliciously warm, there were lovely carpets on the floor, lace curtains adorned windows without bars, and the air smelt of furniture polish. It reminded Elly of a hallway in one of the many hotels through which she had once happily roamed—a past life that was beginning to feel more and more like a dream.

Miss Bland unlocked another door. A cloud of lavender, talcum powder, and perspiration (the scents of Miss Bland herself) enveloped them, and Elly realized she had penetrated the old lady's lair. It was full of heavy, old furniture, and—echoing Miss Bland's untidy person—overstuffed with chipped china figurines, odd knick-knacks, mismatched carpets, framed mottos atilt on the wall, and vases full of wilting flowers.

But all this Elly sensed, rather than saw. For her eyes were fixed on one particular piece of furniture that dominated the room.

A piece of furniture with a keyboard.

She approached the instrument in a trance, Miss Bland trailing behind. It had a most peculiar shape, like a sideboard that wanted to be a piano, and she saw at once it had fewer keys than any piano she had ever played. Impulsively she reached out and played an E-major chord.

A lovely, crystalline sound. Bright yellow, tinged with orange. She held the notes down, watching the colors shimmer, then fade. Her heart was beating fast.

"Can you play it?" blurted Miss Bland in a doubtful voice.

For answer, Elly climbed onto the bench, laid Mr. Hoppy beside her, put her fingers on the old, yellowed keys...

She hardly knew what she was playing. Bits of one song, scraps of another. At first slowly, savoring the glorious sounds. Then faster, as the joy of doing the thing she was born to do took hold of her. Until she was flying over the keys, lost in the music, forgetting where she was, who she was, all the world only music, wonderful music...

After a long time she stopped, breathing hard, kicking her legs with excitement, thinking of what to play next. Miss Bland had pulled up a chair next to her, and was hunched forward with her elbows on her knees and her long powdered face in her hands, mesmerized. Abruptly she stood, snatched at some music from a pile atop the instrument, and placed it in front of Elly. She glanced at the title—"The Dying Poet"—and plunged into it. There were lots of difficult passages with chords she had to roll because they were too big for her hands, and she wished her mother were there to push the pedal down. But she played all the important notes.

When she reached the end, Miss Bland stared at her for a very long time. Elly had an impression there were tears in the old woman's eyes, and she avoided looking into them. Finally Miss Bland jerked to her feet, placed an entire book of songs on the piano, and opened it to the first page...

They went on this way for some time, Elly playing whatever Miss Bland put before her, until there was a soft knock on the door. Miss Bland gave a low moan, tottered to her feet, and—pulling Elly by the hand so quickly she barely had time to grab Mr. Hoppy—opened the door to reveal Henry. Without a word Miss Bland put Elly's hand in his, and he led her back down the hall. This time they took a different staircase, through another door, and she found herself in the empty dining room. It was the same door through which the two old ladies made their grand entrance when the girls ate, and it gave Elly an illicit thrill to walk through it herself.

Finally Henry led her out to the hallway leading to the dayroom. He let go of her hand. She looked up into his broad, dark face. As always, it had no expression. But there seemed to be kindness leaking out of his eyes.

He turned and walked away without a word.

.　　　　　　.　　　　　　.

Hattie opened up *Little Lord Fauntleroy* and began reading the chapter in which Cedric sails to England from America. It was the second time she'd read it, and Drooly rolled her eyes. But soon enough the descriptions of salt air and seagulls and glorious ocean vistas became too much for Hattie. She closed her book.

"Oh, if only we could get away from this place!" she cried.

"Cain't," said Gladys. "Winders all gots bars," she added, pointing toward the window and winking frantically.

Hattie tossed her book in Drooly's lap. She stood and went to the window, grabbed hold of the bars, and stared outside with a fierce expression. "Yes," she intoned, "we are all just prisoners. Like the Count of Monte Cristo."

Elly got up and stood next to her. The buggy sat mired in mud from recent snows. Behind it a line of skeletal trees stood starkly outlined against a dirty gray sky. They watched Henry lead the horse from the stable and begin hitching it to the buggy.

"What if we tried to escape?" said Hattie.

"Wooden git fer," said Gladys.

"Sure, they'd recognize you by your uniform," agreed Brenda in a rare moment of mental clarity.

"But…but not if I wore a disguise!" said Hattie.

Elly knew about disguises—they were rather like costumes—and listened with interest.

"I should disguise myself as…as a *boy*!" cried Hattie, delighted at the thought. "I would take this beastly helmet off, cut off all my hair, and wear boy's clothing. Old clothing, so they would think I was only a hobo. Like in *The Prince and the Pauper*—no one ever bothers you if you're raggedly dressed."

"A hobo—what an *eccentric* idea!"

All of them turned their heads around in surprise, and found Amelia standing behind them. It was the first time she had spoken to them since her arrival.

"Do you think it would work?" asked Hattie, eager to keep the conversation going.

"Ah didn't say it was a *good* idea," said Amelia sulkily. But the ice had been broken. "So, why do you wear that stupid thing on your head, anyways?"

"Oh, isn't it just beastly!" cried Hattie. "They say it's to protect me, because I get excited sometimes—"

"Gets the jumps," said Gladys.

Amelia frowned. "And what about you?" she asked Gladys. "Hows come you're always pickin your nose, or scratchin yourself, or makin goofy faces?"

Gladys shrugged without taking her finger from her nose.

"Sure, she's Satan's puppet," Brenda suggested.

Amelia gaped at her. "Well Ah do declare, y'all sure enough do have eagles in your skylights."

Outside they watched Mr. Wong climb into the back of the buggy. With his arms tucked inside his sleeves, his quilted jacket resembled the canvas coat the Bruiser strapped them into. Miss Pitts strode through the mud, leaning forward like a general reviewing his troops, and hauled her thick body up into the front seat unassisted. Henry handed her a long whip, and she lashed the horse into motion.

"That Miss Pitts, she talks all sugary," said Amelia. "But just look at the way she whipped that horse."

"She'd as soon do the same to you," agreed Brenda. "Bein as she's the devil's handmaiden."

"Ah do believe you have got devils on the brain," said Amelia.

"Miss Bland is quite nice, though," said Hattie.

"What, that old ghost?" Amelia frowned, pulled at a lock of her curly brown hair, and twirled it around a finger. "Oh, what in the world am Ah *doin* in this place? There is nothin at all the matter with my head. Ah mean, y'all don't even realize that Ah'm a van Allen."

When nobody said anything she sighed, and continued:

"Of the Montgomery van Allens? Daddy only moved us here from Alabama to start a big shipping company on the Sacramento. It was my mother that got me sent to this place. Tellin lies about the things Ah did. Uh-huh, Momma just despises me. Well the feelin is mutual, believe you me. In fact, Momma, Ah can rightly say Ah *hate your guts*."

This dazzling confession caused Drooly's mouth to go slack, unleashing a font of saliva onto her frock.

"What things?" asked Gladys. "What things they says you did?"

But Amelia was watching with fascinated loathing as Hattie wiped Drooly's mouth with a rag. "What about that one? Isn't she about ready for the crypt?"

"That's a truly hateful thing to say," said Hattie.

"Ah mean, if Ah looked like that," continued Amelia, "why Ah declare Ah'd just end it all."

"Gah!" sputtered Drooly. "Gah…wah!"

"She says, 'Go away,' you hateful thing," said Hattie.

If a cat had spoken to her, Amelia couldn't have looked more amazed. "Well Ah'm just callin a spade a spade," she finally stammered. "But Ah can sure enough tell when Ah'm not wanted. And believe you me Ah just can't get away from y'all fast enough," she added. "Cause here comes that old darkie again to fetch this one."

She nodded toward Elly, and flounced away.

·   ·   ·

Every day except Sunday, Henry came to fetch Elly and lead her up to Miss Bland's apartment. She'd soon worked out that he came as soon as Miss Pitts left for town, and that it was Henry's job to keep a lookout for her return. Then he would lead Elly back downstairs before Miss Pitts could discover her—which Elly somehow knew would be a very bad thing.

Upon her arrival, Miss Bland might offer her some bit of food—a piece of sausage or a slice of bread smeared with real butter. Elly always meant to save some to share with her friends but was usually unable to refrain from gobbling it all up on the spot.

Then it was time for music.

She and Miss Bland had quickly settled into a very cozy relationship (that Miss Bland shared her own distaste for speech was a decided asset). Elly was willing to play most of what the old lady placed before her. But some things Elly disliked. When confronted with them, she would shake her head, and Miss Bland would whisk the music away without a word. It was also allowed that Elly rummage through the piles of music for her favorites. Miss Bland likewise had her own favorites, and they discovered—to their mutual satisfaction—a shared love for the volume of Stephen Foster songs. And almost every session would include "My Old Kentucky Home" or "Jeannie with the Light Brown Hair," which Elly performed with the memory of a certain cornetist's lovely phrasing in her mind.

Miss Bland would sit leaning forward with her chin in her hands, or sprawled untidily in her easy chair, munching on chocolates (which, to Elly's irritation, she never shared). Sometimes she became dreamy, waving her hand in languid circles (which bore no relation to the music's rhythms) while sipping from a bottle of bright red liquid. At such times she was liable to break into song, and Elly would be forced to stop playing in order to silence her.

Finally Henry would come to lead her back downstairs to the empty dining room. His hand was large and soft and enfolded hers in a way that made her feel safe. Sometimes the door to the kitchen was propped open, and she would notice Mr. Wong eyeing them. One day he stepped out to confront them.

"You!" He pointed at her and she froze. He held a long knife and his apron was bloody. He pointed at the ceiling and made a curious sound—"*bim bim bim bim*"—with a melodic sort of lilt.

Henry chuckled softly. "*Um-hmm,*" he said. "She don't talk, but she make some powerful noise."

Mr. Wong made a face of exaggerated surprise, then darted back into the kitchen. "Good," he said, opening Elly's hand and putting something inside it. "Numbah one!"

She found the other girls in the exercise yard. All of them were intensely curious about where Elly went every day, and Hattie decided to broach the subject.

"Maudie, we've all worked out that you must be with Miss Bland, because we never see her when you're gone. But what on earth could you and she be doing together?"

"They've formed a witch's coven," suggested Brenda darkly.

Drooly snorted.

"And you know," continued Hattie, "quite often, when you're gone and we're outside, we can hear that music in the distance—oh, don't tell me Miss Bland plays music for you!"

But Elly only smiled to herself, and licked her peppermint stick.

·   ·   ·

They were finally getting close to the end of *Little Lord Fauntleroy* when Hattie opened the book one day—and suddenly began to wail.

"Oh Rena Jacobs, I hate you! Look"—she held up the mutilated book—"she's torn out the last chapters. Now we'll never know how it ends!"

Rena flashed them a twisted grin from across the room.

"Ah know how it ends."

Through the entire reading of the book, Amelia had always sat nearby, and they'd speculated that she was listening. But since their falling out, they had never again spoken with her.

"Do you, Amelia?" cried Hattie. "Oh do tell us—"

"Boy dies," said Gladys.

"Oh now Gladys, you know that can't be right—"

"Drownded," said Gladys, obstinate. "In a rain barrel."

"Oh do please tell us how it really ends," pleaded Hattie.

Amelia shrugged. "Well, you know, it ends just like you think. The old man forgives Cedric's momma, Cedric becomes a Lord—Ah mean, that's the name of the darn book, for goodness sake—him and his momma are rich as Rockefeller, happily ever after the end."

It was a lot to absorb, and struck them all mute for a moment.

"You know"—Amelia laid her head on her knees and spoke without looking at them—"Ah'm just awful lonely. If Ah don't find someone to talk to Ah really *will* go crazy. Do you think maybe we might still be friends? Ah mean"—she lifted her head and looked at Drooly, and they saw there were tears in her eyes—"Ah'm just so sorry about those things Ah said."

It was a pretty apology, and Drooly writhed her acceptance.

·   ·   ·

As it turned out, Hattie would never again have to worry about Rena Jacobs mutilating her books.

Nobody was ever sure who the tattle-tale had been. But one night, after the lights were out and the girls were doing their visiting, the lights suddenly blazed back on, and Miss Pitts and the Bruiser burst into the room. Mrs. Wong followed behind them, rubbing her eyes and looking confused. Girls everywhere were jumping out of each other's beds, but Miss Pitts ignored them. Instead she marched directly to Rena's bed and yanked away the blankets.

Rena and Bertie lay in a tangle of limbs, stark naked.

"You filthy-dirty girls," shrieked Miss Pitts. "FILTHY-DIRTY!"

Elly was confused—the two naked girls looked as clean as any of them.

Nightgowns were hastily thrown over the sobbing girls, and they were marched away.

Neither was ever seen again.

·   ·   ·

One bitter morning in February, they awoke to find the mousy girl, who was always crying "it hurts!" and bringing Mrs. Wong's wrath down upon them, had died during the night.

That very evening they watched the ghostly procession carrying her coffin.

Everyone agreed they were glad.

CHAPTER ELEVEN

THE GREAT CHARIOT RACE

Meg, the Irish maid in charge of the baby's ward, had gone from being shocked by Brenda's fantastical outpourings to finding them amusing. Though after laughing at some assertion of Brenda's (such as her claim that the Bruiser "danced naked jigs and reels with Satan and his minions nightly"), she always crossed herself.

Two more of the young Irish maids from County Cork (all of whom Amelia had declared to be "right off the potato farm") worked in the west wing taking care of the imbeciles. Elly and Brenda sometimes saw them hauling their own loads of sheets and oversized diapers to and from Mrs. Wong's boiling kettles of laundry, both looking hollow-eyed with exhaustion.

"And no wonder," said Meg, who—in a certain mood—could be quite chatty. "Desperate overworked they are. Fifty imbeciles to take care of, day and night, and none of you lot allowed in there to help em. Not that you're all that much help." She rapped both of them affectionately on the head with her knuckles. "Many's the time Cora and Kathleen come back to our room so fagged they can barely speak. Cause the imbeciles, they're not tiny babes like these, who most of em can't even stand up in their cribs. They're big girls, some of em. Girls without a speck of sense, who could run around and be gettin into any kind of mischief if they wasn't…well, Kath says the only way they can keep any kind of order, it bein just the two of them, is to keep em chained up."

"Chained up," echoed Brenda, nodding wisely. "So that Lucifer can come in the night, and steal their souls at his Satanic leisure—"

Meg slapped her.

The two stared at one another, both of them shocked. Meg had gone pale. Brenda began to silently weep.

"Bejesus, I'm sorry," said Meg, biting her lip and squeezing Brenda's shoulder. "I know you can't help yourself. It's just that…what you said… Because that's what Kath told me they're doin. Miss Pitts and Miss Klee." She looked quickly up and down the hallway, then bent to Brenda's ear and said, in an urgent whisper:

"They're *stealin girl's souls*."

She crossed herself and rushed away.

For a long time Brenda was struck atypically mute.

"Sure, tis the Devil's doin," she finally muttered.

For once, Elly was inclined to agree.

.   .   .

It turned out to be one of the last references Brenda ever made to the Devil or his minions. Because the very next day she was whisked away by Dr. Phelps, and returned two weeks later a changed girl.

What Phelps was now calling a "course of treatments" (leading Elly to think of menus and golfing) was still mysterious to them all, because none of the girls (unless you counted Brenda's fanciful imaginings) ever remembered what had been done to them. But whatever the process was, it had proved to be as magically effective as Phelps had promised. Though Elly sometimes wondered if, in purging girls of behaviors that other people found unsettling, babies might have been thrown out with bathwater.

Gladys, for example, had been rid of her constant twitching and grimacing. Yet her amusingly off-kilter remarks had disappeared as well, and left her a dumpy, rather plain, yet otherwise boringly ordinary little girl. And surely Brenda found a world that no longer teemed with fascinating supernatural beings a much less interesting place? Elly for one found she missed those lurid bulletins from the netherworld. Though there had still been something veiled and secretive in Brenda's green eyes, just before she left, which suggested she was only biding her time.

For yes, the unthinkable had actually occurred: both girls had been pronounced cured and returned to their families.

After a further round of treatments, Hattie too had been cured of her fits. The odious helmet was long gone, her long auburn hair had been beautifully arranged by Amelia, and her movements were more languidly graceful than ever. But Hattie's bubbling brook of bright chatter had become a placid stream, her tendency to read the same page twice had worsened to where Amelia had been forced to take over the job of story teller—

And, of course, she had no family to return to.

She still did not know this, however, for Phelps claimed to have written the promised letter to Hattie's parents. Elly was there when he produced the purported reply. Written on cream-colored stationery in the florid hand Hattie recognized all too well, it claimed that Hattie's parents had just that month left on a round-the-world cruise, and were not expected to return for more than a year.

"But…but I just don't understand," Hattie stammered through her tears. "My mother hates traveling by ship, she gets terribly sea-sick—"

"Oh, but I'm certain they'll be just on fire to see you as soon as they return!" Miss Pitts gushed.

The news left Hattie heartbroken—and Elly utterly disgusted. And in more of a quandary than ever about whether to reveal the terrible truth to her friend.

.   .   .

Soon after Brenda and Gladys left, a new group of girls arrived.

All of them were from wealthy families and, like animals of the same species, herded together. Even the most severely afflicted of them—a girl as cut off from the world as Elly had once been (but now only pretended to be)—knew enough to gravitate to the others. For they were the elite: the girls who had come especially to receive Dr. Phelps's revolutionary new treatment.

From what Elly overheard, it had all come about because of a "paper" Dr. Phelps had written. Though she found it hard to understand how a mere piece of paper could, like flypaper, attract girls from such great distances.

One of them, a girl named Lucy Unsworth, had come all the way from Chicago. She was a brittle, nervous girl, the same age as Hattie, and suffered from a compulsion to mock and insult everyone around her, barbs she delivered with smirking glee. But her eyes sometimes burned with desperation, as though another, kinder girl were trapped inside her.

Her first examination by Dr. Phelps and Miss Pitts proved memorable.

"You're nothing but a quack," she spat at Phelps, as he gazed at her intently. "Quack quack quack."

"Yes?" Phelps was quite calm. "And what makes you say that?"

"And her"—Lucy's wild eyes darted to Miss Pitts—"I can smell her filthy underthings."

Miss Pitts gasped. The girls sitting near Elly had to stifle their laughter.

"And *lewd*!" continued Lucy, grinning savagely. "Yes, I can hear the obscene thoughts scrabbling through her filthy brain like blind dung beetles—"

"That will be quite enough, Miss Unsworth," said Miss Pitts sternly.

"Patience, Beulah," said Phelps, chuckling in spite of himself. "For we're in luck! This girl is ripe for a course of treatments."

"Ripe!" cried Lucy. "Ripe for the plucking, am I? Well I've got news for you both—I shan't be plucked! Neither by you, Doctor Quack, nor your fat filthy friend—"

But her words dissolved into a flurry of shouted oaths (of the sort girls are not supposed to know), and then into screams, as she was indeed plucked from her seat by the Bruiser, and carried away.

•   •   •

With the arrival of the new girls, Dr. Phelps's campaign to improve their lives had at last borne fruit. But it was fruit of a bittersweet variety.

For a long time—save for their new uniforms and blankets—nothing had changed. Perhaps it was because Phelps was so focused on his work, to the exclusion of all else. Now and then he might make a flying visit to sample one of their unpalatable meals. Or he would be clomping down the hallway, lost in thought—then suddenly jerk to a halt, blinking at the sight of a gang of small, exhausted girls hauling mops and buckets. But his subsequent harangues about "food not fit for dogs" or "enslaving girls to do the work of staff" were delivered in such an impotent and whining tone that Miss Pitts found them easy to shrug off.

It was clear that Miss Pitts's spartan economies stemmed from an utter obsession with money, and she finally realized she could make even more of this precious substance by hawking Dr. Phelps's treatments to the rich. Since girls of that class would not stand to be treated like ill-fed serfs, she hit on the ingenious solution of having the wealthier girls sit at a separate table in the dining room, as though the institution were a ship, and they all first class passengers. And so, while Elly and the other charity cases (the "steerage passengers," as it were) continued to eat the same dreary and meager fare, they watched the new girls feasting on real bread and butter, pancakes with maple syrup, bacon, beefsteaks—even ice cream. And of course, they were all exempted from having to work.

That Dr. Phelps acquiesced to all this (after only a token display of fuss) only added to Elly's growing contempt for him.

·   ·   ·

One day Elly sat in the dayroom, watching the twins.

The two girls sat facing one another. They had curiously blank faces, with features blurred as if half-erased, and they gazed into each other's eyes, engrossed in the game of which they never seemed to tire.

One of them (nobody could ever tell them apart) intoned a long number:

"Seven thousand four hundred ninety-nine."

The other stared back at her for a very long time—then finally blinked. A subtle smile lit both girls' faces simultaneously; it was as if a single girl had eaten a bite of ice cream while gazing into a mirror.

Again their faces went blank. Minutes went by. Suddenly the second twin recited another number. Her sister stared blankly back, then finally blinked. The same enigmatic smiles…

Elly looked quickly around. Nobody was watching them.

"Five thousand two hundred seventeen," she blurted.

Both twins swiveled their heads toward her, stared blankly for a minute, then blinked rapidly. At the exact same instant they cried out together, in scornful tones, "SHUT UP!"

Chastened (and more than ever convinced there was some pattern to their pastime she was unable to divine), Elly stood up and wandered over to sit with Hattie and the new girls.

Being from a wealthy family herself, Hattie had been allowed to eat with them. And Elly's friendship with Hattie gave her an entrée into this glamorous group. For Hattie's face had filled out with her new rich diet, making her the prettiest of them all and quite popular. She smiled at Elly, stealthily handed her the buttered roll she had saved for her, then turned back to the others. Because Hattie—pretty, pleasant, but void of volition—was now just another pale moon orbiting the bright sun that was Amelia.

In retrospect, it was inevitable that Amelia would become their new leader. Having recently turned thirteen, she was the oldest, and (with Rena's departure) sported the most womanly shape. She had been kissed, and even attended charm school; she knew how a lady was supposed to sit, how to pinch one's cheeks to obtain a rosy complexion, how to walk while balancing a book on one's head to develop a "graceful carriage," and was expert at doing hair. Once Amelia had overheard Gladys saying that babies were "growed from cabbages," and laughed so hard she had to lie down on the floor. But even though Elly was pretty certain that the answer to this mystery was yet another bit of worldly knowledge that Amelia possessed, she had refused to say any more on the subject.

Drooly sat slumped in her chair on the other side of Hattie. Amelia had done her hair into quite fetching (if rather greasy) ringlets. But in spite of their reconciliation, Amelia had never really overcome her distaste for poor Drooly's loathsome affliction, and Drooly's inclusion in the inner circle of elite girls was (just as in Elly's case) a measure of Hattie's status.

When Hattie had suggested to Dr. Phelps that Drooly receive a course of his treatments, his reply had been witheringly blunt:

"She has a deteriorating condition for which there is no cure."

Over time, Elly had learned more about Drooly's sad case.

"So how's come you call her Drooly, if you're her friend?" Amelia had asked Hattie early on. "Ah mean, that can't be her real name?"

"No, it's Dooley—Martha Dooley. Except she never liked Martha, because her father always called her Missy. But when I got here, she'd already been called Drooly so long that she was used to it, and"—Hattie shrugged, embarrassed—"I guess I got used to it too."

"She told you all that?" Amelia was unable to hide her surprise.

Drooly was sitting right there, and twitched a "yes."

"Oh, Drooly used to talk oodles better than she does now! In fact, she was once perfectly normal. When she was five years old, she could swim, she used to climb trees, she rode horses…"

Drooly's pretty eyes had taken on a wistful expression.

"Well that's just tragical, is what it is," Amelia had pronounced. "Ah declare, seems like all of us here have just got the short end of the stick."

But this begged the question of what in fact was actually wrong with Amelia, whose manifest normality was another reason the other girls deferred to her.

Elly remembered the day Dr. Phelps and Miss Pitts had first examined her.

"Dear, dear Amelia—oh Doctor, don't you think a course of treatments might help cure her problem?"

But Miss Pitts's maternal cooings had seemed more false than ever, and Phelps had shaken his head impatiently. "There is nothing whatsoever neurologically wrong with this girl. No, I'd say this is a case for Dr. Frood."

He barked a laugh.

Amelia began having private sessions once a week with Dr. Phelps to receive something he called a "talking cure." She was bragging now about the experience to the girls gathered around her.

"Oh, y'all should see it! He's got this room all fixed up with Turkish carpets and a mahogany humidor and Tiffany lamps—Ah recognized them cause Momma once took me to the Tiffany showroom in New York City—and scads of thick books, some of them in German, and this just *exquisite* velvet divan he makes me lie down on."

This last detail had the girls all agog.

Lucy Unsworth's compulsion to sneer at the world had been somewhat curbed by her first course of treatments, but far from extinguished. She curled her lip.

"Oh yes? And then what happens? Does he *ravish* you?"

Elly had no idea what ravishing was. But whatever it was, the suggestion got Amelia flustered.

"You…you need to shut your dirty mouth," she stammered.

"Ah! I thought not. I mean, considering how plug-ugly you are."

Being called ugly by a girl with a beanpole physique and a mole on her forehead was so ludicrous that Amelia laughed and rolled her eyes.

"Lucy Unsworth, if I didn't know you were crazier than a bedbug… Look, it's called the 'talkin cure' for a reason. And the reason bein that that's what we do—we *talk*. Except it's mostly me does all the talkin."

"So what do you talk about?" sniffed Priscilla, who never stopped weeping (because, she had once confided, her cat had died. Though when pressed, she admitted this tragic event occurred five years ago).

"Well,"—Amelia's eyes darted away—"he asks me questions."

"Questions about what?"

"Different stuff."

"She's afraid to tell us," sneered Lucy.

Amelia sighed deeply and picked at a loose thread on the sleeve of her uniform.

"He asks me questions about the lies Momma told that got me locked up in this place. And how Ah feel about her—Ah hate her guts, thank you very much—and how Ah feel about Daddy, and about my dreams, and…oh, Ah don't know, just lots of stuff."

"And what does he say back?"

"Oh he hardly says anything. Just stares at me with those big ol glassy eyes, or writes in this bitty little notebook."

"So why doesn't Daddy just tell them Mommy's lying"—Lucy's eyes flashed with malice—"and get you out of this place?"

Amelia's face twisted. "Because that's exactly what she's lying about, about me and—oh never mind, y'all just wouldn't understand. So,"—she picked up a thick volume and began energetically flipping through the pages—"where'd we get up to?"

"Fie," sputtered Drooly.

"That's right, we were just starting chapter five…"

The new book was one Hattie had received for her thirteenth birthday. It was called *Ben-Hur* and was very long and quite adult. But Amelia had been reading it with dramatic fervor, and the girls had gotten caught up in the exciting story.

The book had come wrapped in a box, along some pretty hair ribbons, a tortoise shell comb, and a card written in the florid hand and flowery style Hattie had come to loathe.

"Oh Maudie, I just can't tell you how much I hate them, all those silly, empty phrases—'for my darling girl on the joyous occasion of having attained her thirteenth year.' How could Mother ever have allowed anyone to write such drivel?"

Hattie had recently taken to visiting Elly alone at night in her bed and, in her newly quiet and decorous manner, pouring out her heart. Just the other night she had confessed how distressed she was by Drooly's deteriorating condition.

"She's getting worse and worse, now she can hardly speak at all, and…well, sometimes she has accidents during the night."

Hattie had long taken it upon herself to help Drooly get out of bed and dressed every morning.

"But if she starts losing control of herself during the day…"

The thought had been too dreadful to contemplate. But tonight, as so many nights, it was the mystery of her parents' silence that consumed Hattie.

"Oh Maudie, it just doesn't make any sense! Because if they sent me all these nice things for doing my hair—why, surely they must know I don't have to wear that helmet anymore. I mean, even when you're travelling by ship, you can still receive letters, isn't that so? So someone must have written to them about how improved I am. But then why haven't they sent me any postcards? Not one single postcard! Oh Maudie, does it make any sense to you?"

Sadly, it made perfect sense to Elly. And, perhaps because they lay together in the dark, just the two of them, their faces so close together Elly could feel her friend's hot breath, she dared to answer Hattie's question with a tiny nod.

Hattie emitted a squeal that threatened to rouse Mrs. Wong, then began whispering, with something like her old vivacity:

"Oh Maudie, I just knew it! So you really do understand everything I say?"

Elly nodded again. It was both terrifying and exhilarating.

A conversation of sorts ensued, with Elly nodding or shaking her head.

"So Maudie—do you think my parents are really on a round-the-world cruise?"

(No.)

"So, you think Dr. Phelps and Miss Pitts lied to me?"

(Yes.)

"Oh Maudie, Maudie— Do you think…do you think there's some other reason, some very good reason, my parents never write or visit me?"

(Yes.)

Hattie had put her hand on Elly's cheek to better read her answers in the dark, and she stroked Elly's face as she pondered all this. Impulsively she leaned over and kissed Elly's cheek, then whispered into her ear:

"Do you think it's really Mother's secretary who sends me all these things?"

(No.)

"Oh, but who on earth could it be?"

Suddenly there was a burst of raucous laughter, followed by a shriek.

They pulled the blankets away and sat up. A few beds away they could see the shadows of two girls. One was beating on the other and sobbing. The girl underneath her was fending off the blows, while gasping, in a paroxysm of mirth: "Her CAT…got his HEAD STUCK…in the COMMODE!"

The lights flashed on, revealing Priscilla, wailing louder than ever and beating on Lucy, who was rolling on the bed, helpless with laughter. Mrs. Wong burst through the door, looking wild and disheveled, and marched toward them, swinging her paddle. Girls everywhere were sitting up so as not to miss anything.

The overworked and exhausted Mrs. Wong had no real taste for punishing them, but was only put into a rage by having her precious sleep disturbed. A single swat to Priscilla's behind broke up the fight (and gave the permanently weeping girl yet another thing to cry about). But Lucy continued to roll on the bed, clutching herself, and squealing gleefully about the cat, the secret of whose ignominious death she had apparently weaseled out of poor Priscilla.

"Her kitty!" she shrieked. "He…he died in the SHITTY!"

Mrs. Wong stared at her a moment, nonplussed, then yelled something in Chinese and slapped at Lucy's shoulder.

It wasn't even a hard blow. But in an instant Lucy was up on her knees and screaming:

"You FAT FUCKING SLANT-EYED WHORE! You keep your FILTHY CHINESE FINGERS off of me, or I'll CHOP THEM ALL OFF—you hear me? CHOP-CHOP!"

Mrs. Wong stood utterly still, gaping at her. The room had gone deathly still. Even Priscilla had stopped sobbing to see what would happen.

What happened was more horrible than anyone could have imagined.

Abruptly her legs gave out. Her bottom hit the floor with a loud smack. She leaned back against the bed with her legs splayed in front of her. Her face collapsed, her narrow eyes squeezed so tightly shut they seemed to form a single horizontal line—and she began to weep.

Her cries quickly rose into a loud and continuous wail, an eerie sound like a siren. Even Lucy looked appalled. One of the girls who massaged Mrs. Wong's feet every night approached her timidly and touched her shoulder. Mrs. Wong swatted her away. Like a big baby having a tantrum, she beat her thighs on the floor and wailed louder than ever…

The astounding scene became only more so when the Bruiser rushed in. Her braids were pinned up and she was dressed in her nightgown. Mrs. Wong tried to beat her off, but the bigger woman finally pulled her to her feet. Mrs. Wong threw herself into the Bruiser's arms, sobbing against her shoulder. The Bruiser cradled her like a child, whispering in her ear and tenderly stroking her head.

Mr. Wong was silhouetted in the doorway. He wore a nightshirt from which his skinny legs comically protruded. The Bruiser led his wife to him. Mrs. Wong stumbled, still clutching the bigger woman, then fell into her husband's arms. He patted her back clumsily. It was the only time the girls had ever seen them together, much less embracing.

Finally they led her away.

.   .   .

"So then you lift up the hem of your skirt like this, and shake one leg, while you hop…on the other leg…like this…then shake the other leg…like…this…"

Spring had come—a few weeks of crisp, cool weather when wildflowers bloomed overnight in the exercise yard before being plucked by the girls or trampled by their boots—then, in the blink of an eye, it was summer. The ground enclosed by the tall iron fence had baked and hardened into concrete, and the air shimmering in the heat rendered the distant mountains a mirage.

Due to Mrs. Wong's breakdown, the Bruiser had been pressed into emergency service doing laundry, and Miss Bland had been enlisted in her stead to supervise their outdoor play. The old lady sat in a chair in the shade and dozed with her mouth agape and her long skirt indecorously spread, as though her bony knees were tent poles. Into this vacuum of authority the girls' play had expanded with unfettered exuberance, and a group of the elite girls were eagerly watching Amelia demonstrate how to dance the "can-can." A ragged chorus line had formed beside her. Elly remembered that the Twin Sisters had done the same steps in their act and longed to join in. She cast her eyes around for the Troll, and saw her sitting in a heap beside the fence. The Troll snatched up Mr. Hoppy and cradled him protectively in her fat arms, and Elly ran breathlessly back.

An unsynchronized riot of skirt-flapping and leg-shaking was now in progress.

"TAH, ta ta ta ta TAH-TAH, ta ta ta ta TAH-TAH, ta ta ta ta…" sang Amelia, the tune half-drowned in squeals and laughter. Elly tried her best to copy Amelia's motions.

The twins squatted nearby, absorbed in their endless game. Lucy Unsworth lost her balance and suddenly went dancing off in a diagonal, tripped over the two of them, and went sprawling in the dirt.

"SHUT UP!" shrieked the twins in unison (except for numbers, these seemed to be the only words they knew). Then they began to bawl.

The can-can disintegrated. Instinctively all the girls glanced at Miss Bland. She yawned, and smiled at them vaguely.

"I know," cried Amelia, "we should have a chariot race!"

Just this week they had finally reached that exciting chapter of *Ben-Hur*, and the girls were galvanized by the idea.

Amelia ran over to Miss Bland, who was sipping her medicine in a furtive manner.

"Miss Bland, oh Miss Bland, can we have a chariot race?"

Miss Bland put the stopper back in her bottle, and blinked up at her, bemused.

"You see, we've been reading *Ben-Hur*, and…well, it would be educational."

Miss Bland chewed her lip. "Yes, um, I suppose it would," she finally allowed.

"So we can?"

"Well, um," Miss Bland nodded uncertainly, "I can't see the harm…"

Amelia raced back.

It was decided the wheelchairs would be the chariots, and each chariot would have a team of two horses. As there was no way for the horses to pull the chariots, they would have to push them instead. The finish line would be the back of the fence (but well away from the haunted area where all the girls were buried).

Feverish excitement as the five wheelchairs were lined up and teams of horses chosen. Elly found herself paired with Hattie behind Drooly's chair. Miss Bland had been seized by girlish enthusiasm, and tottered over to watch.

The girls all tucked their skirts into the waistbands of their bloomers so they could run, and lined up behind the wheelchairs.

"Miss Bland," said Amelia, "you get to be the starter."

Miss Bland actually giggled. "Well, all right. Is everyone ready?"

They all nodded.

"Well, yes, then, um, how do I…? Oh yes, I remember: ready…set… GO!"

The wheelchairs tore over the hard, baked ground, raising clouds of dust. An audience of moaners and shufflers jiggled on the sidelines, shrieking as the chairs bumped and careened along. One chair hit a small rise and the charioteer—a tiny girl with withered legs—went flying through the air and landed in a heap. A moment later two more chairs collided and toppled over, dumping their occupants unceremoniously onto the ground.

Elly was doing her best to keep up with Hattie's longer stride, but their chariot was still teetering alarmingly. Drooly bounced like a sack of potatoes, her greasy curls flapped in the breeze, and she emitted a high, keening sound. The only other charioteer left in the race—a toothy, half-blind girl pushed by the effective pairing of Amelia and Lucy—drew abreast of them. Nearer and nearer came the fence—

Suddenly Drooly's chair swerved, crashed into the other chariot, and both occupants spilled onto the ground. Frenzied spectators circled the scene of the disaster, shrieking. The fence was only a few yards away, and they urged the two dazed charioteers to crawl to the finish line. The toothy girl was far more agile and dragged herself energetically forward by her elbows. Poor Drooly watched her for a moment with dismay, then gamely lurched toward the fence with a writhing, jerking motion.

Miss Bland tottered up and stood among the rest of the girls, looking dazed. The toothy girl had almost reached the fence. But she had cracked her thick eyeglasses in the spill, and suddenly veered blindly off in another direction. Hattie and Elly were on their knees, cheering Drooly on. Her eyes were fixed on the fence as she crawled relentlessly forward, panting. Each jerk of her body brought her a few inches closer—

She bumped her head against the iron fence.

Everyone was screaming. Hattie took Drooly's head in her lap and stroked her face. Both of them were in tears, and Elly discovered she was too.

A shout of alarm made them all look up. Miss Pitts was advancing toward them. Across ground littered with overturned wheelchairs like the aftermath of some battle, past dazed girls sitting in the dirt with their skirts around their waists. Advancing with her face twisted in rage.

"Hazel, Hazel," she shouted, striding up to them, "Hazel, what in the name of God?!"

Miss Bland's lips moved several times before she found words. "I believe it was…they were having a chariot race?"

Miss Pitts eyed her as if she were deranged. "And where—where is that awful smell…?"

Indeed, a terrible stink seemed to be emanating from the vicinity of the victor. Miss Pitts reached down and yanked up Drooly's frock.

"You filthy-dirty girl!"

~

Drooly's head was still lying in Hattie's lap and both girls were sobbing when the Bruiser, her nose wrinkled in distaste, lifted Drooly's twisted body, and bore her away.

Forever.

CHAPTER TWELVE

TRUTH AND CONSEQUENCES

The other girls had long given up wondering where Elly went every day and scarcely noticed when, on one particularly fine day in late September, Henry found her outside in the exercise yard and led her away.

They passed Mr. Wong in the kitchen. Hardly breaking the rhythm of his chopping, he tossed Elly a peppermint stick.

Miss Bland's door opened to Henry's soft knock. Without a word, he handed Elly over to the old lady and left.

Miss Bland put her hand down the lacy bodice of her frock and produced a waxed paper parcel containing four strips of bacon. Elly took the peppermint stick from her mouth and put it in her pocket for later, then quickly devoured the greasy treat. Finally she stoically endured having her fingers wiped with a spitty handkerchief—for only then would she be allowed to touch Miss Bland's precious piano.

At first Elly had wondered why, rather than endure agonies of begging and scheming to procure her pump organ, Miss Bland hadn't just moved her piano into the chapel. But over time Elly came to understand there was a secretive and private side to the old woman's nature, embodied in her overstuffed doll's house of an apartment, and that the lovely old piano was its centerpiece. There were many other fascinating objects as well, which Miss Bland had allowed her to examine. A hat pin with a "real gold nugget from Sutter's Mill" affixed to one end. A giant fossilized egg, presumably from some unimaginably mammoth bird. A delicately carved wooden angel missing half of a wing. And a curious bronze statuette of three monkeys.

"See no evil, hear no evil, speak no evil," Miss Bland had explained in her low, fluting voice. Which Elly came to think described the old lady herself, and her blithe—even willful—ignorance of the horrors around them.

It had been three months since Drooly's banishment to the west wing. Hattie had made a quixotic stab at inducing Dr. Phelps to overrule Miss Pitts and return Drooly from exile.

"I'm afraid with that one it was only a matter of time," he had replied in his offhand way. And Elly was certain he had put Drooly out of his mind forever.

Hattie still missed her friend terribly. And often speculated, when she visited Elly, on how Drooly was being treated.

"But Maudie, I mean—it couldn't be as dreadful in the west wing as the girls say, could it?"

Elly knew it was probably worse.

"Oh, if only we could visit her somehow!"

Elly had considered the same idea. But the door at the end of the hallway was always kept locked, and she couldn't think how it might be accomplished.

Amid such turmoil, Elly's daily sessions at Miss Bland's piano sometimes seemed the only thing that made life worth living. Especially when, shortly after her eighth birthday, Elly made the momentous discovery that—by slumping down with her right leg extended to the utmost—she could just press the pedal down with her toe. Instantly a whole new world of shimmering musical colors had opened up before her, and she now spent the greater part of her time in this cramped position. Though her leg was often so stiff afterward that she could barely keep up with Henry when he led her down the back stairway.

With her fingers finally pronounced clean (if only by Miss Bland's rather eccentric standards), she sat at the piano, wondering what they were going to play.

Her ability to read music at sight had improved to the point she could just about play anything Miss Bland put in front of her. The old lady was fascinated by this uncanny talent, and would set volume after volume before Elly as though feeding an insatiable flame. When they had burned through Miss Bland's store of music, she had Henry drive her into town, and returned with stacks of new books.

The old lady gave her the wide-eyed look that meant she had something up her sleeve, and set a book on the music rack. It was one Elly had never seen before, a thick collection of sonatas by Mozart. She was quite familiar with the name, since she herself had so often been compared to the young boy genius. But she had played only a single easy sonata in C major. Excitedly she thumbed through pages overgrown with thickets of notes. Miss Bland's rheumy old eyes twinkled.

"We should have plenty of time today. Because, you know, Beulah fancies herself quite the horsewoman. And when the weather's fine like this, she stays out longer."

She emitted a fruity chuckle, and reached for her chocolates. Elly took a moment to savor the slyly malicious remark (a side of Miss Bland only she got to see), then attacked the first sonata. It was full of signs for trills and turns and other decorative flourishes she could only guess how to execute. But the music fit in her small hands and had a sparkly beauty that captivated her...

She played for two hours, only dimly aware of Miss Bland munching her chocolates and sipping her medicine. After a very taxing piece called "Rondo alla Turca" left Elly gasping for breath, the old lady whisked away the Mozart like a waiter changing courses and replaced it with the volume of Stephen Foster tunes with which they invariably ended their sessions. Judging by its yellowed cover, it was a book Miss Bland had owned since girlhood. But her movements were rather approximate (as they tended to be when the old lady had been sipping her medicine), and the book fell onto the keys with its cover open to the frontispiece. In the upper corner, floridly written in a still-unformed (but already recognizable) hand, was an inscription:

This Book is the Property of Hazel Bland

Miss Bland set the book back in place and opened it to "Old Black Joe," a tune both of them loved.

And blinked in confusion when Elly refused to play it.

· · ·

"Maudie, Maudie—oh, I've been waiting all day to tell you the news…"

Mrs. Wong had returned to her post, but was still somewhat fragile. So the girls were even more careful to make sure she was snoring peacefully before leaving their beds to go visiting.

A cold snap had arrived just the day before, and Hattie's feet were icy as she burrowed beneath Elly's blankets and snuggled against her.

"It happened this morning, when I was making my bed—and I found this!"

She pressed a scrap of paper into Elly's hand.

"It's too dark to see, but there's a message written on it. At first, I could hardly make it out, it's printed so very poorly—"

Elly felt rather insulted. She knew how to read but had never before attempted to write anything. Moreover, she'd been forced to do her work on the window sill by moonlight with only a stub of pencil; under the circumstances, she thought it quite a respectable effort.

"—but finally I figured it out. And it says: ASK MISS BLAND ABOUT YOUR PARENTS. Isn't that so very strange! Why do you think someone would suggest that? And who on earth could have written it?"

They were not "yes or no" questions, so Elly wasn't forced to answer.

"I was waiting all day, but of course Miss Bland chose not to come. Oh Maudie, do you really think she might know something?"

Elly had long felt complicit in the lie Hattie was being forced to live, and was sure that Miss Bland was the weak link in the dastardly plot to maintain Hattie's ignorance.

She nodded.

· · ·

197

The next day was a Saturday. Normally they would not have seen Miss Bland except at meals. But the old lady wandered into the dayroom shortly after noon with her usual air of benign befuddlement, bearing a book.

The elite girls who clustered around Amelia disdained having anything to do with her. Their treatments were nearly finished, and there had been some astonishing improvements. Weepy Priscilla had dried her tears and, if not exactly jolly, seemed finally resigned to her cat's ignominious fate, and Lucy's tongue, though still sharp, mostly stayed within the bounds of decency. In fact both girls had been pronounced cured, and were scheduled to be returned to their families—but only after the upcoming yearly visit by the examiners, so Dr. Phelps could once again show off the results of his treatments.

So Amelia was the happy center of a flurry of socializing, while the circle of girls pretending to appreciate Miss Bland's ludicrous attempts to entertain them had shrunk to Hattie, Elly, and Tussie, the half-witted girl whose protruding teeth and thick glasses gave her the look of a studious rodent.

The Troll, lurking on the sidelines, made an even more doubtful fourth.

Miss Bland settled herself on the old torn sofa, with Elly and Hattie sitting to either side of her, and opened her book. It proved to be a collection of fables entitled *The Tales of Uncle Remus*. She had tried to read it once before, only to make such a hash of the thick dialect she might have been speaking Greek. So she was either feeling particularly brave or (much more likely) had completely forgotten. But it didn't matter, for she had scarcely stammered out the words "How Br'er Bear Los' His Tail" before Hattie interrupted her:

"Miss Bland?"

Miss Bland looked up in confusion. "Yes?"

"Miss Bland, what do you know about my parents?"

Miss Bland blinked at her. "Your…parents?"

"Yes, my parents. Are they really on a round-the-world cruise?"

Miss Bland nervously smoothed her skirt. "Yes, I…um, yes, I was told…I mean I *believe* that is the case—"

"But my mother gets so terribly sea-sick; I just can't imagine they'd ever do anything like that!"

Miss Bland's eyes darted around. "Yes, um, well..."

"So I don't think it's true," continued Hattie, staring hard at the old woman. "I think there's some other reason they never visit me. And what's more—*I think you know what it is.*"

Miss Bland's eyes were no longer darting around, but were fixed on Hattie's; she might have been a mouse staring at a snake. Her lips started to move, but nothing came out.

Elly reached over Miss Bland's lap and flipped the book to its frontispiece. Yes, just as she'd hoped:

This Book is the Property of Hazel Bland

Hattie glanced down. Her eyes grew huge. She grabbed the book and stared at the inscription, shaking her head slowly, then gave Miss Bland an incredulous look.

"*You.*"

Miss Bland had gone deathly pale.

"*You* sent me all those things," continued Hattie in a quiet but intense voice. "It was *your* handwriting on the cards; my mother never bought any of those things for me."

Miss Bland covered her face with her withered hands and leaned forward, rocking back and forth and emitting a low, bleating sound, like a dying sheep.

"I...I *had* to!" she blubbered. "Beulah *made* me! But I tried... Oh, I tried so hard, so very hard, to find you such nice things, pretty things, nice books I thought you would like...oh I never meant any harm! Oh, never, never—"

"But *why?*" cried Hattie, her pretty blue eyes filled with tears. "*Why* did Miss Pitts make you buy me all those things?"

"Because...because,"—Miss Bland made a choking sound—"oh dear Hattie, it's because...I'm afraid your parents...they both...they both—"

"They've gone away? They disinherited me? Oh please, tell me—"

"Dead," blurted Miss Bland. "They're both dead."

Hattie gaped at her. There was a long silence. The other girls were squealing at something Amelia had said and paid no attention to them. "But…but how?" Hattie finally stammered, "How did they—?"

"It was…Beulah said…an epidemic of typhus."

"Typhus."

"Yes, more than two years ago—"

"Two years ago," Hattie echoed again, dazed.

"—and Beulah was afraid that, in your condition…well, she thought the shock would be too much for you."

"Two years. All this time. All of you lying to me."

"Oh, I'm so sorry, so sorry, so very very sorry," chanted Miss Bland, again rocking back and forth with her face in her hands. She continued to blubber about how very hard she'd tried to find nice, pretty things, books that Hattie might like. And it struck Elly that the old lady had actually tried, in a pathetic sort of way, to be a surrogate mother to Hattie.

Hattie must have felt something similar, because she reached out and gently touched the old lady's shoulder. Miss Bland moaned and clutched at her, and Hattie patted her hand as if it were Miss Bland, and not Hattie herself, who needed comforting. But there was a look of steely resolve in Hattie's eyes. So Elly wasn't surprised when, after giving the old lady's hand a final pat, she abruptly stood up and left the dayroom.

Elly got up and followed her.

It was still early afternoon, and Miss Pitts had not yet ridden to town. They found her in the chapel, assembling her readings for tomorrow's service. She started at the sight of them—then quickly composed herself. Elly sat in a chair and stared at her doll.

MISS PITTS: *(sternly)* You girls are not supposed to wander around like this. *(softening)* Hattie, child, what on earth is the matter?

HATTIE: *(her voice trembling)* Miss Pitts, I…I know about my parents.

MISS PITTS: *(lightly)* Oh? And just what is it you believe you
   know about them?

HATTIE: I know that they died, they died more than two
   years ago, and you've been lying to me all this time, you
   and Dr. Phelps, and even Miss Bland.

(A silence)

MISS PITTS: And how did you discover all…well, no matter.
   Yes, dear Hattie, I'm afraid it is so.

HATTIE: *(still speaking quietly, but her voice trembling even
   more)* Well I think it was a horrible thing to do—

MISS PITTS: Oh dear child, you can't understand—

HATTIE: all the time hoping—

MISS PITTS: decisions regarding your ability to withstand—

(They talk over one another for a time.)

MISS PITTS: *(raising her voice)* Enough! *(a silence)* Oh, my
   dear girl, I know you've had a terrible shock—

HATTIE: Please don't touch me, I don't want you to touch
   me. I want to leave. I'm cured, and I want to leave this
   place at once.

MISS PITTS: I'm afraid it's not so simple.

(A silence)

HATTIE: What…what do you mean?

MISS PITTS: Just that legally—well, I am now your guardian.

HATTIE: What…what are you talking about?

MISS PITTS: You see, at the time your parents passed away,
   you seemed a hopeless case. And, as the executors of your
   parents' estate wished to be assured of your continued
   welfare—

HATTIE: You mean they wished to be rid of me. But I'm fine
   now, really I am, I'm ready to go to school and—

MISS PITTS: It is for me to decide what is in your best
   interests—

HATTIE: But I don't want you for my guardian!

MISS PITTS: I'm afraid—

HATTIE: *(becoming more emotional)* And I'm cured, Dr. Phelps said so, we were only waiting for my parents to return—but of course, both of you *knew* they would never return! So what were you planning to do a year from now, tell me their ship had sunk? *(She laughs wildly.)* But what about our house? We have such a beautiful big house, I can still go home—

MISS PITTS: Oh child, after your parents passed, I'm afraid that several of your relatives laid claim to their estate, and the house was sold. But a certain amount was put into a fund for your welfare, and as your guardian, I am now the trustee—

HATTIE: *(her voice trembling)* But it's *my* money, I can use that money to leave, I can…can use it to pay for school—

MISS PITTS: But as I said, that is for me to decide.

HATTIE: *(beside herself)* Oh you're just a horrible person, you're only after my money, I can see that now! But I'm going to leave, and I'm going to tell everyone how horribly you have treated me, and all about this horrible place, and how you locked poor Drooly away and won't even let me visit her even though she's my very best friend—

MISS PITTS: *(with clucking concern)* Oh the doctor was right; he suspected you'd be having another fit before long.

(Miss Pitts's words strike Hattie mute.)

MISS PITTS: So for now, let's take you up for another treatment. And after that, we'll see what the doctor says about—

HATTIE: Oh no no, please—

MISS PITTS: *Tut tut,* let's not be a baby about it—

HATTIE: But I'm not having a fit, I'm NOT—

A sudden motion made Elly raise her eyes. Miss Pitts had grabbed Hattie by both of her wrists.

"FRIEDA!"

Elly watched, horrified, as Miss Pitts dragged Hattie toward the doorway. Hattie fought back desperately. Miss Pitts continued to cry out for Frieda. Heavy running steps—the Bruiser rushed in and helped pull Hattie out into the hallway. Elly ran to the door and watched the two of them wrestle the wildly struggling girl down the hall. Miss Pitts unlocked the door that led to a stairway to the second floor.

"But I'm NOT! I'm NOT having a FIT!" shrieked Hattie.

Miss Pitts locked the door behind them, and Hattie's shrieks faded away.

．　　　　　　．　　　　　　．

Beulah Pitts's buggy bounced gaily over the rutted track. The October air was brisk, invigorating. The smell of dried grass and wood smoke, with a hint of rotted pumpkin. Overhead a flock of honking geese arrowed their way south.

How she relished her daily excursions! To escape for even a couple of hours the stress and strain of trying to make, out of the bedlam of a vessel Beulah helmed, a tight ship. A chance to stroll through the shops of Marysville deciding on that evening's fare (for, unlike the economies she forced on the institution, Beulah demanded only the finest of ingredients for her own meals). And a chance to practice her driving, for Beulah did indeed fancy herself something of a horsewoman.

She flicked her whip at the animal, and his step became more lively.

She'd been trying to decide how to have Wong cook the succulent loin of veal she had chosen for that evening's meal. Perhaps in a cream sauce? Or simmered in a rich onion gravy?

If it was successful enough, it might be something to serve the deacons next week…

The dinner would be a most important occasion this year, because she and Edgar would be presenting their proposal to fully devote the institution to their revolutionary new electrical treatments. Though really, between the prestige and increased revenue, the deacons could hardly refuse!

She gave the horse another taste of her lash. The way the animal's muscular haunches twitched reminded Beulah of the way the girls jerked and writhed when they were given their treatments. The sight gave Beulah a strange thrill, and Edgar's indifference to the imbeciles in the west wing had left her free to indulge herself. Occasionally she had misgivings about this admittedly rather bizarre enthusiasm of hers. But Frieda had been eager to assist her. Besides, how could one argue against burning the filth out of girls who soiled themselves, or lay naked with one another?

It was regrettable, however, that Beulah had been forced to give the same extreme treatment to Hattie.

The girl who was much more deserving of this fate still eluded Beulah's grasp, and she pursed her lips with frustration. For Amelia van Allen had been caught doing things with her father that—well, which didn't bear thinking about. Her mother averred the child had been utterly brazen in her advances, and the doctors had diagnosed a case of nymphomania. That the girl denied being the instigator counted for nothing, for inveterate prevarication was a symptom of the condition.

How Beulah longed to strap that young hussy to the table and burn the unspeakable shamelessness out of her! But Edgar had insisted on his silly "talking cure." Yet, for all Edgar's affectation of worldliness, the boy was still such an innocent, and the result had been all too sadly predictable.

It was knowledge that could come in handy if Edgar ever tried to balk.

She turned onto the drive, and was mildly surprised to see Henry slumped against the stable wall, asleep. Idly, it occurred to her he was never there when she returned, but always seemed to appear out of nowhere a minute or two later. She saw him wake with a start, looking strangely alarmed, and left him to deal with the buggy.

She had quite decided on onion gravy (perhaps with an accompanying glass of Madeira?), and started up the stairs to her apartment in search of a recipe—when she was brought up short by the sound of piano playing. So it was true what the maid who cleaned their apartments had told her! For the girl had insisted that Hazel played her piano every day when Beulah was gone. But Beulah had never quite believed her, because Hazel's organ playing seemed to be only getting worse, if such a thing were possible.

Yet these thoughts had hardly flashed through Beulah's mind when she found herself pausing on the first step in utter amazement. For the sounds reaching her ears were of such intricacy, such fluidity, such melodious complexity—and as far beyond Hazel's powers as jumping over the moon.

She hurried up the stairway.

·   ·   ·

Since Hattie's disappearance, Elly had been suffering agonies of guilt. If only she hadn't written that message! But surely Hattie would be coming back from her treatment soon?

Like Hattie, Elly had forgiven Miss Bland for her deceptions, and their sessions at the piano had continued as though nothing had happened. In fact, Elly marveled at the old lady's ability to carry on, in spite of everything. Though really, how much did Miss Bland even know about the terrible things that went on here? Not once had Elly ever seen her enter the west wing. And she decided Miss Bland might best be compared not to the three monkeys, but to an ostrich with its head buried in the sand.

Elly's own way of escaping was to bury her head not in sand, but in the sonatas of Mozart. She was tearing through the glorious finale of a sonata in D major when there was a loud knock on the door.

Abruptly she ceased playing. Miss Bland stared at her with a horrified expression.

"Hazel!" More knocking. "Hazel, I know you're in there!"

Miss Bland gave a low moan, staggered up from her chair, and tottered to the door. She opened it a tiny crack and peered out like a terrified animal from its burrow.

P.D. QUAVER

"Hazel, who on earth—" Miss Pitts pushed past her. Elly quickly turned back and stared at the keyboard, her face burning.

MISS PITTS: What…what in the world?! It's not possible, such marvelous playing, surely there's someone else here you're hiding…
(Elly imagines Miss Pitts peering beneath the sofa. Miss Bland sobs quietly.)
MISS PITTS: Hazel, for heaven's sake, pull yourself together—was this child actually playing?
MISS BLAND: (still sniffling) Oh…oh yes, of course.
MISS PITTS: But that is incredible—such dexterity! Can she play any other songs?
MISS BLAND: Oh well, I should say she can play, well…anything you like.
MISS PITTS: Whatever are you talking about?
MISS BLAND: (not without a touch of pride) Well you see, she was playing at sight.
MISS PITTS: No, that's not possible—
MISS BLAND: (gushing) Oh but it is!

Miss Pitts marched over and began rummaging through the music atop the piano. Elly continued to stare stonily at the keyboard. Miss Pitts slapped a book on the music rack and opened it. In spite of herself Elly looked at it. It was a piece with no name but numbered "3," and was in G major. Notes spilled up and down the page in the left hand. She could hear it in her head, and it was very pretty.

"Well, come on then," said Miss Pitts impatiently.

Elly refused to play.

"Oh Maude, dear Maude"—Miss Bland knelt beside her and stroked her face—"oh please play it. Play it just…just for me?"

"Well I thought as much," declared Miss Pitts, turning away. "Just like the book she memorized, a single freakish thing she must have learned."

Seized by a desire to vindicate poor Miss Bland (and wipe the smugness from Miss Pitts's tone), Elly lifted her hands and tore through the piece at a fast clip, touching the pedal with her toe to make the right hand chords sing—

And didn't miss a single note.

.   .   .

"Extraordinary," breathed Dr. Phelps. "A genuine prodigy. So much so, one wonders if she hadn't already achieved some notoriety before she came here. Perhaps by searching through the newspapers, we might determine her identity…"

Elly exulted in his words.

An hour had passed since she had played for Miss Pitts. Phelps had been summoned by telephone, had driven out in his motorcar, and she had played for him as well. This time she hadn't needed to be coaxed; she missed performing, and an audience of three was still an audience. Surely now they would know she didn't belong in this place!

The idea, once so terrifying and unthinkable, that she could just open her mouth and *tell* them who she was, had of course occurred to her. In fact, ever since she'd begun nodding and shaking her head to Hattie's questions, she had felt a pressure growing inside her—as if her brain were a tea kettle nearing the boiling point—to do just that. Happily, her fingers had instead spoken for her.

She picked up Mr. Hoppy and stared into his eyes hopefully. And listened to the three of them:

MISS PITTS: But don't you think, Edgar, the child might be
    exhibited? Surely she would make a sensation—
PHELPS: And a pretty penny for you, eh Beulah?
MISS PITTS: Oh Edgar, how cruel you are! For us, Edgar, *us*!
PHELPS: And besides, I seem to recall there are laws against
    that sort of thing. Stemming from the way Josef Hofmann
    was exploited by his parents as a child—

MISS PITTS: Oh but surely those could be gotten around. I mean, since the girl is otherwise an imbecile, the case could be made that we would be demonstrating a scientific phenomenon.

MISS BLAND: *(hesitantly)* But Beulah, surely… An imbecile? Oh I shouldn't say she's that at all…I mean I've gotten to know little Maude quite well—

MISS PITTS: *(ignoring her)* What do you think?

PHELPS: *(drumming his fingers on the arm of his chair)* There might be something in what you say.

MISS PITTS: And of course, we must have her play for the deacons!

PHELPS: Yes of course, it's the first thing that occurred—

MISS BLAND: *(gushing)* And for the other girls! Hattie especially shall want to hear Maude play. Because the two of them…well they are such very good friends…

(A silence)

MISS BLAND: *(more timidly)* I mean…I mean when she returns from her treatment, of course.

PHELPS: *(absently)* How's that?

MISS BLAND: *(hesitant)* Isn't she…is she not being given…?

PHELPS: You are mistaken.

MISS PITTS: Oh Edgar, I had been meaning to tell you. I'm afraid Miss Limburg suffered a relapse—

PHELPS: WHAT! No, I don't believe it!

MISS PITTS: Nevertheless, it is true. And quite severe—the child actually attacked me! Oh, I could see it coming on.

PHELPS: But…but why didn't you tell me? When was this?

MISS PITTS: Four days ago.

(Phelps makes a gasping noise.)

MISS PITTS: *(lightly)* Oh come now, Edgar, no need for histrionics! I am perfectly familiar with the procedure. Frieda and I have assisted you a hundred times—

PHELPS: Wait... You—you did it *yourselves*?

MISS PITTS: I tell you it was an emergency, and I thought it best.

PHELPS: My God. *(A pause. Elly senses Phelps trying to get himself under control.)* Well, so...and how is she? Still upstairs?

MISS PITTS: No, she's... I have already completed her treatments, and she has been moved to the west wing.

PHELPS: Why in God's name—

MISS PITTS: Well, I'm sorry to say she did not respond as well as one might have hoped.

PHELPS: *(hoarsely)* What...what are you trying to say?

MISS PITTS: Just that...well, I'm afraid Miss Limburg won't be coming back to us.

(A silence)

MISS BLAND: Not coming...I'm afraid I don't... Is she being sent home? But I'd understood that—

PHELPS: My God. Oh my God. Oh you bloody bloody woman—

MISS PITTS: Hazel, please leave us.

(An interval during which Miss Bland, still dithering about Hattie, rushes out of her own apartment. Elly sits absolutely still, staring through a blur of tears into Mr. Hoppy's eyes. As soon as the door closes, Phelps jumps to his feet and starts pacing around.)

PHELPS: Beulah, my God, what have you done?

MISS PITTS: The girl had discovered the truth about her parents and was making threats. I thought it for the best.

PHELPS: But...but she was *cured*! My greatest achievement—

MISS PITTS: Oh pooh, there will be hundreds more—

PHELPS: —and next week, the examiners... Just what do you think Mr. Fisk will say when he sees the girl I touted as my breakthrough, reduced to a vegetative state?

MISS PITTS: *(lightly)* Oh Edgar, how simple you can be! I've already made plans to have her moved to the old nursery on the third floor for the duration of the inspection.

PHELPS: *(sarcastic)* Why don't you just do away with her?

MISS PITTS: *(as though lecturing a child)* In case her family's lawyers should ever enquire, we need to be able to produce the girl—

PHELPS: My God, you've really got it all worked out, don't you? All so that you can continue drawing from her trust fund.

MISS PITTS: *(calmly)* One of us has to have their feet on the ground. And you are becoming hysterical over nothing.

PHELPS: *(pacing even faster)* How can you call it nothing!

MISS PITTS: Oh pooh. And how many of *your* failures are in the same state?

PHELPS: Good Christ, do you not see the difference?! What you did was *intentional*—in cold blood! And how dare you refer to them as "failures!" They were steps on the road to—

MISS PITTS: Oh please spare me, I am sick unto death of your, your precious "scientific method."

(A silence. Despite her horror, Elly again notes the strange intimacy between the two of them, the whining, petulant tone Phelps employs when they argue.)

PHELPS: *(with dawning awareness)* My...God...you've done it before, haven't you!

MISS PITTS: I have no idea what you're talking—

PHELPS: Yes yes—all those girls in the west wing. So many of them in a comatose state, far more than makes any sense!

MISS PITTS: Well, perhaps one or two—

PHELPS: *(muttering to himself)* Oh what a fool I have been not to—

MISS PITTS: Oh Edgar, dear Edgar— *(Elly hears the sound of rustling silk as Miss Pitts rises from her chair, imagines her caressing him.)* Such a silly boy to get so worked up over nothing! When we have everything before us—

Abruptly both of them fell silent. Elly suspected they had completely forgotten her—but now she sensed their eyes on her. She stayed still, her own eyes glued to her doll. And hoped his anchoring presence would disguise the beating of her heart.

CHAPTER THIRTEEN

GÖTTERDÄMMERUNG

On the morning following the scene in Miss Bland's apartment, Elly endured a hair-brushing from the Troll.

The Troll herself would allow no one to touch her own riot of black curls. But she had watched Hattie at work on Elly's tangled locks (as she watched everything) and, with Hattie gone, had taken over the job, which she performed with savage gusto.

Elly tried to distract herself by meditating on the astonishing things she had overheard the previous afternoon.

Much of it had been hard to understand. But it was clear something terrible had been done to Hattie, something Miss Pitts and Dr. Phelps were intent on hiding from the examiners. Just as dismaying was the bitter realization that, so long as there was money to be made from Elly's piano playing, the two of them would never let her go.

Right that instant, she made her decision: she had to escape.

Elly had never forgotten Hattie's idea of evading capture by dressing as a boy in ragged clothes and posing as a hobo; it seemed to her a very good plan. But how to penetrate the thick walls, locked doors, and barred windows of her prison? The Troll's muscular attentions jerked her head around and dislodged a spate of increasingly far-fetched ideas from her brain. She might try to climb the fence in the exercise yard—but it was very tall, and topped with sharp spikes. Floating away in a hot air balloon would be a lovely way to escape—but she had no idea how to construct one. And disguising herself as one of the Irish maids and slipping out the front door was…well, preposterous.

Besides, as far as Elly could tell, it was only Dr. Phelps, Miss Pitts, Miss Bland, and the Bruiser who had keys to the front door. Perhaps, by waiting until Miss Bland was well-stoked with medicine, and playing only dreamy pieces, she could lull the old lady to sleep, and steal her keys…

The Troll slapped her shoulder to signal she was finished. Then it was off to breakfast, and a morning of work in the babies' ward.

.   .   .

The terrible revelations about Hattie had given new urgency to the parallel puzzle of how to get into the west wing, and as she worked, Elly considered the problem afresh.

Her partner in diaper hauling was now the vacuous and rodentine Tussie. She was close to Elly's size, with the steady, mindless plod of a plow horse, and they seldom slopped the contents of their pails. But Brenda's departure meant there were no more whispered asides from Meg, the Irish maid who oversaw them. And thus no chance to learn more about the west wing—and poor Hattie's fate.

The two of them were in the laundry room, washing out their pail so they could haul back a load of clean diapers, when Kathleen, Meg's friend who worked in the west wing, emerged from behind a thicket of hanging sheets with a basket of soiled bedding. As always, she was pale and hollow-eyed with exhaustion. Elly watched her empty her basket into one of Mrs. Wong's steaming cauldrons, and was struck by a thought.

The hanging sheets concealed a narrow passageway, a back way into the west wing. She knew there must be a thick door somewhere along the route, because whenever the maids came and went, the sounds of the imbeciles would suddenly go from faintly audible to loudly echoing, then again become muffled. Elly was sure the door was kept locked with one of the heavy brass keys that dangled from their waists. But—exhausted and carrying their heavy loads—did they bother to lock it both coming and going?

Kathleen was piling clean bedding in her basket, and would soon be returning—there was no time to lose. Mrs. Wong was hanging sheets, oblivious. Elly glanced at Tussie. Fishily unfocused eyes, magnified by thick spectacles, blinked back at her. Elly dismissed her as a threat, scuttled across the floor, and ducked beneath one of the sheets.

As quietly as she could, she fought her way through all the hanging laundry, then darted down the open passageway. It was long, narrow, and dimly lit, and she made her way cautiously forward. With each step the faint sounds of gibbering and shrieking grew louder.

At the end there was a turn—and suddenly she was confronted by a heavy oak door. The cacophony muffled by the door was mixed with the sounds, echoing behind her, of approaching footsteps. Her heart was trying to pound its way through her ribcage.

She grabbed the door handle and twisted it—

It was unlocked.

She pulled the door open, slipped inside, and quietly closed it behind her.

The noise was now deafening. Another hallway, with open doors on each side. No time to think—she raced down the hallway and ducked inside the first open door.

A room full of oversized metal cribs, like animal cages. She dived beneath one of them and crouched, catching her breath. Foul odors, the rattle of chains, demented howling—she might have been surrounded by wild beasts.

She had scarcely gathered her wits before another pair of legs appeared in the doorway. A basket dropped to the floor beside them, and Kathleen bent down and lifted out a pile of sheets.

Elly watched Kathleen's legs as she began going down the rows, changing bedding. Whenever she got too close, Elly scuttled away to crouch beneath a different crib.

The inmates had grown boisterous, rattling their chains and gibbering.

"Move, ya eejit!"

A loud slap.

"Don't ya dare to bite me, or you'll get what's what."

Crazy laughter. A girl began to sing, a high, tuneless, eerie croon. A smacking sound, as if someone had slapped a mud-pie against the wall. Kathleen made an exasperated noise and her legs moved quickly in Elly's direction. The girl above Elly's head screeched, and Elly cowered beneath her crib. The sounds of a beating.

"You better learn quick to stop doin that," panted Kathleen.

The girl's screams had turned to a pitiful wail. There was a strong smell of excrement in the room.

"That one throwin her shit again?"

Another pair of legs in the doorway—Cora, the other maid. Elly tried to make herself even smaller.

"Bejesus," said Kathleen, "next time I'll sic Miss Pitts on her, then she'll be sorry. Hear that?" she addressed the wailing girl. "Turn yez into a turnip."

Cora gave a mirthless laugh, and ducked out of the room. A minute later, she was back with a bucket and began to scrub the wall. "Speakin of the turnips, we got to move one of em tomorrow. Up to the third floor."

"Whatever for?"

"I've no idea. Something about the inspection."

They worked together, continuing to chat, their conversation punctuated by slaps, howls, the rattling of chains. Elly scuttled from crib to crib to keep out of their way—even as the conversation took a terrible turn.

"Lor', as if we haven't enough to do tryin to make em all presentable."

"That new one, she's the one we're to move."

"It's jokin ye must be—why, she bein the prettiest one, they'll be wantin to show her off!"

"Won't stay pretty for long."

Their words tore at Elly's insides.

"I moved her to the window," added Cora. "She likes seein the sky."

"However can you tell?"

"I just think she does. She seems...*nicer* than the others. Looks at me so sweet when I change her, the lamb."

Kathleen gave a snort. She was at the rear of the room. Elly had worked her way back to the front, near the doorway.

"Wonder what she did," mused Cora, still scrubbing, her back to Elly.

"Who did?"

"The pretty one. To make em do that to her."

"Whatever tis, she won't be doin it no more."

More laughter.

Elly crawled to the doorway, and escaped into the hall. She stood, moved quickly to the next open doorway, and looked inside.

More cribs. Several hideously emaciated girls were sitting up, yelling and gesticulating at one another. Their wrists were chained to the bars of their cribs.

Elly looked behind them toward a row of windows, but there were no cribs sitting beneath them. She was about to try another room, when something about the figure in a nearby crib arrested her attention.

She lay on her side, facing Elly. Skeletal arms folded like the wings of a bird, knees to her chest. Eyes glassy and unseeing. Deep-set eyes in a face so emaciated it was all but unrecognizable. Eyes with only a whisper of their former beauty.

The mattress near her mouth shiny and damp.

Elly's own eyes filled with tears. She knelt so that their faces were level and gazed at her friend through the bars of her crib. Her wrists were unchained, for it was obvious she could hardly move at all. Her eyes stared back at Elly for a long time, looking through her as if she weren't even there. Then they seemed to focus. But Drooly must have still thought Elly only a dream, because she just looked sad. Then suddenly she blinked several times, her eyes widened, her mouth jerked open and closed. In a voice scratchy from disuse, she croaked: "Maw!"

Elly gave a tiny nod.

Drooly grimaced a sort of smile. They were both crying. Elly put her hand through the bars and touched her friend's damp cheek.

Footsteps in the hallway. Elly jerked her hand away and ducked beneath Drooly's crib. Kathleen entered again carrying her basket, and began changing sheets. When she got to the back of the room Elly made a crab-like dash for the door. At the threshold she turned and waved at Drooly—Drooly twitched feebly in reply—and ran back into the hallway.

The next room was much quieter than the others. The girls all lay supine in their cage-like cribs. One of them buzzed her lips, another moaned.

At the back of the room, one of the cribs had been moved close to a window.

Elly walked toward it, her heart pounding.

Hattie lay on her back, gazing at the blue October sky. A bright, cloudless blue, already whispering of winter. One of her wrists was chained to the iron bars of her crib. Her pretty auburn hair was plastered to her forehead in greasy ringlets, and her face already looked thinner. But she still seemed much like herself, and Elly felt a pang of hope.

She leaned farther over.

Hattie's pretty eyes blinked, then slowly settled on Elly's face. They were the same chill blue as the October sky. Elly dared to look directly into them. A vague smile pulled at the corners of Hattie's mouth. Elly tried nodding at her. Hattie's eyes flickered, her brow furrowed as though in perplexity. There was a shiny spot on one of her temples, as if she had been burned, and on the opposite side of her head, a curious indentation, like a tiny belly-button.

Elly felt her eyes burning. Her lips began to move.

"Hattie," she whispered.

Hattie stared at her. A single tear dribbled from the corner of one eye. She blinked it away. Then her eyes shifted, and she returned to staring serenely at the sky.

"Bejesus! How the devil—"

Cora froze in the doorway—then strode quickly toward Elly. Elly ran a zig-zag course, ducking under cribs, and made it as far as the door—only to be nabbed by Kathleen.

"Fookin hell," she said, squeezing Elly's arm in a hard grip. "Ain't she one of the ones—"

"In the laundry, she must've snuck through the door."

They marched her to the door she'd "snuck" through. Kathleen knelt and looked hard at her. Elly stared at the floor.

"Look, I don't know what possessed yer to sneak in here. But yez better not try it again—"

"Unless yez wantin to stay," put in Cora, with a cackle.

"Right. Cause if Miss Pitts ever knew you got in here, well she'd turn yez into a turnip and double quick. Do you hear?"

Elly set her lip stubbornly.

"She's touched," suggested Cora.

"They're all touched," sighed Kathleen. "All right then"—she opened the door and swatted Elly's behind—"off with ya."

"I'd run, I was you," added Cora.

Elly ran.

·   ·   ·

The days preceding the examiners' arrival were colored by the same feverish scrubbing, prettifying, and superficial improvements as the previous year. The girls endured another dousing in kerosene and were given shiny, stiff new boots. Another gang of Chinamen—perhaps the same ones?—repaired the building's brickwork. And the elite girls, who would testify to the success of Phelps's treatments, were provided with expensive frocks. Though it seemed they would not be attending the private dinner.

Elly overheard Miss Pitts and Dr. Phelps discussing their reasons for this decision when they met again in Miss Bland's apartment to choose the program she would be playing. Luckily Miss Bland knew the songs Elly especially liked, and insisted they include her favorite Mozart sonata, as well as a medley of Stephen Foster tunes.

"But don't you think," Miss Pitts had suggested, "we might invite Miss Unsworth and Miss Poundstone to the dinner as well? They are both so much improved."

"Oh, I think not," drawled Phelps. "I may have excavated the real Miss Poundstone from underneath a bizarre and crippling fixation on a dead cat. But the real Priscilla Poundstone is an insipid wallflower. And *you* may be willing to trust that Lucy Unsworth won't take it in her head to call Deacon Diddy a witless, antediluvian—"

"Yes yes," Miss Pitts had hastily agreed, "I take your point."

So it was Elly alone who would be rewarded for her playing by dining with them.

On the appointed day, the examiners arrived in the antique carriage (which Henry polished once a year for the purpose, and drove himself, attired in an equally antique suit of livery), and made their grand entrance into the dayroom. It gave Elly a peculiar feeling to see the two deacons again, dressed in the same sober black suits, and Mr. Fisk in the identical gray serge. As if she'd only blinked her eyes, and a year had gone by.

At once, Dr. Phelps directed them to the group of preening, expensively-dressed girls clustered around Amelia. Elly looked up from Mr. Hoppy and peered at them from across the room.

"My prize specimens, these," he exulted. "I have taken the liberty of having copies made of the diagnoses with which they arrived here"—he pulled some papers from a briefcase and passed them around—"and it should be quite clear, the enormous improvements—"

"Oh, if you'd only seen poor Miss Poundstone when she first arrived," said Miss Pitts, reaching out to stroke Priscilla's cheek. "Weeping, weeping the live long day."

Priscilla flinched and chewed her lip.

Mr. Fisk looked rapidly from the page he was reading, to Priscilla's face, then back again.

"Most impressive," he murmured.

"And how do you feel, my dear?" enquired Deacon Radcliffe in his deep, fruity voice.

Priscilla grimaced. "Fine."

"This one looks to be in particularly splendid form!" enthused Deacon Diddy, bestowing on Amelia a kindly leer.

"Oh, but she's not one of us," said Lucy Unsworth. "She's only getting a 'talking cure.'" Her eyes flashed.

"How's that?" said Fisk.

"A different sort of case," said Phelps lightly. "More a psychological than a neurological problem."

It occurred to Elly that Amelia never talked about her sessions with Dr. Phelps anymore. But she must have looked forward to them, for she always did her hair with special care on the days they met.

Deacon Radcliffe was reading one of the files with close attention, and nodding gravely.

"But as you say, she's made splendid progress," agreed Phelps. He gave Amelia's shoulder a squeeze, and a curious look flashed between them. It reminded Elly of the way her parents would glance at one another backstage just before the curtain rose.

Deacon Radcliffe peered at Lucy Unsworth. "And what was this young lady's complaint?"

Miss Pitts cleared her throat. "Miss Unsworth—"

"But I had no complaint," said Lucy brightly. "It was other people complaining about *me*."

"Yes?" said Fisk. "And why is that?"

"Because I liked to tell rude lies about them."

"But," said Miss Pitts quickly, "that was before! And now—"

"—they still complain about me," finished Lucy. "But now it's because I tell the truth." She smiled sweetly.

Deacon Radcliffe seemed to recoil.

"A rare gift," mused Mr. Fisk. "But somewhat of a social liability."

They spent a perfunctory minute with the rest of the girls, then left. Elly guessed they would make straight for the second floor, lingering where Phelps gave his soon-to-be-famous treatments, then pay the briefest possible visit to the imbeciles. Just as in the previous year, the girls in the dayroom spent an interminable hour tormented by the savory aromas wafting through the building, before the Bruiser finally marched them off to dinner (a dinner in which the girls in steerage would for once sample first class fare), while Elly was led off to be changed into her finery.

The same Mrs. Faircroft had sewn her a new satin frock of a different fruitish hue, this time peach instead of apricot. Meg dressed her, chatting in a friendly way (which suggested rumors of Elly's talents were circulating among the staff), then led her to the same parlor as the year before.

That morning Miss Bland had watched in a blither of apprehension as Henry, Mr. Wong, and two other Chinamen carried her precious piano downstairs, and the room had been rearranged into a tiny concert hall. Patty, the same Irish maid as the previous year, entered with a tray full of *hors d'oeuvres*—this time buttery crackers adorned with a variety of tempting toppings—and set them on a sideboard. Elly could not take her eyes off them.

"I heard ya playin this morning," said Patty. Her normally pinched features softened. "Uncommon sweet, it was." She followed Elly's eyes. "Ya want to eat a few now? I'll move em around after, they'll never know."

Elly remembered the admonishments of the previous year, and savored both the fruits of her new fame—and several of the delectable morsels. Patty brought out a second platter, took a few from that, laid them on the first tray, and rearranged them all. She grinned conspiratorially at Elly, said "Good luck!" and ran off.

The distant thunder of boots—the girls' dinner was over. A minute later her audience filed in.

"…and as we mentioned, there's a special surprise in store for you all!" trilled Miss Pitts, as she ushered the deacons into the room. Miss Bland leaned precariously on Deacon Diddy's arm. Dr. Phelps and Mr. Fisk trailed behind.

Elly dropped her eyes to her doll, and listened.

DEACON RADCLIFFE: *(jovially)* Why, it's the girl who recited to us by memory! So, are we to hear more of Alice's adventures? *(the question tinged with a certain disappointment)*

PHELPS: Gentlemen, you are about to hear something truly extraordinary. For we have discovered the girl's gifts extend in other directions.

FISK: *(presumably taking in the piano)* Musical gifts, am I to infer?

MISS PITTS: Oh, the child is a prodigy! Whose talent Hazel contrived to keep a secret, for some silly reason.

MISS BLAND: But…I'm sure I never meant…I wasn't trying to…

MISS PITTS: *(gaily) Tut tut,* you can't deny it!

PHELPS: The girl can play anything one puts before her. At sight.

DEACON RADCLIFFE: I must say, that seems rather hard to believe.

MISS BLAND: *(wistfully)* We were just so happy, the two of us…

DEACON RADCLIFFE: Though I suppose, if the music were simple enough—

PHELPS: I tell you, the most difficult stuff. Limited only by the size of her hands.

FISK: *(leafing through the music atop the piano)* We are to test her, then?

MISS PITTS: First she shall play a short recital, then you may all choose any piece you would like her to play.

DEACON DIDDY: Am I to understand this child plays the piano?

(Miss Bland laughs as if he has made a joke.)

DEACON RADCLIFFE: *(sitting heavily in the chair nearest the trays of* hors d'oeuvres*)* Well, if there is to be a recital, I suggest we begin!

The others found their seats. Miss Bland led Elly to the piano, and gently turned her around to face her audience. Condescending applause, during which Elly studied the carpet. Indulgent chuckles as she laid Mr. Hoppy on the piano bench and sat down beside him.

Deacon Radcliffe began loudly munching crackers.

Elly frowned—and attacked the fifth Hungarian rhapsody of Brahms. It was one of the most difficult pieces in Miss Bland's collection, and (despite the old lady's inability to conduct in time) she had somehow managed to impart, with her wild elixir-fueled gyrations, something of the music's gypsy spirit. Elly exulted in its taxing physicality. Indeed she felt herself possessed by it, her body flung gymnastically around by notes that needed, *demanded* to be played.

The last three brutal chords. But for the sound of her own panting, the room was briefly silent—then filled with more applause than six people seemed capable of producing. The noise was powerfully evocative of Elly's previous life, and, like the professional she was, she rose to the occasion; her medley of Foster tunes was inspired, the lovely variations of the Mozart sonata in A major sparkled, and by the time she stormed to the finish of the "Rondo alla Turca," she knew she had (as her father would have said) "wowed them."

A minute later her audience was clustered around the piano, testing the assertion that she could play anything at sight. But she was in a transcendent mood, and nothing was beyond her powers.

"Astounding," murmured the usually-reserved Fisk, after she raced through the particularly difficult "Spinning Song" of Mendelssohn. "The girl is truly a phenomenon."

"Ah," said Deacon Diddy, with a crafty air, "but can she play *this!*"

It was a simple song called "Flow Gently Sweet Afton," which Elly tossed off as easily as scratching her nose.

"Incredible," muttered Diddy.

At the concert's conclusion there was no end of fuss. Deacon Radcliffe made Elly sit on his knee (an indignity he made endurable by stuffing her with *hors d'oeuvres*) and they all drank wine and speculated about her.

"But it's obvious the girl could be on the stage," said Fisk. "Such freakish ability is truly rare."

"Our thoughts exactly!" gushed Miss Pitts. "People would *pay* to hear her!"

"Perhaps she could be taught to whistle while she plays," mused Deacon Diddy. "Now that would *really* be something…"

Elly again felt an urge to just open her mouth and tell them who she was; it was like a balloon swelling inside her and longing to burst into words. But the idea was still terrifying. And besides, her mouth was full of crackers.

"Beggin your pardon," said Patty shyly, "dinner is served."

●   ●   ●

The same elaborate dinner setting. This time Elly found herself sitting between the two deacons. Miss Bland sat on the other side of Deacon Diddy, and Miss Pitts beside Deacon Radcliffe. Dr. Phelps and Mr. Fisk sat across from Elly.

It turned out to be a good thing she was already stuffed with *hors d'oeuvres*, because the salad had been rendered inedible by some sort of blueish cheese that smelt of old socks, and the main course ruined by something Miss Pitts called "onion gravy." Elly was forced to use a portion of her precious mashed potatoes to dam off the offending sludge before she could sculpt the pitifully small remainder into a perfect circle. This she dispatched in a few bites, then sat, staring at Mr. Hoppy in her lap.

And listened.

(Sounds of contented eating)
FISK: Absolutely delicious.
MISS PITTS: I'm so glad.
PHELPS: I have to agree, Wong has outdone himself.
DEACON RADCLIFFE: *(smacking his lips)* Ambrosial. The food of the gods!
DEACON DIDDY: Wasn't that the name of one of Wagner's operas— *The Food of the Gods*?
(Phelps snorts.)
FISK: I believe you are referring to *Götterdämmerung— The Twilight of the Gods.*
DEACON RADCLIFFE: Last year you told us you attended Bayreuth, Doctor. Did you ever—?
PHELPS: Oh of course, I saw the entire cycle. Twice. Spectacular! And the "magic fire" effect—truly stunning!

Done electrically, of course. In fact all of the theater's stage mechanisms have been converted to take advantage of the latest electrical technology—

FISK: *(musingly)* Something to those old myths, you know. The burning of Valhalla—the gods themselves undone by their own hubris. Reminds one that it was electricity that enabled Dr. Frankenstein to animate his monster.

PHELPS: *(lightly)* Are you implying my new technique is another case of man meddling where he ought not?

FISK: Not at all. In fact, Doctor, I think we can all agree, your results this year have been powerfully persuasive.

DEACON RADCLIFFE: Hear hear.

MISS PITTS: *(eagerly)* I think it's time we presented them with our plan, don't you Edgar?

PHELPS: I do. What we've been thinking of—you see, we have in mind a large expansion…

(Even with her eyes cast down, Elly can tell he has abandoned his relaxed sprawl and is leaning forward, making impassioned motions with his hands, as he outlines a bold plan to devote the institution entirely to his new treatments. Miss Pitts interjects excited predictions regarding the revenue they would thus generate. Deacon Radcliffe rumbles his approval. Patty is clearing away the dinner plates. On the other side of Elly, Deacon Diddy fidgets, and suddenly interrupts Phelps's spiel.)

DEACON DIDDY: Say, whatever became of that other girl?

PHELPS: *(nonplussed)* Other girl?

DEACON DIDDY: She was so very charming! The one that sat next to me last year…

MISS PITTS: *(brightly)* Oh, but aren't you finding Miss Smith an equally charming dinner companion, Deacon?

DEACON DIDDY: *(considers Elly doubtfully)* Well, to be sure, but…

DEACON RADCLIFFE: Wait, I remember her! What was her name, Hannah?

FISK: Hattie, I think it was. Hattie Limburg.

MISS PITTS: Such a memory, Mr. Fisk! And such a happy
    ending for Miss Limburg. You see, when her parents
    received the news of her recovery, they happened to be on
    a round-the-world cruise. They'd just arrived in—Edgar,
    where was it they had just arrived?

PHELPS: Where was it? *(He takes a sip of wine.)* Malta, I
    believe it was.

MISS PITTS: Malta! And they were so eager to see her again,
    they sailed straight home on the first available ship—

DEACON RADCLIFFE:—to be reunited with their
    daughter! What a wonderful story.

*(Elly peers up from her doll at Miss Bland. The old lady is
staring blankly into space.)*

DEACON DIDDY: Such a joyous reunion it must have been!

(Elly finds her mouth forming a word—but no sound emerges.)

DEACON RADCLIFFE: And another feather in your cap,
    Doctor.

(Again Elly's mouth moves, and this time she whispers aloud):
No.

(An astonished silence)

DEACON RADCLIFFE: Did she—did the child speak?

FISK: I believe—I believe she did!

*(Another silence. Elly feels them all staring at her. She gazes
into Mr. Hoppy's button eyes. And, as though telling him the
story, says, in a small, clear voice):* Hattie's parents never came
for her. Because they're both dead.

DEACON RADCLIFFE: What in God's name…

MISS PITTS: Why, the child is spouting nonsense—

(Several people begin talking at once.)

FISK: Will you all please be silent and let the child SPEAK!
    (He himself speaks with such uncharacteristic vehemence,

they all fall silent.) Now, Miss Smith, what is it you were
    saying?

ELLY: *(staring hard at Mr. Hoppy and gathering her courage)*
    She's...she's not gone. She's still here—

PHELPS: Why, it's clear—well it's absolutely clear, isn't it? The
    child is undergoing a psychotic event—

FISK: Doctor, will you PLEASE be quiet and—

MISS PITTS: Really now, you are foolish if you put any
    store—

(They are all startled into silence by a loud, bleating noise.)

MISS BLAND: *(through her sobs)* No no no...she's
    right...she's telling the truth!

(Another shocked silence.)

DEACON RADCLIFFE: Hazel, what on earth—do you mean
    to say, Miss Limburg's parents actually *are* deceased?

MISS BLAND: Yes, yes... More than two years ago. Of a
    typhus epidemic, Beulah told me.

MISS PITTS: *(sighing)* All right, yes, it's true. You understand,
    we didn't want to ruin your lovely dinner with the sad
    story. But the child is utterly deluded about Hattie still
    being here—I'm sure she wishes it were so, the two of
    them were such good friends—but after Miss Limburg was
    pronounced cured, she was released to her guardians.

MISS BLAND: But...but I can't believe—

MISS PITTS: It was only last week; I'd forgotten to tell you,
    Hazel. We'd just given her a final treatment—isn't that so,
    Edgar?

DEACON RADCLIFFE: But if she was cured, why another
    treatment?

PHELPS: A mere touch-up.

MISS BLAND: You never even let me say goodbye!

DEACON DIDDY: Rather shabby, if I may say.

(Elly has been shaking her head.)

FISK: Miss Smith does not agree with you.

PHELPS: Oh why must you continue to—?

FISK: Because so far, the child has only spoken the truth. Now, Miss Smith?

ELLY: She's still here. Because Miss Pitts… She stole Hattie's soul…and turned her into a turnip.

(Laughter—interrupted by a tremendous crash, as Patty drops a tray full of plates.)

PHELPS: *(still laughing giddily)* Well, it's clear as day now! The child is not in her right mind—

PATTY: *(in a terrified whisper)* She's tellin the *truth*! *(She busies herself cleaning up.)*

FISK: *(seriously)* So, Miss Pitts stole Hattie's soul, Miss Smith?

MISS PITTS: *(laughing along with Phelps)* You know, it's really quite simple: if Miss Limburg were still here, you gentlemen would have seen her today.

DEACON RADCLIFFE: *(chuckling with relief)* Well, of course, how silly of us!

FISK: *(imperturbable)* And what do you have to say to that, Miss Smith?

Elly raised her eyes from her doll and looked across the table at Mr. Fisk. His bland blue eyes regarded her without condescension. The dam that had blocked her speech these long months had been swept away, and her words, driven by anger and indignation, flowed freely:

"They've hidden her away. In the old nursery on the third floor."

"Such an imagination!" Miss Pitts attempted a laugh. "She really is most amusing—"

Mr. Fisk stood up. "Well. I should say it's time to pay a visit to the third floor."

Dr. Phelps slapped his hand on the table. "Oh for pity's sake—"

"If you attempt to stop me…"

Everyone began talking at once. Voices were raised and threats made. Finally Dr. Phelps flung a set of keys at Fisk with a disgusted air. Deacon Radcliffe rose to join Fisk, and looked at Deacon Diddy.

"No no, I don't feel up to climbing any stairs," said Diddy in a querulous voice. "And it's more important that I remain here to comfort poor Hazel. Who has undergone a shock—a *dreadful* shock. And been a model to us all with her brave honesty."

He patted Miss Bland's hand. Miss Bland assumed an expression of decorous sorrow.

"I should say the truly brave individual this evening has been Miss Smith," said Mr. Fisk. He met Elly's eyes, then he and Deacon Radcliffe departed.

As soon as the door closed behind them Miss Pitts turned her cold gray eyes on Elly. Elly's courage failed her, and she looked back down at her doll.

MISS PITTS: Edgar, such an incompetent imbecile you
     are—assuring me this child was catatonic! And all the
     time she's been listening to everything, the devious little—
PHELPS: Oh will you just shut up! You have only yourself to
     blame for this fiasco.
MISS PITTS: And heroic Hazel! Who would have been much
     more heroic if she could have kept her mouth shut.
DEACON DIDDY: Such language is entirely uncalled for!
     Why, I'm even beginning to get the feeling there's been
     something not quite aboveboard going on here, some sort
     of skullduggery—
*(Phelps breaks into demented-sounding laughter. Diddy's words
dry up. Patty finishes loading the broken plates on her tray and
rushes from the room. The rest of them sit in silence. The fire
crackles. Dr. Phelps guzzles wine. Finally Mr. Fisk and Deacon
Radcliffe rejoin them.)*
DEACON RADCLIFFE: What in the name of God have you
     done to that poor girl?

MISS PITTS: Well, I'm afraid it's time to confess, wouldn't you say, Edgar? You see, the poor child had a relapse after all—

PHELPS: Yes, it's true what she's saying, it was so very distressing, after how close we came—

FISK: *(wearily)* You are both lying. The terrible marks on the child's forehead are very plain—

DEACON RADCLIFFE: Appalling, utterly appalling—

FISK: —and I think I can promise you, Doctor, I shall be doing my damndest to outlaw this pernicious and unproven treatment—

PHELPS: Oh you fools!

Elly looked up, as startled as the rest, as Phelps jumped to his feet and began pacing the room.

"You myopic, small-minded, imbecilic—it wasn't me! It was HER!" He stopped and pointed an accusing finger at Miss Pitts. "SHE'S the one who did that to poor Miss Limburg! *Intentionally* misusing my treatment—"

"Oh Edgar, shame! Trying to blame *me* for your own failure—"

"—intentionally, I say! Just as—and I have only just recently learned this—she has wantonly destroyed the minds of many of the girls in the west wing, for reasons I can hardly—"

"I've done nothing but use your own techniques—"

"Destroying my good work—you gentlemen have seen what miracles I have wrought with your own eyes! But this woman is a monster, polluting my work with a perversion of my methods—"

"A *monster*?!" Miss Pitts laughed harshly. "Shall we talk, Edgar, about you and Miss van Allen?"

Phelps went pale. "Just…just what are you implying—"

"Ask him! Ask him about the unspeakable things he has been doing—"

"Beulah, my God—"

"What"—Deacon Radcliffe sputtered—"what fresh outrage is *this*?"

"—a thirteen year old girl, entrusted to his care—"

"Beulah, I command you to SHUT UP! Don't listen to her—"

"—long suspected as much"—Beulah spoke over him—"so I stood outside and listened through the door when Edgar was giving Miss van Allen her supposed 'talking cure.' Well! I can assure you, gentlemen, there was very little *talking* involved—"

"The woman is completely deranged!" cried Edgar in a hoarse voice. "You must pay no attention—"

"ENOUGH!" roared Deacon Radcliffe.

The room fell silent. Absentmindedly Radcliffe used his napkin to mop his face. For a long moment words seemed to fail him. When he finally spoke it was in a hushed voice quivering with emotion.

"Such criminal abuse of authority, such…such *filth* and *decadence* are beyond anything I have ever experienced. I think I can guarantee you both that the church will be completely withdrawing its patronage from this tainted institution." He threw his napkin on the table and rose to his feet. "I wish you a good night—and pray God has more mercy on your souls than I would!"

Still shaking his head, he strode heavily from the room.

Mr. Fisk now rose.

"And I—I shall be recommending your license be immediately revoked." The clipped tones with which he delivered this verdict had a steely finality. "In addition, I shall be contacting the families of both Miss Limburg and Miss van Allen about filing lawsuits. And should either of you ever try to move to some other state to conduct your obscene experiments and outrageous transgressions, I shall do my best to stop you."

He gazed at Dr. Phelps and Miss Pitts for a long moment. His mild blue eyes were cold as ice. Finally he turned to leave—then caught himself.

He walked around the table and knelt beside Elly.

"You are a very brave, and very talented girl. If you could please be patient for just a couple more days, I promise I shall move heaven and earth to close this place down—and set you free."

He kissed the top of her head, and left.

Deacon Diddy rose unsteadily from his chair, and gave Miss Pitts a befuddled glance.

"Yes, um, well… Thank you for the lovely dinner," he offered.

"Should you like me, Horace," murmured Miss Bland, "to walk you to the door?"

Diddy gallantly offered his arm, and the two of them tottered off.

"Well!" cried Phelps, with mad ebullience. "And how does it feel to have destroyed both of our lives—*Mother*?"

He spat the word. Miss Pitts made a guttural sound as if she had been punched in the stomach.

"Why, what's wrong?" Edgar's voice was mocking. "Don't care to be so addressed?"

"You"—Miss Pitts shook her head weakly—"you know how I hate it."

"Just as you hated *being* my mother. Oh the *shame* of it! The shame of bearing a child out of wedlock!"

"I…I did my best to raise you—"

"You did nothing of the sort, you paid *others* to raise me—"

"—footed the bills for your schooling—Groton, Harvard, nothing but the best! Always scrimping and saving—"

"Cheating, stealing, treating your charges with criminal negligence—"

"Oh Edgar, Edgar"—Miss Pitts staggered from her chair and rushed toward him—"please don't turn against me, I couldn't bear it. You're everything to me, don't you see I did everything for *you*, all for *you*—?"

He pushed her violently away and fled from the room. Miss Pitts emitted an agonized sound, the roar of a lioness that has lost her cub. Then her eye suddenly fell on Elly.

"You!" she hissed.

Elly shrank in her seat.

"If it hadn't been for *you*"—Miss Pitts began moving toward her—"yes, it was all because of YOU—"

"Beggin yer pardon, mum."

Miss Pitts whirled around. Patty stood in the doorway.

"I'm finished with my work. Shall I take the child and put her to bed?"

Miss Pitts stared at her. Patty flashed her eyes at Elly. Elly slid from her chair and raced to the girl's side.

As they left she could feel Miss Pitts's gaze burning into her back.

.   .   .

Next morning Elly endured another hair brushing from the Troll, went to breakfast, did her job, ate lunch, than sat in the dayroom. In other words, it seemed like a normal day, as though the tumultuous events of the previous evening had never occurred.

Yet things were not normal at all.

All the staff continued to go about their business. But they had a shocked air, like victims of enchantment whose spells were wearing off. At work, Meg was skittish and distracted, and Elly often felt herself being stared at. Finally Meg burst out:

"So Patty tells me yer can talk!"

Elly saw she couldn't deny it, and nodded. Then, realizing that was hardly proof (and needing to prove to herself it hadn't been a fluke), she murmured: "Yes."

Meg grinned crookedly.

"Always suspected there was more in that noodle than yer was lettin on." She rapped Elly's head affectionately with her knuckles. "But Jaysus," her face fell, "what's to become of us all now, I'd like to know…"

The two old ladies did not show for either breakfast or lunch—only the Bruiser's intimidating presence kept the meals from descending into anarchy—and by late afternoon it was clear that Miss Pitts would not be making her customary buggy ride. These disruptions of the institution's inviolable routines made the girls uneasy, and Elly overheard Amelia and her friends speculating that something must have happened the previous evening.

"Maudie would know," said Amelia, nodding toward Elly. "She was there."

"Yes, I'm sure she could tell us all about it," said Lucy sardonically (and unwittingly upholding her claim of the previous day by telling the truth).

Elly looked up from her doll and glanced at the Troll. Should she speak? The deluge of attention this would bring down on her head was a frightening prospect.

The Troll's moon of a face gazed back at her, as expressionless as ever.

And besides, what would she say? All the things she had learned were still confusing to her. The girls had all been told Hattie had been released—she would have to reveal the terrible truth. She would have to tell them the church would no longer pay for them, and their license was to be taken away. But she had no clear idea what a license was, and what would happen to them all. Mr. Fisk had promised to get Elly out—but he'd said nothing about the others.

Dr. Phelps seemed to have done something bad to Amelia. But Elly couldn't fathom what it was, and so didn't know how to tell her about it. Then there was the truly flabbergasting news that Miss Pitts and Dr. Phelps were mother and son! Which confused Elly as well: shouldn't she then be *Mrs.* Pitts? Though Elly had an inkling, gleaned from vaudeville routines and backstage gossip she had heard over the years, that things weren't quite that simple...

She was still turning all these questions over in her mind, when she suddenly realized the room had gone deathly quiet. She looked up.

Miss Pitts stood in the doorway.

She looked ten years older, her gray hair piled up haphazardly, no trace of grandmotherly concern in her haggard expression. The girls all froze in mute horror as she peered around the room. Her gray eyes burned with something like madness.

They settled on Elly.

Elly felt her blood run cold.

The Bruiser stood next to Miss Pitts. She followed the old woman's eyes and grinned.

Miss Pitts gave a curt nod, and the Bruiser started for Elly.

By the time Elly jumped to her feet, the big woman was already advancing with her arms wide, cackling. Elly tried to dart to one side. The Bruiser swiped at her and snatched Mr. Hoppy from her arms. Elly shrieked and grabbed at him. The Bruiser held him out of reach, then waved him enticingly.

"Here he ish, here he ish!" she crooned. "Ya shwant him, ya gotsh ta get him!"

Elly made a great leap and grabbed her doll, and the Bruiser clamped a meaty hand around her arm. The girls in the room were all shrieking. Miss Pitts shouted something—

The Bruiser pitched forward and fell on her face.

Elly was thrown clear. She looked up in amazement. The Troll had pulled the Bruiser's legs out from under her and climbed onto her back. The big woman tried to get to her knees but the Troll lifted her fat rump and drove her back into the floor. She reached forward and grabbed the Bruiser's long braids. Grinning savagely, she yanked the big woman's head back—then shoved it into the floor.

The girls in the room were all shrieking, the moaners and shufflers dancing around. The Troll gave another vicious yank on the Bruiser's head—blood streamed from her nose, Elly heard something crack—then drove it into the floor again. The big woman lay still. One of the shufflers ran up, kicked at her inert form, danced away shrieking, then came back for another go. Others began to join in…

A minute later one of the maids began frantically herding all the girls from the room. Elly cast a last look over her shoulder. The Troll was still perched atop the Bruiser's motionless body, grinning and pounding her bloody face into the floor. Henry and Mr. Wong, directed by Miss Pitts, were warily circling her.

They were given a cold supper and put to bed early. Elly lay under her blankets, hugging poor Mr. Hoppy and fingering what had flown out

Grinning savagely,
she yanked the
big woman's head back.

of the Bruiser's pocket when she fell. Something very precious that, unnoticed in all the excitement, Elly had managed to snatch up and put in her own pocket. She ran her fingers over them again and again, in wonder:

Keys.

Chapter Fourteen

Escape

She woke up suddenly, and looked out the window. The skies were clear, and a friendly moon smiled down on the mountains. From its position, she guessed it was near dawn.

The previous evening she had lain awake a long time, fingering the keys, trying to decide what to do. She did not doubt that Mr. Fisk would fulfill his promise to "move heaven and earth" to get her out of this place. But even though the Troll had thwarted Miss Pitts's plans, her bed was empty, and Elly suspected she had suffered the fate meant for Elly herself—a fate that filled Elly with horror. What the Troll did to Frieda Klee could only have intensified Miss Pitts's thirst for revenge. Perhaps she herself would snatch Elly up that very morning?

Now, as the sky behind the mountains glowed with the promise of another day, Elly realized the decision had been made for her:

It was time to escape.

Still, to set off all alone was a terrifying thing. Without the moon's cheerful presence she would never have had the courage to do all the things she was doing now: to get dressed, pull the sheet from her bed, grab Mr. Hoppy, creep past the row of sleeping girls, then past Mrs. Wong, slumped at her post. Then down the hallway, through the dining room, and into the kitchen.

The grease-stained windows let in barely enough light to find the knife she needed to hack her hair off. This turned out to be a difficult and painful operation, rendered even more awful by the kitchen's dark shadows, and the thought that any minute now—for it was beginning to lighten outside—Mr. Wong might burst in to begin preparing breakfast. But by twisting her hair into tight plaits and sawing at them determinedly, she at last succeeded.

She hid the severed tresses behind the stove, grabbed a loaf of bread along with the knife, and made her way back through the dining room and down the hall to the back door. Coats hung from pegs on the wall for the girls to wear outside. She chose one that fit, along with a couple pairs of leggings from a pile in the corner. She pulled on one pair and wrapped the other—along with the bread, knife, and Mr. Hoppy—in the sheet she had taken from her bed and tied it all up in a bundle.

Hobos carried their bundles over their shoulders on the end of sticks. It somehow seemed an important part of her disguise, and she ran out the back door into the exercise yard. The sun was already peeping up over the mountains and making the frost on the ground glisten, and she was terrified someone would look out a window and spot her. She found a stick the girls used in their play, rushed back inside, and tied the bundle to the end of it. With her hair cut off, her ears had been cold outside. She found a shapeless cap in the pile of clothes and pulled it on.

She crept to the front door, set her bundle down, pulled the keys from the pocket of her frock and, her heart beating fast, began to try them. There were six of them. She went through them all—and none of them worked. Frantically she tried them again, jiggling them harder, terrified of the noise she was making—when a hand suddenly clamped around her wrist.

She looked up into the face of Mr. Wong.

He took the keys from her hand, then pulled the cap from her head. At the sight of her hacked-off hair, his eyebrows shot up. Finally he examined the things in her bundle. He found the loaf of bread and knife, and stared hard at her.

Elly cast her eyes down miserably.

He grabbed her hand and pulled her down the hall. She thought he was taking her to Miss Pitts, and was confused when he led her instead through the dining hall and back into the kitchen. He set the loaf of bread on a counter and, using the knife she had stolen, cut it into thick slices. From a larder he pulled out a block of cheese and a ham; Elly recognized them as toppings to the previous evening's *hors d'oeuvres*. He sliced them with the knife and made up four thick sandwiches. He found a jar of mustard and showed it to her with raised eyebrows. She shook her head, and he put it away. Finally he wrapped the sandwiches in waxed paper, used another piece of paper to wrap up a handful of peppermint sticks, and put everything back in the bundle. At the last minute he held up the knife, shrugged, wiped it off, wrapped it an old dishcloth, and put it in with the rest of the things.

Holding his finger to his lips, he led her back to the front door. He managed to get it unlocked and opened it for her.

Elly looked up at him. Looked, for the very first time, directly into his eyes.

"Thank you," she whispered.

Mr. Wong's smooth face wrinkled into a toothy grin. He nodded, gave her shoulder a squeeze, and shut the door behind her.

She put the bundle over her shoulder, began to walk quickly away, and was just breaking into a run when the barn door swung open and Henry emerged.

He stopped, blinked, then walked to where she stood rooted to the ground. He looked down at her with his expressionless face.

"You runnin away?" he said finally.

She nodded.

Somewhere a rooster crowed. Henry looked off into the distance, lifted his hat, and scratched his head. Finally he replaced his hat and fished in his pocket.

"Here," he said. He put something in her hand. She opened it and discovered a shiny silver dollar.

When she looked up again, he was walking away.

~

She turned in the same direction that Miss Pitts always drove into town. The rutted dirt track was lined with bare trees and ran parallel to the distant mountain range. After a few minutes, she saw a cloud of dust coming toward her. She ran to the side of the road and crouched behind a clump of weeds. A wagon loaded with bales of sweet-smelling hay rumbled past.

She got up and continued on, glancing behind herself now and then. She was fearful of long stretches of road where she might be easily spotted, and kept an eye open for places to hide. But there was little traffic on the road. She passed a ramshackle farm, warily watching for signs of life. A big dog suddenly appeared, streaking toward her, woofing excitedly. Terrified, she swung her stick at it—and the bundle flew off. Smelling the sandwiches, the dog snatched it up. Mr. Hoppy's desperate plight gave Elly sudden courage, and she swung the stick at the dog's hindquarters with all her strength. It dropped the bundle and limped off, yelping.

She retrieved her bundle and continued down the road. The sun had grown warm, so she took off her cap and leggings and stowed them inside the bundle. She wanted to take off her coat as well, but dared not expose the striped frock of the asylum. Her shoulders were terribly sore—carrying loads hobo-style had turned out to be hard work—so she decided to eat one of the thick sandwiches.

She had just pulled it from her bundle when she realized the dog had followed her. It sat a few yards away, watching her with a look of wounded indignation—which changed to keen interest when she unwrapped the sandwich. She tore the sandwich in half and tossed part of it to the dog. The animal devoured it with frightening speed. She began walking away again, but the dog followed her, eager for more. To make it go away, she fed it the rest of the sandwich in her hand. The dog swallowed it in one gulp but refused to leave. Desperate now to be rid of the beast, which really was quite big and scary, she had no choice but to feed it the other three sandwiches. The dog made short work of them all. Finally she gave it all the peppermint sticks. The animal crunched them up like bones, then looked up expectantly.

"That's all," she said, and rather crossly, because it was.

The dog must have divined the truth of this statement, because it trotted back home.

~

The road crossed a small stream, which Elly guessed must be flowing down from the mountains in the distance. She was terribly thirsty, so she left the road, clambered down beside the wooden bridge, squatted next to the clear, burbling water, and cupped her hands to drink. The water was heavenly but astonishingly cold, and she wished she had brought a tin cup.

She had just climbed back up to the road when she heard fast hoof beats. She threw herself behind some bushes and peeked through the leaves. An instant later Miss Pitts flashed by in her buggy, lashing the horse with her whip. Henry sat behind her.

Then they were gone.

She sat a long time, her heart beating violently. Beyond the stream, a road branched off toward the mountains, where Miss Pitts would never find her. For a moment she was tempted—then, far in the distance in the direction of the town, she heard the sound of a train whistle.

It seemed like a sign, because if she was going to be a hobo, she needed to find a train. She remembered the time her father had pointed to a group of ragged, dirty-looking men running furtively between the cars of a freight train sidled next to them at some station.

"Hoboes," he had said. "Ah, that's the life! No practicing, no mercenary managers, no worries—"

"And no money," her mother had dryly added.

So she continued on toward Marysville. She had picked up another stick to defend herself against the dogs that continued to bark and chase after her at the farmhouses she passed. But these were as infrequent as the traffic on the road. Her mind began to float, her thoughts circling around themselves like the hawk soaring in the distance.

She thought about poor Drooly and Hattie. She had grown fond of Miss Bland (even if the old lady hardly ever shared her chocolates) and wished she'd been able to say goodbye to her. She thought about Albert Jenning, and Smiley Hobson, and Esta and Molly. But most of all she thought about her parents, and wondered how in the world she would ever find them.

There had been a very troubling conversation soon after Amelia had arrived. Elly had been induced by Hattie to show off her memory of *Through the Looking Glass*. Amelia had followed along with the book, her eyes widening with amazement, until she finally interrupted:

"Why Ah do declare, with a brain like that, why ever is she in this place?"

"They found her in San Francisco," Hattie replied.

Elly stopped reciting and stared at her doll, listening.

"San Francisco! Was she in the earthquake?"

"I think so." Hattie dropped her voice to a whisper: "I heard Miss Pitts say she's an orphan."

"An *orphan*!" Amelia had whispered back. A silence, during which Elly imagined the two of them exchanging meaningful glances. Then Hattie (who still had no idea she was an orphan herself) had brightly suggested Elly recite some more from the book. But she had refused. In fact, it was the last time she ever told the story.

Elly had only vague ideas about earthquakes. But she knew that if you were an orphan, it meant your parents were dead. Surely she would remember anything so terrible and momentous!

But she didn't. She did remember San Francisco. Remembered Mr. Barnhold's animals running around crazily during their act, and a wonderful party with Molly and Bret Crawley, and a man singing very loudly while Elly played the piano, and people dancing. But mixed in with all this were terrible memories of Mr. Barnhold staring at her with his bulging eyes, and cattle stampeding down a street. Memories she had decided were only dreams, just like all the other terrible dreams she often had of buildings crumbling and horses swallowed up by the earth and fire all around her…

Only now, as she trudged down the road, unsure of where she was going or what would happen to her next—only now did it occur to her those might not have been dreams.

The traffic began to increase—carriages, wagons, people on horseback—and she was increasingly forced to hide by the side of the road. She saw Miss Pitts and Henry returning, Miss Pitts lashing the horse more furiously than ever. In the distance she saw church steeples and knew the town was up ahead. To walk through it, she would have to show herself. And realized that—despite her bundle and hacked-off hair—the striped asylum frock peeping out from below the hem of her coat rendered her hobo disguise pathetically inadequate.

Behind the next farmhouse, she caught a glimpse of clothes hanging on a line and decided her situation justified desperate action. She crept around the side of the house (luckily there were no dogs) and saw, hanging between a man's shirt and an enormous pair of lady's bloomers, a pair of boy's overalls. She hid behind some bushes and watched the rear windows of the farmhouse for signs of life. Finally she screwed up her courage, darted from her hiding place, and snatched the overalls from the line.

Back behind the bushes, she stripped off her coat and frock, pulled the still-damp overalls on, and found that, with the cuffs rolled up, they fit well enough. But she needed a shirt to wear underneath them and was forced to return and pull one off the line. While she was at it, she grabbed two pairs of socks and an undershirt. All the time her eyes were darting back toward the farmhouse—and now she noticed that, sometime during the last few minutes, a pie had materialized on a window sill. Feeling recklessly brave (and terrifically hungry), she snatched it as well, wrapping it in the clothes she had just taken, because it was still hot.

She raced back behind the bushes, put on the shirt, wrapped everything up in the bundle, swung the heavy load over her shoulder, and was creeping back along the side of the house when she was suddenly overwhelmed by the wrongness of everything she had just done.

She reached into the bundle, pulled the silver dollar Henry had given her out of her coat pocket, and ran back and left it on the window ledge.

After only a few minutes of walking, the pie's aroma overcame her, and she squatted by the side of the road and burned her fingers and tongue on what turned out to be a blackberry pie—and the most delicious thing,

Elly decided, she had ever eaten. She ate half of it, staining her hands and the front of her overalls, and wrapped the rest of it in her frock to keep from staining the other things in her bundle, for a purple frog would never do.

In her new overalls, Elly felt disguised enough to risk staying on the road and letting the traffic pass her by; to her relief no one gave her a second glance. The asylum, where she had been locked away for more than a year, had been a sort of prison; for the first time she allowed herself to savor the taste of freedom. She looked with interest at the signs of the approaching town: a shop where carriages were repaired, advertising "Finest Workmanship, Lowest Prices"; a liquor wholesaler, selling "Spirits by the Barrel"; an unpainted wooden building leaning at an angle with the crude hand-lettered sign, "Church of Holy Redemshun."

She began to see people. A trio of old men sat on a bench outside a general store. An ugly dog with hair missing in patches jumped off the front steps and began sniffing at her bundle. She chased it away with her stick. One of the old men said something and the others laughed.

She passed two tiny, half-naked boys squatting in the dirt in front of a broken-down shack and arranging stones in a circle. They swiveled their heads as she walked past. One of them threw a stone at her, and they snickered.

The houses began to be bigger and better cared for, there were trees, a wooden sidewalk—and suddenly she was in the town. Two girls about her age walked toward her, carrying books, and she realized school must have just let out. They stopped and stared at her, then burst into laughter.

"What—what is it?" shrieked one.

"Lookit that haircut!" cried the other.

"I seen dogs with better haircuts 'n that!"

Elly hurried away from their jeering voices. Up ahead, more children were approaching. Desperate now to avoid them, she turned down an alley. Passing by a window, she looked at her reflection—and saw her hair indeed stuck out in all directions. She tried to pat it down, but it stubbornly resisted taming.

She sat down, leaned against the house, took off her ill-fitting boots, and rubbed her throbbing feet. She was tired and thirsty, and there was nowhere in the wide world she belonged. She laid her head on her knees and wept.

·　　　·　　　·

Someone kicked her foot. She realized she'd been asleep.

"Hey."

A boy her age, in short pants and stockings with holes in them, stood staring down at her. The sun was almost gone, the alley in deep shadow.

"Hey, whatchoo doin here?"

Elly avoided his eyes and said nothing.

The boy pointed to her bundle. "You runnin away from home or sumpin?"

She nodded.

"Whatchoo got in there?" he said, squatting down and fingering her bundle.

Elly's tongue was still rusty from disuse. "Pie," she finally answered.

"Gimme some that pie."

She untied the bundle and unwrapped the pie. The boy began greedily scooping out the filling with his fingers. Elly looked at Mr. Hoppy and realized he needed to be petted. The boy finished all the pie and licked his fingers.

"What's that?" he said.

"Mr. Hoppy."

"Lemme see him."

"No," said Elly, hugging Mr. Hoppy close.

"Yer a pansy," sneered the boy.

Somewhere a voice called, "Clyde, supper!"

The boy stood up. "I'm gonna tell on you," he said, grinning. "Gonna tell on you runnin away from home, just see if I don't!"

He disappeared around the corner of the house. Frantically Elly pulled on her boots, retied her bundle, and hurried away.

She turned randomly from street to street trying to lose herself, and became lost in the process. She passed by a window on the side of a house and stopped, transfixed by the cozy, lamplit scene of a family eating dinner. A pretty girl with a big bow in her hair was watching her father carve a roast. A baby in a high chair kicked its legs as its mother fed it. The girl said something that made her father laugh.

Elly felt tears coming to her eyes. How she longed to be that girl! The father was now putting a slice of meat on her plate, and Elly realized how hungry she was. Why had she let that boy eat all her pie? How she hated him! She trudged away, walking aimlessly now. It had become cold, and she was pulling her coat from her bundle, when she suddenly became aware of a deep rumble that made the very earth tremble.

The sensation touched something deep inside her, and she was filled with terror—which changed an instant later to fresh hope:

A train.

She threw on her coat and began to run, chasing the sound—and there, at the end of another alley, she saw the cars of a freight train winking rhythmically past, one by one. She ran down the alley as fast as she could, thinking she might jump on the train, for that's what hoboes did. But before she could reach it, the caboose had gone by.

The train had been slowing down, and she walked along the tracks in the direction it had disappeared. She stepped from tie to tie, counting them as she strode along. By the time she reached two thousand, she found herself amidst lamplit streets and the backs of tall brick buildings. In the distance, she saw the caboose of the train, and beyond that, what looked like a station. Miscellaneous train cars were parked on several other tracks. A man was walking toward her swinging a lantern.

She started walking toward him when she heard a low whistle. She turned and saw a dark figure crouching in front of a shack by the side of the tracks and waving its arms at her.

"*Psst!* Kid! Over here!"

She stepped off the tracks but was afraid to go any closer.

"C'mon, ya dope—afore he lays his peepers on yez!"

She walked a few more steps. A hand shot out, pulled her roughly down, and covered her mouth. They lay still as the man with the lantern went by. Finally, the person who had pulled her down released her and let out a long breath.

"Holy jumpin turnips, don't ya got no brains at all? This burg's hostile. Pete says the dick's the meanest ol devil ever went without a tail."

"What's the rumpus?" came a voice from inside the shack.

"Aw, some kid bout got us pinched."

"Well haul him in here, we'll give him a souvenir to remember us by."

Elly was pushed roughly into the shack, which smelled of mold and pee and unwashed bodies. A match was struck, lighting up a lizard-faced man with a hand-rolled cigarette between his thin lips. He eyed her from beneath the brim of a misshapen hat as he lit his cigarette.

"Goddamn, Jimmy. You caught yerself a tadpole."

"Haw! Reckon I oughter throw him back?"

By the match's light, Elly saw that the man who had grabbed her was really just a boy with a leather patch over one eye. An older man with white stubble on his chin sat on the ground leaning against the wall, clutching himself and shaking. The match went out, and all three of them became vague shapes.

The old man let out a moan.

"Don't mind him," said the lizard-faced man. "Got hisself a case of the snakes."

The boy named Jimmy was still holding Elly and studying her in the dim light. "Damn Pete, I've et chicken legs fatter 'n this kid's arm."

Pete sucked on his cigarette, making the tip glow.

"Kid, jus how old are ya?"

"Eight," said Elly.

"Holy jumpin turnips!" said Jimmy, laughing.

"So what happen," said Pete, "lose yer punkgrafter?"

Elly stared at him.

"You know," said Jimmy, "yer jocker. Like Pete here's my jocker. I mean, ain't yer got no one t'watch out fer yez?"

Elly shook her head. She saw the two exchange a look. The old man moaned again.

"Whatcha got in this here bundle?" said Jimmy, squeezing it.

"Clothes," said Elly. She pulled the bundle close, worried about Mr. Hoppy.

"So what they call ya?" asked Pete.

Elly had been thinking someone would ask her this and had settled on a name.

"Albert," she said.

Jimmy snickered.

"Well now, Bert," said Pete, "it looks to me like yer jus startin out. Maybe runnin away from home, thought you'd try a bit of hoboin, life of adventure, all that dime novel bunkum—am I readin ya right?"

Elly nodded. The boy had finally let go of her arm, and all three of them were squatting in the doorway of the shack. The buildings across the way were silhouetted black against a deep indigo sky.

"Well Bert, it's an exciting life all right, but a rough one. And a tadpole like you, well he's liable to get his tail caught if he ain't got nobody to watch out fer him."

"Picnic Pete'll watch out fer yez," said Jimmy quickly. "He's been ever-where, he knows the ropes, an we eats good. An he can fight—I watched him kill a man with a razor oncet."

Picnic Pete was nodding his head. "I treats my boys straight." He stood up. "So what'll it be, Bert? Ya comin?"

Elly felt like she had no choice and nodded.

~

All four of them set out. Pete carried all their bundles (but not, to Elly's disappointment, on the end of a stick) while Jimmy helped the old man hobble along. They skirted the railroad yard in a wide arc through back alleys, while Pete kept up a running commentary on the city.

"This ain't no town—it's a disease. Last time I come through, the dick caught two boes I was with. I got away an hid under a car an watched that sumbitch blackjack them two defenseless bums to the ground afore he hauled em away. Wait—"

He grabbed Elly by the shoulder, peered around a corner, then pointed.

"See that bridge? Train'll be a-crawlin when it goes acrosst, an it's a short drop to the top of a boxcar."

"Ol Pete, he knows all the tricks," enthused Jimmy. Now that they were standing up, Elly saw he was thin and not very tall—probably no more than twelve or thirteen—and his eye patch was tied on with a shoe-lace. She wondered if there was a big hole underneath it.

They scuttled toward the bridge, which crossed a wide, dark river, and set out across it. The spaces between the railroad ties led straight down into the blackness of the river. After a few yards, they reached a lad-der that led up into the ironwork of the bridge. The rungs were thin and widely spaced. Jimmy went first, pulling the old man behind him. Pete passed their bundles up to Jimmy, then took Elly's bundle from her and passed it up as well.

Elly watched all this with dismay.

"C'mon, Bert," said Pete, pulling his hat on tight and bending down, "climb aboard."

Again Elly felt she had no choice. She crawled on his back, her arms around his neck, and they started up. They found the other two squatting on the lip of an iron beam directly over the track. On the other side of them was a third man, a stranger.

"Hey Pete," said Jimmy, "this here gent knows yer tricks!"

"Hello, bo," said the stranger. "How ya makin it?"

"Oh, I'm a-havin a picnic," said Pete, setting Elly down beside him. She was afraid to move an inch and kept hold of his tattered coat.

"Ya wouldn't," said the old man in a shaky voice, "ya wouldn't have a drop on yez? I got the snakes, I do. Got em real bad."

The stranger reached into his coat. "Got some corn licker take the hide off a mule," he said, pulling out a tin flask. He took a drink and passed it to the old man, who grabbed it with shaking hands. He took a long pull and wiped his mouth with the back of his hand.

"Well I guess it would," he said. He let out a little cackle and took another drink.

"Pass er here," said Pete. He took a drink and (to Elly's surprise) passed the flask to Jimmy, who drank as well.

"She does kick," said Jimmy, giggling. He passed it back to Pete. "Don't she kick, Pete?"

Pete took another drink and swirled the liquor in his mouth, as though considering. "Make a hummin-bird fly slow," he pronounced, and Jimmy giggled again. The old man was eyeing the flask like the dog had eyed Elly's sandwiches that morning, and Pete passed it back to him.

"Let him finish it," said the stranger.

"We's much obliged to ya, bo," said Pete. The old man nodded agreement without taking the flask from his lips.

"Call me Montana Red," said the man. The old man gave him the empty flask, and he returned it to his coat pocket. He was a big man, his coat tight in the shoulders. Even by the dim light coming from the town, Elly could see the shock of red hair spilling out from under his hat.

The men began a conversation about burgs they had been in and dicks in the yards and jolts they had done in pens, and Jimmy said he'd "never let em send me back to the ref." Elly had no idea what they were talking about. She did figure out that the word "bo" was short for hobo. The moon was rising above the trees where the river disappeared around a bend. Slivers of moon danced in the water.

The shriek of a train whistle interrupted their talk.

"She's a-comin, boes," said Pete. The men gathered their bundles. There was talk of which cars might be empty and when to jump before the train got too fast. Once again Pete directed Elly to climb onto his back.

"Now when I jump, you hold on tighter than a tick," he told her, "lest you wants your hoboin days to end afore they begin. You hear me?"

Elly nodded against his back. The train was chuffing toward them. Its light was so bright she had to shut her eyes, then it blinked out as the train thundered beneath them. The noise was deafening, the bridge shook, and clouds of steam enveloped them. She clutched Pete's neck with all her strength. There was a yell—and abruptly they were falling through space.

The shock of impact threw her violently to the side, and a hand grabbed her arm just before she slid off the sloping roof of a boxcar. "Hold on a this!" Pete yelled in her ear, putting her hands around a pipe running down the center of the roof.

The old man had landed on the same car. Elly watched half-dazed as Pete, holding on to the pipe with one hand and the old man's ankle with the other, dangled him over the side of the jolting, tipping car, which was accelerating at a frightening rate. The old man yelled out, "She's locked!" over the roar of the train, and Pete hauled him back up.

On the car behind them, Montana Red and Jimmy were doing the same thing. Jimmy dangled over the edge, and Red held his ankle while keeping all their bundles from flying off the careening train. Jimmy yelled something, and Red hauled him back up. Then Jimmy reversed himself, let himself over the edge feet-first, and disappeared. Red waved at the rest of them and began passing the bundles over the edge of the car.

Again Elly clung to Pete as he climbed like a monkey down a ladder at the end of the car, then up another. Drink seemed to have made the old man spry, and he scrambled behind them. The train was now thundering through the night at a furious pace. Pete gave a shout and lowered Elly down the sloping roof of the boxcar. For a terrifying moment her legs were dangling out in space—then hands were grasping her, and an instant later she found herself lying on a wooden floor smelling of oil and sawdust. Pete lowered himself in, followed by the old man, who almost went tottering out the open door before Montana Red grabbed him. Someone rolled the door shut, cutting the cold wind and plunging them into darkness.

Pete lit a cigarette and by its light, Elly spied her bundle. After all these dangerous exploits, Mr. Hoppy was sorely in need of comforting, so she liberated him and cradled him in her arms. With growing contentment she listened to the sounds of the train, sounds she had grown up with. And—with each click-clack, click-clack—dared to believe that the

Marysville Benevolent Christian Asylum for Unfortunate Girls was growing farther and farther away…

.   .   .

It grew colder. The men tore up some empty crates and built a fire in one corner, then stood around it, warming themselves. Montana Red nodded at the tiny boy asleep against his bundle with a doll in his arms.

"What the hell, Pete. Guess you like to start em out young," he observed.

"Haw," said the old man.

"Still playin with dollies," jeered Jimmy. "Calls hisself Al-bert," he added in a mincing tone.

Pete squinted at the boy. "Aw, he'll do, I expect." He nodded to himself. "Yeah, we'll have ourselves a picnic with ol Bert."

He took out his tobacco and began rolling another cigarette.

CHAPTER FIFTEEN

HOBOING

In the middle of the night Elly was awakened and made to climb on Pete's back, and the men all jumped from the train, running when they hit the ground to match the speed of the slow-moving train as it pulled into a town. They stealthily skirted the rail yard, Pete still carrying Elly on his back, and she listened to the distant booming sounds of freight cars being detached and new ones joined to the train until she fell asleep. She was rudely jogged awake by Pete's heavy footsteps as he ran beside an empty boxcar and passed her up to the others. It was very cold, and she huddled against one of the bundles and fell asleep again, and all of it was like a dream.

She awoke to find a bright ribbon of daylight shining through the partly open door of the boxcar and trees and bushes flashing past. The old man and the boy were asleep against their bundles. Pete and Montana Red were squatting by the open door smoking cigarettes and talking in low tones. Elly badly needed to pee and had no idea what to do about it. But they were slowing down, and a few minutes later, Pete woke the others. They gathered their things and jumped from the train. As soon as Pete put her down, she ran behind a clump of bushes. She could hear them laughing at her.

They set off walking. Elly could see it was a very big rail yard, with a big town in the distance. Jimmy walked beside her carrying his and Pete's bundles. Now and then he glanced at her with his good eye. It was pale gray and scared her more than the eye patch.

"Why don't you never talk none?" he finally said.

Elly felt herself blushing. "I don't like to." Even those four words she had to pry from her brain.

"Huh," said Jimmy, considering this. "Well now, listen here—don't spect me to do all the gabbin, you got to share the load. Cause some these housewifes now, they spect yez to sing for yer breakfuss, an ya got to have a yarn or two up yer sleeve. Ol Pete, he's tole me lots a good ones, an they works real good. I'll teach em to yez…"

Elly was finding it hard to listen, because she didn't really understand what Jimmy was talking about. Besides, even as he mentioned breakfast the air was filled with the smell of fried meat. She couldn't remember when she'd ever been so hungry.

They came to a weathered building on the edge of the rail yard with CAFE printed on the side in faded gray letters.

"Boes," said Pete, "I got a little scratch so I'll stand treat."

"You're on," said Red.

They went inside, put down their bundles, and lined up at the counter. Elly sat between Pete and Jimmy. Pete ordered eggs on toast, sunny-side up. The sour-faced man at the counter yelled, "three on a raft with their eyes open" through a hole leading into the kitchen. Jimmy ordered the same. "Make that two," bawled the man. The other two men placed their orders, and Pete looked at Elly.

She gathered her courage. "Hamburger steak. With mashed potatoes."

Jimmy let out a whoop. "What in the hell kinda breakfuss—"

Pete lifted a hand. "Bert wants hamburger steak, he gets hamburger steak."

"No gravy," added Elly.

"Like a man knows what he wants," said Red.

The men drank coffee. The sour-faced man poured some for Elly as well, but she asked for milk instead and Jimmy snickered. The food came quickly. It was the first time Elly had eaten her meal in such a long time, and—hungry as she was—she savored the inviolable ritual of shaping her mashed potatoes into the required circle. The whole time she felt Jimmy's good eye staring at her with disbelief, but she didn't care. When she finally began to eat, it was even better for the waiting.

They ate in silence. When they finished, Pete rolled cigarettes and passed them around. They lit up and Pete asked the man, who was wiping the counter, what the scoffin was like in Fresno.

"How the hell should I know," he said impatiently. "I ain't no bum."

"Well now," said Red conversationally, "seems to me like that's your loss. I mean you could be out there free as a firecracker enjoyin this beauteous day stead a cooped up in here grease-jockeyin for diddly-doo."

"Some of us got to work for a livin," muttered the man.

"Now brother, that's where you're wrong," said Red. Elly noticed again how big he was, his coat so tight around his shoulders that its armpits were ripped. He leaned forward and his face, under the shock of red curls, had a stubborn, bulldog look to it. "It's the rich men bleedin the rest of us dry that makes men gotta work their damn lives away. Why, if the workin man was to own the means of production, he could work just a couple hours a day and take the rest of the time off to enjoy God's wonderful world. Just two hours—it's all been sci-en-TIFF-ickly proven." He slapped the counter for emphasis. "The whole rotten system is just a big con to make the workin man a slave."

The man behind the counter looked unimpressed.

"So what are you, some kinda socialist?"

"You bet I am, brother. And I'm a-castin my vote for Eugene Debs like every other workin man in this country with any brains."

"Cept I don't see you workin," said the man.

The old man cackled.

"C'mon, boes," said Pete, putting some coins on the counter and standing up. "Time to prove this man wrong and go to work."

~

Outside they separated. Montana Red and the old man headed toward a clump of trees in the distance, while Pete, Jimmy, and Elly struck out for the city.

"They's goin to the jungle," Jimmy informed Elly.

"We'll meet em there later," added Pete.

Elly was alarmed. She had never been in a jungle but knew them to contain snakes and wild beasts.

They trudged along. The houses they passed were mostly shacks with chickens and goats and scruffy dogs that growled at them. Jimmy threw stones at the dogs. Pete seemed to be appraising the houses. He gave them both instructions.

"Now Jimmy, Bert here's new to this game, so you got to show him the ropes. Bert, your job is mostly to jus smile at the ladies and look pitiful."

"But Pete," said Jimmy, "He don't *never* smile! And with his hair a-stickin out ever which way, he don't look pitiful—he looks *tetched*! Why them ladies is liable to take fright at the sight a him."

"Well now, yer one to talk with that fuckin pirate patch," said Pete.

Jimmy kicked at a stone, pouting.

Elly had been desperately needing to pee for a very long time, and when Pete and Jimmy casually stepped up to a fence and began to unbutton their trousers, she ran behind a tree.

"I do believe ol Bert has got a case of the trots," remarked Pete, chuckling.

They came to a two-story house more prosperous looking than the others around it. Pete nodded toward it, leaned against a tree, and began to roll a cigarette. Jimmy dropped their bundles beside him and reached to grab Elly's bundle as well. But she had taken a dislike to him and held it tight.

Jimmy cast an aggrieved look at Pete.

"Bert," said Pete, sighing, "ya got to leave it here."

Elly felt her face burning but stubbornly stood her ground.

"Lemme show him what's what, Pete," said Jimmy, grabbing Elly by the shoulder.

Pete held up his hand, and Jimmy reluctantly let go. Suddenly a crafty gleam came into Pete's eyes.

"It's that there ragdoll," he said. "He wants his ragdoll—don't ya, Bert?"

Elly stared straight ahead and said nothing.

"Well now, go ahead and get out yer ragdoll, Bert. We wouldn't wanta take a feller's ragdoll, now would we, Jimmy?"

Jimmy gave him an incredulous look.

"But Jimmy, don't ya see," said Pete, his eyes laughing, "it'll make it even better."

~

Elly followed Jimmy around the back of the house, clutching Mr. Hoppy to her chest. Through a screen door, they could see a woman's dark form at the kitchen counter. Jimmy knocked. She came to the door and frowned at them through the screen.

"Mornin, Ma'am," said Jimmy in a honeyed voice Elly didn't recognize. "Me an my lil brother here, well, we's awful hungry, an we're on the way to Albuquerque to see our Aunt Sary on account a our folks is dead—they up an died of the pneumonyer. An I—I mean *we*—we been travelin such a piece, and we ain't got no money, and we're jus powerful hungry, an if yer could jus give us a handout, why I—I mean *we*—we'd be jus ever so much obliged to yez…"

The woman said nothing. She had a red face and blue eyes so piercing that Elly had to look away.

"Wouldn't we, Bert? Wouldn't we be jus ever so much obliged?" said Jimmy, kicking her.

Elly nodded, staring at the ground.

The woman stood a long moment with her hand on her hip, made a sort of *hmph* sound, then opened the door. "Sit down," she said, nodding at the kitchen table.

"Yes'm, thank you ma'am, we're jus ever so much obliged to yez," said Jimmy, sitting down. "Ever since Ma and Pa up an died on us, an our pore lil baby sister too, jus two years old she was, an pretty as a angel—"

"You save your guff for the next house, I ain't buyin none of it," snapped the woman, busy at the counter. Jimmy cast his eye on Elly and kicked her under the table, mouthing, "Say somethin." Elly set her jaw and held Mr. Hoppy tight. She watched the woman slice bread with angry motions and put the slices in a paper sack, along with two apples and some pickles wrapped in waxed paper.

"Here," she said, slapping the sack on the table and holding the screen door open. "And don't come back."

Jimmy grabbed the sack (Elly noticed he didn't bother with any more "much obliged" talk now that he had it) and they left. As soon as they were out of sight, he swung his fist at her and knocked her to the ground.

"You ain't no use a'tall," he yelled at her and stalked away.

Elly got up. Her shoulder ached from where she had been slugged. Mr. Hoppy was as uncomplaining as ever, but she brushed him off anyway. Out front she found Pete sitting against the tree and Jimmy yelling things and pointing in her direction.

"...didn't never say a single word—an *smile*? Why he wouldn't even look the woman in the eye—"

"Uh-huh," said Pete, dumping the contents of the sack on the ground and pawing through it all with a disgusted look.

"He's tetched, I'm tellin yez," concluded Jimmy. His single eye glared at Elly. She glared back at it.

"Well now, Jimmy," said Pete, unwrapping the pickles and munching on one, "maybe it's true. Maybe ol Bert is a might tetched. Ain't sayin it's so," he added, eyeing Elly speculatively. "But let's say he is. What we got to do is use that to our advantage."

He stood up and, as they gathered their bundles and continued on, began outlining a new plan of attack to Jimmy. Elly trudged along behind them. She was angry and terribly embarrassed to find that being a hobo meant begging. They tried several more houses. At three of them the doors were shut in their faces. At the fourth, no one even came to the door (even though they saw an old woman peeking out from behind a curtain). Finally, a young woman with a smooth, bland face and sympathetic eyes listened to Jimmy's speech and, at the mention of their parents who had "up an died" cried, "Oh you poor things!" and invited them inside.

She wore a pretty flowered apron and, as they ate big pieces of apple pie and drank glasses of cold milk, stuffed a large sack full of food. Jimmy watched her out of the corner of his eye and continued to lay it on thick.

"Yes ma'am," he said, finishing his pie and wiping his mouth with his hand. "When our Pa died, an then Ma right after well, pore lil Albert here, he jus up an went all to pieces. Stopped talkin, won't look nobody in the eye…"

"The poor lamb," said the woman, putting two large pieces of fried chicken into the sack and looking at Elly with glistening eyes. Elly drank her milk, her face burning, and clutched Mr. Hoppy.

"An now, well he jus can't let go a that there ragdoll, on account a it was the favorite dolly of our pore lil sis Matilda what got carried away by the pneumonyer right after Ma an Pa…"

This was too much for the woman, who knelt beside Elly and stroked her hair.

"Oh Albert, brave little Albert," she cooed. Elly sat rigidly and stared at the table.

When they left, she gave them two dollars.

·   ·   ·

They went at it all morning and part of the afternoon and struck a few more good ones (though none so good as that). Elly was exhausted and so stuffed with pie and cookies and bread and butter she was about to burst. They were up to almost six dollars and fifty cents (which Pete declared was "almost good as Christmas") before they finally headed back. Pete bought some whiskey, and he and Jimmy passed it back and forth, Jimmy crowing over and over about how all those "ignorant housewifes" just ate up anything he dished out about "pore lil Albert." Pete laughed and drank and laughed some more.

Elly trudged behind them, fuming.

A wisp of smoke was struggling up from beyond the clump of trees where Elly had been told there would be a jungle. Instead she found a clearing littered with boards and rusty pieces of sheet metal. In the center of the clearing, a circle of raggedly-dressed men were squatting around a fire. Montana Red sat with them. The men looked up at their approach with hard faces, but when Red said, "It's all right, boes—this here's my friend, Picnic Pete," they all relaxed.

Pete sat down beside Red and handed him the bottle. Jimmy sat on the other side of Pete like a faithful dog by its master. Elly sat on a stump outside the circle, watching.

A hawk-nosed man was standing over a cast-iron pot suspended above the fire and stirring the contents. He had dark skin, and Elly suspected he was part Indian. The smell from the pot made her full stomach queasy.

"Whatcha got in that sack?" somebody asked Pete.

"Well boes," said Pete, "I figured we'd just have ourselves a picnic." He dumped the day's take on the ground with a flourish.

A heavy-set man with one arm whistled. "You's a damn good moocher," he said.

"Them Fresno farmers is closer than fleas on a dog," said a dried-up little man with no teeth. "How the hell'd ya skin em?"

"My boys was workin em," said Pete. He squeezed Jimmy's shoulder, then looked around for Elly, but she avoided his eye. Hands were reaching for the pieces of fried chicken and sandwiches. The hawk-nosed man appropriated a sausage and began slicing it into the pot. The bottle was going around, and the old man they had traveled with appeared out of nowhere. The shadows grew, and the air turned chill. Elly put on her coat and cap and moved closer to the fire. The woods lost their form and became a blackness, and the sky was strewn with stars. The talk grew loud and full of laughter, and Red sang a song about a hobo's idea of heaven:

> *Where the chickens crawl into the skillet*
> *and cook themselves nice and brown,*
> *and the cows churn butter in the morning*
> *and squirt their milk all around.*
>
> *Where the lunches grow on bushes*
> *and bump the boes in the eyes*
> *and every night at eleven*
> *the sky rains down apple pies…*

The other men added their own verses, and the song went on and on. Elly sat staring into the fire. Despite all the talk and laughter, she had never felt so alone. She pulled Mr. Hoppy from her bundle, held him in her lap, and stroked his face. Suddenly she felt an arm around her shoulder and saw Pete was sitting next to her.

"Bert, hey Bert. Ya done good today. Real good." He squeezed her shoulder. Elly risked a quick glance at his face. In the flickering firelight, his lizardy eyes looked almost kind. "We had ourselves a picnic, huh Bert? Didn't we jus'!"

Elly nodded. After a while something inside her gave way, and she leaned against his side. A few minutes later she was asleep.

.   .   .

She woke up terribly stiff and cold and for several long moments had no idea where she was. She lay on her coat on a piece of rusty sheet metal with her bundle under her head and a greasy blanket on top of her. Above her, a flat piece of wood she decided was the door of a boxcar was propped up on two sticks. Outside the ground was frosty, and birds were having morning conversations in the trees nearby.

She pulled on her boots, which were hard as ice and just as cold, stumbled stiff-legged to the edge of the forest, and squatted down. She was just finishing her business when Jimmy stepped from behind a nearby tree, buttoning his fly—and burst into raucous laughter.

"Haw! Lookit them drawers! Looks like a girl's bloom—"

His words died on his lips, and his single eye widened.

"Pete!" he yelled, "Hey, Pete!"

Elly was frantically pulling her overalls up over her asylum bloomers when Pete arrived. He listened to Jimmy's excited babbling then reached over and pushed them down again. And—as Elly stood there, angry and ashamed—burst into laughter.

.   .   .

On days when the weather was fine and Pete was in the mood, they worked Fresno some more, and Elly got a little more used to it. Now that Pete and Jimmy knew she was a girl, they were different around her. Jimmy especially she would sometimes catch staring at her with a troubled expression. Until one cold, rainy, dreary day, when they both sat under the boxcar door huddled in damp blankets and Pete was passed out drunk beside them, Jimmy suddenly blurted:

"I'm sorry I walloped yez, Bert. That one time. I didn't know yer was a girl, see? Ya can't blame a feller fer what he don't know, now can yez?"

Elly shook her head.

Jimmy nodded, relieved. "See, I thought it were a sissifed thing, you playin with dollies an such, but now I understand it, see, an I ain't blamin yez. So things is straight with us now, ain't they? I mean, we's partners now an all?"

Elly glanced at Jimmy's eye. It had a pleading look. She nodded.

"Shake on it."

They shook. Jimmy let out a deep breath. The rain drummed on the boxcar roof and smeared the edge of the forest in a pretty way. She looked again at Jimmy's pale gray eye, which—now that he wasn't being angry or impatient—was actually quite nice.

"What happened to your other eye?" she asked him.

Jimmy glanced at her sideways, and let out a funny laugh.

"Well now, that's from when I was in the ref."

"What's the 'ref'?" said Elly, determined to get to the bottom of some of these mysteries.

"The ref, you know, the reform school."

Elly still looked confused.

"It's like a prison, but fer kids, like."

She nodded; this was something she knew about.

"Right, so when I was in the ref, I got into a scrap with this other kid on account a he called me a bastard, and he got me down on the floor an dug my eye out with a spoon. But me an my pals, we jumped him later and bout killed him, so I guess I come out ahead."

Elly considered this. "Let me see it," she said.

Jimmy lifted his patch and she examined the hole, which was mostly shut and scared her less than if there had been an actual eye staring out of it. "What's a bastard?" she asked as an afterthought.

"Holy jumpin turnips, you don't know nothin, do yez? A bastard's a kid ain't got no daddy."

Elly frowned. "Everyone has a father," she said.

"Oh yeah?" said Jimmy. "Show's what yer know—cause that kid, that kid were right after all!"

And he laughed himself silly.

.   .   .

Pete and Jimmy hadn't told the other hoboes she was a girl. Pete said this was for her own protection.

"An yer name ain't really Albert, is it?"

Elly had shaken her head.

"But you don't wanna say what yer real name is, that it?"

She nodded.

"Well now, I'm sure ya got yer reasons," said Pete, nodding along with her. "So we'll jus leave er at that."

The other hoboes in the jungle were constantly changing as some left and others took their places. Elly began paying more attention to their conversations and slowly started to decipher their talk. A "jolt in the pen" was time spent in prison, and the "S and P" was the Southern Pacific Railroad. "Dicks" were bad men who made hoboes get off the trains and put them in prison. They had funny names for cities; she knew "Cincy" must be Cincinnati and "Indy" was Indianapolis. But where was this "Shy" they talked about so much? And what on earth was "The Big Easy"?

She heard lots of stories around the fire as well, including one she would never forget. Even though she wished she could.

It was already dark when a new man approached. He murmured a few words to set them all at ease and sat down outside the group, drinking from a bottle in a paper sack. Elly watched him for a while. But beneath the brim of his slouch hat his face was in deep shadow, and she turned her attention back to the conversation.

"So, who's ya votin fer, boes?" A silly-looking young man with a crooked face atop a scrawny neck repeated the question he had asked before the new man's arrival. "Taft, or this feller Bryan?"

Elly listened with interest; Teddy Roosevelt had been president her entire life, and now it seemed there was to be someone new. But the man's question was greeted with snickers.

"Hell's the difference," someone muttered.

"All them bums is cut from the same cloth," agreed a man in a torn engineer's cap.

One man—not Montana Red, who was long gone—suggested Eugene Debs.

"Might as well sell your vote as throw it away on Debs," countered another.

This started some lively talk about the possibilities of selling one's vote in a big city, with many stories of prior success. The men had about decided to head as a group to Los Angeles and try their luck when the original asker of the question, the crooked-faced young man, said, "Well I'm fer Taft. Cause any man that ol Teddy's behind is good enough fer me."

He swiveled his head with its silly smile around the circle as though daring anyone to disagree.

"T.R.?" said a voice. It was the new man sitting in the shadows. "May the devil absorb him. And his stooge Taft as well. And all the rest of the politicoes in this God-forsaken country."

There was a long silence.

"Them's strong words," said someone at last.

"Not half so strong as I'd like," retorted the man. He lifted his bottle and took a long drink.

"Well now, see here," said the young man, his adam's apple bobbing up and down on his scrawny neck, "you've no call to be a-runnin down our great country like that."

"Yeah?" said the man. "Well I went to war for this great county, didn't I? And I've seen how the 'Land of the Free' sees fit to treat the rest of the world."

"Was you at San Juan with Teddy?" asked someone.

"I was in the Philippines," said the man.

"Well hell, I don't care you was in Timbuktu," said the young man, smiling fatuously. "It still don't give you the right—"

The man in the shadows drained his bottle and suddenly smashed it to the ground. Everything became very still.

"Gonna be a fight!" Jimmy whispered to Elly gleefully.

The man lifted his head, and for the first time the fire's light revealed his face. A scar ran from his forehead to one corner of his mouth, lifting his lips and exposing three teeth in a ghastly sort of permanent leer.

"The right?" he repeated in a chilling voice. "I don't have the right?"

There was a silence.

"So, what—was you wounded over there?" said the silly young man. "Well, I guess that's a shame. But I still say it don't give you—"

"Yeah, I was wounded all right," said the man, cutting him off. He took a deep breath and stared up at the stars. "Shot in the face by another American soldier."

That seemed to shut the young man up.

"So how'd it happen?" someone asked.

The scarred man stared into the flames for a long time. The others all waited. Finally—still with his terrible fixed grin—he began to speak.

"Before I joined up I'd never been anywhere. And the Philippines—well, to a farm boy from Illinois, it was pretty close to paradise. People there are about the loveliest people you ever want to meet, and after a while I had me a girl. Only sixteen, but they get to be women early over there, and a finer gal you never…"

He looked down at the ground for a long moment, then continued.

"She was set to have my baby. Soon as I got my discharge, I was fixin to marry her and settle down. We had us a place just outside the barracks. But she was from some village about thirty miles away. Took me there to meet her people. About eight months gone she was, by this time. She was such a little slip of a thing, made her about as wide as she was tall. Her folks were nice, simple people. Lived in a hut with a dirt floor. They made a fuss over me. Killed a chicken in my honor."

He chuckled mirthlessly.

"I had to get back for duty, but she stayed on for a visit. Couple miles outside the village, I run into a division of cavalry goin the other way. There'd been some rebel action in the area, so I didn't think anything of it. Figured they were on their way to some encampment.

"Not much later I hear all hell break loose behind me. Go racin back—fast as you can get a mule to race—and find the U.S. army circled around that village and blasting holy hell out of it with machine guns. I go tearin for my girl's hut. By that time, troops are in the village settin fire to the huts and gunnin down the stragglers—I'm talkin about men, women, and children. There were people lyin all around in pitiful heaps. Some paunchy private with a cigar and a smokin rifle comes runnin out of my girl's hut, and when I get there, I find the whole family dead. My girl lyin there with her brains spattered all around. And that baby, sweet Jesus, that baby was kickin inside her, tryin to get out."

He became silent and stared up at the stars again. Tears ran down his face and glistened in the firelight before disappearing into the leering hole around his mouth.

"I was bending over her body. Didn't have my uniform on, so they must have thought I was a native, and I took a bullet in the face. Knocked me out cold. Wish to Christ they'd left me there to die. But someone must have taken a closer look, because I woke up in a hospital, and when they got the bandages off my face—well, this is what it looked like.

"Soon as I got out of the hospital, I tracked down the general who gave that order and told him what I thought of him. Showed him too—I guess he lost a few teeth. For that they gave me five years in Leavenworth."

He looked down again. His face was once more in shadow.

Nobody said a word.

"Yeah, far as I'm concerned," he muttered, standing up, "this whole country can get swallowed up by the cold, chilled steel hinges of hell."

And he wandered off into the night.

CHAPTER SIXTEEN

IN WHICH ELLY AND JIMMY BECOME A COMMODITY

Next morning Pete roused them early.

"Pack it up, you bums," he said genially. "Someone heard some yard men gabbin at the café. Meat wagon comin through this AM, bound for Los Angeles." He grabbed the piece of broken glass he used to shave with and, whistling tunelessly, disappeared.

"Meat wagon's a fast un," said Jimmy, as he rolled all their stuff up into one bundle. "Don't sidetrack fer nothin but passenger an mail trains."

Elly stuffed Mr. Hoppy down the front of her overalls, and they joined a few others who had heard the news and were headed for the rail yard. The silly man with the crooked face was with them but not, Elly was relieved to see, the man with the terrible scar. The wind was cool and the sky overcast. Beneath her overalls she had on both pairs of leggings, because Pete said the way they would be riding, it would get a lot colder. They moved stealthily along the edges of the rail yard and hid behind a boxcar. The men sat smoking and not saying much. The silly young man tried to start up another conversation about the election, but nobody was buying any.

In the distance they heard the train arrive. Through the rumble of cars being pushed from sidings and the deep booms as they were attached to the train, Elly could dimly make out the lowing of hundreds of cattle.

It took a long time and she became bored. She looked around—and suddenly caught her breath.

Behind them, half-obscured by bushes and trees, stood an ancient locomotive.

She stared at it for a long minute. It must have been there so long the trees had grown up around it. Mesmerized—hardly aware of her actions—she pushed her way through the overgrowth, and gazed in awe at the mountain of rusted metal. She reached out to touch one of the long rods connecting the engine to a wheel and examined how it was attached. Soon she was crawling underneath and all around the enormous machine, imagining all its frozen parts in motion. And once again trying to divine the secret of how something so manifestly inert could be put into thundering motion by a wisp of water vapor…

The booming in the distance had ceased, but she failed to notice. She hauled herself laboriously up the side of the engine. The door to the firebox was frozen ajar, and the black cavity still smelt of burning coal. She climbed a set of steps to the cab. The leather seat that folded down from the wall was torn and moldy, and the space was strewn with leaves and trash, but it still seemed a place of magic. She grasped handles and levers; imagined pulling them and bending the machine to her will. Rubbed the tarnished brass gauges with her sleeve to reveal arcane sets of numbers, their purpose a tantalizing mystery…

She heard the soft *chuff* of a moving train—for a marvelous instant it seemed the locomotive had come alive—then two short blasts of a whistle. An instant later, she was clambering down from the engine in desperate haste. She scrambled through the thick bushes, bruising her knees and scratching her face. The men were all crouched behind the boxcar with their bundles. The train slowly advanced toward them, screeching and hissing and snorting steam like an angry beast. Jimmy was waving frantically at her, and she raced across the clearing. The men began creeping through the tall weeds toward the track. When the locomotive thundered past them, they broke cover.

She ran up, breathless, jumped on Pete's back without a word, and in an instant they were loping along beside the train. She had a confused glimpse of hair, horns, and rolling bovine eyes through the slats of passing cattle cars before Pete grabbed a metal railing and hoisted them up with a smooth motion. He climbed a ladder, and suddenly they were sitting on top of the car in the wind and the smoke. Jimmy climbed behind them with their bundle tied to his back and sat down next to Elly. He punched her lightly on the shoulder and pulled her cap down over her eyes. When she pushed it back up, he was grinning at her.

All around them, other hoboes were climbing onto the top of the train like fleas onto a dog's back. Fallow fields stretched off into infinity. Fence rows flashed by in hypnotic procession as the train gathered speed. The cattle moaned and bawled beneath them. The locomotive sent happy smoke signals to the fluffy white clouds overhead.

Pete had somehow managed to roll and light a cigarette. He smoked and squinted at the endless horizon, now and then pulling out a flask and sipping from it. The train was flying now, rocking beneath them like a ship in a heavy sea. Jimmy's eye patch fluttered in the wind. A cinder flew into Elly's hair. She brushed it away, pulled her cap on tighter, and smiled to herself. For this was just what she had always dreamed being a hobo would be like.

The meat wagon was in a rush to get the cattle to market and, as Jimmy had predicted, made few stops. They pulled over onto a siding once to let a passenger train go by and lay flat to avoid detection. In the windows of the other train, Elly watched people in bowlers and tall feathered hats flash by, and thought wistfully of her past life. At Bakersfield, they jumped off the train as it was slowing down and hid beneath the wheels of a car. The brakeman came so close when he walked by that Elly could have reached out and touched his striped overalls. When the clank of cars ahead of them showed the train was beginning to move, they bolted from their hiding place and scrambled back on top.

They left the flat fields and entered an area full of high hills. A herd of shaggy horses watched them from a bluff, and Pete said they were wild mustangs. The sun sank, and it grew cold and dark. The hills disappeared and became night. Elly huddled between Jimmy and Pete and fell asleep. She was still half-asleep when Pete made her climb on his back, and they

leaped from the still-moving train. It was still dark, he stumbled and fell, and she hit the ground. She looked up, dazed. Lights were jiggling in the distance, and she heard shouting voices.

"C'mon," hissed Pete. He grabbed her hand, yanked her to her feet, and pulled her down a sandy embankment. Jimmy was just ahead of them.

"There's some more of em!" yelled a voice.

The caboose was going by. From its light Elly caught a glimpse of an eerie landscape of wrecked train cars and twisted metal. Abruptly Jimmy seemed to disappear, and an instant later Pete pulled her to the ground. They rolled beneath a massive car half-sunk in the sand and burrowed like animals as deep as they could go. Jimmy was already there. All three of them huddled together, gasping for breath. The running footsteps came closer—then stopped.

"Where the hell'd they go?"

"Shine a light under that car."

A beam of light snaked toward them. Pete tried to jerk his legs away, but it flashed on his boot.

"There they are!"

"Come on outa there." A pause. "Come out, or we'll start firin down in there, and the devil take the consequences."

Pete gave a long sigh. "All right, all right, don't blow a gasket, I'm a-comin," he said. He gave Elly's shoulder a squeeze and then crawled outside. Sounds of clanking chain and something clicking shut.

"Where's the rest a ya?"

"Hell if I know, cap'n, I'm the only one here."

"Shine that light again, Jake."

Jimmy pulled Elly close to him. They held their breath as the light danced toward them, then away again.

"Guess that's all of em."

"What I tell ya—"

There was a thump and a gasp.

"You shut yer pie hole lessen I tell ya. Check around those other cars, boys. They can't have got too far…"

The footsteps and voices faded away, then Elly heard a snuffling sound.

Jimmy was crying.

.　　　　　.　　　　　.

They spent the night huddled together beneath the car. Sometimes they slept; sometimes Jimmy talked in a low moan. "Aw Pete," he said over and over, "Pete, why'd yer have to leave me, Pete?" Or he'd curse the men who took Pete away. "Pete, don't you worry, Pete—I'm gone kill them sumbitches, gone kill ever last one of em." He told her about the time he'd had the fever "strong enough to kill a Haitian darkie," and Pete had nursed him back to health. And a confused tale of how Jimmy and Pete had once stolen a pig. Before they butchered it, Pete had gotten drunk and tried to ride it; Jimmy had "bout bust a gut" laughing. But now the story only made him cry some more, and they hugged each other. She could feel his heart beating in his chest.

She awoke feeling thick-headed. There was a murky sort of light, and she guessed it must be morning. Jimmy was gone. She scrambled outside, blinking in the sunlight, and found him sitting against the side of the car staring at nothing. The tall buildings of a distant city appeared dreamlike in the morning mist. The smell of damp sand, cattle, and—from somewhere unseen—the sea. She brushed the sand from her hair and clothes and saw Jimmy looking at her.

"Bert," he said.

She waited.

"C'mon, Bert." He grabbed their bundle and stood up. "We gotta find him."

They walked toward the city. Beyond the rail yard were huge pens full of bawling cattle. Jimmy pointed to a long, squat building and said it was a slaughterhouse. From its direction came an eerie keening sound; Elly guessed they must be the collective screams of dying animals.

They found a pipe trickling rusty water into a pool. They cupped their hands to drink, then washed their faces. The sun had burned away the mist and it was getting warm, so they stripped off their extra clothing. Elly no longer felt any embarrassment pulling her leggings off in front of Jimmy. Neither did she feel any compunction against looking at him, and noticed with interest how pale his body was compared to his sunburned face and hands. They rolled everything up in the bundle. Not for the first time, she wondered if hoboes ever washed their clothes.

Jimmy pulled out a bit of sausage and divided it up, and they ate as they walked along. Soon they were in the outskirts of the city. It was pretty much the same as other cities, but with palm trees. People tried to avoid them, but Jimmy asked anyone he could corner which way was the jail, and they got pointed in the right direction. Before long they were downtown. The streets were full of people, and Elly had never seen so many automobiles. Somewhere a brass band was playing.

The jail turned out to be a dark, three-story building with bars on all the upper windows. It scared Elly, and from the way Jimmy paused at the bottom of the steps, it must have scared him too. He took a deep breath. "C'mon," he said.

She followed him up the steps. Inside it was cool and echoey. A fat, red-faced policeman with a white mustache sat behind a high desk and peered down at them doubtfully.

"Yes?" he said.

"I come here to visit my pa," said Jimmy.

"Oh?" The man tapped his pencil on the desk. "And what about him?" he said, nodding toward Elly.

"He's my brother. We both come."

"Ah." He tapped his pencil some more. Elly saw his eyes dart toward their bundle. "And why aren't you in school?"

The word seemed to unsettle Jimmy. He squirmed and looked at the floor.

"Please, mister, we jus wanna see our pa, yer gonna let us see him or not?"

"Visiting hours are on Saturday," said the man, turning away from them.

"But…but can yer jus tell us if he's here?" Jimmy sounded close to tears.

The policeman glared at him, then sighed. He opened a large register. "Prisoner's name?"

"Pete."

"Yes yes. And?" More pencil tapping.

"Er…Picnic Pete."

"Picnic Pete," repeated the man. He was not writing.

"Uh-huh," said Jimmy. "Jus ask around. Ever-body knows ol Picnic Pete," he added hopefully.

The man stared at him a long moment. Then he leaned over his desk with a strange smile and whispered, "Get the hell out of here."

They got the hell out.

~

They walked all around the building, Jimmy shouting Pete's name. None of the shadows behind the bars shouted back. There were crowds of people on the street and the brass band was still playing somewhere in the distance; with all the commotion, Elly doubted anyone could hear them anyway.

Finally they sat on a curb. Jimmy slumped over with his head on his knees.

"You should have told him his real name," said Elly.

"I don't KNOW his real name," moaned Jimmy. "He never TOLE me his real name."

From down the block, an electric streetcar rattled toward them. Red-white-and-blue bunting streamed from its sides, and men were hanging out the windows and yelling. A sign on the back said VOTE FOR TAFT and underneath in smaller letters, "You can vote for Bryan anytime." The car stopped, and the men piled out and joined the big, entirely male crowd collecting outside the building across from them. A plaque identified it as the LOS ANGELES COUNTY COURTHOUSE.

The brass band had been getting louder and was now playing "Columbia the Gem of the Ocean." Suddenly it appeared around the corner with volume redoubled, and even though the clarinets were shrilly out-of-tune, the thundering drums sent a thrill through Elly. Another gaily-decorated streetcar disgorged a group of dowdily dressed women carrying placards. They assembled on the sidewalk and advanced on the courthouse with grim purpose. A strongly built man in a torn coat detached himself from the crowd of men and faced them, waving a bottle with one hand and yelling something that made the men behind him laugh. He turned around and bowed, doffing his misshapen hat and spilling a mop of red curls.

"Montana Red," murmured Elly.

Jimmy lifted his head from his knees just before a line of flutists marched in front of them and blocked their view.

"Holy jumpin turnips—it IS him!"

He grabbed their bundle, and they threaded their way across the street, dodging men in sweat-stained, red coats blowing trumpets and tubas. They found Red prancing in front of the women and playing to the crowd.

"Sisters, the good Lord in his wisdom made you for bakin cakes and birthin babes—"

"Haw!"

"You tell em!"

"—and he left all the cogitatin and governatin to us menfolk. It's called 'division of labor'—"

"We shall not rest," cried a strident-voiced, young woman in spectacles, "until the other half of the human race is given a voice in its own destiny!"

"Tell him, Sister Caroline!"

"I'll give you somethin," retorted Red. "A swift kick in the rear that'll bounce ya right back to the kitchen!"

He mimed a kick, and the men laughed. Elly had been reading the signs: WOMEN'S VOTE NOW; END FEMALE SLAVERY; WOMEN'S SUFFRAGE—NOT SUFFERING. Red was opening his mouth for another go at the women, when he felt someone pulling at the tattered tail of his coat. He looked down into the face of Jimmy.

"Hey!" he said. "Well, if it ain't, er—" He took a drink to refresh his memory. "So, where's ol Pete?"

"Aw Red, Pete got hisself pinched!" Jimmy sounded close to tears.

Red smacked his forehead in a pantomime of shock. "Say it ain't so!" he cried, glancing down at Elly. She nodded solemnly. "Ain't no justice in this world," said Red. "Ol Pete was a peach," he added, hoisting his bottle in a toast.

"He's gotta be in there," said Jimmy, pointing to the jail.

"Yeah well, then you can kiss ol Picnic Pete goodbye for six months at least. Once this city's got its hooks into ya, it don't fool around. Yeah, it's the chain gang for ol Pete."

Jimmy was speechless.

"But hey, you boys stick with me. I'll get ya squared away. And don't you worry bout ol Pete. He'll do his stretch, and you'll meet up with him again down the road a piece. Meanwhile, you got to look out for yourselves—that's what ol Picnic Pete would want, am I right?"

Jimmy nodded glumly.

"That's the cheese." Red squeezed Jimmy's shoulder. "Now you boys hang tight, I got some business to attend to."

A group of raggedly-dressed men had formed an equally ragged queue before a rather more prosperous-looking man in a derby and striped vest. He held a clipboard and was scribbling information on slips of paper and passing them to the men, who then headed up the steps of the courthouse. The woman with the piercing voice was standing on the steps and giving a speech, which the other women were applauding. Red got his slip of paper and headed up the steps, doing a little mocking dance as he passed the women. They ignored him. To Elly, they seemed both silly and curiously heroic.

Another marching band turned the corner and headed toward them playing "The Battle Hymn of the Republic" and drowning the woman out. The glorious tune seemed to fill Elly's very soul with golden light, and she felt herself floating toward the sun…

"Bert! Bert—c'mon!"

Jimmy was pulling at her arm. Red had emerged from the courthouse and was heading, with a group of other men, toward a streetcar creeping behind the marching band. Jimmy and Elly hurried behind him, and they all jammed inside.

"Bert," said Jimmy, "Bert, I swear sometimes I think you *are* tetched. Standin there a-starin into the sky like that, give a body the heebie-jeebies."

The men were all yelling and joking and passing around liquor. The streetcar turned a corner, and Elly listened to the music fade until it was only playing in her mind.

.   .   .

The day became a confusing procession of crowds and queues and streetcars as they trudged along with Red from one voting place to another. Once Elly got close enough to the man with the clipboard—for there was always a man with a clipboard—to hear what he was saying:

"Okay, your name is John H. Schenk," he told the man in front of Red, scribbling as he talked. "You live at 312 Melrose Place." He handed the man his slip of paper, and Montana Red stepped up. "Okay, you're Isadore Cohen, you live at—"

"Wait a minute," said a weasel-faced man behind Red, "how can you give him a name like that, with a mug out of a St. Paddy's day parade?"

"He's right," said Red. "Let him be Cohen, he looks more like a kike than me."

The man with the clipboard shrugged. "Okay, your name is Caleb Pendergrass, you live at…"

When Red came back out of the building, another man, wearing a derby and smoking a cigar, laid a silver dollar in his palm.

"Did you," said Elly, as she and Jimmy crowded into yet another streetcar with Red, "did you vote for Eugene Debs?"

"Debs? Why'd I want to do a fool thing like that? Ain't nobody payin nothin for Debs."

278

"But you said," replied Elly in her curious monotone, "that you were a-casting your vote for Eugene Debs like every other working man in this country with any brains."

Red looked down at her with drink-bleared eyes.

"Bert's right," said Jimmy. "'S'what yer said."

"Yeah, well," said Red. He rubbed his face and looked away. Jimmy grinned at Elly and pushed her cap down over her eyes.

Outside the streetcar, black clouds had blotted out the sun and hastened the evening's arrival. People began putting up the windows just as fat raindrops splattered on the streetcar's roof. Out in the streets, people were holding on to their hats and running for cover.

A few blocks farther on, the glistening sidewalk reflected the brightly-lit windows of a string of saloons. Red jumped out, and Jimmy and Elly ran after him. He pushed open a brass-handled door—then suddenly appeared to remember them.

"Come on in, sport," he said to Jimmy. "Let's you and me go on a whiz. I'll stand treat." He jingled the silver dollars in his pocket.

"What about Bert?" said Jimmy.

"Bert?" Red regarded Elly and scratched his head. "Bert's a mite runtish for this breed of establishment. Better wait out here." He opened the door and swaggered inside.

"Bert," said Jimmy, "I'll try an make him push the wind." He looked doubtful. "An, an I'll get yez somethin to eat and bring it out to yez."

He ducked inside.

Elly pressed her face against the window. She could make out Red's mop of flaming hair amidst a crowd of men at the bar, and saw he was already telling some story. The men broke into laughter. She saw Jimmy burrowing his way into the crowd with his bundle tied to his back, nobody paying him much attention. And she knew she was going to be out there a very long time.

Through the rain's hiss and splashing clop of horse's hooves she could make out the muffled sounds of someone playing a piano. She pressed her face to the window again but couldn't see any sign of it. The door opened and a man emerged, but the sound got no louder.

She splashed down the block following the music. Water soaked through her old boots and wind-driven rain splattered against her coat. The piano was louder now, a lively song she didn't know. She pressed her nose up against another window. Across a crowded room she spotted a man in a derby hammering away at a tall blond upright.

She pushed the door open. Rain dripped from her clothes and puddled on the floor. Vaguely she sensed heads turning her way as she made her way across the room. Something about the song was familiar. She pushed through a crowd of men, and found them gathered around a toothless old man doing a buck and wing. His hat was askew and his face set in comically grim concentration as he lashed his tired old legs into motion. The men clapped and cheered him on.

She edged along the circle and stood next to the piano. The piano player raised his eyebrows at the sight of her. He was a squat little man with stubby fingers, but he was making the piano dance. There was a mug of beer beside him; the head of foam jiggled in time to the music. Elly recognized the tune from a song in one of Miss Bland's books called "The Merry Peasant," but with a lot of extra notes. There was a chorus that someone began to sing:

> Now the moon shines tonight
> > on pretty Red Wing,
> The breeze is sighing,
> > the nightbird's flying,
> And afar, 'neath his star
> > her brave is sleeping,
> And Red Wing's weeping
> > her heart away...

The chorus was repeated, more people sang along, and the clapping got louder. The old man shuffled for all he was worth. The piano player was stomping his foot as he played. Elly watched his hands, mesmerized, the harmonies flashing ruby red in her mind.

Big finish. Whoops for the old man. The piano player swigged from his beer and eyed Elly over the top of the mug.

She had the whole song learned now and wanted to try it out.

"I can play it too," she said.

The piano player put down his beer. "What was that, sonny?"

For answer, Elly reached out her hand to the keyboard—then felt herself being grabbed by the shoulders and spun around. A tall man in a dirty apron was frowning down at her. "You lookin for your pa?"

She shook her head.

"You here with someone else?"

When she again shook her head, she found herself being unceremoniously lifted in the air, carried through the bar—and suddenly she was standing outside again in the rain. The man looked down at her and shook his head, then closed the door.

The piano was playing again, and she pressed her face to the glass. Rain dripped from the awning and down the back of her neck. When the music finally stopped, she sat down against the side of the building in a puddle of water and felt for Mr. Hoppy beneath her overalls. She wanted to pull him out but knew he'd get wet. So instead she hugged his shape.

And wept.

.   .   .

"Bert, Bert, what in blazes, whatcher doin down there?"

Jimmy reached down to pull Elly up, got her halfway to her feet—then suddenly they were both lying in the puddle. Jimmy's eye patch was askew, and he laughed stupidly.

"Bert, holy jumpin turnips Bert, I'm fair snockered, I am. Jus flat out snockered."

Now it was Elly who helped Jimmy to his feet. The rain had mostly stopped. They went back down the block, Jimmy walking unsteadily and going on and on about someone named "the perfessor."

"Spends two dollar words like he's swallowed a goddamn dictionary. Just wait'll you hear…"

The saloon was nearly empty, the bartender wiping tables. At the back sat Red and another man. Red was telling a story that involved extravagant hand motions and sound effects. The other man was leaning back and nodding with his eyes half-closed.

"Yes, yes," he murmured. "How cunning."

"An then," cried Red, "an then the whole rig just BLEW—*ker-PSHHH!*" He demonstrated the force of the explosion by kicking out his legs and tossing his hat in the air.

"Great catamounts," said the other man. His crinkly eyes opened wide.

Jimmy laughed, bent to retrieve Red's hat, and fell on his face.

"It would seem," remarked the man, "young James is reaping the benefits of his debauch."

"So my pals and me, we took off a-runnin'"—Red's hand skittered across the table on running fingers—"an never looked back."

"Discretion the better part of valor," drawled the man, nodding.

"Didn't I tell yez!" said Jimmy, grinning at Elly.

"Oh hey, here he is," said Red, grabbing Elly by the waist. "This here's, this here's, uh…"

"Bert," said Jimmy.

"Right," said Red, squeezing Elly painfully.

The other man regarded Elly, and she regarded him back. He wore a tattered hat from which spilled thin, greasy strands of gray hair. Sunken cheeks covered with gray stubble, a long and interesting nose, very little chin, and two large yellow upper teeth. It was like being examined by a rather large rat in a fedora.

"These two together," Red was saying, "well, they's jus the jooka-lorum when it comes to moochin. You jus sit back and make like Rocky-feller and watch the greenbacks pile up."

"Capital!" said the man, holding up a long finger. "In both senses of the word."

"Uh-huh," said Red uncertainly. He poured the last of a bottle of whiskey into his glass and drained it in a swallow. The other man had only a glass of beer, mostly untouched.

"Bert," he said, musing on the name. "Are we to infer, Albert? Moniker of the late prince consort himself?"

Elly had actually named herself after her friend Albert Jenning, but she nodded anyway.

The man smiled his rodent smile and nodded along with her.

"He's a perfessor," said Jimmy. "Perfessor Carp."

"At the moment unattached to any university, alas" sighed the professor. "A ship without a port. A sort of 'Flying Dutchman' of academia, if you will." He made a vague gesture with a long bony hand.

The bartender was wiping the table next to them and glaring in their direction. Red appeared to be making a supreme effort to muster his wits.

"So, perfessor, whatya say? Thirty's cheap. Thirty for the pair."

"Yes," said Carp, nodding thoughtfully. "I think I can say we have come to terms."

Money was exchanged.

~

A few minutes later, Jimmy and Elly were back outside following Professor Carp through damp, shining streets.

"Why aren't we going with Red?" asked Elly.

Jimmy staggered along beside her with their bundle, his legs weaving. "Well Bert, I'd say that's cause, cause we done been sold."

And he giggled stupidly.

CHAPTER SEVENTEEN

TRAVELS WITH PROFESSOR CARP

The news was exciting: they would be leaving Los Angeles in a "dead head"—an empty passenger car the railroad was moving from one city to another.

"Yes, for once I shall be traveling in a style befitting one of my exalted station," said Professor Carp airily. "Albeit society seems blind to my qualities at the present moment," he added. He lay sprawled in one corner of the wrecked boxcar that had been their home for the past several weeks. His shoes were off, and his feet added a crowning touch to the boxcar's stink. Long, yellow toes protruded from the holes in his socks like bunches of bananas.

All around lay piles of moldering old newspapers. Elly missed reading terribly and had been avidly perusing them. Jimmy had challenged her to read something aloud. This she had done in her toneless voice, and he had been amazed. She offered to teach him how, but he had colored and said he'd tried before but the letters "jus danced around and wouldn't hold still long enough for me to make any damn sense out of em."

Professor Carp, too, had been surprised at Elly's reading skill. Jimmy had also caught her humming to herself, and—when she was in the mood—they could sometimes get her to sing songs (though she didn't much care for the sound of her own voice).

"*Music hath charms to soothe a savage beast,*" quoted Carp. "Or in this case, *two* savage beasts." He grinned toothily at Jimmy.

Elly imagined herself singing to a wolf or a bear and savored the thought.

"Actually a misquote of 'savage breast,'" added Carp with scholarly punctiliousness.

The professor had also discovered the secret of Elly's sex (a fact that, considering their circumstances, Jimmy felt compelled to reveal early on).

"Could it be?" Carp had cried, his eyes widening as though he had been suddenly awakened from a dream (which, in a way, he had). "Our young Albert is, in fact, an Albertina?"

Elly had blushed and nodded.

"Now don't you go lettin on to no one," said Jimmy, in the hectoring tone he had already adopted with the professor. Who, he had quickly decided, was "crazy as a bedbug an bout as useless."

Carp had declared his lips were sealed, her secret "entombed in the stygian depths of my soul."

Jimmy rolled his eyes, as he did at most of the things that came out of Carp's mouth. (The professor took no notice, for he had already drifted back into his dream. "Papageno and Papagena," he murmured, smiling to himself. "Birds of a feather…the cock shall shed his comb…") This was because, as Jimmy had informed Elly after only one day in his company, the professor was a hophead.

"Yer know, a dope fiend," he had explained. When Elly was still confused, Jimmy said this meant the professor liked drugs the way Montana Red like whiskey. "Saw it in his eyes last night in the bar—didn't yer feature how black they was? An he hardly touched his beer."

They were standing outside a drugstore, having completed their first day of begging in Los Angeles and given the proceeds, some three dollars and change, to the professor. He had listlessly dragged himself around all morning. But after he emerged from the store and ducked into an alley for a few moments, his lethargy had been magically transformed into feverish ebullience.

"Great catamounts!" he exclaimed, standing with hands on hips and beaming into the distance. "*Then felt I like some watcher of the skies, when a new planet swims into his ken…*"

Jimmy gave Elly a look. She stole a glance at Carp's eyes, which were indeed all dreamy blackness.

Since then Jimmy, in his growing contempt for the professor, had begun to withhold some of their earnings, a thing he had never dared do with Pete. Elly felt bad about this, especially since Carp sometimes passed back part of what they gave him with a grand gesture, like a duke tipping a servant. Elly used her money to buy a pair of hardly-worn boots from an old man in a black skullcap ("He's a kike," Jimmy had warned her, "don't let him gouge yez") as well as a faded union suit and other underclothing she desperately craved. She bought soap as well and tried to wash her clothes (and herself) in a muddy stream surrounded by cottonwoods behind the hobo jungle.

Jimmy sat on the bank idly watching as she stood knee-deep in the water wearing only a pair of wet drawers. "Why yer botherin?" he asked. "Jus gonna get dirty again."

"Because," said Elly, "we stink." She wrung her overalls out as best she could and hung them over a branch to dry. "That's why they won't let us in the door sometimes."

Jimmy's brow wrinkled, and Elly could see him working out the monetary implications of cleanliness.

"Ya reckon?" he finally said.

A minute later she was washing Jimmy's clothes as well and watched with amused satisfaction as he reluctantly scrubbed his pale body. She made him cut her hair with the pair of scissors she had bought, then did her best to trim his shaggy locks.

"Well ain't we jus a couple of swells," marveled Jimmy.

It was when they got back to the boxcar that Carp told them about the "dead head."

"The gent who informed me had it on best authority. Brakeman himself. Horse's mouth, as it were. Going all the way to Flagstaff. Christmas amongst the mesas and mesquite. Most picturesque." He extracted a packet of white powder, shook some of it into his cupped fist, inhaled with an explosive snort, then he and Jimmy left to join the other men around the evening campfire.

Elly stayed behind to pore over the stack of newspapers she had not yet looked through. She had been clipping out pictures with her new scissors—images of actresses and alligators and the Taj Mahal—intending to make a scrapbook. The papers were from 1906, almost three years old. She found a fascinating article about a steam-powered automobile built by the Stanley brothers that had set a new speed record of 128 miles per hour on a Florida beach. She clipped out the photograph of the amazing vehicle, which looked something like an inverted canoe, and added it to her collection. The light was fading, and she was about to join the others around the fire when she happened to glance at another old, yellowed front page—and froze.

THOUSANDS DEAD IN EARTHQUAKE AND FIRE, screamed the gigantic headline. Then underneath in smaller type: "San Francisco Reduced to Rubble and Ashes." Beneath was a photograph of hundreds of people standing with their backs to the camera, looking down a steep-hilled street that ended abruptly in a black wall of billowing smoke. She stared at the picture in horrified fascination:

It was an image straight out of the nightmares she still had.

Feverishly she read every scrap of print and pored over more pictures of burning buildings and fleeing crowds, until the light finally faded. Distant laughter reached her from the men around the fire as she carefully folded the paper and put it with her clippings. She lay down with Mr. Hoppy, wrapped herself in a blanket, and looked through the hole in the ruined boxcar's roof. And saw not a jaggedly-shaped patch of sky, but a hotel folding like a house of cards into a cloud of dust.

As if a dam had broken, more awful images flooded her mind. Molly Doyle lying beneath a pile of bricks. A man with huge staring eyes chasing Elly through streets that swallowed horses whole. And—over and over—the hotel in which her parents had been peacefully sleeping, crumbling before her eyes. Nightmare images she suddenly knew, with a terrible certainty, were actually memories…

When her sobs finally subsided, she took a shuddering breath, and squeezed the last tears from her eyes with her fists. In the patch of violet sky, a single star was struggling to wink itself into existence. Around the campfire someone began to play "My Old Kentucky Home" on a harmonica. And Elly decided she was finished crying.

She hugged Mr. Hoppy to herself, and sang along.

．　　　　　．　　　　　．

The sun was just coming up as they crept with their bundles toward an old rusty passenger car. It sat on a siding with its window shades pulled down, unattached to anything, looking utterly forlorn.

"That ol car looks like it's set there for a hunnert years," said Jimmy, disgusted. "An it's fixin to go fer another hunnert."

"Nevertheless, I was assured it shall be leaving this very morning," said Carp, sounding doubtful. "And I have kept it under my hat, as it were. We are the only ones privy to the information." He glanced furtively around, then tried the door. It was stuck fast. "Rusted, it seems." He jerked it harder. to no effect.

The blind covering the window beside the door suddenly rose up a crack. An eye peered at them. They heard the sounds of something being jiggled, then the door jerked open.

"Get in," hissed a voice.

They squeezed inside with their bundles, and the door clanked shut. Inside, it was dark and smelled of rust and mildew. The man who had let them in was busy wiring the door shut again. Their eyes began to adjust to the dim light, and the professor chuckled.

The whole car was full of bums.

They went down the aisle with their bundles and passed tramps of every description. There was another boy about Jimmy's age and a long-haired tramp in a corduroy cap Elly suspected was a woman. They found two empty seats. Their velvet cushions were ripped and covered with mold. Elly sat next to the professor, and Jimmy found a seat across the aisle next to an old man with a long, gnomish beard. They had just settled their bundles beneath their seats, when they heard the sound of a locomotive starting up in the distance.

"She's a-comin'," yelled someone. "Everybody lay low."

All around them people began scrambling for the floor. A shaft of sunlight pierced the darkness. "Keep them blinds down, fer fuck's sake!" hissed a voice. Carp pulled Elly down next to him. There were shouts outside, the locomotive grew louder, then the car gave a lurch as it was hitched to the train. Someone outside began pulling on the door. Everyone held their breath.

"It's okay," they heard a shout. "She's rusted shut."

There were more jerks as more cars were attached. Then another long wait. Finally they began to move, slowly at first, then faster and faster…

All around them, people were taking their seats and pulling up blinds, and the car was flooded with light. Elly turned around in her seat and gazed at the scene with delight. The carload of shaggy, unkempt passengers was like a looking glass picture of her former life. The journey was cock-eyed as well. Hoboes strolled the aisle and traded stories, or sprawled snoring on the luxurious seats. But every time the train slowed for a station, there was another mad scramble to pull the blinds down and hit the floor.

"Alas" said the professor, crouching next to Elly, "first class is not what it once was."

"Shut up, ya idjit," hissed a voice behind them.

Then the door would be tried again, found to be "rusted shut," the train would start up—and everyone would return to their seats like nothing had happened.

Someone tried to get a drink from the water tank at the front of the car, only to find it dry.

"Ya wants service, ya gots to pay extree," the gnomish old man called out to hoots of laughter.

Elly looked around for Jimmy and found him talking to the other boy. He was scrawny and missing several teeth, and his pants were held up by a rope over one shoulder. His face had a feral look, and he talked in spasms as though unaccustomed to speech. Next to him, a grizzled man lay with his head back and his mouth open, and his breath was that of a corpse.

Jimmy said as much.

"Naw, he ain't dead," said the boy. He sounded disgusted by this fact.

"Ain't he treat yer right?" said Jimmy.

The boy jerked his head. "Beats me," he said. He leaned forward and pulled up his shirt. His back was woven with scars like a basket. "After we gets back to Oklahoma, I'm gone kill him."

At the back of the car, a group of colored men sat together, passing around a bottle and laughing. It reminded Elly of the colored cars on the trains she used to ride.

"Well looky here," said one of them, catching sight of Elly. "The conductor done come for our tickets."

"Well, I'm jus so sorry Mr. Conductor man," said another, "I seem to has *mislaid* mine somewheres."

They laughed and Elly understood it was a joke. She gave the closest thing she had to a smile, skipped away, and plopped down next to the professor. He was reading from a tattered volume whose loose pages were normally bound up with twine, for she had seen him pull it out before. She looked at it curiously.

"Ah, tis young Albert, come back to the fold. And wondering what tome the dotty old professor holds so dear as to carry next to his bosom."

Elly filed away this reference to the masculine bosom as Carp flipped the book's loose leaves to the title page: *Walden, or Life in the Woods*, by Henry David Thoreau.

"In this book, Albert, are words to live by," said Carp, tapping the page. "A paean to the life of men such as ourselves. Men—er, in your case I use the term loosely—who refuse to begin digging their own graves as soon as they are born. Men who are not slave-drivers of themselves. In short, men who are *free*, Albert—*free!*" The professor's yellow eyes were ablaze. "And," he continued, riffling through the pages, "men who are a minority, an elect!" He stabbed at an underlined passage. "Read!" he commanded.

"'The mass of men live lives of quiet desperation,'" read Elly.

"Ha! Ha!" cried Carp. He shuffled the pages and pointed anew.

"'Beware of all enterprises which require new clothes—'"

"'—and not rather a new *wearer* of clothes,'" finished the professor. "D'you see, Albert? Doth it penetrate?"

Elly thought about it. "It means," she concluded, "don't judge a book by its cover."

Carp went bug-eyed. "Great catamounts!" he exclaimed, slapping his knee. "The child has a mind!"

"And you got a mouth," murmured a voice behind them.

The professor took no notice, for he was lit. He expounded on Thoreau's philosophy, touched on his relationship with Ralph Waldo Emerson, elucidated the tenets of something called transcendentalism…

Elly listened, rapt. The ideas were confusing, and she had to ask for some definitions. But Carp's enthusiasm was contagious and the words themselves like music. Occasionally he would ask her to read another passage or repeat a definition he had given her a half hour earlier. Only to explode, after her word-perfect responses, in yet another firework display of erudition…

Outside, the day was winding down. The setting sun had transmuted an empty, arid expanse of sand into shimmering gold. Carp, too, seemed to be winding down. His eyes fluttered, and his head fell to his chest. But thoughts continued to dribble from his mouth like air from a leaky balloon.

"Beginnings of…anti-materialism…American thought," he mumbled. "Influence…Marx and Engels…suspected but…not confirmed…"

The book slipped from his fingers, and the pages fluttered to the floor. Elly gathered them up. She ordered them, rebound them with the piece of twine, and put the book back in the professor's hand. He opened a bleary eye and regarded it, then looked at Elly. Nodding to himself, he handed the book back to her.

"You are a scholar now," he said. "And this shall be the first volume in your library."

He leaned back, closed his eyes again, and smiled.

·   ·   ·

All through their travels together, Carp continued to tutor Elly. For texts, they raided libraries. The professor would choose a book, then distract the librarian (he could, Jimmy said, "spin a load of bull like nobody's business") while Elly slipped the desired volume down the front of her overalls. They pinched Voltaire, Plato, Montaigne. On all these Carp could—and did—lecture for hours. Timing was of paramount importance, however. Too early and he was listless, impatient, abrupt; too late and his speeches became fantastical, and Elly could make little sense out of them. From time to time, he went on patent medicine binges, guzzling whole bottles of the stuff Hazel Bland had taken in ladylike sips; at such times he was possessed by dreams and quite useless. But when he was in fine form, the thoughts flew from his brain like sparks from a blacksmith's hammer.

Jimmy could hardly contain his disgust at the turn things had taken.

"Bert, that ol fish got yer plum bamboozled with all his gab. Don't yer see it's all a bluff? I swear, the other boes is pissin theyselves fer laughin at him."

Yet Jimmy had to concede that Carp had his points. His scientific approach to begging, for instance.

"In any town," the professor had explained early on, "the most pious folk will be found living near a church. Sadly, said 'piousness' most often manifests itself as priggishness and hypocrisy. Yet a predictable percentage of these people will possess that traditional Christian attribute known as charity."

Jimmy had frowned, trying to make sense of the professor's words (and when he finally did, had scoffed as usual). But soon enough he realized the old dog was right. For, by making straight for the nearest steeple in each town and working the houses around it in expanding circles, they had surprising success.

It was in Mobile that Elly and Carp (having managed to pinch a volume of Gibbons from the local library) were walking back down the main street, when they passed a store window featuring a display of Edison talking machines.

The professor stopped and examined them with interest.

P.D. QUAVER

"A wonder of the age, Albert. One of the fruits of our enlarged brains" (they had been studying Darwinism) "thus setting us even farther apart from our apish ancestors."

Elly stared at the strange contrivances. Something in her look made Carp's eyes widen with surprise.

"Don't tell me you've never had the experience?"

Esta Sangley had promised to play Elly her own recording of "I Don't Care." But you couldn't play cylinders on a moving train, so they'd never gotten around to it.

She shook her head.

"Ah!" The professor's jaundiced eyes took on a mischievous gleam. He straightened the brim of his tattered fedora, and they entered the store.

Given the state of their clothing, Elly was sure they would be immediately thrown out—and indeed, the pasty-faced young girl at the counter looked ready to do just that. But before she could get the words out, the old rascal released his silver tongue like a ship getting off the first broadside.

"My dear young lady! This poor child—possessed, I should point out, of an uncommon musicality—has never had the good fortune to hear one of these extraordinary devices in operation. Such a deficit in her experience surely needs to be rectified, do you not agree? So if you could find it in your heart to provide her with a demonstration, well"—a courtly bow—"we should be forever in your debt."

As though hypnotized, the girl nodded dumbly, pulled a shiny grooved cylinder from a cardboard box, and inserted it on the spindle of one of the machines. She cranked a handle and released a switch. But when the cylinder began to rotate, what emerged from the machine's brass horn was not a tinkly music box tune but "The Stars and Stripes Forever." And though the sound was scratchy and distorted—a sort of aural Frankenstein's monster—Elly had not the slightest doubt she was listening to the memory of real people playing real instruments.

Her mouth fell open in astonishment.

Carp tapped his fingers on the counter to the rhythm and grinned at her. The trombones, transmogrified by the device into something akin to bass kazoos, stuttered out the interlude leading to the trio. Carp picked up the cardboard box and examined it. "The master himself at the baton," he exclaimed. "Imagine, having John Phillip Sousa at your beck and call—"

"Margaret! What on earth—" A hefty, red-faced man in shirtsleeves and striped vest had entered the store. "I go out for five minutes—and return to find you serenading a pair of filthy tramps!"

"But Daddy—"

"Go on! Out with you!" cried the man, making shooing motions as if they were a species of vermin.

The professor remained unruffled. He thanked the girl, doffed his hat ironically to the man, and—just as the trumpets began to repeat the chorus with piccolo *obbligato*—marched smartly out of the shop with Elly trailing behind.

"Well!" he exclaimed, standing on the sidewalk and smoothing his frayed cuffs. "That is one establishment we shall not be patronizing in future."

.   .   .

For a year and a half, the three of them traveled, moving from place to place on a whim, following the weather. The professor pontificated on the histories of the various cities they passed through. His favorite topic was the War Between the States. At the age of fourteen, he had run away from home to enlist, he told them, but—to his eternal regret—the conflict ended before he saw any action. Yet the Blue and the Gray must have still been battling it out in the professor's brain, for he seemed to have the war's entire history at his command. He pointed out Lookout Mountain in Chattanooga and spun colorful accounts of the burning of Atlanta and the terrible trench warfare at Richmond.

Jimmy listened to these speeches in spite of himself. He warmed to Carp still further when the professor—having decided Elly's diet of philosophy might be leavened with the occasional novel—read aloud, with much panache, *The Adventures of Robinson Crusoe*. From the first mention of cannibals, he had Jimmy's undivided attention. Elly, for her part, was excited to finally discover what the Twin Sisters had been singing about (though vaguely disappointed that the promised "wild women" never materialized).

Jimmy was so captivated by the book, he tried to get Elly to act it out with him, a hobo jungle standing in for the real jungle. But when he told her she had to be Friday because "yer the one with the nigger hair," she scowled and refused.

Tom Sawyer was an even greater success, Jimmy delighting that here was a book where "folks talk like folks talk." He made Elly reread the whitewashing of the fence chapter the next day, laughing again in all the same places.

"Well ain't Tom a swift one!" he exclaimed, leaning back and chewing on a blade of grass. "Jus look at him work that ol dodge!"

They sat together on a hillside overlooking the Saint Louis waterfront. It was late summer. They had set off from Vicksburg (which, the professor had informed them, never celebrated the Fourth of July, that being the day the city had fallen to the Union) and reached the city after a leisurely journey by freight train. Their open boxcar had offered a view of the Mississippi that the professor proclaimed "superior to anything in first class," and Elly had to agree. The mighty river shimmered in the heat like a mirage, and every new turn revealed a tow boat pushing a string of coal barges or a magnificent paddlewheel steamer like a floating wedding cake. From their vantage point above the levee, they looked down on a score of steamboats huddled against the city's flanks like a litter of suckling pigs.

"Where'd yer say ol Tom's from again?" asked Jimmy, when Elly had finished the chapter.

"Hannibal. It's north of here." Elly had been studying maps, and asked a question she'd been wanting to ask for a very long time. "Where are you from?"

"Me?" said Jimmy. He sounded uncomfortable. "I'm from Pittsy."

"Pittsburgh."

"Uh-huh."

"That's where the Monongahela and the Alleghany rivers meet to form the Ohio," said Elly, showing off.

"You say so." Jimmy picked up a pebble and threw it aimlessly.

"Is your family still there?"

Jimmy made a disgusted noise. "Family—huh! Ain't never had no family. Had a mama was a drunk and a stepdaddy I like to have killt. Big ol fat Dutchy. Sposed to be a ironworker, but he had spells so he couldn't keep a job. Jus set around all day an drunk his schnapps, and when he got drunk enough he'd beat on us fer nothin, jus fer sport, and laugh while he done it. Mama tried to make do with sewin, but she was mostly too drunk, an he'd beat on her fer not gettin any money. She got to where she was shamed to go out an look for work, she was that bruised up. So I had to pinch stuff so's we could eat. Bout the only fun me an Liddie ever had was watchin the Dutchy havin one a his spells. His eyes'd roll up in his head, he'd flop around some, an yer could hit him then all yer wanted cause he never remembered nothin after. Yeah," said Jimmy, laughing crazily, "me an Liddie would whale the bejesus outa him. Hit him in the belly oncet with a big ol stick whilst he was a-floppin around. Shoulda went fer his head." He shook his head ruefully and tossed another pebble.

"Was Liddie your sister?"

Jimmy let out a long sigh. "Uh-huh."

"What was she like?"

"Liddie?" Jimmy lay back on the grass and looked at the sky as though some fleecy cloud might hold the answer. "She was bout three years older 'n me." (Jimmy's age was a mystery to himself. Around the other hoboes he claimed to be sixteen, but he had once confided in Elly he was "probly nearer bout fourteen an a half.") "They was two others, but they died," he added.

"Was it the pneumonyer?" asked Elly.

"*Pshh!*" said Jimmy. "Pneumonyer! One of em got run over by a dray full of iron bridge girders, an t'other one got into the cornmeal. Et so much her stomach swole up an she choked on her own spit. Pneumonyer!" He twisted a strand of grass in his fingers, still staring at the sky. A long way off the calliope of a passing steamboat began playing "My Darling Clementine." The mournful, whistling tones seemed to shimmer in the heat like the air over the river.

"She was pretty," said Jimmy suddenly. "Liddy. She could pretend like she was the Dutchy talkin his Dutchy talk an make me bout sick with laughin. Guys is sposed to hate they sisters, but me an her was pals. I tole her when I got outa the ref, I'd kill that ol Dutchy an we'd run away together."

Elly waited. "What happened?" she finally asked.

Jimmy sighed. He sat up, pulled off one of his boots, lifted the leather insole, and extracted a square of folded cardboard. He handed it to Elly without a word.

She unfolded it. It was a postcard with a picture of a railroad car parked on a mountainside at an impossible angle. "Pikes Peak Cog Railway" was written in white script in the corner. She flipped the card over. It was postmarked "Manitou Springs, Colorado" and addressed to "James McGann, Reading Industrial School for Boys, Reading, Pennsylvania." Next to it was a message written in a clumsy, childish hand. "Read it," said Jimmy. Elly read:

> *Dear Jimmy*
> *I got maryed to John Skeets we ar going to Cripple Creek*
> *John has a pal there with a staik hope you ar fine*
> *Lydia*

Jimmy mouthed the words as she read. He nodded, folded the postcard back up, and returned it to his boot.

"Who is John Skeets?" asked Elly.

"Hell if I know."

There didn't seem much else to say. The calliope music was now so distant, it was like they were dreaming it.

"Sing me that song," said Jimmy.

Elly looked at him.

"That one bout the girl with the light brown hair."

"Jeannie."

Jimmy nodded. "Liddie had light brown hair," he said. "It makes me think of Liddie."

"I can change the name," suggested Elly.

Jimmy nodded again. He lay down and stared at the sky again as Elly began to sing in her thin, clear voice:

I dream of Liddie with the light brown hair,
Borne like a vapor on the summer's air…

They took the streetcar back to the rail yard, stopping first so Jimmy could buy some whiskey. Elly didn't like when he did this. But today they had plenty of money, and Jimmy was in the mood to celebrate. The professor was on one of his binges, so they had gone back-door begging without him that morning. And at one house, they had a windfall.

A nervous, raw-boned woman, who smelled of onions, let them in. As they sat down at the kitchen table, Elly hugged Mr. Hoppy and Jimmy went into his spiel. The two of them were as smooth and practiced now as a vaudeville team, which was how Elly tried to think of what they did. As she stared with a stony expression at nothing at all (as her part dictated) she found herself looking through a door propped open for the breeze into the interior of the house. And her heart leapt at the sight of a piano in the parlor.

She saw them often, in those rooms to which they were never invited, and the sight always filled her with bitter longing. While Jimmy rattled on with his gab, a girl about Elly's age suddenly came into the parlor, sat down at the piano, and began to play.

Except she couldn't play.

The piece she couldn't play was Beethoven's "Fur Elise"—a simple thing Elly could have tossed off in any key blindfolded. But the silly girl could not play a bar without a wrong note and her rhythms were all mangled: to Elly it was like watching a pretty doll have its limbs savagely torn off. She longed to knock the inept child from the bench and play the song the way it needed to be played. But instead, she had to sit and listen as the girl attacked the poor piece again and again like a never-sated sadist…

Fat tears ran down Elly's cheeks. Dimly she sensed a sudden break in Jimmy's speech and realized both he and the woman were staring at her, the woman with pity in her eyes, and Jimmy with amazement. But Jimmy was a pro, and a moment later he was milking the situation for all it was worth.

"…an now poor Albert here, ever since our lil sis done died, well he jus never talks a word. Jus carries around poor lil Matilda's dolly, won't never part with it, and never stops crying the live-long day—"

And the woman had burst into tears herself, hugged Elly, and given them five whole dollars. All the time, the girl kept up her ungodly hammering, and Elly just wanted to kill her.

"Holy jumpin turnips, Bert," cried Jimmy when they left, "that was the hell-firingest piece a work I ever seen!"

Elly had scowled in response (and, to Jimmy's disappointment, was unable to repeat the performance in any other houses). Nevertheless, they were now flush, and Jimmy swaggered into the hobo jungle like a conquering hero. They stopped to check on Carp. The professor lay shaded by a piece of tin with his shirt off. His withered chest was as pale yellow as a snake's belly and glistened with sweat. Empty patent medicine bottles littered the ground. His eyelids flickered, and one of his arms slowly rose in greeting; the effect was of a corpse coming back to life.

"All that we see or seem," he intoned, *"is but a dream within a dream…"*

Jimmy ignored him and strode off toward the fire, eager to show off their take to the other bums. Elly got the professor a drink of water and sat with him a while, politely listening to him ramble on until it became clear he had no idea she was even there.

The sun had set when she wandered over to the fire. A scruffy pack of bums was busily devouring a mess of the ubiquitous hobo dish of whatever-is-at-hand known as "Mulligan stew." They ate it out of tin cups and cracked bowls. One old man poured his into an old shoe and was trying to eat it before it dribbled out of the cracks. From the aroma—more palatable than usual—Elly suspected the sack of food they'd bought featured heavily in the recipe. One look at Jimmy's flushed, beaming face confirmed this. And confirmed as well that he was drunk.

"Purty good eatin," said someone, breaking the silence.

"You betcha," said another.

There was a loud belch.

"Kid, we's obliged to ya," said the old man, spooning the last morsel from his shoe and tossing it aside.

"Like I said it was—hey, there he is!" said Jimmy, waving toward Elly. "An see, he's got his dolly, jus like I tole yez!"

"Well so he does!"

Elly hugged Mr. Hoppy, embarrassed. On the other side of the fire, a huge, ugly young man with flaming red hair had stopped eating his stew to stare at her.

"Jus like I tole yez!" repeated Jimmy, waving his bottle. "He's a twenty-four carat goldmine, ol Bert! Jus sets there bawlin an them housewifes fall over theyselves loadin us up with grub and silver dollars. Sometimes we can't hardly haul it back it's so much!"

Elly was more embarrassed than ever. The huge red-headed youth, a giant with the face of a demented child, was still staring at her in a way that bothered her. She gave Jimmy a disgusted look and wandered back toward their camp.

.   .   .

Jimmy slept late. When he finally staggered out from under their sheet metal lean-to, the sun seemed to cleave his skull. He made it to the creek, lay down with his face in the water, drank until he about burst, then drank some more. He splashed water over his head and got shakily to his feet.

Back at the camp, the professor was squatting and drinking coffee from a tin cup. When he raised it to his lips his hand shook. He poured a cup for Jimmy from a chipped enamel pot, and they sat sipping in silence.

Jimmy tried to remember the evening before, but much of it was hazy. He knew he had been gassing it up something awful and was vaguely ashamed. There had been some funny talk, but he couldn't remember much of it. Someone had asked a bum with a peg leg how he could chase trains, and he said he could "get er goin fast enough to outrun the whole pack of yez"—that had been a good one. There'd been a whole family of dagos, woman with a kerchief and a kid who looked sickly, but they didn't stay around the fire long. That old man who ate his mulligan out of a shoe—ha! And that big ugly kid, big as a giant he was, who never said a word. Jimmy thought he was a Dutchy with his orange hair, but someone said he was a Swede. Face like a Halloween pumpkin carved by a blind man. The way he had stared while Jimmy was gassing about old Bert and his doll. Give a body the creepy-crawlies…

"Where's Bert?" said Jimmy.

Carp wasn't much for talk in the morning, which counted for a heaven-sent miracle. He shrugged.

Jimmy wandered over to the fire. The man with the peg leg was grilling a rabbit on a stick over last night's embers. He looked up.

"Tole ya I could get er goin," he said. "Caught this little feller—jus straight outrun the sumbitch."

Jimmy wasn't buying his guff, but he sat down anyway.

"You don't look so hot," said the bum cordially.

Jimmy shrugged.

"Saw yer little buddy early on. One with the dolly. You rentin him out or sumpin?"

Jimmy stared at him. "What yer say?"

"Saw that big, dumb Swede leadin him by the hand—"

"What?" said Jimmy. He was suddenly wide awake.

"Sun barely up, couldn't see too good. But I'm sure it was him, only one around here that big. They was goin that way, toward the yard—"

"Why you ol cock-eyed lizard, why in the name of Christ didn't yer stop him?" cried Jimmy. He was standing over the man with his fists balled. The old bum squinted up at him.

"You talked that boy an his dolly up pretty good last night." His eyes gleamed with malice.

Jimmy gave a strangled cry and ran back toward camp.

The man laughed and began to chew on his rabbit.

CHAPTER EIGHTEEN

IN THRALL TO THE GIANT

Torkel Lunberg lay stretched out in the bottom of the empty coal car, lulled by the rhythm of the train, watching the sky through the narrow opening above. It seemed to Torkel like a big blue eye looking back at him.

He was proud of himself for how well things had gone. He swiveled his head lazily to the side and looked at the boy. He sat huddled in the shadows cradling his doll. How lucky it was that Torkel had remembered the doll! It would have been so easy to forget, for Torkel found it hard to keep two things in his mind at once. And indeed, the act of clapping his hand over the boy's mouth and lifting his struggling body had been so satisfying—so like landing a large, wriggling fish—that he would have forgotten the doll if it hadn't fallen from the boy's arms and lay there, staring up at Torkel in the dim morning light.

He was proud of himself, for the doll was important—the other boy had said so. The doll made people give them food. And money to buy whiskey, for the boy had whiskey. And a big sack of food—Torkel saw it with his own eyes. Though why the doll should make them do this mystified Torkel. Perhaps it had a magic power?

He reached over and grabbed the doll from the boy. The boy tried to grab it back so Torkel cuffed him one. He held the doll in the shaft of light slanting down from above and examined it. It was just a doll. A funny-looking one, though. He squeezed it all over, then looked at its face. It looked back at him. This bothered Torkel. Perhaps the doll's power was in its eyes? He pulled one off and scrutinized it. The boy made a sound and reached for the doll, so Torkel cuffed him again. The eye had somehow turned into a button. He pulled off the other eye, but it did the same thing. Bored, Torkel threw the buttons away and tossed the now-sightless doll back to the boy. But the boy lay as motionless as the lumps of coal littering the floor of the car, and Torkel decided he had fallen asleep.

The train stopped several times but they did not get off, for Torkel wanted to get far away. The boy awakened, examined the doll wordlessly, then stuffed it inside his overalls. By mid-afternoon, the car had become an oven and Torkel grew thirsty. The train began to slow down. Torkel stood up and the boy cowered. Torkel slung him over his shoulder, grabbed his bundle, leapt up to grasp the lip of the opening, and hauled himself to the top of the car with one arm. He clambered down the iron ladder and stood on the lowest rung waiting for the right moment. The broad river's silvery surface winked at him through the trees. He jumped and hit the ground running, letting out a whoop of pure animal happiness.

He found a stream that fed the river, and they both drank and washed coal dust from their faces. One side of the boy's face was purple and swollen, and Torkel dimly wondered if this would affect his begging. He was eager to try the boy out because he was getting hungry. Torkel himself could not beg because people were afraid of him, so he was reduced to stealing or taking things by force. Occasionally he got jobs as a day laborer, but these seldom lasted because the men he worked with were afraid of him too. It might have gone better for him if he talked more, he thought. But though he understood English well enough (he had understood about the boy and his doll and how they went in the back doors of houses and people gave them things), Torkel was afraid to speak it, because people laughed at how he sounded. Even Swedes laughed at the way he spoke Swedish.

As eager as he was to try the boy out, it was getting late with no houses in sight. So he set off along the tracks toward the city. Torkel could feel the boy wanting to run and kept an eye on him. The river glimmered in the late afternoon sun. There was no wind. The air was thick and smelled of things breeding and rotting in the heat.

After a while, the water Torkel had drunk ran through him, and he stopped to relieve himself. Sure enough, as soon as he got a good stream going, the boy took off, running as aimlessly as a scared rabbit. It made Torkel laugh. In no particular hurry he buttoned his trousers, caught up with the boy in a few giant strides, and cuffed him to the ground. The boy lay a long time without moving. Torkel became impatient and hauled him to his feet, but he would not stay up. So he threw the boy over his shoulder and continued on.

He came to where another, smaller river emptied into the big one. It was getting dark and he could see the lights of the city in the distance, but the only way across the river was the train bridge. It was a long way across, and he didn't want to be caught. He put his ear to one of the rails but couldn't hear anything, so he loped across the bridge with the boy on his shoulder.

A little farther on, he came to a group of hoboes gathered around a fire. He put the boy on the ground; he crawled a few feet, then collapsed in the dirt. No one said anything, and he saw they were afraid of him. He sat with them. They gave him some food, which he wolfed down, then passed him some corn liquor. The boy was sitting up now. Torkel offered him the jar of liquor, but he just stared at the ground. Torkel laughed, and the men sitting beside him slowly sidled away from him. After a while, he reached across the fire, grabbed the jar of liquor again, and drank the rest of it in one go. No one said anything. The stars spun around in circles and made Torkel laugh some more. He began to sing a song his mother had sung to him. It was the only song he knew, and he could only remember two lines. So he sang them over and over:

Vem kan segla förutan vind,
Vem kan ro utan åror…

Over and over he sang them, and the fire blazed, and the stars spun round in circles. After a while, he realized the other men had all left. He picked up the boy and stumbled into the darkness and found a spot. He used the rope tying his bundle to tie the boy's hands and feet. And Torkel fell asleep dreaming of all the food and whiskey he would have tomorrow.

·   ·   ·

It was funny, thought Jimmy later, how there had been no talk between him and Carp about what to do. They both just up and went at things, like going after Bert was the only possible thing. And Jimmy had to hand it to the old buzzard: as worthless a gasbag as he usually was, he put all that gabbing to harness now and worried all of those bums like a terrier at a rat to find out what they knew.

The more they learned, the worse it got.

"Seven foot tall, strong as a ox, and twicet as dumb," said one.

"Don't know nothin bout him," said another. "An I don't wanna know."

They found two other men who had seen the giant Swede leading Bert toward the rail yard, and both agreed it was just before sun-up. "Looked like they was out to catch the Big Four freight. Leaves every mornin at six A.M. for Cincy," said one, and the other nodded agreement.

It was late afternoon, they must have interrogated thirty bums, before they finally found a wizened little tobacco-chewing tramp who knew him.

"Yeah, I run into that big dumb Swede before," he said. "I'd stay away from him, I was you." He spat for emphasis.

"And why is that?" asked Carp. They squatted next to the old bum and watched as he sewed a patch onto a pair of trousers with, Jimmy thought, pansy-ish delicacy.

"Why is that?" repeated the little tramp. He interrupted his stitching to give the professor the once-over with his yellow cat's eyes. "Why, because he'll kill ya, a course." He chuckled, spat, and resumed sewing.

"Tell me about him," said Carp. He gave a little nod to Jimmy, who pulled out the bottle they'd been using to loosen tongues. The old man grinned, put down the trousers, and took a most unpansy-ish slug. He wiped his mouth and nodded.

"Don't know his name. Don't hardly talk and when he does, folks wants to laugh, but mostly they don't dare. Ain't just that he's so big, and strong enough to push a train off the tracks. It's cause he's wrong in the head. First time I lamped that Jack-o-lantern noggin a his, I knowed it. Like somebody carved out his head and stuck a animal inside, and it's lookin outa the eyeholes at ya."

He took another slug of whiskey, and continued.

"Saw him beat a man to death in Chatanoogie. Least I think he died—I didn't hang around long enough to find out. Beat him to bloody meat over who's turn it was at the liquor barrel someone stole off a wagon—over nothin at all. Fought like a mick at Donnybrook Fair, used those mitts a his like sledgehammers. We left the rest a the barrel to him and welcome to it."

The old man passed back the bottle and bit off a chaw of tobacco. He picked up the trousers again and squinted at his handiwork.

"Did he do any punk-running?" asked the professor.

The bum jerked his head up and stared. "Punk-running? Him? Be like givin a kitten to a oranger-tang!"

He chuckled and spat.

.   .   .

They woke up early to catch the same train east. Coal cars were always empty going this direction, and Carp—despite his unhealthy, skeletal look—hoisted himself up onto one with surprising agility; he was, after all, an old hobo. When the train crossed the river and slowed down into Cairo, they jumped off and spent the rest of the morning talking to the hoboes there. In the afternoon, they hopped a drag further east to the next big town and made more inquiries.

But no one had seen the giant Swede.

.   .   .

Elly could feel herself starting to slip into a dream world, a seductive place where there was no pain, no rope chafing her wrists, and no giant tearing

Mr. Hoppy's eyes out—a giant whose own eyes were so scary that to look into them was to lose herself…

She knew this world, had been there before. It was the place she had gone after watching her parents die in the earthquake. On that occasion her dream world had perhaps saved her. But this time something told her she could not go there and survive.

She forced herself to stay awake and pay attention.

With her one eye not swollen shut, she could see tall buildings rising above the trees ahead and knew they were walking toward a city. Pain pierced her side with every step, and her head felt like it belonged to someone else. But she struggled to keep pace with the giant to avoid another beating.

They came to a house on the outskirts of the city, an unpainted place with a rusted tin roof and sagging porch. The giant stopped and tilted his huge round head with its shaggy, orange mane down toward her, and his mouth spread in a horrible imitation of a smile. Elly realized with utter despair what was being asked of her.

"Begga," said the giant, pushing her in the direction of the house. "You begga."

As though to her own execution, Elly stumbled around the house toward the back. It wasn't even the right kind of house, she noted, for she and Jimmy had become expert appraisers of begging potential. Smoke came from a stove pipe, and there was a smell of baking bread. Clutching poor, blind Mr. Hoppy, she crept up to the screen door. Inside the kitchen, she could make out a dark figure. She gave a timid knock. The person inside rattled pots and pans around and took no notice. Steeling herself, she knocked louder. A large woman came to the door. Elly took in bare, sweaty arms mottled with flour but could look no higher.

"My Lord, what in the—?" cried the woman in a shocked voice.

Staring at the ground now, Elly began reciting Jimmy's speech in a soft monotone—

She got as far as the word "hand-out," when the door slammed in her face.

·   ·   ·

When she returned, the giant was grinning at her. But at the sight of her empty hands his face fell, and he let out a moan and knocked her to the ground. Then he hauled her to her feet and marched her to the next house…

The terrible day dragged on. One woman was moved to pity and let Elly inside and bathed her battered face. Over and over she asked, "Who did this to you, child? For pity's sake, tell me!" But Elly could only repeat Jimmy's spiel while staring at the floor. The woman clucked her impatience, and sent her back with only an apple to appease the giant.

The giant stared at the apple with an empty expression, then ate it in a few bites. He had stopped beating her, his rage replaced by despondency. But Elly had no doubt that if things kept on like this, a truly terrible reckoning awaited her.

They continued their hopeless quest. In the afternoon, another woman let her inside. She had blonde braids tightly pinned to her head and spoke with an accent. She listened to Elly's listless lies with a look of incomprehension, staring at her battered face. As she had all day, Elly was reciting the tale of "poor little Matilda" in Jimmy's exact words. But they made no sense—for how could she say she never spoke, and here she was chattering away? But she had no idea what else to do.

While talking of Matilda's doll, she held out Mr. Hoppy. The woman leaned over to examine him.

"*Ach!*" she exclaimed, brushing at the loose threads that marked where his eyes had been. "*Wo sind die Augen?*"

She rushed away and returned with a sewing basket. Together they chose two matching buttons that the woman sewed on, murmuring about "der poor froggy!" They weren't exactly Mr. Hoppy's eyes—they gave him a roguish and knowing expression he had never had before—but Elly was very pleased and tried to twist her swollen face into a smile. The woman gave her a glass of milk and a slice of buttered bread, which she could hardly chew. But she was so hungry she ate it anyway, even though she knew she should give it to the giant. She was sent away with even more food in a paper sack, as well as two shiny new quarters.

The giant seized the sack and was devouring the bread and sausage when he caught sight of Mr. Hoppy. He gave a yell, dropped the sausage, and grabbed the doll, staring into his new eyes with amazement. Elly watched with despair, certain Mr. Hoppy was about to be blinded yet again. In desperation, she thrust out her hand and revealed the quarters. Another yell from the giant. He snatched up the coins, lifted Elly into the air, and did a sort of dance. Then he put her down, returned Mr. Hoppy to her arms, and pointed to the next house, grinning eagerly.

Once again, Elly went around to the back of the house, had the door slammed in her face, and trudged back empty-handed. The giant held out his hand, grinning horribly. Elly shook her head. The giant's face underwent a terrible change. He let out a low moan and raised his fist…

~

Torkel had been so sure that with its eyes magically restored, the doll had regained its power—the money had proved it! But now he understood nothing at all. He kicked at the boy, but he would not rise. With a cry of rage, he threw the boy over his shoulder and headed back toward the jungle, stopping along the way to buy some whiskey with the money.

He dropped the boy on the ground and joined the hoboes sitting around the fire. All but one of them got up and walked away. The one who remained was a skinny fellow in a derby, with one eye higher than the other. He held out his hand for the bottle. Surprised and happy to find someone who didn't seem to be afraid of him, Torkel passed it over. The man took a swig and turned to examine the boy.

"You runnin him?" he asked.

Torkel nodded dismally.

"Ain't moochin too good, is he?"

Torkel shook his head.

The man nodded. "Cain't hit em like that, they don't run good," he said. "You likes to hit em, you gotta do it where it don't show."

The man reached for the bottle again, and Torkel gave it to him. He was listening carefully.

"I used to have a boy," continued the man. "He mooched real good afore he run off on me. If I ever catch him, I'll make him think twice before he does it again." He wiped his lips. "Had me a real good dodge goin towards the end. Got tired a walkin all over town, so I figgered out a way to set in one place and let the boy do the work. People would look at him settin there all pitiful, and the money just poured in. Um-hmm, it was a real good dodge."

The boy was sitting up and watching them listlessly. "You give him anything to drink?" said the man. When Torkel shook his head, the man got up and gave a dipper of water to the boy from a rusty bucket. "Gotta feed and water em," he observed. "Just like horses."

So much work keeping a boy, thought Torkel with dismay.

"You know," said the man, returning to the fire and accepting another drink, "your boy's such a young un, that dodge a mine would work real good. A course," he added, squinting his eyes in a way meant to look crafty (but instead, with their uneven slant, looked demented), "a course you gots to make yourself a sign."

Torkel had been listening eagerly. But at the mention of something that needed to be written, his face fell.

The man was watching him. "Still got that sign," he said casually. He unwrapped his bundle and extracted a wooden shingle. Torkel stared at the crude lettering formed of thick, black paint. And, when the man explained the words, knew he had to have it.

"I might could make you a deal," suggested the man.

In the end, Torkel traded his elk horn knife and a brass buckle with the image of an eagle for the precious sign.

"Best thing for this dodge," said the man, when their business was concluded, "is a big city, not this two-bit burg. I'd go to Cincy, I was you. Head on downtown, where there's the most people. Then just pick you a spot—and roost!"

Torkel listened closely. The man knew so much! They drank some more whiskey, Torkel sang his song, and the man laughed. But when the whiskey ran out, he left.

Torkel was not drunk enough, and he was hungry. The sight of the worthless boy, who had fallen asleep, filled him with fresh rage. He carefully stashed the sign in his bundle, picked up the boy, and found a spot to sleep. He was just about to tie up the boy, when he jumped up and ran into the bushes. Torkel ran after him and found him crouching with his

P.D. QUAVER

overalls around his knees. And saw as well, by the moon's light, that he had been cheated—it wasn't even a boy at all!

With a savage snarl he drew back his foot.

~

Elly had been forced to soil her clothes the night before, and had decided that even if she were beaten for it, she would not do it again. But as the giant's shadowy form hovered over her and she braced herself for the coming blow, an idea came to her.

She had never forgotten the professor's words: *Music hath charms to soothe a savage beast*—and the giant was surely as savage a beast as she had ever encountered. She had heard him sing his little song many times over. And though he sang it so out of tune it was agony to listen to, she had figured out what the melody was supposed to be.

All this flashed through her mind like lightning. As the giant drew back his enormous boot, she shut her eyes and in a high, pure voice, began to sing:

Vem kan segla förutan vind,
Vem kan ro utan åror…

At the first note, the giant froze. When she finished the song, he dropped to his knees and grabbed her by the shoulders, staring at her face and whimpering. Shuddering at his touch, she forced herself to sing again. Tears poured down the giant's cheeks, and he tilted his face to the moon and began to howl. Astonished, Elly fell silent. The giant yelled and shook her violently, and once again she forced herself to sing. The giant stroked her face, then lay down and put his head in her lap. As Elly continued to softly croon the lullaby over and over, he fell asleep.

She stopped singing and sat in a daze. Fireflies lit up the humid night air with their mysterious journeys. The giant's head was like a boulder in her lap, and pinned her to the ground. Exhausted, she lay back and asked the moon if she should try to run.

But she never heard the answer.

· · ·

"The Wabash," said the professor, pointing to the river below them. They were on a bridge, hanging from the side of a coal car. So of course the old goat decided this was the right time to break into song:

Oh the moonlight's fair tonight
along the Wabash,
From the fields there comes the breath
of new mown hay…

sang Carp in a quavery tenor, and Jimmy wanted to throttle him. They had crossed the river where it flowed into the Ohio, and a while later the train began to slow down as they approached another city. The professor jumped and Jimmy tumbled after him. They followed the tracks toward what Carp said was Evansville, though all these river burgs looked alike to Jimmy. Through the trees they caught glimpses of the Ohio. The sun was so bright the world seemed bleached, while the two of them were so covered in coal dust they looked like black-face minstrels. The professor said something about forming a vaudeville team, but he was as dead-beat as Jimmy, and the joke fell flat.

They found a stream and drank like camels and washed their faces. The sun was setting as they trudged into the jungle. There were three men around the fire cooking something in a pot. They looked up suspiciously, but when Carp murmured, "Hey, boes," they relaxed. Jimmy threw their bundle down, and they joined the men.

"Hotter than blazes," said Carp conversationally.

"Too hot to work, that's sure," replied a dumpy, little tramp in a filthy, checked suit.

"Aw, when you ever work?" said another, a scrawny bum in suspenders over a torn undershirt. "You're too lazy to scratch yourself when you're lousy."

The man stirring the pot, a swarthy fellow with a shock of coal-black hair, snorted.

"Hey, I work," protested the man in the checked suit. "Cept my work is seasonal."

"Yeah? What kinda work is that?"

"I'm a Christmas tree decorator."

The man stirring the pot snorted again. "It's this hot, it's fixin to rain." He glanced at the sky. "Yep, be a big thunderstorm. Sometime tomorrow—I can feel it comin."

The man in the checked suit said, "That lightning starts up, you better not be near them tracks. Draws that lightning like a magnet. Saw a tramp once got hisself burned blacker than a Jew's derby."

The others nodded; it was common knowledge.

The ice was broken, and Carp started in:

"Say, any of you boes run into a big, red-haired Swede? Giant kind of fellow?"

"Yeah, we seen him," said the man in the torn undershirt.

Jimmy and the professor glanced at each another. Jimmy felt his exhaustion evaporate.

"Runnin a little punk," said the man in the checked suit. The man stirring the pot scowled.

"That's him," said Carp. "He still around?"

"I felt for that little feller," continued the check-suited tramp. "Oughter be a law."

"You said it, brother," agreed the other. "Naw, they left—when was it, Clem? Day before yesterday?"

"Round about."

"Why is it you say," said Carp quietly, "there ought to be a law?"

The man stirring the pot snorted. "Cause he bout killed that little slip of a kid, that's why. Brought him here all beat up. None of us could stand to be around him."

"Cept that cock-eyed feller," said the man in the checked suit.

"Why in the hell didn't yer stop him?" blurted Jimmy.

The men wouldn't look at him.

"So where'd they go?" asked the professor.

"Well now," said the man in the undershirt, rubbing his chin, "best thing to do is ask the cock-eyed feller."

"Only one who talked to him," agreed the check-suited tramp.

"And where might this cock-eyed fellow be found?" asked Carp patiently.

"Went fishin, didn't he Clem?"

"He did." The check-suited tramp pointed toward a stand of trees in the distance. "Hole over yonder."

"Little cock-eyed feller in a derby," the man in the undershirt called after them as they started toward the woods.

The man stirring the pot snorted.

.   .   .

They found him sprawled on the bank beside the fishing hole with his derby covering his face. A limp fishing line ran from his big toe to a wooden float bobbing placidly in the water. Carp bent over and lifted the derby off the man's face. The man blinked, and Jimmy saw he really did have one eye higher than the other.

"Sir," said Carp, squatting down next to the man, "a word with you if we may."

The man reached for his derby and clapped it back on his head as he sat up. He squinted at them.

"I understand you spoke to the big, red-haired Swede before he left," said the professor.

The man rubbed his chin. "Might," he drawled.

"And further," continued Carp in the same conversational tone, "it was suggested to me that he may have revealed to you where he was next headed."

"Might," said the man again.

Fast—so fast Jimmy could hardly register it—the professor had gripped the man by the back of the neck and was holding a straight razor to his throat.

"Now then," he murmured softly into the man's ear, "if you would please try to remember."

The man's derby had fallen over his eyes, and his lips were covered with spittle. "C-C-Cincy," he sputtered. "Went to Cincy. Swear to Christ he did."

Carp said nothing. He pressed the razor more firmly to the man's neck until a bead of blood appeared. The cock-eyed man began babbling.

"It was a c-c-couple a days back, maybe three. Told him to go to Cincy—him and his little p-p-punk. Told him to t-t-try his luck downtown, where there's lots a folks walkin around. G-G-God's truth, mister!"

They left him straightening his derby with shaking hands. Jimmy kept trying to catch the professor's eye so he could say…he had no idea what. But Carp wouldn't look at him.

By the fire, the other boes handed them plates of grub, and Carp quizzed them about trains to Cincy. It was full dark when Jimmy grabbed their bundle, and they headed for the yard to catch a "drag"—a slow freight. They got aboard and found a boxcar where three other bums were already holed up. They caught a bit of sleep, but in the middle of the night, a brakie with a pistol woke them all and shook them down for a buck a piece. The other bums coughed up, but Jimmy and the professor were flat broke. The brakie told them to jump. Jimmy could feel the train was moving too fast, but with a pistol at their back there was nothing for it.

He grabbed their bundle, and the two of them leapt from the speeding train into blackness.

They hit rough—Carp got the worst of it—and bedded down by the tracks. But the land was half swamp, their blankets got soaked, and the mosquitoes ate them alive; Jimmy couldn't remember when he'd spent a more miserable night. By first light, they were all swollen up and pretty well frazzled. They beat it on foot maybe five miles down the tracks to a siding. An hour later another drag pulled over to let an express by, and the two of them climbed into an empty gondola, Jimmy pretty much dragging Carp by the scruff because the old goat was about all in.

They lay in the bottom of the car. Carp looked like a dead man, and Jimmy felt about the same. The drag stopped as often as an old woman with the trots, and it was late afternoon before they pulled into Cincy.

Gray clouds smothered the city like a hot blanket, and it was a chore to breathe.

They caught a streetcar and headed straight for downtown, hanging from the outside and scouting the streets, saying hardly a word. Carp had revived some, and his rat nose twitched like he was on the scent. The sky was darkening, and Jimmy knew the bum yesterday had been right—a real cloudburst was coming. It was a big city, and they ran up and down the main streets for an hour, jumping off whenever a conductor came their way, catching another streetcar and searching some more. Jimmy was just thinking how hopeless it all was—

When he spotted them.

Or rather, it was the giant Swede's orange pumpkin head he spotted, in flickering glimpses behind the people hurrying by on the pavement to beat the coming rain. Carp saw him at the same time and squeezed Jimmy's shoulder. Without a word, they dropped from the moving streetcar with the practiced skill of hoboes and headed back on the opposite side of the street, mixing with the crowd of homeward-bound office workers and shopgirls.

It was the giant Swede all right. Sitting on the sidewalk with his knees up and a rag tied around his eyes. Beside him sat a frail child with a battered face, a pathetic little doll—and a sign hung around her neck.

"Christ Jesus," muttered Jimmy.

~

BLIND AND MOTHERLESS was what the sign said.

At first Elly was so mortified by it she cried, and this may have helped because the first day, they made enough money to appease the giant and get him drunk. But on the following days, in spite of her efforts not to, she began slipping more and more often into her dream world. They made less money, and this made the giant angry. Sometimes policemen made them move. Elly tried to look them in the eye and saw them frown. But she was afraid to say anything and didn't know what she would say anyway. And today they'd made less than ever, because it was so hot and the same people saw them every day.

The giant was sure to be very angry.

When she sang to him, he always stroked her face and howled at the sky and didn't beat her. But he must have resented this power she had over him, because now he struck her without warning, while they were walking along or when she was trying to eat the little bit of food he now and then tossed at her. She might have tried to run away, but now she could barely hobble without falling.

The direness of her situation had driven her back into her dream world. But a sudden gust of cool air brought her out of her trance. Towering above the buildings across the street was a wall of black cloud. All around them people were scurrying. The giant whipped the rag from his eyes. He gathered up their few coins with an angry grunt, hauled Elly to her feet, and strode off in the direction of the jungle. Elly stuffed Mr. Hoppy inside her overalls and staggered to catch up to him.

~

Torkel gathered up the coins and saw it was less than ever. All day he had been thinking of what to do about the boy (he had in fact forgotten the boy was really a girl), and decided he didn't want him anymore — neither him nor his magic doll (which had turned out to have no magic at all). In fact, the boy was now a liability, for not only did he have to be fed, but the beatings Torkel gave him made the other hoboes shun Torkel more than ever. He had tried to follow the man's advice and beat him where it didn't show. But sometimes he couldn't help himself, because beating had turned out to be all the boy was good for. That and the singing.

But these things weren't enough to make up for all the aggravation, and Torkel had decided to get rid of him. He'd decided to leave this city as well, which had brought him nothing but bad luck. Leave tonight on the mail run south, for the summer was almost over, and get rid of the boy on the way. How easy it would be — and fun as well! — to pitch him from the top of the train and watch him sail through the air. Perhaps while they were crossing a bridge, so he would fall even farther. And no one would ever know…

Excited by his plan, he looked back at the boy, limping along desperately behind him. Torkel cuffed him one — then laughed aloud. Yes, this he would miss!

This, and the singing.

~

They watched from a distance as the giant Swede knocked Bert to the ground. Even from here they could hear his mad laugh, and it was all Carp could do to stop Jimmy from rushing to her rescue and getting himself killed for his efforts.

"Wait." He squeezed Jimmy's shoulder. "Wait until they get to the jungle. We'll get more men on our side—you've seen how popular he is with the others."

"Aw," said Jimmy, twisting under Carp's surprisingly strong grip. Now that he was off the drugs, everything about Carp had been surprising Jimmy. The way he had whipped out that razor...

The Swede had thrown Bert over his shoulder and was loping away. Jimmy remembered the way the big Dutchy would beat him and his sister Liddie, laughing in the same crazy way. He fingered the clasp knife in his pocket.

They followed the giant as he crossed an empty lot toward a stand of trees. Rain-scented wind blew the weeds sideways and sent trash skittering across their path. The black cloud closing in on them rumbled as though clearing its throat. The giant disappeared into the woods, and Jimmy and the professor broke into a trot, close on his heels.

They reached a small clearing. A wind-whipped fire was still burning. But there was no one around, and no sign of the giant Swede.

A quick search revealed a pack of bums sheltering in the lee of a rough lean-to.

"Come on in, boes," called a man in a torn tophat. "Plenty of room."

"We're looking for the Swede," said Carp.

"Big feller?"

"That's the one."

"Just saw him a minute ago," said a second man. "Runnin towards his camp. Over yonder somewheres." He gestured toward the trees.

"You got somethin agin him?" asked another.

"We're gone kill him," said Jimmy, pulling out his knife.

Somewhere nearby, a train was jerking into motion. They heard a series of booms as the cars pulled taut.

"He's been a-beatin on that punk a his somethin shameful," said the tophatted tramp.

"Well, why the fuck didn't you—" cried Jimmy.

"So who among you"—Carp cut him off—"who will help us rescue the poor child?"

An embarrassed silence, broken by the shriek of a train whistle. Wind-driven raindrops splattered against the lean-to's tin roof like shrapnel.

"Fixin to rain somethin fierce," said the man in the tophat. "You'd best be stayin here, least for a while—"

"There they are!" yelled Jimmy.

Through smudged half-light the giant Swede, carrying both Bert and his bundle over his shoulders, was briefly visible running along the edge of the tree line before disappearing down a path.

"Headed for the yard," said one of the men.

"Catchin the mail run south, must be. Hell of a night for it."

"Well he *better* run, cause she's a-leavin—"

By the time Jimmy and the professor burst from the trees onto the yard, it was raining blue cats with feathered tails. They could just make out the giant's indistinct form as he swung himself aboard the rapidly accelerating train. Jimmy dropped their bundle, and he and Carp raced through a wall of water. They just managed to catch the last car before the caboose. They hauled themselves up and stood in the space between the two cars, gasping for breath. Carp had lost his fedora and looked exactly like a drowned rat, and Jimmy felt like one.

For the first time it occurred to him that they might be at a disadvantage.

They waited a few more minutes, hugging the iron brake beam and struggling to collect their wits. Night was coming on fast. The train thundered onto an iron bridge, a flash of lightning revealed the Ohio for a lurid moment, then everything became a rainy blur again.

"Well," said Carp, "let's go."

Jimmy had been hoping for some kind of plan, but there didn't seem to be one. He followed Carp up the ladder on the side, and they started working their way forward over the tops of the mail cars. The train was still picking up speed, barreling into the dark Kentucky mountains and doing its best to shake them off its rain-slick back. They gripped the iron pipes running down the center of each car, battered by wind and rain. They both knew the cars on mail runs are always locked, and the Swede was undoubtedly perched between two cars, escaping the rain. Each time they reached the front of a car, the professor slowly peered over the edge.

Jimmy wondered what he would do when he found the giant Swede staring back up at him.

It was full night now. But lightning was flashing all around them, giving stark, lurid glimpses of the long train snaking its way through black mountains, and revealing another bridge in the distance. Jimmy had just started down between two cars behind the professor, when another flash revealed the Swede climbing up two cars ahead of them. His back was to them, and Bert was over his shoulder.

He raced down and yelled the news into Carp's ear. The professor nodded, climbed the ladder to the next car, then slowly peered over the top. Another flash of lightning, and he disappeared over the edge.

Jimmy scrambled up after him.

He poked his head above the top. Rain stung his eyes. There was nothing but blackness—then a flash of light revealed, as though it were a photograph, an image of the giant Swede kneeling on the car ahead of theirs with Bert under his arm, and Carp inching forward on his belly like a snake.

Jimmy crawled after him. The bridge was fast approaching. Thunder boomed and echoed all around him like cannon fire. He reached the end of the car and descended one last time. Carp clutched his shoulder and shouted in his ear:

"Surprise! That's our advantage."

A flicker of light illuminated the open razor in Carp's hand. Before Jimmy could think, the professor was pulling himself up the side of the car and over the top. Again Jimmy scrambled after him. He stuck his head over the edge. Rain hit his face like a solid thing. A flash of lightning showed the Swede, still facing away from them, and Carp again creeping toward him. Huge iron bridge girders loomed ahead of them. Jimmy pulled his knife out and opened it. He crawled after the professor, gripping the water-slick pipe with one hand, clinging desperately to the hurtling, juddering train.

Everything had again gone dark—then another flash revealed the giant Swede standing on his feet with Bert in his arms. They thundered onto the bridge. Lightning flashed crazily, illuminating a deep gorge beneath them. The Swede lifted Bert over his head. Above the roar of the train Jimmy could hear his mad laughter—

Carp yelled something, and the Swede whipped his head around. Another series of flickering images: The Swede, hair plastered blood red to his pumpkin head, gaping in astonishment… Bert lying on the roof of the car… The Swede facing Carp and grinning… The professor's scarecrow body doing a tap-dance atop the shuddering car… The Swede swinging at him… Carp tipped on one leg and slashing crazily with his razor—

Then blackness again.

The train made a sudden lurch. Jimmy stared desperately ahead, struggling to pierce the darkness. Lightning flashed again, a deafening sound as if the very fabric of existence were being torn asunder—

And the professor was gone.

The professor was gone, and the giant Swede was crawling across the roof with a terrible grin on his face, inching his way toward Jimmy. Jimmy said a silent prayer and raised his knife. Lightning flickered continuously like a madman was at the light switch, revealing a series of progressively more astounding images: Bert up on her feet behind the giant, and running toward them… The grinning Swede on his knees before Jimmy with a giant fist poised to belt him into oblivion… Bert perched on the Swede's back with her mouth to his ear… The Swede with his head thrown back, howling into the rain—

Jimmy slashed with his knife across the giant Swede's throat with all his strength.

Warm blood mixed with cold rain splattered his face. The Swede clutched his throat with a wild look. Bert was crouching behind him, and Jimmy waved her to get back. When she was safely away, he gripped the iron pipe and aimed a vicious kick. The Swede tumbled sideways, arms flailing—

With a gurgling scream, he disappeared into the night.

CHAPTER NINETEEN

REVELATIONS

The night was endless. They rode between two cars, standing on the bumpers. Jimmy gripped the rusty, rain-slick, break beam as Bert clung to him. Wind whipped between the cars with a banshee shriek, tearing at their clothes and doing its best to snatch both of them away.

After a while the rain finally stopped. The air turned frigid, and Jimmy's hand began to cramp up. He knew he couldn't hold on much longer, but the train hurtled through the mountains like a mad dragon with no sign of ever stopping. In desperation, he took off his belt and, balancing precariously, managed to attach it to the brake beam. He wrapped the other end around his wrist and took some of the strain off his fingers. But he still had to stay awake to balance on the shifting bumper. Bert was so exhausted and limp she threatened to drag both of them down into the wheels thundering beneath them, and the wind whipping their sodden clothes chilled them until they both shivered convulsively. Which was probably, Jimmy thought later, what kept him awake and saved their sorry carcasses.

The eastern sky was glowing dully behind the mountains like a purple bruise when the train, climbing a high grade, finally slowed enough for them to get off. Bert clung to Jimmy, and they jumped and rolled on the ground together. They lay there without moving, more dead than alive. Both were half-frozen, and they huddled together for warmth, Jimmy silently cursing himself for dropping his bundle in the race to catch the train.

It was the last coherent thought he had before dropping into exhausted, oblivious sleep.

.   .   .

When he finally awoke, the sun was high in a clear blue sky. The air had been fresh-scrubbed by the storm and the whole world sparkled. Bert lay curled up beside him. He shuddered to see in broad daylight how beat up she was.

"Aw, Bert," he said and lightly stroked her bruised face.

Bert's unswollen eye slowly opened and looked right at him in a way Bert's eyes seldom did.

"You lost your eye patch," she said in a thick voice.

Jimmy felt his face and realized it was true. He shrugged. Bert's eye closed, and Jimmy felt the urge to drift off again fighting with the sudden awareness of a raging thirst. Thirst won out. He staggered to his feet. It felt like he'd gone ten rounds with John L. Sullivan. At the bottom of a ravine, he found a puddle of rainwater. He drank from it, then walked a long time along the tracks until he found half a broken beer bottle. He used it to bring water to Bert, making several trips. He pulled up a bunch of weeds and formed them into a thick pile. When they lay down again it seemed soft as a feather mattress. Again they slept.

When he woke again, the sun was going down, and it had turned cold. Jimmy thought if they walked a spell, they might find a jungle with a fire and hot food, and he helped Bert get to her feet. But watching her try to walk was so pitiful it made him want to find the giant and kill him all over again—and only now did Jimmy fully realize he had actually killed a man. And it did feel fine.

They stumbled drunkenly along together, Bert leaning on Jimmy and Jimmy conjuring up roast beef and hot buttered biscuits in his mind. But it was soon clear Bert couldn't go much farther. So when they saw the outline of a building that looked dark and abandoned, he thought they might break in and spend the night.

As they came near, he saw it was a simple frame building with a row of windows and a door on one end. A schoolhouse, he decided, disappointed—for that meant there would be no food or bedding. But there was a stovepipe silhouetted against the darkening sky, so they could at least build a fire. He tried the door—to his surprise it wasn't locked. Inside, it was almost too dark to see. But he remembered where the stovepipe was and went along one wall in its direction. He became accustomed to the gloom and could make out rows of benches and a pot-bellied stove in the corner. There was a stack of wood and a box of kindling. He used his knife to carve some shavings, then struck the blade against the piece of flint he carried and got a flame going.

It was wonderful how having a fire changed things. He left the front of the stove open, and—while Bert sat and stared into the flames—used the light to explore. He quickly realized it wasn't a school at all, but a church. A simple one, with rudely built pews and tatty old hymn books. Up front, behind the pulpit, he found a row of chairs with seat cushions, and used them to make a pallet in front of the stove. He stoked the fire, closed the stove, and they lay down together. The heat and the soft cushions were fine things, and soon they were asleep.

His sleep was laced with vivid and violent dreams. Twice in the night he was awakened by them, and he used the opportunity to stoke the fire. Toward morning his visions softened, and he found himself dreaming of his lost sister, Liddie. She was dancing in a long white dress to the most beautiful music Jimmy had ever heard. When he finally opened his eyes, he lay for a long moment, stupefied.

The music from his dream was still playing, more beautiful than ever.

Jimmy thought he'd sure enough gone loony. He turned his head and looked for Bert, but she was no longer beside him. He stumbled to his feet. The sun had just risen; its beams slanted through the tall windows, filling the church's interior with dappled light. For a long time he stood still, just staring. And listening. In wonder and amazement.

The music was coming from Bert. Bert, seated in front of a big old piano and playing it like nobody's business. Playing the song about Liddie and her light brown hair, waving her arms around and making it sound so pretty. He crept closer until he stood right next to her and stared at her fingers spidering over the keys, mesmerized. And decided he must still be dreaming after all.

Elly was lost in her own dream. It was the first time she had played in almost two years, and at first, she had been dismayed to discover how stiff her fingers felt. But soon they began to fly to the notes as she heard them in her mind, just like they used to, and all the pain in her body seemed to magically disappear as she teased shimmering colors out of the air—

"Bert—Bert, holy jumpin turnips, Bert!"

She jerked to a stop, startled.

"Christ Jesus, Bert, don't stop—play er again!"

So she did, adding big sweeping arpeggios in the left hand, doubling the melody in octaves—and quite forgetting about Jimmy again until she reached the last quiet chords and he suddenly yelled, "Hoo-EEE!" and asked her if she knew any more songs, did she know "Oh Sussaner?"

She nodded and played it for him. Jimmy went so bug-eyed that even his empty eye socket was wide open, and he came right back at her with "Danny Boy" and "Dixie." So she played them as well.

"Bert—holy jumpin turnips, you never *tole* me! Where'd you pick all that up?"

Elly couldn't think of anything to say that wouldn't lead to questions about her parents and what happened to them and other things she didn't want to talk about. So she didn't say anything but instead began to play one of the Mozart pieces she had learned on Miss Bland's piano, the fast and exciting "Rondo a la Turk." Jimmy danced around her, spinning in circles, stomping his feet, and letting out little whoops. When she hit the final crashing chords, he grabbed her by the shoulders—and she almost passed out. She stumbled from the piano bench, and Jimmy helped her lie down, babbling all the while. But she could hardly hear him for the pain, and soon she was asleep again.

•   •   •

They stayed in the church three more days as Elly slowly recovered. Jimmy went out begging every day, but he told her the pickings without her and Mr. Hoppy were "plum pitiful." He added to their meager fare with raids on a local orchard, so they had all the apples they could eat—though Jimmy had to slice them for Elly because she could hardly chew.

Each day she played for longer periods, reveling in the return of her powers. All the songs she had learned on Miss Bland's piano were like old friends, and it felt like music itself was healing her. She no longer had to slump to reach the pedal and realized she had grown taller. Her hands, too, had grown, enabling her to play octaves and big chords more easily.

Jimmy listened to it all with unceasing amazement. Sometimes he asked for songs but more often was content with just whatever poured out of her, for she never seemed to repeat herself.

On the third night, he got a good fire going and lay on the pallet listening to her play, munching apples and forming vague plans in his head. Next morning she was at it again early, so he knew that even though her face was the color of an unripe eggplant, she was getting better. He was having a hard time tearing himself away to go out begging, because Bert was just exasperating that old piano like she had five hands, showing it what's what. Then suddenly there was a new sound that didn't fit with the music—the rhythmic clip-clop of horse's hooves—and Jimmy looked out the window to see a buggy driving up.

A moment later a man and woman were standing in the doorway. Bert played on, oblivious. Jimmy was in a sweat, trying to work up a good story, but they hardly noticed him—just stood gaping as Bert beat that old piano seven ways to Sunday. Which was, of course, thought Jimmy, what it must be: Sunday. He cursed himself for a fool for not checking.

They were creeping up on Bert, and Jimmy studied them. The man was fairly old but burly, with a square head and bushy, gray hair all over. He wore a black suit with a vest and watch fob. Jimmy figured him right away for a preacher and the woman—a bony affair in a plain gray dress and old-fashioned bonnet—for a preacher's wife. Bert hammered a slap-bang finish on her work. The woman cried, "Oh child!" and grabbed her all huggy, and Bert about jumped out of her skin. Then the preacher—had to be—started in nattering about the Lord having sent Bert to them. And Jimmy saw real quick how to work the thing.

The woman was kneeling next to Bert now and stroking her back and asking what happened to her. But Bert kept her lip buttoned and wouldn't look at either of them. Jimmy saw his chance, stepped up and said, "She don't talk a whole lot—"

"She!" cried the woman, staring at Bert, and Jimmy cursed himself for a fool once more. "Is the child a girl?"

Jimmy was trying to figure how to dig himself out when Bert gave up the game by nodding. Jimmy about wanted to kick her.

The preacher was looking hard at him. "Young man, did you beat this poor little girl?"

"Me!" cried Jimmy. "Tweren't me, it were—"

"The giant," said Bert.

The man's eyebrows, which were as bushy as the rest of him, jumped up like startled mice.

"That ol giant like to killt her," said Jimmy, jumping in. "But we got the best a him. Then we like near froze to death, but the Lord, well he stepped right in an brought us to this here church—"

"Praise Jesus!" cried the woman.

"Praise His holy name!" said the preacher, one-upping her some.

"—an then we finds this ol pianer, an she suddenly starts in a-playin the bejesus—er, I mean playin the hell outa her. And don't yer know, that's gotta be the Lord's work too—cause *she ain't never played before in her life!*"

Well the preacher's eyebrows twitched something fierce at that, and the woman got all discombobulated, so Jimmy said, "Come on, Bert, do yer stuff—show em how the Lord's got into yer fingers an all."

Bert looked at him kind of funny. But she was on the ball cause she let fly with a real knuckle-buster, and Jimmy could see they were taking the bait. Then the preacher asked if the Lord had seen fit to show her how to play "The Old Rugged Cross," and she went right at it. They both dropped to their knees kind of moaning and swaying and crying about how it was a miracle, and the hook was good and set. Then they asked for more hymns, and when Bert played every one of them, Jimmy figured they were landed, gutted, and in the frying pan.

All this time, folks were coming in and joining in the fun, and pretty soon old Bert was about drowned out what with all the yelling and praise-Jesusing and carrying on. The preacher made her stand up on the bench facing all the people and preached a sermon on her, and some folks got so worked up they threw themselves on the floor and rolled around like the old Dutchy having one of his spells. Bert looked uncomfortable, and it was all Jimmy could do to keep a straight face. Then the preacher set her down again and made her play a heap more hymns, and they sang and shouted and rolled around some more.

And Jimmy knew they were in the clover.

When it was over, the folks about smothered Bert with all their fussing. Jimmy got the leftovers on account of he knew her but felt pretty much like a sidekicker. There was some fighting over who got to take them home, but the preacher, whose name was Reverend Pike, got top dog's rights. They got in his buggy, and driving up to his house there was the smell of baked chicken, and Jimmy thought he'd die from it.

They sat down, and an old colored woman brought out the food. Jimmy seized a drumstick and had just got it to his lips when Reverend Pike's head suddenly fell to his chest and he launched into a prayer. It was so long and drawn out (and fattened even more by Mrs. Pike's "Praise God"s and "Hallelujah"s) it looked set to turn into another sermon. But at last Pike gave the all clear and they went at it.

Jimmy knew he was eating like a damn wolf, but he couldn't help himself, and Bert looked like chewing was coming back to her real quick. But Mrs. Pike didn't seem to mind and kept pushing food at them. Then there was apple cobbler, and it was like the plain apples they'd been eating were a dog house and this was a solid-gold mansion.

Jimmy had been pleased to see the Pikes took their eating serious, for all through the meal neither had said a word (beyond the "pass the butter please" variety). But now they looked set on conversating. Jimmy, though, was so full to bursting he could hardly talk, and had to let Bert carry the load until he could catch his breath.

Which turned out to be a mistake.

"So, young lady," said Reverend Pike, dabbing at the grease on his beard with a stained napkin, "you have not yet told us your name."

"Elly," said Bert.

Jimmy about choked up his cobbler.

"Elly," said Mrs. Pike. She had a sharp nose and a quick way of jerking her head that gave her the look of an inquisitive bird. "Such a pretty name."

They asked Jimmy his name, and he told them. All the time he was trying to catch Bert's attention, but she wouldn't look at him. But there was a gleam in those dark eyes of hers. You had to know her to see it, but to Jimmy, it was plain.

"And where are your parents?" asked Mrs. Pike, darting her sharp nose from one to the other of them as though searching for a worm.

"I'm an orphan," said Elly.

Jimmy's mouth fell open.

"Oh, how terrible for you," said Mrs. Pike.

"We's both orphans," said Jimmy, recovering himself. "Ma and Pa, they up and died of the—"

"My parents died in the earthquake," said Elly. "In San Francisco."

She looked straight at Jimmy for the briefest instant—and he knew with a terrible certainty that it was the truth. He couldn't think what to say. Not that he could have gotten a word in, the way the Pikes were fussing over Bert (or whoever she was). And Jimmy was forced to admit it: The truth had turned out to be the best story after all.

·   ·   ·

Elly wasn't sure exactly why she suddenly decided to tell the truth about herself. It was something to do with everybody knowing she was a girl and playing the piano again. But she was glad she had, because to finally say aloud what she had long known made it easier to accept. And it was nice to hear people calling her by her real name. Even Jimmy was forced to do it when other people were around. Though the way he said it—"Pass me them pickles, would yer, EL-LEE," rolling his eye—made her laugh inside.

But when they were alone, it didn't take.

"Holy jumpin turnips, Bert—ain't we struck it though!" he said that first night.

He wore an old shirt of Reverend Pike's and sprawled like an emperor on the feather mattress the Pikes had fixed up for them in the attic. Elly wore one of Mrs. Pike's flannel nightgowns, lifting the long hem like an elegant lady when she had to walk around. Mrs. Pike had filled a tub in the kitchen with hot water that evening and bathed Elly, clucking over the bruises covering her body. Even though it had hurt, it was heavenly to be clean (though judging from the sounds coming from the kitchen when it was Jimmy's turn, he thought it was hell).

Mrs. Pike had taken their clothes and given them to the colored woman for washing. "Though burning would better suit them," she had sniffed.

Perhaps that's what she did with them, for they were never seen again. Instead, she and Jimmy arose next morning to find Mrs. Pike had already been to a neighbor's house and returned with clothes their children had outgrown, including a linen shirt and pair of corduroy trousers for Jimmy (both somewhat faded and patched, but to Jimmy's thinking quite elegant). And for Elly—to her intense delight—a flower-print frock with lace trim. Mrs. Pike helped her button it up and went at her hair. It was already pretty long for a boy but pitifully short for a girl, and (like everyone who had ever tried to brush Elly's snarly hair) Mrs. Pike complained the whole time. But she did manage to attach a big yellow bow to the back. And when Elly looked in the mirror, she saw a ten year old girl who was—in spite of bruised face and hacked-off hair—rather pretty.

She wasn't sure exactly what Jimmy saw when she finally came downstairs. But whatever it was struck him dumb, and she caught him staring at her all day from the corner of his eye. Mrs. Pike had asked about his other, missing eye, and he told her some story about being captured by wild Indians and how he'd lost his eye patch fighting with the giant. She sniffed at both stories but went to work and sewed him a new eye patch out of some scraps of black sateen. And now it was Jimmy who couldn't stop admiring himself in the mirror, crowing that he looked like "a real desperado."

It was not far from the Pike's house to the church (in fact, Jimmy confided to Elly, it had been Pike's orchard he'd been stealing apples from), and Mrs. Pike walked there with Elly every afternoon so she could play the piano. Jimmy stayed on the farm helping Reverend Pike and told Elly she was lucky she'd turned into a girl because the old buzzard fair worked him to death and preached at him the whole time, which made it "twice as worse."

The second day Elly went to play, there were people there to listen. Word spread and each day there were more. Jimmy's claim that she had never played piano before she entered the church had first startled, then amused Elly—and seemed to unleash a devil in her, for she delighted in playing the fastest, most complex pieces she knew for her awed listeners. By Sunday the church was so full that folks lined the walls and spilled out the door.

The men all had long beards, the women wore old-fashioned bonnets, and the children carpeting the floor were mostly barefoot. Elly sat up front between the Pikes, and everyone's eyes were on her. So it was a relief to finally turn her back on them and play. She did a medley of hymns Mrs. Pike had suggested (Elly knew them all from Miss Bland's books—could see the music and turn the pages in her mind), and she tricked them out in ways to make the chords rich and the piano fill the room. In the silence behind her, she could sense the raptness of the crowd. But it wasn't long before someone shouted, "Praise the Lord!" and it was like they fired a starting pistol the way the room erupted in noise. By the end, there was so much carrying on she had to thunder out the melody in octaves to be heard.

Then Reverend Pike preached another sermon on her, working himself into a lather. He undid his tie, threw off his jacket, rolled up his shirtsleeves, and seized Elly's head between his sweaty hands. "The Lord has struck this child with his power like a bolt of holy lightning!" he roared.

People were yelling, "Praise Jesus!" and throwing themselves on the floor. Pike's entire body trembled as if Elly were giving him an electrical charge. "I can feel it—Christ Jesus, the holy spirit is *just a-bustin outa her!*"

The aisles were so full of people flopping around, it was like being back in the asylum. Elly felt dizzy from having her brains shaken up (and rather like a fraud), so again it was a relief when the sermon was over and it was time for more music. And even though the people continued to make a commotion, it was still an audience—the first she'd had since she gave her little recital at the asylum—and she went at the music with all she had. When the congregation began to sing along to "How Great Thou Art" (which had been Miss Bland's favorite), with one woman's sweet, pure soprano floating over all the rest, the room seemed to fill with golden light. So that even though Elly considered herself a transcendentalist (and thus thought God was everywhere all the time), she couldn't help but wonder if Reverend Pike might actually have summoned up the deity for a special visit.

Afterward, there was a big dinner with several guests and far too many questions for Elly's taste, most of which she pretended not to hear. Through it all she could feel Jimmy's eye on her and knew he was itching to talk to her. But it wasn't until later up in the attic that they were finally alone. Jimmy blew the candle out. They lay together on the feather mattress in the dark, and he started in:

"Bert, yer got no idea what's really goin down with these here Pikes, so I got to tell yer what's what. Now yer couldn't see nothin on account a yer had yer back turned. But after he preached on yez and yer was aggravatin that ol pianer again, they was passin a plate around. When it come back up front, ol Mrs. Pike got her mitts on it double-quick and dumped it in that big ol carpet bag she brought. But I got a gander at it, and I'm

tellin yez, there was nigh thirty or forty dollar in it. And I can guarantee yez that's money you ain't never gonna see—even though it was you what earned it fair an square."

Elly thought about how many days of begging that might represent. "That's a lot of money," she conceded.

"Bert, yer said a mouthful," said Jimmy, warming to his theme. "It fair knocked me off my perch. An ever since, well, I been studyin on a plan..."

Elly listened to his idea, but was dubious at first. After all, she pointed out, the Pikes had fed, clothed, and housed them and let her play the piano every day. But it did seem like she was being used, Jimmy's enthusiasm was infectious, and the prospect of making money without ever having to beg again was intoxicating.

"An we won't need no punkgrafter no more," said Jimmy, "cause from now on *I* can take care a yez. After all, yer seen what I done to that ol giant."

It was true, thought Elly. Jimmy had been growing fast and was almost as tall as a man now.

"An so," concluded Jimmy, "I say we hop a freight to the nearest burg an—"

"No," said Elly.

"Huh?"

"No more hoboing."

"Whatcher on about!" cried Jimmy.

Elly explained that since now she was a girl again, she couldn't hop trains in a dress (leaving out that her experience with the giant had turned her against the whole hobo enterprise). Jimmy argued until he was hoarse, but she wouldn't budge. Giving up on that, he went to work on her about leaving right away (he was anxious to avoid even one more day of work) and finally won her over.

They decided to leave the very next morning.

.   .   .

Reverend Pike was an early riser, so they were up before dawn. They rolled up the blankets from their bed into a bundle with Mr. Hoppy snug inside (Jimmy said it was the least the Pikes owed them after all the money they'd made off of her) and crept down the ladder from the attic. Reverend Pike's snores filled the house but stopped abruptly when Jimmy lifted the door latch. They froze. There was a long moment of silence, then the snores started fitfully up again, got up a good head of steam—and they were out the door.

They walked quickly, both to get away and to warm themselves, for the air was brisk. Birds twittered the news about the coming sunrise. The road climbed a hill, and shafts of blinding light pierced the pines and warmed them for a moment before they descended again into chilly shadow.

When the sun was full up, they got a ride on the back of an empty hay wagon pulled by a pair of mules. When the wagon reached a field studded with haystacks, they walked some more, then got a ride with a man and woman in a buggy. The man asked them where they were going, and Jimmy said, "Jus to a town, some burg what's got saloons an such." The woman got all tight-lipped, and that was the end of the conversation.

They got let off at a town, but it was pitifully small—just a church, a few houses, and a general store. A train track ran through the center of town. Jimmy looked at it wistfully and raised an inquiring eyebrow at Elly, but she ignored him. The general store had a barrel room in the back, and Jimmy ducked inside it. There were a few men drinking, but that was all, and he knew they needed a bigger town.

They were both hungry, and Jimmy murmured something about begging. But Elly was so aggrieved by the very suggestion, after all the promises he had made, that he said no more about it and instead traded his clasp knife to the man running the store for some soda crackers, cheese and sausage, pickles, several cans of sardines, and two bottles of ginger beer.

The day had grown warm, so they ate their food sitting in the shade of a big oak tree. They had no knife to slice the cheese, and Jimmy had to break it up with his fingers. Elly thought about how proud he had been of the precious knife that had killed a giant.

"Aw hell," said Jimmy, as though she had spoken aloud, "we'll make enough in a day or so to buy ten knives."

Elly nodded and hoped he was right. They ate in silence for a while. The sound of a train whistle in the distance made them both look up, and a while later, a freight rolled through the town. It was so slow they could have hopped it with their eyes closed. Jimmy made a great show of ignoring it as he wrapped the remains of their meal inside their bundle.

"Well," he said, swinging the bundle over his shoulder, "wherever we's goin ain't gonna come to us." And he began walking down the dusty street away from the train tracks.

Elly smiled to herself and followed.

~

They got a ride with a wild-eyed old man in a filthy Confederate cap. He said he'd been with the Army of Tennessee at Chickamauga in sixty-three under General Bragg and lifted his cap to show them where a minie ball had plowed a furrow through his scalp, so deep you could have planted a row of corn in it. He told them it had scrambled his brains some, and it must have been true, because the old guy would not shut up. But he took them a long way, all the way to a much bigger town. When they jumped off and watched him ride away he was still talking to his horse.

The sun had long set, and it was cold again. They walked along the wooden sidewalks of the main street, peering into the windows of pool halls and cafés. They seemed to be the only businesses still open. The smell of hot food made Elly wonder if they'd been rash in leaving the Pikes after all. The businesses petered out, and Jimmy made a disgusted sound.

"Aw Bert, don't tell me we're in some dry burg—"

Elly touched his arm. He stared at her—then suddenly he heard it too. They walked faster, the sound grew louder, and they came to a side street filled with horses and buggies hitched in front of a string of saloons. A confusion of sound poured into the street as they strolled past each one, peering through the open doors. In the first, a fiddler and banjo player had set the legs of a few half-hearted dancers into motion; in the next, a man with a guitar was singing of lost love in a high keening voice and seemed to have lost his audience as well.

From the last one came the sound of a piano.

The impossibly doubled notes suggested a twenty-fingered pianist, and Elly knew at once it had to be a player piano. A glance through the open door confirmed a hulking, playerless instrument dimly visible at the rear of the smoke-filled room. It was grinding out "My Bonnie Lies Over the Ocean" to a sparse crowd of disinterested drinkers. Raucous laughter came in waves from a table of bearded, rough-looking men.

"We's still in hillbilly country, an that's a fact," observed Jimmy. He gathered his courage and walked rather uncertainly toward the bar with Elly trailing behind. The bartender was a very short, balding man with a red face and luxuriant blonde mustache. He raised an eyebrow at their approach and seemed to have trouble understanding what Jimmy was getting at over the noise of the bar.

"What—your sister? She does what? Plays the pianah, you say?"

He filled a tray of shot glasses from a whiskey bottle with practiced motions.

"I'm tellin yer, she'll tear that ol pianer apart," said Jimmy.

"Haw—that lil thing?" said a cross-eyed man leaning against the bar.

The bartender finished pouring and peered over the bar at Elly.

A thick-waisted woman with dark eyes set in a doughy face reached for the tray of drinks—and stopped short.

"What ya doin in here, sweetie?" she asked Elly, not unkindly.

"Feller here says she plays the pianah," said the bartender.

"Like nobody's business," said Jimmy.

"Huh," said the woman. She stared at Elly doubtfully. "Ain't ya got school tomorrow?"

Elly shook her head.

"Aw come on, Cora," said the cross-eyed man. "Let the lil lady play us a tune."

Cora glanced at the bartender, who shrugged.

"All right, what the hell," she said finally. "You can play us one song, sweetie. Then you better git on home." She smiled at Elly distractedly and headed with the tray toward the table of loud men.

Jimmy and Elly made their way to the piano just as a song was ending. A tall bearded man in knee boots and overalls was poised to feed another nickel into the machine. He stared in confusion as Elly hopped onto the bench.

"She's gonna play a tune," said Jimmy.

The man's brow clouded. "Oh no she ain't," he said, waving his nickel. "I got er fust."

A trio of men at a nearby table stopped talking to watch them.

"What song yer gonna play?" said Jimmy, a little desperately.

"What song?" said the man stupidly. He was clearly drunk. He peered at the celluloid window with the list of songs on the roll, moving his lips. "Bird in a Gilded Cage," he said finally.

Jimmy looked at Elly. She gave a little nod—it was a song Esta Sangley had sung in her act. The man lifted his nickel again, but before he could drop it in the machine, she plunged into the introduction. Dimly she was aware of the man next to her frozen like a statue with his nickel in the air—then lost herself in the lilting rhythms of the verse. Her slender body swayed as she made the piano waltz, and when she came to the chorus, she imagined Esta singing along in her high quavery voice:

She's only a bird in a gilded cage…

The man in tall boots stared at her, stupefied. The three men at the table behind them gaped as well, then suddenly jumped to their feet as if they'd all been goosed at the same time and clustered around the piano with their drinks. The table full of loud men turned their heads at the commotion and, unable to make sense of what they were seeing, rose as one to investigate. And by the time the song was ending, half the room was crowded around the piano, marveling at the slight young girl coaxing all that music out of the instrument, calling her the "damndest thing they ever seen," and shouting out requests for "Swanee River" and "Silver Threads Among the Gold" and "My Darling Clementine."

Jimmy saw his chance. "Boys," he said grandly, "Miss Elly here, she don't play for nothin."

Coins were slapped down, "Swanee River" won out for a quarter, and Elly went at the song in a way that just made you want to dance. One old man pushed his hat down kind of stylish and started in tapping his boots on the floor, the crowd clapping him on. The barmaid named Cora stood at the edge of the crowd, gaping. The bartender walked up and stood beside her. He was a head shorter than her, and Jimmy saw Cora flash a look down at him that said plain as day, "Well how was I supposed to know?"

When the song finished, the bartender put an empty pitcher on the piano, tossed in a whole fifty cent piece, and said, "Play 'Dixie.'" Elly jumped right on it and didn't the whole bar let out a real rebel yell! And by the time she finished, the place was so worked up it was like to turn into a Confederate uprising.

That pitcher started the ball rolling all right, and pretty soon the songs were coming so fast (Jimmy marveling all over again at all the songs in Elly's brain) that he could hardly keep track. Someone bought him a beer and then another, and after a while he couldn't keep track of them either. Cora brought Elly root beers, which she sipped between songs, never looking at anyone, hardly looking up from the piano at all. But her face was shining.

As the night went on, the word spread. People came from other saloons and the bar grew crowded. Men fought to get close to the piano, and there were a few painted women among them, which got Jimmy's attention. The competition to get songs played drove the prices up like it was a damn auction, and he watched the pitcher fill up. The fiddler from the other saloon showed up and started in sawing away at Elly, but there wasn't a song he threw at her she couldn't pick it up and throw it right back at him. The place had thinned out some, but those that stayed Jimmy figured for the real music fiends. One man had a real high, pretty voice, and when he sang "Liddie with the Light Brown Hair" (except he called her "Jeannie"), Jimmy had to wipe the tears from his eye.

It might have gone on all night, but Elly suddenly announced she was tired (and Jimmy would come to know that after she said that, wild horses couldn't drag another song out of her). So the place emptied out until it was just Jimmy, Cora, and Zed, the bartender. And Elly asleep at a table with Mr. Hoppy for a pillow.

.   .   .

Cora let them sleep in a storeroom in the back of the bar, and they packed the place four more nights. They had more money than they'd ever seen before, and ate huge meals in the cafés. But soon there was too much talk in the town about a child playing in a saloon (this, they would soon discover, was how things usually went), and Cora told them they'd have to leave.

Before they left town they went on a shopping spree. They split the money fifty-fifty (Elly wouldn't have it any other way), and Jimmy bought himself a Stetson, new boots, a stiff pair of canvas pants, and a belt with a brass buckle engraved with an Indian head. Elly bought a red sateen dress for performing in, a pair of matching shoes with red bows, a coat trimmed in rabbit fur (for winter would soon be upon them)—and the most expensive clasp knife she could find, with a mother-of-pearl handle.

Jimmy turned the knife over and over in his hand, marveling. "Prime, Elly," he said (the name had finally taken). "Jus prime." He pocketed the knife, pushed his new hat back, and scratched his head. "So, when yer reckon we oughter strike out fer Chattanoogie?"

"Tonight," said Elly.

"Yer think? Seems a bit late for snaggin a ride out of town—"

"There's a train leaving at six-fifteen."

Jimmy stared at her, confused. "But I thought yer said no more train hoppin?"

Elly gave the closest thing she had to a smile. And the train departed the station that evening with two proud paying passengers.

THE END OF VOLUME ONE

CONTINUED IN VOLUME TWO:
ELLY ROBIN AND THE COLORADO GOLD CAMP

AFTERWORD AND HISTORICAL NOTES

The Ordeals of Elly Robin was conceived as a sort of multi-volume, historical fantasia. The title intentionally echoes *The Perils of Pauline*, an early movie serial. And the publishing strategy harkens back to the days when novels were commonly published in serial form. Thus, though the books can be read separately, they together form a single vast novel—and a multi-sided portrait of the United States at the dawn of the twentieth century.

It was a fascinating period characterized by enormous change. Horses were replaced by automobiles and live theater by a virtual reality of flickering images. Rickety machines built of wood and canvas took to the skies. And the United States was in the process of becoming an industrial and—with the advent of the First World War—military powerhouse that would dominate the world.

This growing industrial behemoth was fueled by what seemed a bottomless supply of poor immigrants, joined by the "great migration" of African-Americans from the rural South to the factories of the North. In the cities, these polyglot populations lived cheek-by-jowl, and the United States became an unprecedented de facto social experiment: could the peoples and races of the world, with all their ancient prejudices, unite into a harmonious whole? Even a hundred years later, many would say the jury is still out; back in 1906, when our story begins, the putative "melting pot" had barely begun to simmer.

It made for a lot of fear and distrust, and anyone reading source material from the time will find the ethnic slurs we now so abhor being tossed around with breathtaking casualness. So in attempting to recreate the speech of the period—to give that sense of having gone "back in time"—I have had to throw political correctness out the window. These same tensions fueled a rich vein of comedy, begun in nineteenth century minstrel shows and continuing into vaudeville, which traded in broad ethnic stereotypes. But in laughing at other people, you are at least acknowledging their existence. And perhaps the heat generated from laughter made the melting pot a touch warmer.

Adrift in this turbulent landscape is Elly Robin. Her travels, adventures, and—yes—ordeals will take her (and the reader) from vaudeville stages to hobo jungles to mining towns to the gilded palaces of the rich; she will witness the San Francisco earthquake, the birth of jazz, the horrors of the First World War; Zelig-like she will encounter the likes of Emma Goldman, Louis Armstrong, Jack London and George Gershwin.

It will be an extraordinary journey, undertaken by a most extraordinary girl. A pianistic prodigy on the level of a Mozart, Saint-Saëns, Joseph Hofmann, or (in our own time) Evgeny Kissin, she is also, like many thus gifted, "different": inarticulate, obsessive, expressionless of face and voice, and loath to look people in the eye. In fact, Elly would now clearly be classified somewhere on the autism spectrum; back then she was merely "touched."

Elly's talents are integral to the story, and her musical influences—everything from Chopin to ragtime, Stephen Foster to the blues—comprise a sort of musical melting pot. And here is where I must confess that I am myself a professional pianist. And that the impetus for writing these books was not just a fascination with the historical period (and its music), but the conviction that no novelist (at least none I've discovered in a lifetime of searching) has written about the life of a musician and gotten it right.

Elly's development mirrors that of the typical musical prodigy. Early on she demonstrates (as illustrated in the first chapter) uncannily perfect pitch, and the common feeling of those so gifted that her abilities are nothing special. In addition, she has the ability to "see" sounds as colors, a phenomenon known as synesthesia (for more about this—and other fascinating music/brain lore—see Oliver Sacks's book, *Musicophilia*).

Elly's fellow vaudevillians are all fictional creations, though some are based on actual people. Eva Tanguay—the real "I Don't Care Girl"—was not in San Francisco for the earthquake, so I have given some of her attributes (and her song!) to Esta Sangley. Smiley Hobson bears some resemblance to Bill "Bojangles" Robinson. Sadie Jacobs is a fictional but typical practitioner of the ethnic humor of the time; details of her act come from other real acts. And there was an actual "Barnhold's Animals," whose act did climax with a monkey driving a paddy wagon.

The real "Great Profile" was of course none other than the great John Barrymore; I have conferred some of his attributes (and one of his liabilities) on the fictitious (and odious) John Humphrey Davies. At this time the youthful Barrymore was beginning his career as a Shakespearean actor (his "Hamlet" would later create a sensation) and matinee idol. In later years he was ravaged by alcoholism, but his charisma (and hypnotic power over women) is still vividly evident in the 1931 film *Svengali*.

Vaudeville purported to be wholesome family entertainment, with cultural pretensions here embodied by both Davies's act and that of Elly and her parents. But acts like the Twin Sisters (a real pair), whose scanty costumes and double entendres pushed the bounds of decency, were enormously popular.

Moving pictures (the "chasers" shown between shows) were only a novelty in 1906, and many future film stars were working in vaudeville. These would include the Brits Charlie Chaplin and Stan Laurel; Albert Jenning is a sort of amalgamation of the two.

Buster Keaton, another great clown of silent film, was a child vaudeville star, part of a knock-about act in which he was thrown around the stage by his battling parents; from his story I learned about the cat-and-mouse game child vaudevillians had to play with the Society for the Prevention of Cruelty to Children—Elly's dreaded

"Gerries." As Edgar Phelps mentions, it was the great child piano prodigy Josef Hofmann's exploitation by his parents in the late nineteenth century that spurred the society's formation.

It may seem far-fetched that the police wouldn't have realized there must be an itinerant killer in Elly's vaudeville troupe. But the entire concept of "serial killers" was only just beginning to take hold at this time, with only one sensational case in the United States (that of James Holmes and his "Castle of Horrors" at the Columbia Exposition of 1893) for precedent.

Animals have been noted to have an uncanny ability to sense an imminent seismic disturbance; thus the misbehavior of "Barnhold's beasts" on the eve of the San Francisco earthquake. Likewise, many people noted, like Elly, strange lights flashing in the sky that night. At the party, Elly meets a tenor from the chorus of the Metropolitan Opera; they did indeed conclude a production of *Carmen*, starring the legendary Enrico Caruso, just a few hours before the quake. (Incidentally, the two tipsy women dancing in bed sheets are devotees of the rather fanciful "classical dance" popularized by Isadora Duncan.)

In depicting the sensational events of the Great San Francisco Earthquake, I incorporated many details from eye-witness accounts. There *was* a stampede of cattle being led to market, and someone saw a man gored to death. The Valencia Hotel collapsed in exactly the accordion-like fashion as Elly's hotel. A hastily assembled militia of armed rabble added to the chaos, looting and dynamiting buildings in an ineffectual attempt to stop the fire that soon engulfed the city. Lucy Fisher was a real nurse who wrote an account of the mass evacuation of casualties by private motorcar; this is sometimes cited as the first time the automobile proved it could be more than just a rich man's plaything. The chaotic scene at the Oakland ferry terminal did feature drunken whores singing "A Hot Time in the Old Town Tonight." And the military did erect a huge tent city for the masses of refugees.

Though the Marysville Benevolent Christian Asylum for Unfortunate Girls is—thankfully—a fiction, the terrible conditions rampant in the asylums of the period were all too real. Anyone doubting this should read *Ten Days in a Madhouse*, an exposé published in the 1880's by the intrepid investigative reporter, Nellie Bly, from which I have lifted a few lurid details. (Though any similarity between Elly's hallucinatory vision of Mr. Hoppy strutting the stage while belting out "Hello, My Baby," and the classic Looney Toon "One Froggy Evening," is of course entirely coincidental.)

Electro-convulsive therapy (popularly known as "shock treatment") did not come into general use until the 1930's. But a man named Battelli (with whom the fictional Dr. Phelps studied) did indeed experiment on dogs as early as 1903, and during the First World War, victims of shell shock were sometimes treated by being strapped into an electrical device known as a Bergonic chair.

So in stumbling upon (and refining) the process in 1907, Edgar Phelps is a man slightly ahead of his time. In his use of human beings in trial-and-error experiments though, he is sadly *of* his time, suggesting what can happen when the thirst for knowledge is allowed to run roughshod over ethical considerations. At the same time, I have tried to depict the genuinely beneficial aspects of this still-misunderstood therapeutic tool, which is still in use.

For insight into the many varieties of mental dysfunction, I am again indebted to Oliver Sacks and his marvelous book, *The Man Who Mistook His Wife for a Hat.* It was in those pages I learned how aphasiacs (such as the Troll) compensate for their inability to understand speech with a preternatural sensitivity to vocal and visual cues. And how the severely retarded can sometimes display gifts as astonishing as the twins' ability to generate prime numbers.

In 1906, there was as yet no real regulation of addictive drugs, and many so-called "elixirs" sold over-the-counter were laced with morphine. Thus Hazel Bland's unwitting addiction (and tragic befuddlement) was an all too common phenomenon.

Many people have forgotten that before the two wildly popular films of *Ben-Hur* (the incredible chariot race in the silent version is, incidentally, worth checking out), there was the equally popular novel published in 1880 by the ex-Civil War general, Lew Wallace. Another of Hattie's books, *Little Lord Fauntleroy* (by Frances Hodgson

Burnett—she of *The Secret Garden* fame), was also very popular. But the book's illustrations of its anodyne protagonist—a sort of male Pollyanna—were often mocked for his long girlish locks, which inspired these immortal lines by James Whitcomb Riley:

> Mighty glad I ain't a girl—ruther be a boy,
> Without them sashes, curls and things that's worn by
> Fauntleroy!

Roads at this time were still quite primitive. But an extensive rail network enabled an adventurous subset of the nation's downtrodden to travel across the nation's underbelly like fleas on a dog. For the lore and colorful slang of this fascinating fraternity, I am indebted to Jim Tully's *Beggars of Life*, a popular account, published in the twenties, of his life as a hobo at the turn of the century.

"The Dutchy," as Jimmy called his odious stepfather, was probably not Dutch but German, just as "Pennsylvania Dutch" was in fact a German dialect.

Though the terrible tale told by the scarred ex-soldier around the hobo campfire is a fiction, the brutal suppression of the rebel insurrection that followed the war in the Philippines—a part of the Spanish-American War—was so tainted by atrocities it sparked moral outrage amongst the intellectuals of the day (Mark Twain wrote a scathing indictment) and could almost be thought of as a sort of proto-Vietnam.

A final thought: I'm a lifetime lover of literature who has come late to the craft of writing; it has been a fascinating and humbling experience. My lodestar has been the simple idea of writing a book I'd want to read, trusting there are others it will appeal to. If you are one of them, and eager for the further adventures of our plucky heroine, I am equally eager for your thoughts and comments!

Sincerely,
P.D. Quaver
contact at: pdquaver.com

SUGGESTED LISTENING

The "Elly books," as I privately refer to them, are steeped in references to music. Should my readers care to steep themselves in the real thing, here are a few suggestions (in the e-version of this book, all the YouTube addresses are linked):

Fritz Kreisler—"Liebesleid"

If *The Ordeals of Elly Robin* were to become a miniseries (dare to dream!), this would undoubtedly be played over the opening and closing credits. Music that suggests a *fin de siècle* Viennese cafe, "Liebesleid" (love's sorrow) was one of many enormously popular musical bon-bons that Kreisler composed for his own inimitably expressive and insouciant performances. Along with John McCormack and Enrico Caruso, Kreisler was one of the first three recording superstars; this is one of the many recordings he made of this piece. For those seeking more modern recordings, Joshua Bell is one of the carriers of the torch of this particular performance style.

Jascha Heifitz — Rimsky-Korsakov —
"The Flight of the Bumblebee"

Sumi Jo — Offenbach —
Les Contes d'Hofmann — "Doll Song"

Kissin plays Chopin
"Fantasie-impromptu" op. 66 verbier festival

These are the other selections from the act Elly does with her parents. Evgeny Kissin's wonderfully sensitive recording of the Fantasie-impromptu is especially suited to this list, not because Elly would have played it this expressively (at the age of six, dividing the notes of the melody between her two hands, even a prodigy like Elly would no doubt have played it somewhat mechanically), but because Kissin himself was an astonishing child prodigy, and (as pointed out in Andrew Solomon's book *Far From the Tree*), shares some of Elly's autistic traits.

Kissin plays Chopin at age 12

An astonishing example of a true child prodigy, suggesting Elly's abilities.

Scott Joplin — "Rag Time Dance"
(Orchestra — New England Ragtime Ensemble)

The piece Smiley Hobson dances to in his act. As performed by Gunther Schuller's ensemble, which provided the soundtrack for the movie *The Sting*. And providing a good idea of what the orchestra of Elly's vaudeville troupe might have sounded like.

Eva Tanguay sings "I Don't Care" — recorded 1922

The real "I Don't Care Girl," singing her theme song. Recorded when she was past her prime (and even her prime was, reportedly, none too prime), but fascinating nonetheless.

John McCormack sings Stephen Foster's
"Jeanie with the Light Brown Hair," 1934

The second "theme song" of the Elly books, played in the book by Brett Crawley on cornet, and reminding Jimmy McGann of his lost sister Liddie. Here sung by the wonderful Irish tenor John McCormick, toward the end of his recording career, but still in fine voice.

"The Dying Poet," by Louis Moreau Gottschalk

The piece with which Elly first demonstrates to Miss Bland her amazing ability to read at sight, and a typical example of "parlor music." Gottschalk was a fascinating American composer/pianist, whose book, *Notes of a Pianist*, a sardonic account of the life of a mid-nineteenth-century traveling virtuoso, is well worth checking out.

John Phillip Sousa conducts "The
Stars and Stripes Forever"

Sousa's fame in the early twentieth century cannot be overstated: he was a superstar. This is the 1909 recording heard by Elly and Professor Carp.

Mitsuko Uchida—Mozart Sonata in A
K331 "Rondo alla Turca"

The piece with which Elly concluded her recital at the asylum (and that later made Jimmy dance around the Pike's empty church), performed by the foremost Mozart interpreter of our time.

Acknowledgments

Many friends read the first drafts of "the Elly books," as I often call them, and offered countless valuable suggestions. I would like to especially thank Doc D., Al H., Fred K., "Swede," Mike G., Michael B., and Kevin U.

Elly's most devoted (if not entirely unbiased) fan was my mother, whose delight in the first four volumes of my tale kept me going. Though she passed away when the work was yet unfinished (as it still is as I write this!), she remains my "ideal reader."

Finally, five people deserve special mention: My irreplaceable friend Sandy K.; Steve C., ace researcher; Kathy O., who graciously agreed to offer her skills as editor; and my two hyper-literate and discerning brothers. Without the love and support of this formidable quintet, Elly would never have been brought to life; I can never thank them enough.

Sincerely,
P.D. Quaver

ABOUT THE AUTHOR

P.D. Quaver is a retired musician. In a long life as a professional pianist, he has played everything from Bach and Beethoven to jazz, ragtime and blues, including most everything the fictional Elly Robin performs in his books. In addition to "The Ordeals of Elly Robin" series, he is the author of the young adult thriller *Unplugged*. He divides his time between Colorado and Washington State.

Made in the USA
Coppell, TX
21 March 2025